ELLIOT **YORK**

DARK

A LOGAN
COOPER
NOVEL

LIES

DARK LIES

Copyright © 2022 by Elliot York

All rights reserved.

No part of this book may be reproduced in any form or by any electronic or mechanical means, including information storage and retrieval systems, without written permission from the author, except for the use of brief quotations in a book review.

ISBN: 9798364125347

Imprint: Independently published

PROLOGUE

His will be the last face I see.

The monster in sheep's clothing. A true predator.

I went through all the stages of grief. Whizzed through them in record time. All those times I wondered what it would feel like to sit across from a stone-faced doctor and have him give you the news. It's cancer. Terminal cancer. Only I got the shortened, drive-thru version of that scenario. No cancer. Just assured death. No 'get your affairs in order'. No 'we'll support and comfort you'. Just straight to a nightmare end.

Denial lasted all of a minute. He used handcuffs, the good ones. None of those playful, fuzzy ones lovers used in a sexy game of submission. I yanked so hard, my arm popped free of my shoulder. The skin peeled away from my hand. Like a glove, I thought. Hadn't there been a book like that, where the person freed themselves from a handcuff by peeling off their skin? Or was I thinking about that story with the guy who'd cut off his arm to save his life? That took far longer than the fifteen minutes I had before water seeped in around me. That ended denial. It was happening. Death was going to meet me at the other end no matter how hard I tried.

Isolation came next but that was easy. I was alone in the car. The monster stayed on shore, lingering to watch as I drowned. I was absurdly glad his features, his evil smirk were muted by the surrounding night.

Frigid, slimy water rolls over the tops of the open windows. It pools around my feet, around my flip-flops. They'd find me in flip-flops. Should have worn better shoes. The funny things you think of when it's all going to shit.

Anger. That was a given. I screamed at him through the half-open windows. Hollow threats that *they* would get him. That he would be brought to justice. He is smart. True evil requires brains. Bargaining came next but it was fleeting. I begged for my life only long enough to realize that a murderer's version of orgasm was hearing their victim plead. What was a horrific murder without a little begging?

Will it be called horrific? Will anyone miss me? Have I pissed off enough people to produce a few 'how tragic' comments murmured behind fake tears?

Cold water pools around my ankles. It's only water but it looks murky and menacing. I swallow and taste the rusty, decaying scent of the water. By morning, the sun will heat the surface of the lake. Boys will come fishing with their dads. Young lovers will tease each other to distraction during a mid-day swim. Birds and squirrels will land on the beach to take sips of the cool water. The water has a musty smell. It reminds me of swimming with friends in the pond behind our house. My hair would smell of moss for a week. 'Becca, you smell like sewage,' Dad would say. He was always a fucker.

Depression came with its own story. It seems the myth is true. Your life passes before your eyes when you face certain death. Once the true darkness sank in, I was suddenly that girl again, in my small, pathetic hometown. The girl everyone wanted but no one could have. My friends were so envious of my popularity. No one ever asked me if I wanted it. If someone had given me the choice between having my pick of the boys in town or an entirely different family, I wouldn't have thought twice. It would have been the family every time.

My free hand drags through the water as if I am checking the temperature of bathwater. I am going to miss bubble baths. Maybe most of all. The thin scribble of ink, a tattoo from my teens, is illuminated by the streaks of moonlight. They teased me as the girl no one could have, but there had been someone. Just one. No one knew. I hid the tattoo under a watch.

The tattoo takes me back again. I can't seem to stay out of my past. Is this part of it all? Part of dying?

I'm sitting in my dad's big armchair. It smells of his stale cigarettes and the general stench of my hateful old man. Any other day, I never would have sat there. Any other day, he would have yanked me by the arms and thrown me across the room. But that day, the day of my grandmother's funeral, I stared at him as I sat in it, letting him know I was going to sit in his chair and that was that. Nonna was the only person I cared about, the only anchor in my life, and when she died, I was lost, alone. Neighbors and friends floated in and out of the house bringing coffee cakes and casseroles, none of them staying long. They all loved my grandmother. They spent hours quilting and baking and having coffee with her. My parents were better in very small doses, if at all. Through the haze of my grief, I kept staring at Greta Harvey's glasses. They were crooked, leaning severely to the right. I stared at her tilted glasses as she carried a pot of beef stew into the kitchen, as she leaned over to give my mother a stiff hug. I stared at them as she bent down to touch my cheek, her own ample cheeks rolling up into a sympathetic smile. I sat on my hands to keep myself from reaching up and straightening out those damn glasses. The funny things you think about when it's all going to shit.

The water reaches my knees. My feet are numb from the cold. Blood trickles from my torn up wrist, the wrist that is going to be the cause of my death. In tenth grade, Samuel Peters grabbed my wrist. He told me it was so small he could break it into a million pieces with a good squeeze. I dared him to do it. That was me. Not the girl who yanked her wrist free to give him the slap he deserved. I was the girl who dared him to do it. If only Samuel were here now, crushing my wrist so that I could fold my hand and pull it free from my shackle.

I stare down at my thighs. The blood is mixing with the clammy water. The sliver of moon somehow manages to find me in my watery grave, to illuminate my imminent death. Summer shorts. I am going to die in my denim cutoffs. It is exactly what I would choose to wear if someone told me, 'you're going to die today, choose your wardrobe wisely'. I would have skipped the flip-flops. The funny things you think of when it's all going to shit.

The water level reaches my belly button. Why is it taking the car so long to sink? Aren't cars impossibly heavy? My heartbeat races as some of the earlier rage reappears. What a bastard. What a goddamn bastard. His image is only a silhouette now, a familiar silhouette. His elbows stick out as his hands casually rest in his pockets as if he is just somebody's dad or thoughtful boyfriend, out for an evening stroll, out to watch the stars peel out of the darkness. The only thing missing is the cup of coffee in his hand.

The car is filling faster now. Water weight brings it to the bottom of the lake. How deep is it? Will they find me? I hope they don't. I prefer to spend eternity with the fish in the lake. I imagine them using the car as a reef, a coral reef. Did that only happen in salt water? Why didn't he drown me in the ocean where I could become part of a coral reef? The funny things you think of when it's all going to shit.

I stretch my neck as long as it will go. A bit of denial comes back to tease me, then acceptance washes over me again. Just like the cold, slimy water that has nearly filled the cab. A moment of terror seizes me as I think about what it will be like to have that same slick, mossy water fill my throat, my lungs, my body. Then I remind myself—relax, this won't be so bad.

After all, this isn't the first time you've died.

CHAPTER
ONE

Logan stared down at the lump at the end of his arm. It had only been two days, but he'd nearly forgotten what his hand looked like, the rounded knuckles, the slim veins, the dent from his wedding ring that never seemed to go away. Swelling made moving his fingers pure torture, and the deep cut, where the medic had removed the asshole's front tooth, seemed to be oozing something that shouldn't be oozing from any part of his body. The medic, a young kid who looked as if he was still closer to acne than to razor burn, asked if it was worth it. Logan hadn't hesitated. He'd nodded. "Yeah, it was worth it."

All of it was still in his head, crystal clear as if his brain had captured everything on video, in high definition. Clearest of all were those brown eyes, the eyes of the five-year-old girl staring up at him from the cage her father kept her in, the four by four prison complete with chains and a flat dog bowl filled with filthy water. The horrid smell of the place, human waste, mold, stale food was stuck in his nostrils. The seven-year-old was right next to her, in her own chain-link prison. She was as small as her sister, both girls too malnourished to grow. Worst of all, their dead mother was lying on the floor next to the cages. And then there was dad, the man who should have protected them, cared for them, fed them, loved them. He sat on the crumbling front steps of his rundown house, his hands bound behind his back as he yelled at the police to get off his property. When the social worker tried to walk past him to enter the house, the scumbag shot his foot out, dislodging the unsuspecting woman's kneecap. She collapsed, screaming in pain.

It had been the last straw for Logan. He snatched the creep by the collar and pounded him, using his weaker left fist as a precaution. The right would have killed him in three blows. And every blow was pure delight. As he obliterated the features, as the cheekbone gave way and the nose sank into the cavity between the two beady eyes, as the teeth broke out, one landing right in Logan's knuckle, as blood covered his hand and the asshole's face so heavily it was impossible to know the source, Logan told himself this would probably cost him his job. But it was worth it.

Castillo's voice rumbled through the thick glass panes of his office. Someone on the other end of the phone had him plenty mad. That was going to make it worse for Logan. He leaned his head back against the cold plaster wall behind him, closed his eyes and adjusted his ass on the hard bench. It was that day in tenth grade all over again. Sitting outside Principal Halbert's office, his hand tucked in the ice pack the nurse had wrapped around it, waiting to be suspended for throwing his fist into Caleb Dixon's face. Dixon had deserved it too, only Logan's motive for hitting him hadn't been for the right reasons. Jeremy West had always been teased mercilessly. He was the quintessential nerd. Every high school had one, but Jeremy was really top of the line. Becca had had it with the teasing. She shoved Caleb hard and he shoved back, hard enough to push her down. Logan's fist shot straight into Dixon's jaw. He wasn't protecting Jeremy, but he should have been. Jeremy never deserved the shit he got. Never.

"Coop, my man. Hang in there, buddy," Detective Gregor's voice jarred Logan from his grim thoughts. He was always wearing that same clownish grin. "Hey, we're all pulling for you. That animal deserved everything you gave him and more." Gregor was one of those good ole boys who liked to be liked. He was that guy who always sat at the popular kid's table, and they let him because he brought his mom's chocolate chip cookies to share. Without the cookies he would have been toast. He was an okay guy who probably talked far too much about the 'amazing' sex he was having with his girlfriend, but he was a sloppy detective. He left too many stones unturned. He was too busy wanting everyone to like him to worry about nailing shut a case.

Gregor glanced down at Logan's hand and swallowed hard, pretending he wasn't grossed out. "Wow, that's gnarly." His gaze shot toward the captain's office to make sure Castillo wasn't witnessing the interaction. After all, Logan was that kid on the bench in front of the principal's office, and Gregor was the kid who wanted to be pals with everyone as long as it didn't get him in trouble. "Good luck, buddy."

Logan nodded. Gregor had never been his buddy. Logan couldn't see any scenario in any period of time in any place in the world where that would've been the case. Castillo was still cussing someone out on the phone. Maybe he'd blow off all his steam on the call and have nothing left, Logan thought as he leaned forward, resting his arms on his thighs. His head was pounding.

The clamor in the precinct wasn't any different than any other day. The woman whining at the front desk, pestering the police technician behind the glass window to arrest her neighbor for constantly allowing his sprinklers to hit her car. The drunk guy sitting outside the processing room, trying futilely to get free of his restraints while spitting and cursing at the arresting officers. The phones ringing endlessly and the mix of voices and occasional laughter, it all played continuously like an infinite loop. The chaos never stopped. Normally, Logan could tune it out, but his hand throbbed and his head ached and he just wanted to be at home on his threadbare couch with a cold beer at his side and his feet up on the wobbly coffee table.

Logan's phone vibrated. Out of habit, he reached for it with his left hand, stopping just short of shoving it painfully into his pocket. He leaned back and reached across to pull it free. Vicki. Seeing the name gave him the usual charge in the chest, the twinge, the twist that came knowing he was going to hear her voice.

"Hey, Vick. What's up?"

"Did I catch you at a bad time?" It was a soft, silky voice. One that Logan just couldn't free from his head no matter how hard he tried. "It sounds like you're at the station."

"Sitting outside the principal's office," he said wryly.

"What?"

"Nothing. What's up?"

"You sound down. Are you taking care of yourself?" she asked.

"Not sure what you mean. I eat. I sleep. I shit. Guess I'm doing everything that I'm supposed to be doing." And all of it without you, he thought afterward.

She clucked her tongue. "I'm going to take that as a no." A pause followed. It was long enough that Logan pulled his phone from his ear to see if the call had been dropped. He heard his name again, slipping off those soft pink lips, lips he'd never kiss again. He pushed the phone back against his ear.

Vicki's breath whispered through the phone. "I wanted

to tell you before you heard it from a family member or mutual friend—"

Logan chuckled. It was short and dry. "There aren't any mutual friends, Vick. They all ended up in your court. Tell me what?" Castillo's voice was a low rumble. He seemed to be finishing the call. Logan was waiting to be slammed once he stepped inside the captain's office. What he wasn't expecting was to be slammed as he waited outside the door.

"I'm pregnant," she said it fast as if blurting it would soften the impact. "Rick and I are expecting a boy in October. I thought you should hear it from me. I didn't want to send it in a text."

Polite of her. I'll drive the ice pick into your heart over the phone and not in a text.

"Logan?" she said tentatively.

Logan sat up straighter, suddenly finding it hard to catch a decent breath in his slouched position. "Yeah, wow, October. That's only a few months away." He stared down at his hand hoping he could focus on how badly it hurt. It would lessen the sting of the conversation.

"I didn't want to take a chance by announcing it too early. We've been keeping it to ourselves. I've been camouflaging it as much as possible. I didn't want to let people know just in case—well—you know."

Logan knew, he knew so fucking well that he could taste bile in his throat just thinking about it. The first time was short. They'd barely had time to absorb it when suddenly the baby was gone. It hurt but it had been just a mere whisper, a few weeks of nervous joy at the prospect of having a baby. The second time fate was a little crueler. They'd told everyone and even allowed themselves the fun of debating whether it would be a boy or girl. Vicki had started reading parenting books and there were brochures on the safest cribs and car seats. Logan woke in the middle of the night to sobbing. Vicki was in the bathroom. The doctor hadn't confirmed it but she knew. Baby two was gone. The marriage was growing more fragile. Third time wasn't a charm. Logan remembered every detail of the night when Vicki's mom called him. It was raining and they'd just found a body in the bottom of a ravine. He saw Margaret's name on the screen and he knew. It was over... again. This time he hadn't allowed himself to imagine himself a father, to imagine himself cursing and throwing tools as he tried to put together the crib, to imagine himself sitting up at night cradling a baby, his baby. But Vicki had. She'd felt a kick. She'd connected with the tiny life inside of her. This time she wanted answers. She needed to know why. One young doctor, a confident, cocksure guy with a narrow face and long nose had mentioned incompatibility. One word and that was it. The marriage fell apart so fast, Logan had no chance to stop it.

"Cooper, get in here!" Castillo bellowed loud enough that every head in the precinct turned.

"I've got to go, Vick. I'm really happy for you both."

Apparently, Rick and Vicki were compatible. Maybe it was the rhyming names. "Take care."

Logan hung up and put the phone away. Castillo had already turned around and gone back into his office. Logan pushed up from the bench. Standing made the pressure in his hand worse, and it seemed to shoot right up to his aching head. If he was fired, he'd take a long vacation. Maybe somewhere remote. Somewhere ex-wives, angry police captains and kiss ass coworkers couldn't find him.

CHAPTER
TWO

Captain Castillo didn't look up from the folder on his desk as Logan walked into his office. The dank little space smelled of anger and sweat and the menthol cough drops Castillo was always sucking on. Logan had surmised the drops were to soothe his throat from all the yelling. Logan had worked with Castillo out in the field. He was a good detective, one of the best. He moved up the ranks quickly. More than once Logan had heard him mutter that he would have preferred the field to his office any day. Castillo had allowed himself to get pasty white and pillowy soft sitting in that chair behind the desk. He was only fifty, eleven years older than Logan, but his hair was thinning and he was always sweating. Even today, with the noisy air conditioner in the room blasting out cool air, there was a sheen of sweat on his forehead, a forehead that grew more exposed from hair loss each day.

"Close the damn door," Castillo barked even though

Logan was already pushing it shut. Logan figured he was in for a yell session. The door didn't need to be open. This half of the precinct would hear it anyhow.

Castillo picked up a pen to sign his name on something. "Take a seat, Coop." There wasn't as much anger in his tone as Logan expected. Maybe that was because the next words were going to be 'turn in your badge'. That didn't need yelling or anger. Those words could be said without any emotion, just a straightforward command.

Logan picked the chair on the right because the one on the left was so wobbly it rocked back and forth with every movement. He didn't mind it on days after a successful investigation when he was feeling cocky and sure of himself, but with the pain in his head and hand and the prospect that he had just ended his career, he wanted four steady legs beneath him.

Castillo put down the pen with a clamor and rested back. His chair squeaked as if he'd just sat back on a family of mice. He peered at Logan over the mountain of paperwork on his desk. "Do you think the job I have is easy, Cooper? Do you think I'm in here painting my fucking fingernails and answering calls from sweet little grannies who can't find their lost cats?"

Logan stared back at him for a long moment. "I'm going to assume those are rhetorical questions."

"Are they?" Castillo's voice was raised a few decibels but still not at its usual pitch for a good shouting session. "Cuz it seems you think that's what's happening in here.

Otherwise, you wouldn't pull shit like you did. Otherwise, you wouldn't have decided to go all fucking vigilante on that scumbag. Now I've got internal affairs breathing down my neck. They want to know why my detective, my best detective I might add, decided to turn someone's face into hamburger."

"He deserved it."

Castillo sat forward so fast the chair rolled into the desk. "Don't you think I know that? I saw the photos of those little girls, treated worse than people treat their dogs. Fuck, far worse. My dog has his own couch. Can you imagine that? The wife bought him a designer couch to match the furniture in the living room. But guess where that dog is laying every time I go to sit down in my easy chair." Castillo grabbed a lozenge and fiddled with the cellophane wrapper. "Shit."

Logan figured he'd brought up the dog story to soften the blow when he asked for his badge.

Castillo was about to stick the clear red drop in his mouth but thought better of it. Yelling at someone wasn't as effective with one cheek stretched out with a cough drop. Logan would just as soon not have to perform the Heimlich on the sweaty captain.

"The point is, Logan," his voice had lowered, and he was calling him by his first name. Maybe he'd used up all his rage on the phone call after all. "Any one of us would have liked to pound that asshole's face into pulp, but we don't do it. Do you know why?"

"Because it hurts." Logan held up his hand.

Castillo flinched. "Jesus. Not because it hurts. Because it's not protocol. We don't beat the shit out of suspects because that's not how things work."

"Should I turn in my badge?"

"Give me a good reason not to ask for it?"

"You just said it. I'm your best detective." The dull ache in Logan's head seemed to be spreading over his entire skull. If he was being fired, he just wanted to get it the fuck over with. Drop the guillotine blade already.

"Do you like this job, Coop?"

What was with all the off-brand questions? Castillo was normally straight to the point. Maybe this time the point was more painful than a reprimand. Maybe this time he was working up to some shitty news. Turn in your badge and get a lawyer. That would do it. That would put the topper on Logan's day.

Logan thought about Vicki's phone call. He thought about his crummy little apartment that didn't allow pets yet still smelled like urine. Vicki had taken the dog too. It was for the best she'd kept insisting. Logan looked up from his pulpy left hand. Castillo had shoved the cough drop in after all. His cheek stuck out like a hamster's.

"This job is all I've got." The words that were supposed to stay packed in his head rolled out of his mouth.

What was that in Castillo's face? Genuine concern? Not possible. "Then why do you take such chances?" The desk phone rang. Castillo held up his finger. "Don't move. We're not through yet."

"Castillo here." His dark brows moved up and down on his sweaty forehead. He sucked on the cough drop as he listened to the voice on the other end. He nodded as if the person could see him. "Right, then that's the way the report will read. Yep. Yep." Castillo glanced briefly my direction. "He's in my office right now. Right. Right. Yep." He hung up.

"The suspect is dead."

Logan felt the breath go out of him.

"Not from injuries," Castillo continued, "so you can take that look off your face. The officer we positioned outside his door got distracted by some squabble down the hall. Probably staged to distract him. In the meantime, someone slipped into his hospital room and turned up the morphine drip. That asshole had it easy. Just drifted off in a nice, cushy drug induced sleep. They're investigating it. Once the story got out about how those two little girls were treated—let's just say, he wasn't a respected member of society."

Logan sat forward. His head felt like a lead ball. Numbness was wearing off, and his hand was starting to feel as if someone was hammering it consistently with a mallet.

"We're writing it up as resisting arrest. The suspect became violent. That poor young social worker, who needs a whole new knee just to walk again, can attest to that."

"So that's it?" Logan asked.

The cough drop crunched between Castillo's teeth. "Nope. The higher-ups have made it mandatory that you attend therapy sessions to deal with your anger issues."

Logan stood up. "No fucking way am I sitting on a shrink's couch pouring out all my mommy and daddy issues. That therapy crap is bullshit."

Castillo held out his palm. "Then hand over the badge."

Logan stared down at Castillo. The captain didn't flinch or show even an ounce of emotion as he stared up at him. He was serious. It was therapy or the badge. It took Logan longer than he would have expected to make the decision.

"Fuuck." Logan turned to leave. The captain tossed another zinger before he could escape. That couch and cold beer were calling him more than ever.

"Your first session is tomorrow," Castillo said. Logan turned back around. His head and hand hurt too much to argue. "You'll go twice a week for six months or until the therapist signs off on it. I'll text you the contact information once I get it. Report back to duty next Monday, and that hand better look like a hand and not a clay sculpture my four-year-old might make."

"Right. I'll get to work on that," Logan said dryly.

Before he could turn to the door, Castillo had one more blow.

"Your new partner starts Monday." He tossed the next bomb out as if he was just telling Logan that it was hot outside.

"No partner," Logan said. "You know I work better without one."

"New protocol. Chief wants everyone partnered up. That way detectives are safer. It also keeps them from going rogue—you know—beating the shit out of suspects."

"Christ," Logan muttered. "Not Gregor. Don't pair me with Gregor."

"It's not Gregor." He shuffled through the papers on his desk, pushing aside thick folders until he found the page he was looking for. "Detective Reggie Hawkins is from down south, from Los Angeles."

"Shit, not one of those tofu eating, Kumbaya clowns from Southern California. Fuck, what did I do to deserve —" Logan cut himself short. His throbbing hand was an instant reminder of what he'd done to deserve it.

Castillo held the slightly crumpled paper in his hand. "It says Reggie graduated first in her class from the academy. Detective Hawkins comes with high recommendations from her superiors."

Logan froze to the spot and stared at Captain Castillo. "I'm going to assume you said 'her' accidentally."

Castillo tossed the paper aside. "Assume all you want. By the way, Google Santa Cruz in the 1960s if you want to know where the Kumbaya bullshit came from. You're working right along sidewalks and beaches that were once covered by hippies. Don't know where tofu started but once a week, Gina tries to stick it in a casserole or stew, thinking I'm not going to notice. By the way, the transfer paper says Hawkins has a positive attitude. I'm hoping it rubs off on you."

Logan laughed but cut it short when the reverberation hit his aching skull. He reached the door.

"And, for fuck's sake, get a life. If this job was all I had, I'd be pounding faces too," Castillo barked.

"Thanks for the pep talk, Cap'n."

"I'll send you the contact information for the therapist as soon as I get it."

"Great." Logan walked out of the office. Plenty of curious expressions turned his direction.

"How did it go?" Gregor popped out from nowhere. He must have been lingering in the hallway waiting for Logan to leave the office.

"How does any meeting with Castillo go?" Logan left him with the answer that wasn't really an answer at all. Therapy and a new partner. Why the hell didn't Castillo just ask for his badge?

CHAPTER
THREE

The morning fog hadn't cleared. Usually it clung to shore until lunch. Today it had drifted inland, filling every crack and crevice with a cold, wet haze. Shiny marble, steel and glass were all competing to be the most pretentious part of the two-story façade. The building was cold and stark, one of those contemporary designs that lacked style and character. Logan wondered if he'd think the same thing about the doctor. Dr. Benjamin Webb to be exact. It sounded like a cold, stark name.

The emergency room doctor had prescribed a painkiller for his hand. Logan swallowed two as he reached the building. He figured the whole session would be more bearable if he was feeling good.

The ten foot tall glass doors at the front of the building were locked. A small brass plaque read 'push the intercom to be let inside'. He pushed the red button and a man answered. "Yes?"

"Logan Cooper. I have an appointment with Dr. Webb."

The door buzzed and Logan walked inside. The whole place smelled of a forced fragrance, one of the flowery, annoying smells that came from a plug-in air freshener. The downstairs was sparsely furnished with two blue upholstered benches. A pair of tall rubber plants sat in bright green pots on each side of the elevator. There was no receptionist. The downstairs seemed to be deserted.

A brass plaque next to the elevator said Dr. Benjamin Webb second floor. Below was the name Dr. Francis Jordan second floor. They seemed to be the only doctors in the building.

Logan stepped inside the elevator and hesitated before pressing two. He would have done anything else, community service, all the holiday and weekend shifts for a year, even taken Gregor on as a partner if it meant avoiding therapy. The last thing he wanted was to spend an hour bullshitting with a complete stranger, a stranger who would pretend to be neutral and non-judgmental. There just wasn't any way that was true. Logan always imagined all the psyches getting together somewhere for cups of coffee and to compare notes to see who was dealing with the biggest wackos that week.

The ride to the second floor was over before he could take a decent breath. The pills had kicked in. There was just enough of a melted butter sort of feeling going through Logan's brain to make him think he could get through the next hour.

Only two doors on the second floor had signs. Dr. Jordan's office was right across the hallway from Dr. Webb's. Logan knocked. The door buzzed again. It reminded him of entering the high security area of a prison. Electronic doors that required someone on the other side to buzz people through.

The front room of the office had lime green chairs that were not the least bit inviting. But then Logan wasn't there to sit or relax. There was a desk in the front room with an appointment book sitting on it. Silver framed diplomas boasting Webb's educational background hung on the wall behind the desk. The door to the inner office opened. Webb looked just as Logan expected with his collegiate gray sweater and neatly combed hair slightly dusted with white.

"Mr. Cooper," Webb said with a practiced smile. "May I call you Logan, or I understand people call you Coop?" He strolled over to the appointment book, flipped it open and checked something off. Logan's name he presumed.

"Logan is fine." Coop was his name at the precinct. It would be weird to hear it coming from this posh, properly polished shrink.

"Great. Come inside."

Logan's gaze swept around the inner office. Some designer had gone overboard trying to make the place sleek and modern. The furniture looked like something from a futuristic movie set. The Jetsons popped into Logan's mind. He couldn't stop his smile. The pills were working.

"Something amusing?" Webb asked. He had gray eyes that reminded Logan of storm clouds. Webb stared right into Logan's eyes. "Oh, I see. You took some pain relievers before you came up. Your pupils are dilated."

Logan didn't know whether to feel ashamed or impressed.

"Yeah, sorry." Logan glanced down at the left hand hanging at his side. Wrapping it would be pure torture. It was on full display.

"That looks very painful. Please have a seat." Webb waved to the couch. "Can I get you a glass of water or a cup of coffee?"

"No, I'm fine."

"I know the building looks rather deserted, but I only just signed the lease on it. I'm planning on renting out offices as soon as I have time to interview prospective tenants."

Logan was already bored. He wondered how much of the session had already passed with small talk. Maybe they could pass the entire forty minutes with Webb talking about his newly leased building.

Logan's gaze drifted to the large window behind the oak desk. The haze was drifting past in ghostly looking flurries. The sun was working hard to break through.

"Well, Logan?" Webb's deep, smooth tone penetrated

his thoughts about the weather. It seemed he'd asked a question only Logan had been busy thinking about the haze and the sun and, if he was honest, about the burger he planned to grab on his way home. The pills were working too well.

"I'm sorry," Logan said. "I didn't catch that."

"I thought we could start with you telling me a little bit about yourself." Webb crossed his legs at the knees and picked up a notepad and pen from a shiny glass table.

Logan couldn't believe how fucking uncomfortable the couch was, as if someone had covered a slab of cement with navy blue fabric. He had a hard time deciding where to place his left hand so that it wouldn't throb or rub or feel anything except the air circulating around it. Even that tended to be irritating. He finally rested it as lightly as he could on his thigh.

Webb looked pointedly at it. "Maybe you should start with that hand. Would you like to talk about the incident?"

Logan shook his head. "Not today."

Webb put down the pen. "Look, Detective Cooper. I know this wasn't a choice for you. I'm sure you'd rather be anywhere else, but you're going to need me to sign off on your release from therapy. I won't do that until I think we've made sufficient progress."

"Right." I'll play the game, Logan thought. Let the doctor think he's done his usual miracle work so this can end quickly. "Where do I start? Wait, I think I know. It's always got something to do with the past." Logan could hear the snarky, abrasive tone. He almost felt guilty about it. Almost. "I can give it to you in a nice little summary, but I have to warn you there won't be any big ta-da moments."

Surprisingly, Webb didn't look disgusted by Logan's attitude. It probably wasn't the first time he had to work with a client who was only sitting on the couch to keep his job.

"Big ta-da moments?" Webb asked to clarify.

"You know, the creepy uncle or the controlling mom or the abusive dad, the thing that helps the person sitting on this blue couch discover just why they're so messed up."

"And are you messed up? Aside from the obvious— your hand?" Webb set down his pen, apparently deciding this session wasn't going to produce many worthy notes.

Logan shrugged. "I think I'm more messed up than some and less messed up than others." There, Mr. Psyche degree. How was that for a non-committal answer?

Webb's mouth turned in. He picked up the pen to write something. Logan wondered if he was just writing the word 'asshole' over and over again. That was what Logan would be writing if he was sitting in the straight-backed chair.

"Let's get back to the past, the one with no big ta-da moments," Webb said. Logan had to admit, he didn't hate the guy. He was far too polished and looked as if he spent ten minutes just flossing his teeth but he wasn't unlikable.

"I grew up just east of Monterey in a little farming

community. It was one of those towns where everyone knew everyone else's business. I have an older brother, ten years older so he didn't pay much attention to me. Never see him much now. I was just the scrappy little brat who borrowed his stuff and broke his skateboard when I tried to jump off a curb. My dad was an accountant."

"Really?" Webb asked.

"Yeah, really. Why? Is that a profession people like to lie about? I mean I could see if I said he was a rock star, lead singer of some famous band but accountant? He liked numbers. Still does. I send him my taxes every year. My parents, Harris and Jennifer, live down in Palm Springs."

"What was he like as a dad?" Webb asked.

I smiled and nodded. "Ah ha, I see where this is going. Once again, I'm going to have to disappoint you."

"Actually, you haven't disappointed me at all, Logan. I'm learning a lot. So we know he liked numbers." He left the rest open.

"He was quiet as far as dads go. If he was watching my soccer game, he wouldn't cheer me on like the other dads did for their kids."

"Did that bother you? Not being cheered on?"

"Not at all. To be honest, the other kids' dads were embarrassing. Aside from cheering, they would yell too, when someone messed up. My dad just sat and watched the game and then took me out for an ice cream afterward. We never even talked about the game. Sports weren't really his thing."

"But you were athletic?" he asked.

"I liked sports. Soccer, football, skateboarding."

"Did it bother you that you couldn't talk about it with your dad?" Webb was really going after the dad-son angle.

"Nah, I had a lot of friends. It was a small town, but there were a lot of kids my age. We all hung out together."

"That all sounds rather ideal."

"It wasn't ideal but it wasn't terrible. Both my parents worked a lot, and I was home alone for most of the evening. I liked it. Made me feel independent, mature. I had it better than some, you know?"

"You mean some of your friends?"

"Yeah, kids around my age. Some of them had it pretty rough." Some hard, dark memories surfaced as Logan talked about growing up in Layton. Logan worked quickly to clear them from his mind rather than allow them to get a stronger hold.

"Were there suicides?" Webb asked. It seemed like an off-the-wall question. Logan's face must have shown it. Logan had to hand it to him, the man knew how to read expressions. "I only ask because those are quite common with teens in small towns."

And then a reaction Logan wasn't expecting. His throat thickened. For a brief moment, that day, one of the worst days of his life, flickered through his thoughts. No way. He wasn't going there. He'd come to the shrink's office to race through a few therapy sessions, get a signature and leave for good. "Yeah, there was a suicide."

"A good friend?"

Logan shook his head. It was a lie. He had no doubt Webb knew it, but he didn't prod any further.

"You mentioned your brother ignored you and your parents were always working. Did you feel neglected at all? Lonely?"

"Like I said, I liked my independence. My dad's job was an hour away. He had to work long hours. His boss, the owner of the accounting firm, was an asshole, a real Scrooge. My dad worked late on Christmas Eve. He never spoke up. My mom would tell him, 'Harris, you need to tell that man that you need Christmas Eve off'. But my dad let the guy walk all over him. He let a lot of people walk all over him. The neighbor would borrow his tools and return them broken. Dad would just tell him thanks for returning it. That was just his way. He didn't like to ruffle feathers."

"How did you feel about it?"

Logan laughed. "Hell, I wanted to go over and throw the broken tool right through the neighbor's window. I wanted to call up that Scrooge boss and tell him he was a genuine asshole."

"So, in a sense, you had the opposite reaction as your dad. You were angry. You wanted to speak up for your dad because he refused to speak up for himself."

Logan sat back against the hard cushion and nodded

at Webb. "Well, lookie there. You've already gotten to the heart of my anger issues. It was all about daddy, after all. I guess that's it then, huh?"

"Nice try, Detective Cooper. By the way, have you ever been hypnotized?"

Logan laughed. "No and no offense to your skills, Dr. Webb, but there's no way you'd be able to put me under."

A faint smile crossed Webb's face. "Interesting. It's always the people who are confident that they can't be hypnotized who go under the fastest and the hardest. We might try some in our next session."

"I'll think about it. So, is this it?"

"I think we can stop for the day. I need you to come back feeling a little less glib from painkillers. Then we can do a serious session."

Logan didn't stick around to argue the point. After all, he'd been called a lot worse things than glib. One down, Logan thought as he made a beeline for the door.

CHAPTER
FOUR

Logan drained the last of his coffee as he pulled into the parking lot. He lifted his hand off the steering wheel to get a better look at it in the early morning sun. The knuckles were returning one by one. His hand was looking less like a ball of clay and more like an appendage he could actually use. After five days off, with most of that time spent slumped on his couch eating pizza and binge-watching television, he felt surprisingly ready to get back to work. During those blissful hours of not thinking or paying attention to the world outside, he'd forgotten about his new partner. He'd almost managed to push the therapy crap out of his head too. He was determined to get through it and fast. With any luck, Webb would get tired of seeing him and sign off quickly just to get the pain in the ass detective off his couch.

Logan spun the steering wheel and headed toward his usual parking spot. Before he could slide his truck into it, a motorcycle yanked in ahead of him. It was the last of the parking spots reserved for detectives. The detective's badge didn't come with all that many perks, but a prime parking spot was one of them.

Logan rolled down the window. "Hey, visitor parking is on the other side of the entrance."

A long leg wrapped in vintage style bell-bottom jeans swung over the seat of the Ducati. Black gloved hands reached up and pulled off the full face helmet. A brunette ponytail fell out of the helmet. The face that turned his direction was the kind that you definitely turned to look at in a store or at a party. She was young. Too young, Logan chided himself. Big brown eyes, full lips, it was all there. But she was still in his parking spot.

"Hello, sorry but these spots are reserved for detectives. Like I said, visitor parking is on the other side."

She smiled. It went right along with the big brown eyes and full lips. She reached into her white and green motorcycle jacket and pulled out a badge. A red and black striped backpack bounced on her back as she headed on long legs to the precinct door.

"It can't fucking be," Logan muttered. His tires chirped as he parked in one of the patrol car spots. He climbed out, slammed the door and lumbered across the lot, spinning every kind of objection he could think of in his head.

The newest member of the force had already caused a stir. People were huddled in groups muttering snippets of gossip. "Holy shit, Coop, why do you always hit the lotto?" Garcia cooed. "Not fair." It would figure Garcia was already scoping out the new hire. Creepiness was his go-to move when it came to women.

Logan headed straight down the hallway to Castillo's office. It was rare when he didn't at least knock before barging in, but this was a special occasion. The door was slightly ajar. Logan took that as an invite to burst inside.

"I'm not going to fucking babysit some fresh out of the academy junior cheerleader," Logan barked.

"Detective Cooper," Castillo said, far too formally, before he waved to someone who was now hidden by the door. "This is your new partner, Detective Hawkins."

Hawkins stepped forward with a gracious smile. "We've already met, Captain Castillo. Detective Cooper was telling me all about the visitor parking. Thank you again, Detective. Now I'll know where to send visitors."

Logan felt the heat of anger in his face get slowly replaced by the heat of embarrassment. He wasn't about to let this very shitty start get in the way. "Glad I got the visitor parking thing all cleared up for you, Miss—Detective Hawkins. If you don't mind, I need a word with the captain."

Castillo smiled. Logan saw it so rarely, he briefly considered whether or not the captain was having a stroke.

"Detective Hawkins, why don't you go set up your desk. I'll send your partner right out. There's a body in an alleyway at Tuscany and Harbor. Probably a junkie over-dose. The coroner is on his way."

"Sounds good, Captain Castillo." Damn, did she have a smile and damn, did she know how to use it. Castillo nearly melted into a puddle of sweat right in front of his desk.

Hawkins ignored Logan as she swept past, leaving behind a fragrance that reminded him of freshly squeezed lemonade. The door snapped shut.

Logan shook his head. "No, just no. Just fucking no."

Castillo circled around to his chair. The weird smile he'd plastered on for his newest officer was long gone. "You're right, Coop. Oh wait, that's right. You're not in charge. I am. So deal with it."

"She looks like she just graduated high school."

"That's because when you hit middle age, when you cross the ugly line of forty, everyone looks like they just graduated high school. She's thirty-one."

"First of all, I'm not forty... yet. How the hell did she already make it to detective? Wait. Don't tell me. She's the chief's niece or granddaughter. Nepotism. This is nepotism, isn't it? And now I'm stuck making sure this kid doesn't get herself killed, or both of us killed, for that matter. Just put me out there on my own, Cap'n. I promise I won't beat the shit out of anyone."

"First of all, it's not nepotism. I told you she was first in her class at the academy, and she came with high marks and recommendations. She's only been detective for a year."

"Great. A year. Why did she transfer up here? Must have been something that made her request a transfer?"

"You sure you aren't forty because you are as cynical as an old fuck. I don't know why she asked for a transfer, but she's here and she's your partner. So get out there and catch the bad guys."

Laughter rolled down the hallway. It was a loud, collective rumble as if half the force was gathered together laughing at something.

Castillo stomped past Logan. "What the hell is going on?" he muttered angrily and yanked open the door. Logan stepped out into the hallway behind him, looking past his shoulder. His estimate had been off. It wasn't half the force but a good third standing in a huddled group talking animatedly with overdone smiles. The center of their enamored focus was Logan's new partner. Garcia kept smoothing his hand over his hair to bring attention to what he considered his crowning glory, a thick head of black hair. He was right. It was about the only thing he had to brag about.

"What the hell is going on?" Castillo barked. The guys began splintering off as he spoke. "Did all crime and murder in the city stop? Are we suddenly living in a Utopia that needs no law enforcement? If that's the case, then you're all fired." Castillo spun around so fast they would have collided if Logan hadn't stepped back. "And why the hell are you still here, Coop? There's a body. Go and find out why there's a body and wipe off that pout. I'm sick of seeing it." He marched back to his office and slammed shut the door.

Logan's new partner placed a few things in the empty desk she'd been assigned to. It was directly across from Logan's desk. She set the motorcycle helmet on the floor and picked up her backpack. She pulled it on her shoulders.

"Where do you think we're going?" Logan asked. "School?"

"I've got my lunch and a few essentials inside. Is it a problem?"

"I guess it's better than a lunch pail." Logan started walking to the door.

She caught up to him, with her bouncing backpack and the fragrance that reminded him of lemonade. "Can I drive?"

"Nope," he answered as he smacked the door open. She slipped through before it closed on her.

Her ponytail swung back and forth as she strode next to him with those long legs.

"Look," Logan started, "sorry about what I said back there in the captain's office."

She shrugged. "It's all right. They told me you were an asshole. I'll just have to adjust to that."

"Adjust to what?"

"To having a partner who's an asshole."

Logan stopped and turned to her. "Who told you I was an asshole? No, you know what. I don't care."

"They said that too. That you wouldn't care that they considered you an asshole."

Logan unlocked the car. She slid the backpack off her shoulders and dropped it on the floor of the car before climbing inside. Logan sat down in the driver's seat. Just having another body in the seat next to him felt strange, as if his personal space had been invaded. Invaded by someone who reminded him of lemonade. Hell, when was the last time he had a tall, cold glass of lemonade? Could have been worse, he supposed. Gregor smelled like a mix of garlic, cheap aftershave and shameless groveling.

"What should I call you?" she asked.

"Coop is fine. What about you? You don't really fit the name Hawk."

"Call me Reg. That's what everyone used to call me down south."

Logan started the car. "That's easy." He could feel her brown eyed gaze on the side of his face. He was going to have to get used to that again, to not being alone. "What?" he asked.

"Aren't you going to ask me if my name is actually Reggie?"

Logan shook his head. "Should I ask?"

"Not if it doesn't interest you." She reached for her backpack and unzipped it. The sights and sounds of a backpack carried him briefly back to high school. She pulled out a granola bar and offered Logan one. He shook his head. The aroma of roasted nuts and dark chocolate filled the car as she unwrapped it and took a bite.

Logan drove past her motorcycle and looked pointedly at it. "A motorcycle, eh?"

"Cheaper than a car. And more fun too," she said between bites.

Logan's mind went straight to gambling addiction or maybe she was a shopaholic who spent all her money ordering new toasters and expensive purses online. Why the heck couldn't she afford a car on a detective's salary? It wasn't exactly great pay, but it was enough for a damn car.

"I look young," she said, while peering out the window. "I'm thirty-one." She turned back to him. "And I wasn't a junior cheerleader. I was varsity."

"Yeah, well I shouldn't have said any of that. Sometimes, yeah, sometimes, I guess I'm just an asshole."

Reg spun in her seat. "And how old are you? Wait, let me guess." She squinted at him. "Forty-three."

"Forty-three?" Logan asked incredulously.

"Forty-five," she continued.

"Fuck off. I'm thirty-nine."

"Ah, so you're on the cusp," she said and turned back to face forward.

"On the cusp of what? I've still got four months in the thirties."

"Sorry, didn't mean to insult you. Besides, you're sort

of handsome in that grungy, couch potato with beard stubble kind of way."

"Gee thanks. Feeling better by the minute."

She laughed. "You're right. I'm still getting back at you for this morning. I'm sure you clean up real nice."

"Yeah, after I get the grungy couch potato shit off of me." Logan glanced over at her. "Let me see—varsity cheerleader. You grew up in the perfect little family, two amazing parents and maybe a younger sister and an older brother, and the five of you vacationed in the Bahamas every summer. You lived in a two-story contemporary with big glass windows overlooking the beach, and you blew your parents' minds when you told them you wanted to become a cop but you just felt you needed to contribute to society."

"I'm impressed. You're pretty spot on, only you forgot the palomino horse and the pink convertible Corvette I drove to high school. Oh wait, that's right, that was my Barbie doll's life. My Malibu Barbie that my mom bought me at a yard sale for a quarter. She was marked down because her previous owner had already cut her hair thus depriving me of that particular rite of passage."

"Rite of passage?"

"Giving your Barbie doll a haircut. It's a rite of passage. Only we were too poor to buy a new Barbie. And no siblings. Just me and my mom. I had a dad but one day the principal pulled me out of my third grade classroom. I was pissed too because we were cutting out paper pumpkins for Halloween. Anyhow, my mom was there crying, and she told me Dad had gone to the angels. All I knew was that my paper pumpkin wasn't going to have a mouth because I'd only cut out the eyes and nose."

Logan looked over at her. "Your dad was dead, and you were worried about your pumpkin?"

"He was so drunk my entire life, I never really got to know him. He was just this blob on the couch who smelled like sweat and stale beer." She turned again and seemed to be assessing him. "My turn. You came from a long line of cops and military, so you had no choice except to join the force. Every morning you drive through your favorite junk food place and order two breakfast burritos with extra salsa and a hot, black coffee. Two hours later you're popping those chalky wafers because of the extra salsa, but the heartburn doesn't stop you from buying the burritos the next day. You get angry easily hence the swollen hand. You've never been married because of commitment-phobia. And you'd love to get a dog but you don't get one, again, because of the aforementioned phobia."

"I take cream in my coffee." Logan had his good hand resting casually over the top of the steering wheel as he watched the road. Traffic hour was in full swing, and brake lights were splashing on and off like strobe lights in a disco.

"Ah ha, so I was right about the rest?" She sat back with a self-satisfied grin.

"My dad was an accountant."

She spun. "Seriously?"

"Why does everyone say it like that? Yeah, he worked with numbers. And I've been married. We even had a dog, so I guess the whole commitment phobia theory is out the window too."

"Extra salsa?" she asked holding on to a last thread of hope.

"I do like salsa."

She clapped once. "Ah ha!"

"Uh, not sure if that's worthy of a victory lap. You got everything else wrong, including my age. Forty-five. Fuck that."

Logan turned down Tuscany. It was one of those streets that was more dead than alive. Half the shops were boarded up and those boards had been there so long they were covered thick with graffiti. The most popular corner boasted a run-down liquor store that sold beer that was well past its prime, wine that was more vinegar than alcohol and waxy donuts in cellophane wrappers. The owner, Jimbo, as the locals called him, also owned the Laundromat next door and the check cashing hole in the wall next to the laundry. One could say that Jimbo was the Bezos of Tuscany Street.

Logan's new partner had finished her granola bar and moved on to a silver thermos. She took a few swigs and blotted her mouth dry before pushing her thermos into the backpack.

"Is nutrition break over?" he asked.

She zipped her backpack up with extra flair. "Yep, ready to work. Just point me toward the corpse."

The coroner's van was parked at the end of an alley. A cluster of curious onlookers had lined up behind the yellow caution tape, each one straining and standing on toes to catch a glimpse of what was happening.

Logan and Reggie pulled out their badges to flash at the uniformed patrol keeping a check on the spectators. They ducked under the yellow caution tape stretched across the alley and walked past the dumped trash can, the discarded pair of underwear and the dead rat. The narrow passage smelled rank as if someone had taken a piss on a pile of towels and then left them in a wet heap. It made his eyes water.

Reggie crinkled her nose too. "What a hellish place to take your last breath," she said grimly.

The coroner was crouched over a crumpled body. Mitch Oster, fifty something with a double chin and two uneven eyebrows, had once been a prominent plastic surgeon. The ridiculous cost of malpractice insurance convinced him to try a different path. He switched from millionaires searching for the perfect chin, nose and ass to dead people found in alleys, riverbeds and on the sides of freeways. As he once told Logan 'dead junkies don't have the lawyers or the enthusiasm to sue a doctor, mostly because they're already dead'.

"Mitch, what have we got?" Logan asked the coroner.

Mitch spun around. "Coop," he started but stopped abruptly when saw Reggie. "New partner?" he asked Logan as if she wasn't standing right there.

Reggie didn't wait to be introduced. "Detective Hawkins but feel free to call me Reggie."

Mitch tripped over his tongue for a second. "Right, uh, Reggie. Right." It was like watching the school nerd find out that the prom queen was going to be his science partner. The man got elbow and face deep into some of the grisliest murder scenes in the city, but he was losing his shit trying to keep his cool for the new detective.

Reggie, on the other hand, ignored his reaction and stepped closer to the body. Something told Logan she'd learned how to ignore men acting like idiots in front of her. She pulled on her latex gloves and stooped down next to the woman. The victim looked young, early twenties with matted hair and chapped lips. Her face and clothes were streaked with dirt as if she'd been on the streets forever. Her t-shirt had a sparkly unicorn, a kid's shirt, probably from the garbage or a thrift store. It made her look even younger and sadder.

"Looks like an overdose. Jane Doe right now. No identification." Mitch said. "Maybe you could find out who she was so I can wrap this up with a name."

Logan glanced past Mitch's shoulder to his partner. Reggie gently, thoughtfully brushed a stray piece of hair off the girl's forehead as if the woman was just sleeping.

She pushed to standing. Mitch made no effort to hide that he was checking her out from behind.

"Let's see if anyone knows her," Logan suggested. "Maybe we can get a name."

They ducked back under the yellow caution tape. A blazing summer sun had made its way through the early morning haze. The grimy sidewalks were starting to heat up. Jimbo had come out from his liquor store. He always wore a green baseball cap, his lucky cap he claimed. His belly had grown bigger and his gray beard longer than the last time Logan had had to ID a corpse in a nearby alley.

"Detective Cooper." Jimbo always used his most polite tone and most gracious grin. He figured it would help Logan look the other way if one of his semi-legitimate businesses got caught up in police radar. This side of town was a catastrophe, one that the city council had neatly managed to ignore, Jimbo's business practices floated easily under the radar.

"Hey, Jimbo, this is Detective Hawkins."

Jimbo handled the introduction much better than the coroner. "Always nice to have a new hero out here on our humble streets." At seventy something, an ex-marine and a father of six, all from different mothers, Jimbo was always the charmer.

"We've got a young woman, deceased in the alley," I continued.

"Brown hair and wearing a shirt with a sparkly unicorn," Reggie added.

"I figured it was Tawny. At least that was what she called herself," Jimbo said. "You know how it is out here— no one uses their real name much. I thought Tawny sounded like she saw it in a book or something. But I could be wrong. That's too bad. She was a good kid. Hate to say it but I'm not too surprised." Jimbo's gaze swept over to the group that had huddled across the street to watch. Many of them wore that desperate, terrified expression that seemed to be saying 'am I next'.

Jimbo turned back and pulled down the brim of his hat as if that might keep someone from reading his lips. He spoke quietly now, not his usual booming tone. "You need to talk to that kid with the sweatshirt hood pulled up over his head. Tall, skinny one with the yellow shirt." Logan and Reggie glanced casually over their shoulders. "I think he's been passing some bad shit around. I know he and Tawny were friends."

"Right. Thanks, Jimbo." Logan and Reggie headed across the street to the crowd. A few of them peeled away from the group, obviously not wanting to talk to the police. Logan made eye contact with the kid in the sweat-shirt. His eyes rounded before he pushed a woman out of his way and tore off down the road.

"Come up on his right," Logan blurted. He glanced around for Reggie but couldn't find her. "Fucking great." The first sign of trouble and his new partner conveniently disappeared. Logan's feet hit the cement hard as he raced after the kid. He found himself having to dodge people on the sidewalk and hopped off the curb onto the cracked asphalt. He kept the runner in his sights, but the distance between them was stretching. The hood of the sweatshirt flew off revealing a shaved head and a few neck tattoos. Logan jumped back onto the sidewalk to avoid a bicycle. The kid turned a corner. Logan was going to lose him. Breaths were coming fast and short and labored. He was pissed at himself for eating garbage all weekend and blowing off any notion of a workout for the past half year. But he was more pissed at his new partner for managing to lose herself in the crowd when the suspect took off.

Only she hadn't lost herself in the crowd.

Logan's feet had been moving so fast, as fast as the heartbeat in his chest, he faltered forward a few steps before putting on the brakes. It would take a lot longer for his pulse to slow. Reggie stood in front of their runaway suspect. He was already on his knees with hands behind his head as Reggie aimed her gun at him.

Logan was far more interested in how his partner had managed to get so far in front of the suspect while Logan was breathing as if he'd been dragging a wagon of bricks behind him.

He glanced around hoping that there was a bicycle or a scooter nearby, something to make him feel less crappy. "How the hell?" he asked with a head shake.

"Must have been that nutrition break." Reggie put the gun in back in its holster near the small of her back. The kid wasn't going anywhere. Logan pulled out his phone and radioed the patrol officers to come make the arrest. Before he could put his phone away, dispatch rang through.

"Coop here."

"Detective Cooper, you're needed over at Crystal Lake. They've found a submerged car with a body inside. Looks like foul play."

"Right. Just tying up some loose ends over on Tuscany. We're heading there next." Logan hung up. "Well, Flash, we've got another dead body."

CHAPTER
FIVE

Crystal Lake was a twenty acre mud puddle eighteen miles inland from the coast. It had started as a natural lake, a result of uneven topography and rain run-off. Fifty years ago, the surrounding towns decided to turn it into a park where people could fish or kayak. There was even a section roped off for swimming if one didn't mind taking a dip in cold, slimy water.

Logan pulled into the small paved parking lot. There were a few cars, including one that had a boat trailer. Low shrubs grew around half the lake in between sections of sandy shoreline where weekend fishermen could launch their boats or ducks could cluster for a nap. The trash cans at the opening of the parking lot were overflowing with food wrappers, foam cups and all the garbage collected up after a busy summer weekend. The smell of charred burgers, mustard and sunscreen lingered in the air.

Sara Vaughn's gray coroner's van was parked on an unpaved section between a bike rack and a kiosk for cold drinks and bait.

The car that was coated with sludge and weedy lake debris looked to be a silver Camry. It had been pulled to shore by a boat. The chains were still attached to the undercarriage. The driver's side door had been pried off and was resting against the car. Sara was wearing her signature lavender lab coat as she crouched next to a body. Two feet, one bare and the other with an orange flip-flop dangling off the big toe, were all Logan could see as they approached the site.

Yellow caution tape fluttered in the breeze, a gentle air disturbance that caused a slow ripple across the murky surface of the lake. A man and a young boy, maybe ten, stood near the scene but stayed just far enough back to avoid making eye contact with the waterlogged corpse.

Officer Yardley, a newbie on the force, who was always serious and by the book, greeted them before they reached the grisly part of the scene. "Detective Cooper," Yardley nodded. She nodded at Reggie too.

"Officer Yardley, this is Detective Hawkins."

Yardley nodded again. "Nice to meet you."

"What have we got?" Logan asked.

"Two fishermen, Ian Perkins and his son, Kyle, were out on the lake. Kyle's hook got caught on something. Rather than snap his new pole, a Christmas present from his grandfather," Yardley added in unnecessarily. She liked to be thorough. "Kyle jumped in to free the hook. He popped right back up to let his dad know that the hook was caught on the bumper of a car. He dove down once more and this time came up breathless and terrified. He told his dad there was someone inside the car. They called the police. A dive team was summoned and sure enough, this Camry was jammed into the lakebed under about eight feet of water. The coroner thinks the woman has been down there about four days."

"Possible suicide?" Reggie asked as they hiked the grassy knoll down to the shore. From a distance, the water looked almost refreshing on a hot summer morning, but up close it had a musty, fetid odor.

"If so, then she was determined not to change her mind." Sara's cryptic comment was instantly clarified. The limp, bluish hand was missing several layers of skin. A handcuff was still secured to the wrist. "They had to cut her free of the steering wheel to remove her from the car. Looks like she popped her shoulder out trying to escape." Sara pointed out the unnatural slope of the woman's left shoulder. "Scary way to go," she added.

"Ann Robbins." Yardley held up an evidence bag with a wallet. The inside of the bag was smeared with lake water. "Her wallet was in the pocket of her shorts."

Logan glanced briefly at the lifeless body. The coroner had placed her on her back. She was wearing cutoffs, a t-shirt and her left flip-flop.

"Looks like she was going to the beach or for a walk at

the park," Reggie said. "Do you think she was heading here, to the lake? Maybe met up with a crazy—"

"The car was stolen." Office Moore came up from behind. He was a veteran on the force, one who had paid his dues and was counting down his days to retirement. He held up another evidence bag. It contained a plastic sleeve of car registration. "Car belonged to Terrence O'Hara. He reported it stolen four days ago."

Reggie stooped down next to the woman. It was the second time Logan had seen her crouched next to a corpse, a stranger she'd never met, and it was the second time Logan had seen her touch the victim gently, gloved but still with tender fingertips. There was no revulsion or cold, hard examination on first glance. It was one human showing a brief flash of emotion for someone who had lost their life. It could've been something that got in the way of her job, but something told Logan it was just her way of dealing with what came next—putting together their story, piece by piece, until their life became clear, and with any luck, their death became even clearer.

"She's beautiful," Reggie noted as she stared down at the woman. "Like someone a man might become obsessed with." She pushed to standing. "Just tossing out possible motives. It's hard to fathom what kind of monster would do this. Was it just for fun? Seems like we're dealing with a real psycho."

Logan surveyed the area, the lake, the parking lot, the slime covered car. Every detective had their way of dealing with seeing more than a natural or healthy share of dead people. It seemed his new partner liked to make an instant emotional connection. Logan was the opposite. He avoided a connection for as long as possible. He tended to focus on external factors and evidence, leaving the connection to the body on the ground to the last possible moment. Today was no different. Something about the flip-flop hanging off her toe had placed a lead ball in his chest. She was young, active, and so alive just days ago, she'd scooted around on flip-flops. No one could look depressed or sad walking in flip-flops. This woman had not been thinking about her imminent death when she slipped her slender, tanned feet into those damn shoes.

"I'll go talk to the father and son who found her," Logan suggested. It was easier to start out and work his way in toward the main event, the victim. Sara would have time to give the body a thorough look first.

"Coop, I'm going to take a look around," Reggie said. Shit, her voice was already starting to sound familiar like they'd been out on the beat together for years. It felt right. Maybe Logan had needed a partner after all. "I'll see if anything looks out of place. Four days ago would have put her death on Friday." Reggie looked pointedly at the overflowing trash cans. "From the looks of it, there were a lot of people here this weekend. That'll make it almost impossible to find anything relevant but I'll give it a shot."

Logan headed over to the man and his son. Someone had put an emergency Mylar blanket around Kyle's shoulders. It was the middle of July. The sun was starting to get brutal, but the kid had his arms crossed and he shivered beneath the blanket. An unexpected dead person on your morning fishing excursion could do that, and this kid looked young. He'd probably only recently learned that there was such thing as death.

"Mr. Perkins." Logan flashed his badge.

Kyle finally stretched up out of his cold huddle to look at the badge. "Cool. Is that a detective's badge?" he asked. It was reassuring to hear the typical kid question. With any luck and some good strong chats with his father, Kyle wouldn't be too traumatized by the morning's event.

"Sure is." Logan let him get a better look at it. "So, Kyle, I understand you were the person to discover the car."

Kyle nodded. His nose was bright red with sunburn, and his hair was plastered to his head from the water. "My fishing hook got caught." An impish grin appeared. "I thought I'd caught a whale or something. Then it looked like my rod might break it was bending so much, so I jumped in and my foot kicked something hard. I thought it was a rock. I opened my eyes underwater. It's really gross under there. But the car was easy to see. It's so big and it doesn't look like a rock."

"He popped up and said 'hey, dad, there's a car under here'," Mr. Perkins said. "I didn't believe him at first." Perkins pointed to a section of sandy shore that was to the left of the parking lot. "We put our boat in there. There's something about the way the lake is situated, a natural current or a slight drop in elevation. Anyhow, when we drop our boat in on that section of beach, I don't even need to start up the motor."

"That always scares the fish off, then you have to wait for them to come back," Kyle added.

"We just drift right to the middle," Perkins continued. "Not sure how it works with a car but with air in the tires and in the cab, I suppose they could float for awhile. At least long enough to get to the center where the water is deepest."

Logan glanced out at the lake. Sunlight was reflecting off the surface. The wind had died down giving it a glassy appearance. The dive team had dropped a buoy in where the car was found.

"Do you happen to know how deep this lake is?" Logan asked. A good fisherman always knew a lot of facts about their favorite fishing spots. Perkins knew the best place to launch his two-man boat.

"It's about twelve feet in the center," Kyle piped up, happy to share his knowledge. "But never take your boat to the east side, where the kiddie slide and swings are. There's a bunch of submerged tree trunks."

Perkins chuckled lightly. "Trust me, you only make that mistake once."

"Cooper," Sara called.

Logan waved to let her know he'd be right there. "Thanks so much for your help. We'll contact you if we need anything else."

"So we can leave?" Perkins asked. "Unless you want to keep fishing?" he asked Kyle.

Kyle shook his head decisively. "Let's get burgers tonight. After I opened my eyes under that water, I'm not sure I want to eat anything out of that lake for dinner."

"I'm with Kyle on the burger decision." Logan winked at the kid. He headed back to Sara. Reggie had joined her. His new partner was stooped down next to the victim on the right side. She had on her latex gloves as she looked at something on the woman's wrist.

"Want to see something wild?" Reggie called to him. Logan couldn't imagine what could be wild about a four day old waterlogged corpse, but something seemed to tickle his partner. And the coroner, for that matter.

He reached the body.

"She has a name tattooed on the inside of her wrist," Reggie said, again with a teasing tone that was especially strange given the situation. "Not sure what the odds are—" Reggie said to Sara.

Sara shook her head. "It's not a common name, so I'd say slim to none."

"What the hell are you two going on about?" Logan asked.

"It says Logan," Reggie said.

Logan was still trying to decipher just what the hell they were talking about. "What do you mean?"

"Look." Reggie gently took hold of the arm and lifted it.

Logan stared down at the wrist, at the scrolled

writing that spelled out the name Logan. He inadvertently stepped back, stunned, the breath evaporating from his chest. It took all his will to drag his gaze to her face. Seconds ago, she was a dead body, a woman named Ann who had found herself in a nightmare situation and who had undoubtedly died a horrible death. The tiny nose, the perfect lips, now blue with death, the long lashes shadowing the sallow cheeks, she was no stranger. But it was impossible. It was fucking impossible.

"Becca," the name fell from his mouth.

"Coop?" Reggie asked. "Everything all right? Are those breakfast burritos backing up on ya?"

Logan raked his fingers through his hair and spun around to catch his breath. The acrid smell of the rusty car pushed through his nostrils making him feel even more nauseous. He walked a few paces toward the parking lot. The overflowing trash had its own rotten odor.

He turned back around. Sara, Reggie and the other officers were watching him. He wanted to be anywhere but standing on that lake shore. He forced himself to look again at the body outstretched, her torn up hand lying limply next to her side, the unnatural shade of gray on her long legs clashing with the bright green grass. It was impossible. There was no fucking way. It had to be a bizarre coincidence, all of it.

He took a deep breath and ignored the knot in his

stomach. He pulled tight his latex gloves. "Yardley, let me see that wallet."

His reaction had confused everyone at the site. He didn't give a fuck at the moment. Yardley lifted the wallet out of the bag and handed it to him. It was a nice leather wallet with a brass clasp. He opened the wallet and lifted out the driver's license. Ann Robbins was thirty-nine years old. Five foot six. A hundred and twenty-five pounds with blue eyes and brown hair. But it wasn't the information that had every muscle in his body tense as if someone had tased him. The name was different but that didn't matter. It was the face. He would know it anywhere. Someone could plaster a thousand photos on a wall, and he could pick it out.

Logan dropped the wallet back into the bag and handed it off to Yardley.

Reggie pushed to standing. Her brown eyes blinked at him, bewildered. At the same time, a true detective, she was mentally picking apart his reaction. Her bottom lip parted slightly from the top. "This was no coincidence," she said quietly. "You knew her." The words and the tone she used tightened his throat around his Adam's apple. He swallowed to relieve the pressure. "The name on her wrist," Reggie continued. "You're Logan."

Logan found it hard to make direct eye contact with Reggie, with Sara, with anyone standing at the scene. He nodded, still not making eye contact. "Her name is Becca. Rebecca Ann Kinsey." He could feel Reggie's gaze hitting the side of his face. He finally drew in a clean breath and looked at her. "We grew up together."

"I'm sorry," Reggie said quietly.

Logan shook his head and stared down at the body. "I haven't seen her in two decades."

"Wow, what are the odds?" Reggie said again.

Logan looked at her. "I'd say a hundred billion to one. Becca Kinsey died four weeks after her eighteenth birthday."

CHAPTER
SIX

Logan let Reggie drive. He told her not to get used to it. He needed time. Nothing made sense. Becca Kinsey, or Ann Robbins as she would be officially called at the morgue, would be lowered onto the cold metal table, in the icy room where chemical smells and the pervasive odor of death could make the strongest stomach turn in on itself. Memories kept popping up, but Logan squashed them fast. They would only mess with his head.

Reggie kept her eyes on the road. She wasn't familiar with the area. Logan sensed she was memorizing street names and important locations as she drove through town. He also sensed that she had a million questions just waiting to be asked, but she kept them to herself... for now. Eventually, he'd have no choice except to answer them, but at that moment, her silence was exactly what he needed. His head was clear right now, a blank slate of dreary nothingness. He didn't want to think about the dead body they pulled from the lake or the terrifying way she died. He didn't want to think about his teen years growing up with Becca Kinsey, the girl who could steal your heart with a laugh, the girl everyone wanted, the girl who lit up the whole fucking town just by existing.

Logan's phone rang and jarred him from his semi-coma. It was the coroner. He let it ring again.

Reggie glanced his direction. "Do you want me to answer it?"

Logan shook his head. "Hey, Sara, what have you got?"

"The next of kin have been notified." The phrase next of kin unleashed a few of those memories he'd hoped to tamp down. The only kin Logan knew of were Ray and Linda, Becca's parents. Both dead now. Ray was an abusive prick who had no right to ever be called human, and Linda was a woman so broken by her abusive husband she spent her days walking the town dressed in mismatched clothes and shoes muttering incoherent phrases. And the two of them, two people who everyone in town avoided, had somehow produced an incredible daughter.

"Who is it?" Logan asked.

"Her husband, of course."

"Yeah, right. Her husband." It was stupid considering her last name, Robbins, but Logan hadn't even considered that Becca was married. Stupidly, Logan had convinced himself that he was her first and only real love. In his defense, he hadn't expected her to go on with life, with love, with dating, with marriage after she'd been declared dead.

"I thought you'd want to be here when he comes in to identify the body," Sara continued. Words were flowing through the phone, but Logan was having a helluva time comprehending anything. It took him a second to respond.

"Right. When is he going to be there?"

"He's on his way. His name is Gary. Gary Robbins." Images of Gary Robbins flashed through his mind. What was he like, this Gary Robbins, the man who won the heart of the elusive Becca Kinsey? People in town called her the girl everyone wanted but no one could have. She hated the phrase. And Logan did too. No one knew they were together. It was just easier not letting people in their gossip-laden town know.

"We'll be there soon. Thanks, Sara." Logan hung up. "Husband is going to identify the victim." He spoke as if he was talking about any victim, any corpse they might have come across during their work day. "County morgue. It's a block past the precinct." Logan stared out the passenger window. He rarely sat shotgun in his car. It was nice for a change, nice not having to deal with traffic or signals. The sidewalks were crowded with locals and tourists, the latter being the most recognizable because of the constant quest for selfies and the long pauses at shop windows. A large, shaggy dog, with no particular human attached, trotted between the pedestrians and stopped in the doorway of the deli. It made Logan smile, the first of the morning. But it faded fast. He worried he wouldn't be able to continue this investigation. At the same time, it had to be him. He had to find out who did this. He had to do it for Becca.

Reggie still hadn't spoken. It had only been a few hours and she'd stolen his parking spot and told him he looked forty-five, but he liked his new partner. Aside from being remarkably fast in a foot race, she had the good sense to know he wasn't ready to talk about this yet. She was just as involved, this was very much her case too, but she kept all her questions for later. And he would answer them later. He had to. Whoever did this was going to pay. Logan's hand throbbed just thinking how badly he wanted to pound the person who handcuffed Becca to that steering wheel. What was she thinking as the water seeped in around her? Was she screaming with terror? Something told him, she wasn't. That wouldn't have been Becca at all. She would have put up a good fight, and did from the looks of her shoulder and hand, but she never would have let her killer see her fear. She would have kept that inside, hidden from the malicious person who imprisoned her in that car. After all, she had a lot of experience with monsters.

Reggie navigated her way to the coroner's parking lot. It was a gray, nondescript industrial looking building with sparse windows. Logan always considered it wrong to have the place where people came to identify their dead loved ones such a grim looking place. He wasn't picturing a cozy cottage with curtains and flower beds but a building that somehow offered some light, some comfort would have made a horrific situation slightly more bearable. That was what he needed right now. What about Gary Robbins? How had he reacted to the news? How would he react to seeing his beautiful dead wife on the exam table? They were all questions he should be asking as an investigator.

Logan hadn't seen Becca for twenty-one years. In that time he'd had to absorb the heartbreaking news that she was dead, gone from his life for good. It seemed her death now should have had less impact, but he was still feeling as if someone had run him over with a semi-truck. He couldn't imagine how it would feel to someone who was recently in her life, someone who had recently held her in his arms, someone who had recently heard her laugh. Her laugh. There was no sound better than Becca laughing. What if Gary was the killer? They always looked at the husband or significant other first. Gary. Logan didn't like the name. He'd worked with a guy named Gary on the force, when he was still in a patrol car. He was an asshole who liked to bully coffee baristas and donut shop owners into giving him free food. He weaseled his way out of working holidays and weekends by making up family emergencies like sickly parents or grandparents' funerals. He buried a lot of grandfathers.

Reggie turned off the car. She stared at the building. "I

know it's a morgue, but could it look any more depressing?"

Logan smiled again, for a second time, finding it amusing that they were thinking the same thoughts about the morgue. She turned to him. There was a spray of freckles across her nose that he was already fond of. It went along with the fragrance of lemonade that surrounded her, a pleasing scent that seemed to be natural.

"How are you doing?" she asked. It was the first time she'd brought up his obvious state of distress. He needed to pull his shit together. He was on a job, and he needed to be professional.

"Fine. I'm good. Let's go inside and meet the husband. Nine times out of ten, it's the husband." Logan said the word husband through gritted teeth. If Gary had been the culprit, Logan wanted to look him right in the face as he read him his rights.

Sara spotted them on the way inside and came out of her office. "Detectives, the husband is on his way. A friend is driving him. He was too upset to get behind the wheel."

Right, too upset, Logan thought wryly. "Sara," Logan started. He didn't know if it was a good or bad one but he'd made a decision. "Do you mind if I see her..." Logan glanced at Reggie. "Alone," he added, unnecessarily. His intuitive partner had already figured out what he meant.

"I'll keep an eye out for the husband," Reggie said.

Logan followed Sara to the autopsy room. She opened

the door and closed it behind him once he stepped inside. Holy shit, it was a dreadful place. He always hated the metallic, sanitized smell of the morgue, but today he hated it even more. How did Sara spend her day in such a cold, miserable room without going into full depression? He assumed it was interesting to someone like her, a medical expert, a forensic scientist. Drab and metal and cold as it was, this was where she practiced her craft.

Surveying and mentally criticizing Sara's lab, a lab he'd stood in dozens of times, helped him avoid looking at the body on the metal table. Logan could see the outline of Becca's delicate form beneath the gray sheet. It was time. The husband would be there soon. Logan would need to pull back on his detective's hat and force himself to be objective.

Logan willed his feet forward. It felt as if his shoes had been covered in cement as he walked toward the table. He couldn't remember the last time his hands trembled. Or could he? The day Vicky told him the marriage was over. He remembered having to still his hands as she spoke to him through tears and sobs.

Logan reached for the edge of the gray sheet and pulled it back slowly, revealing first the pale forehead, smooth and relaxed in death. The long lashes, the only feature that still made her look alive. How often he'd seen those same lush, sable lashes flutter as Becca lifted her blue gaze to his. Hell, did she have a magnetic gaze. If you were lucky enough to get caught up in it, there was no way you could look away first. She held you there with her magic, those baby blue eyes that could peer right into your soul. Her lips were no longer the dark pink he remembered. Death had erased the color. He could still remember how warm and soft they felt pressed against his mouth. Becca's kiss could draw out any darkness. There was no way to feel sad with her lips on you.

Becca's right arm had slipped halfway out of the sheet. It was almost as if she'd done it on purpose. Her hand, a hand he'd held secretly, under the lunch table in the quad, in the local park after dark, in the middle of the night when she'd snuck out of her house of horrors for the security of his arms. As often as he'd mentally plotted killing Ray Kinsey, taking his thick neck between his hands to squeeze the life out of him or pounding him to oblivion with his torpedo fast right fist, he was never able to save Becca from her horrific family life. Logan had convinced himself she could no longer bear the abuse at home so she walked into the Pacific Ocean and took her own life. But here she was, now, two decades later, most certainly dead. What the hell happened?

Logan's hands still trembled as he reached for her hand. The fingers were icy cold, hard. Nothing like he remembered. "Why'd you leave me, Cricket? I'm sorry. I should have just killed him. I should have taken him out." His fingers grazed over the tattoo. It was only two inches long, but to him, it had been huge. He'd never forget that day. It was marked in indelible ink on his heart just like the ink on her slim wrist.

Becca bites her lip teasingly. She knows it drives me nuts, and this time is no different. "Cricket, what are you hiding behind your back?"

"It's a surprise." Her pink tank top stretches tightly across her breasts as she keeps her hands behind her back. The powdery perfume she always dabs around her throat caresses my sense of smell. My erection presses against the front of my jeans. I lunge for her. She shrieks and backs up with almost a look of fear.

It gives me pause and, honestly, I'm more than a little hurt. "What's wrong?" My mind flashes instantly to her dad. "Did that fucker hurt you again? I swear, Becca, I'm going to take him out. Just get me alone with the asshole." I know my words are bigger than my actions, but while half the guys in town daydream about being with Becca, I dream about killing the man she calls Dad.

Becca brings her arms forward and lifts her right hand. Her wrist is red and puffy, and my resolve to kill Ray Kinsey causes me to nearly bite through my bottom teeth.

"What did he do?" I ask, still clenching my jaw.

Her blue eyes blink with innocence, confusion. "Who? It's a tattoo. I told you I was going to get a tattoo the second I turned eighteen." Again, she bites her lip. "Want to see it?"

"Yeah, of course I wanna see it." I'm expecting a kitten or a butterfly. I stare at the black fancy script trying to break free from the red swollen skin around it. The capital L is easy to see. My heart skips ahead a little faster as I look up at her. Every time I look at Becca, it's like looking at her for the first time. She always takes my breath away.

"Does it say—" My words trail off. It would be too embarrassing to be wrong. I badly want to be right.

"It says Logan." Her warm breath caresses my neck as she presses her body against me. *"Do you like it?"*

"What do you think, Cricket?" My arms wrap around her. *"How the hell did I get so damn lucky?"* I kiss her softly at first, then harder, my arms tightening around her more.

She pauses the kiss long enough to peer up at me. I'm on fucking fire, wanting her, needing her more than ever. *"Guess it's official, Logan Cooper. I belong to you and no one else."*

Sara's light knock on the door jarred Logan from his thoughts. "The husband just arrived." She backed out again, shutting the door, leaving him alone in the room.

Logan's throat tightened as he squeezed her hand for the last time. "I'll find who did this, Becca. I promise. I'll find who did this."

Right, Logan thought angrily. Let's meet this guy Gary.

Gary Robbins was smaller, paler and far less imposing than Logan pictured. It seemed that grief might cause him to crumple into a whimpering pile on the cold tile floor. Logan watched his every move, every mannerism, every expression. It was all part of the routine, to gauge the loved one's reaction, but on this occasion, Logan had an even keener interest. He could only explain it as a weird dose of envy. This was the man who had Becca all to himself. The man she said yes to.

He was not at all what Logan expected. His long face drooped under the weight of despair. He'd tried to keep his glasses steady on his nose, but they became such a burden, especially with having to wipe his eyes and nose, that he finally yanked them off and stuffed them angrily in his top pocket. Yes, he was that kind of man, the kind who wore a button-down shirt. Logan could only assume there had been a tie as well. The top button of the shirt was open where the tie once sat. His gray trousers seemed to indicate there had also been a matching coat. A business suit, a gray business suit complete with dark brown leather shoes. Becca had married a businessman. Gary was the last person on earth Logan would have expected to see shuffle through the glass doors of the morgue. His friend, also a business looking guy but with a sloppier appearance, wrinkled shirt and trousers, had to support Gary Robbins as he stumbled along on unsteady legs. Reggie hurried forward to lend a hand to the faltering husband. Logan was frozen to the spot, in front of the door to the exam room. It was almost as if he was standing guard, not wanting anyone to touch her. Not Sara with her torture implements. Not Gary with his business shirt and ill-fitting glasses.

It looked real, Logan thought. The grief, the anguish, it seemed genuine. Logan had seen some real Oscar winning performances in the building, but this seemed like the real thing. That didn't necessarily mean anything because he'd seen killers break down in utter agony when forced to come face-to-face with their victim. It was a level of remorse only someone who took another human's life could feel. Was that what Logan was looking at right now? Was Gary Robbins sick with the thought that he'd now have to identify his beautiful wife, the wife he sent to a terrible end?

Reggie braced Robbins' elbow while his friend held the other arm. His eyes were bloodshot red, and the color of his skin indicated that he might throw up.

Sara raced forward. "Let's sit him down here on the bench," she suggested. They led him to the wooden bench lining the hallway. He plopped down hard as his legs gave way even with the support on each side. Sara hurried off and returned with a bottle of water. "Here, Mr. Robbins, drink this. We'll let you get your bearings before we proceed."

Robbins shook his head. "I couldn't even swallow it." His voice was low and gravelly. It was a tone that would be hard to fake. Logan stood back, almost as if he wasn't part of this whole scene. Only, on this particular case, he was more involved than ever.

After a few minutes collecting himself, Gary Robbins took a deep, bracing breath. "I'm ready as I'll ever be." His voice cracked as if his throat was as dry as the desert. Sara offered him the water once more. He shook his head weakly. Gary made the short distance to the exam room door look like a journey to the top of Everest. His friend stuck by his side and looked just as faint and pale as Gary. Having to identify remains wasn't something most people endured. After standing in the room watching dozens of family members do just that, Logan knew it was, for most, a day they would never forget.

The journey to the table where Becca lay face up, her foot now free of the flip-flop and her wrist now free of its restraint, was even longer than the one to the door. Reggie swept to Gary's side and offered physical support. She didn't utter a word but was taking it all in, his reaction, his expressions, his mannerisms. She was a true professional. Logan felt like a total heel for going on the ugly rant in Castillo's office. Castillo, he thought right then. What if the captain took Logan off the case? It wouldn't be unheard of. It would be expected. He was going to have to fight to stay on it.

Logan stood like a dark shadow in the background, not saying a word, not offering support like his partner was doing. He was just there. He almost felt as if he was watching the whole thing from some other world, like when someone leaves their body in a hospital room and watches as the doctors try to revive them. None of it felt real. None of it was possible and yet, there she was, on the table, still and gray as a statue. He considered that he should have been happy that Becca Kinsey went on to live twenty more years than he thought, but there were so many questions it was hard to even think it. She still died a horrible death. The perpetrator was still out there. One thing seemed certain, the killer was not in the room standing over the table.

The wails were hard to endure. Logan had witnessed some heartbreakingly profound reactions, usually parents identifying children, but Gary's was in the top five. Who could blame him? Becca wasn't an easy person to let go of. Logan knew that all too well.

CHAPTER
SEVEN

"I can't believe Halbert made us do detention on a Friday afternoon." Nate reaches for the radio and turns up the music. He drowned himself with aftershave this morning and I've been avoiding the smell all day. Now I'm stuck with it. "Whooee, a weekend at the beach. Can't fucking wait." He picks up the bag of red hot cheese puffs and jams his hand inside. "I wish I could take back all the rotten shit I put Jeremy through in middle school. I wouldn't have done it if I'd known his family had a beach house."

I laugh dryly. "So that would have made you nicer to the guy?"

Nate shaved his head recently. I'm still trying to get used to it. I doubt I will. "What can I say, I'm shallow like that. At least that's what Gina told me last week. She said, Nathan Collins," Nate was putting on his best imitation of Gina's high-pitched voice. "You're so shallow. All you want to do is get into my panties."

Nate shrugged. *"I said, yeah, what else?"* He reaches forward again and leaves orange, cheesy dust on my radio knob. *Sometimes I wonder why I am friends with Nate, then I remind myself of the slim-pickings in Layton. Besides, I have a best friend who is amazing. I don't need anyone else. An entire weekend with Becca. I can't fucking wait. She needs it too, getting out of town. Things seem to get worse at home each day. She's determined to get out of the house the second we graduate. I plan to marry her as soon as I get a good enough job to support us. I haven't let her in on that plan yet, but this weekend is going to be the best place to propose. After that, I don't give a damn who knows about us.*

"Can't believe Becca is going to be here this weekend," Nate says. "Do you think I have a chance with her? I was thinking of, you know, making a move."

I squeeze the steering wheel just a little tighter, tight enough to make my knuckles white. "No, she's not here to have you make a fucking move on her," I say with enough anger that he backs right off.

"All right, yeah, yeah, I get it. You want to try and make your move. I'll step aside."

"Fuck, no moves, She's here because she's friends with Jeremy. Becca is the only person who has never teased or bullied Jeremy. He considers her his best friend, and we're not going to fuck that up for him. Got it?"

"Jeez, Coop, calm the fuck down. Touchy subject, apparently. Or maybe you're just cranky because we had to help the custodians clean all the graffiti off the bathroom doors. Talk *about the punishment not fitting the crime. We should only have to clean up that graffiti if we wrote it."*

I take a breath to release some of the anger his comments have built up. It is something I am always working on, my anger. Mostly because Becca asked me to. "What would a punishment for truancy be then, having us skip more classes?"

Nate laughs. "Yeah, why the hell not?" He sat up higher. "Hey look, there's the entrance to the state beach. Looks like something happened down there."

Nate is right. Red spinning lights flash off the surrounding cliffs as a group of emergency vehicles huddle together on the sand.

Nate unbuckles his seat belt and scoots all the way forward to get a better view. "Looks like there are divers and a boat offshore. I wonder if a boat capsized."

The police have part of the parking lot sectioned off with yellow tape. I park my truck at the far end. Nate and I climb out.

"Is this the right place?" Nate asks.

I pull out the note Jeremy gave me with the address of the beach house. His uncle, a wealthy tech guy, has a beach house overlooking the coast. Jeremy managed to snag it for a whole weekend. "It says we'll be at the beach near lifeguard tower fifteen." The sun is almost entirely set. It touches the horizon line and casts only a smoky glow toward the shore. Jeremy and Becca headed out right after school. They planned to start a bonfire in one of the stone pits so that we could make hot dogs and s'mores. Nate and I had been caught ditching school on Tuesday, but Principal Halbert decided after-school detention would be a little more painful on a Friday afternoon.

We walk toward the chaos in the center of the sand, just a few feet away from lifeguard station fifteen. It's the only action on the otherwise deserted strip of sand. It's still early in the season for beachgoers. We were stoked about the idea of having the whole place to ourselves.

Nate grabs my arm. "Shit, isn't that Jeremy talking to the policeman?"

Instantly, my heart sinks to my stomach. We pick up our pace and are running by the time we reach them. Jeremy is white as the sand around us. He's shaking uncontrollably. We get closer and I realize he's wet. Jeremy West is afraid of germs, accidents and alien invasions. In middle school he wore a special suit he created for himself. It was lined with aluminum foil and had a thick canvas outer shell. He was sure it would keep him safe from everything. The only thing it didn't keep him safe from was a Layton heat wave. He passed out during a pep rally from overheating. Nearly died was what he always said about it. He was probably not far off. I can't think of what might have coaxed Jeremy into the icy cold ocean. He spots us running toward him and immediately breaks down in loud sobs.

"She's gone!" he cries. "Becca is gone!" He covers his face and drops to his knees. A policeman brings a blanket and drops it over his shoulders. I freeze to the spot, hoping all of this is a bad dream. But it's not. Becca walked into the ocean for a swim and

disappeared. That was how Jeremy told it over and over again between shoulder wracking sobs and gulps of air.

She was gone. The only person who mattered to me in the entire fucking world was gone. The lifeguards and coast guard searched until there was no light left in the sky. There was no trace of her. Nate, Jeremy and I sat at the fire pit, its flames long since gone, and waited late into the night hoping to see her suddenly, miraculously stroll out of the water with that teasing little sashay she pulled off so well. But she never emerged.

It wasn't until we returned to the house, so cold and numb from the temperature and shock we could barely climb the stairs, it wasn't until we entered the beach house, the place we'd planned to spend two glorious days away from adults and away from Layton, it wasn't until then that Nate noticed a piece of paper sticking out from under the candy dish on the coffee table.

My throat was so thick as I read the note, I could barely breathe.

"I'm so sorry, Jeremy. Tell Logan I'll always be his cricket. Love, Becca."

After ten minutes, Reggie and Sara led a disoriented Gary Robbins out to the hallway. Sara would collect his information. Reggie let him know they needed to talk to him and that it couldn't wait. He agreed.

"I want this monster found and put in front of a

fucking firing squad. Please just give me a few hours. I need to rest."

Reggie glanced toward her entirely unhelpful partner. Logan nodded. She turned back to Robbins. "That's fine. In the meantime, think about anyone she knew, anyone she might have been having trouble with, anyone at all who might have done this to her." Reggie placed a hand on his. "It will be hard, but we're going to need to turn Ann's life inside out. I hope we can count on your help with that."

Gary nodded and looked to his friend to help him out to the car.

Reggie walked over to Logan.

"How are you holding up?" she asked.

"Sorry I wasn't more help. I'm fine. What did you think?" Logan asked. She knew exactly what he meant. It was as if they'd been partners for years instead of only a few hours.

"He seemed genuinely broken," she said. "But then I've seen that before."

"Me too."

"I had a chance to talk to his friend, Hunter. They had just landed at the airport when he got the news. It seems they've been in New York at a business conference since last Wednesday. Get this, Gary Robbins is an accountant." Her brown eyes took on a cocoa color under the fluorescent lights. "Just like your dad."

"Don't say it," Logan said as they headed toward the exit.

"Say what?" she said teasingly. "Oh, you mean—what are the odds? I'm thinking we should buy some lottery tickets on our way out of here. At least you should buy some, but you have to share if you win because it was my suggestion." She was talking lightly, hoping to knock Logan out of his dreary mood and damn, if it wasn't working.

"Let's get some lunch," Logan said. His appetite was returning. He was coming out of his fog. It was time to get to work. This one was for Cricket.

CHAPTER
EIGHT

Reggie and Logan found an outside table near the parking lot and away from the group of teens throwing fries at each other and holding contests to see who could squirt ketchup farthest.

Logan smiled at Reggie's hummus and cucumber on wheat. She bought the sandwich to go with her grapes, an apple and thermos of water.

"What? If you're going to tell me you guessed I'd be choosing the vegan sandwich off the menu, I won't be impressed. There's nine million of us plant only eaters in this country, so the odds were pretty good."

"After this morning's display of preternatural speed, I'm almost thinking I should switch to hummus." Logan picked up his pastrami on rye. "Or I could just remain slow now that I have you as my partner." He took a bite. His stomach had been through every emotion before lunch. The pastrami was probably not the best choice but he was hungry.

Reggie wiped her mouth with a napkin and picked up the dill pickle on her plate. "So, it's time to talk." She took a loud bite of her crunchy pickle.

"Yeah, thanks for not pelting me with a million questions. I needed some time to process all this. It's just so fucking hard to believe."

"You said Becca died four weeks after her eighteenth birthday," she started. "What was that about?"

"Not exactly sure but I think it's going to take a trip to my hometown of Layton to find out for certain. There's someone there who might know more about her miraculous recovery from death. There was never a body. We were all convinced Becca committed suicide by swimming out into the Pacific. She even left a suicide note. The rescue crews couldn't find her. She never showed up, dead or alive. Until now."

"Why would she commit suicide?" Reggie pulled her water from her backpack. Logan made fun of the backpack, but it was starting to become a part of who she was and Logan liked who she was.

Logan placed his sandwich down. Just thinking about Becca's parents put a bitter taste in his mouth. "She had it bad at home. Her dad abused Becca and her mom. He was a first-class asshole. He ran the sawmill at the end of town. Ray Kinsey was a big, mean son of a bitch. People ducked out of his way on the sidewalk and even in church. You just didn't want to cross paths with him."

"I don't understand," Reggie said. "Why didn't the police do something about the abuse? Why didn't they call child services?"

"Ray Kinsey's older brother was the chief of police in our county. People tried to help, but his brother just covered up the problem, made it all go away."

"Shit, that sucks. Is Ray still alive?"

Logan shook his head. "Cancer finally got him about ten years ago."

"Good, I hope it was a long, hard slog to the end." Reggie took another bite. "Did you love her?"

It wasn't a question he was expecting. He nodded. "Me and every guy in town. Layton was this grubby, depressing, sleepy town, and Becca was the North Star. You couldn't help but love her."

Reggie squinted at him over her sandwich. A few of the curly green sprouts fell out onto her plate. "You're not really answering my question. I didn't ask if the whole town loved her. I asked if Logan Cooper loved her, the guy who she obviously loved because writing someone's name on your body in black ink takes some level of adoration."

"We were in love," Logan said. He took a bite, hoping that would be enough.

Reggie waited patiently for him to swallow, then grabbed his wrist before he could jam in another bite. "From the look on your face this morning, Coop, it seemed you'd just had your heart torn out, stepped on and wrung out. You guys weren't just a high school drive up to the look out to make out on Saturday night or hang when there was nothing better to do kind of couple. It was the real thing, wasn't it?" she asked. Her brown eyes were the kind that could coax secrets from a dead man. Another great detective skill as long as she didn't use it on her partner too often.

"I was fucking nuts about her. The weekend she disappeared—" He was calling it that now because it finally dawned on him that he had not lost Becca that horrid afternoon on the beach. She had left him. She wasn't lost. She hadn't killed herself to get away from her monster of a dad. She had decided to leave behind her whole life, including Logan. "I was planning to propose that weekend. We'd both finally turned eighteen. Becca planned to move out as soon as we graduated. I was going to be her knight and sweep in and carry her off to my castle. Only I didn't have a cent to my name. Still, I was sure we could make it on our own. I was willing to do anything to get her away from her parents."

"So her mother was evil too?" she asked.

"No, she was unstable. Some kind of psychosis and it only got worse. She'd always take long walks around town, even in the rain. She'd be soaking wet and wearing a sundress and sandals. Two angels. There were two angels. She was always repeating that. Becca didn't know what she meant by it. We figured she was seeing things and was always seeing two angels. She died a year after Becca disappeared. A broken heart was what my mom told me."

A text came through Logan's phone. It was from Fran, the office assistant and tech specialist who helped him with cases. "Fran says Robbins' alibi checks out. There was a tax accountant's conference in New York. He was even a speaker on Friday. There was no way he could have killed Becca." Another text. "The car was stolen after the owner accidentally left the keys in it. Right out of his driveway."

Logan texted back. "Any camera or security on the property?"

A text popped right back. "Nope. The owner is eighty. Probably why he left the keys in his car."

"Thanks, Fran."

Reggie folded up the second half of her sandwich in a napkin. "The husband's anguish seemed genuine. Guess it's time to talk to him. With any luck, he can give us some details about Ann's life that will lead us to her killer." She paused before standing up. "Are you sure you're up to this case, Coop?"

"Never been more sure."

CHAPTER
NINE

Logan parked the car and sat back. A traditional ranch house in the middle of a green lawn, paved-driveway suburb. It was what he expected for accountant Gary Robbins but not for Becca. She was untraditional in every sense of the word. Reggie noticed his hesitation.

"You all right?" she asked.

He pulled his eyes from the house with its pink rose bushes, brick trim and big front window. "Just can't picture Becca living in this house." He yanked the keys from the ignition. "Let's go."

Reggie picked up her backpack and swung it over her shoulder as they stepped outside. He was already getting used to that stupid striped backpack. He tugged it to stop her progress up the gray slate pathway leading to the house.

Reggie looked back with a raised brow. "It has my notebook and pen. I prefer to write notes."

"Sorry. I wasn't stopping you for that. I just wanted to —just so we're on the same page—let's not—"

"Let's not mention your previous relationship with the victim," she finished for me. "I think that's for the best."

There was a wreath on the front door, a collection of dried lavender and some small white flowers. Becca hung a wreath on her front door. He smiled to himself. At least he thought it was to himself.

"Something funny?"

"Nope." Logan knocked and pulled out his badge. Robbins knew who they were, but it was protocol and since he was already on thin ice due to skirting protocol, he decided to walk an extra straight line. Not that it would be easy considering the circumstances. This murder investigation was going to test him on every level of emotion.

A woman, thirty-something, attractive with short blonde hair and green eyes answered the door. Her face wore the pink puffiness of a good long cry. Logan and Reggie held up their badges.

"Detectives Cooper and Hawkins," Logan said. "We're here to see Gary Robbins."

The woman took a tissue from her jeans and gently wiped her nose. "Yes, he's expecting you. I'm Janey Moore. I was Ann's best friend. Please, this way. He's in the den. Can I get either of you anything, a glass of water or a cup of coffee?"

"We're fine, thanks," Reggie replied.

They followed Janey down a hallway to the den. Becca had a den. It was just as one might expect a den to look. Light blue curtains were drawn back to allow sunlight in through the big front window. The room was filled with a pair of matching floral print sofas, a tan rug and a cherry wood coffee table.

Gary was sitting on the couch staring out the front window, blankly, almost as if in a trance. He'd traded the button-down shirt for a gray tee. It matched his complexion. Everything about the man looked gray as if every ounce of life had been drained from him. Logan remembered that feeling well, having the life drained out of him by heartbreak. Sometimes, it seemed impossible to ever get back to normal. Logan was sure that was what Robbins was feeling right then as he stared blankly out the window. Would his life ever be the same? Would it even be worth living? After it had been concluded that Becca was gone forever, drowned in the icy Pacific, Logan had considered more than once following in her footsteps. He thought it might bring her back to him somehow. He could be with her in death, which, for a long time afterward, seemed like a better prospect than life without her.

"Gary," Janey said softly as if she didn't want to cause him to break into a million pieces.

His movements were slow, languid, the movements of someone in shock.

"Gary, there are two detectives here to see you." Janey

turned back to them. "Should I stay, or would you prefer I go?"

"We'd love to talk to you too," Reggie said.

Janey nodded. "I have to pick my kids up from the sitter in an hour, but I'd be happy to answer any questions. Anything that might help." She sat on the same couch as Gary. Logan and Reggie sat on the opposite sofa. Logan couldn't draw his eyes away from the photo on the wall behind Gary. Becca and Gary were standing on a beach, Hawaii from the looks of it. He was in a dark suit and tie. She was wearing a flowing white dress with a wreath of flowers in her hair, a diamond ring sparkling on her tanned finger. She looked stunning. It was her wedding day. He was supposed to be standing there on that beach, not Gary, Logan couldn't help thinking. Reggie's first question pulled him back to the conversation.

"First of all, we were unable to locate Ann's phone. Do you know where it might be?" Reggie asked.

Gary leaned forward and picked up a glass of water. He took several big swallows, then set the glass down. "I'm sorry, I'm just so parched." His voice was low and gravelly like he had sandpaper in his throat. "Janey and I looked all over for her phone. I was hoping that she might have left it behind when she went out. I figured it would be something you'd ask for. It's not here. I'm sorry. Is there a way you can trace it?" The chat seemed to be pulling him out of his stupor, something to get his mind off his misery. Logan had worried that he'd be too distraught to provide any information at all, but he'd already had the where-withal to search for the phone.

"Possibly. We'll have to get a warrant to get call detail records," Reggie said. "If you could write down your numbers and any other ones that we can eliminate as we're looking at the records that would be helpful." She'd already taken the lead. Logan was good with it. He was still in a bit of a stupor himself, especially knowing that he was sitting on Becca's couch, looking at Becca's blue walls, breathing in the air of the house she lived in.

Janey hopped up. "I'll get some paper and a pen."

"Is it true what they say?" Gary asked, starting apparently in the middle of a thought that was mostly still stuck in his head.

"What's that?" Logan asked.

"That if they don't get a suspect in the first twenty-four hours, then it gets harder? I think I saw that on some crime show somewhere." He paused to rub his face with his hands. "I'm sorry, I didn't mean to imply that you couldn't solve the case. But it will be harder, won't it? Considering it happened a few days ago."

"It can make the case harder," Logan said. "But we won't stop until the killer is arrested." He was telling himself that as much as the husband. "You've been away since last week?"

"That's right. I was at a conference."

"How did the house look when you returned?" Logan

asked. "Anything out of place? Signs of a struggle? Any open windows or broken doors?"

"It was just as you see it, neat and clean. Everything was locked up."

Janey returned with paper and pen. She looked pointedly at Gary. "Have you mentioned what we were talking about earlier?"

"Not yet." Gary gulped more water.

"Is there something you want to tell us?" Reggie asked.

Gary put the water down. "Janey and I were talking. Both of us noticed a big change in Ann these last two months or so. She was depressed. She was usually always happy, carefree, a wild spirit, you might say." His voice trailed off. "It was what I loved about her. You might be wondering why someone like her, someone as beautiful as Ann would have fallen for a guy like me. I often wondered that myself. She told me when she was growing up her best friend's dad was an accountant. She said she always envied their family. She said her friend's father was the only nice man in the neighborhood." Gary grew quiet. "I suppose I should thank that man if I ever meet him."

Logan felt himself sit back, stunned by what Gary was saying, as if the wind had been sucked out of his chest. He so badly wanted to jump into the conversation and talk about her past. It would help his own pain. It might help Gary too.

"I don't think Ann had great parents," Gary continued. "They're both dead now, apparently. I never knew them.

She told me they'd parted ways when she was just out of high school, and she wanted to keep it that way."

Reggie flicked a glance Logan's direction before focusing again on the conversation.

Janey pulled out her own phone and started writing down the contacts they had in common, including Gary's number.

Gary handed over his phone. "Don't forget her work number. It's on my contact list." Gary's face was still pinched, and his eyes were red. "She worked at Morgan's Fine Jewelry. I thought they would have called by now to find out why she's not in for her shift." That statement caused him enough grief that the color washed from his face. "Excuse me. I'm feeling faint."

Janey stopped her task and hopped up. "Lay back, Gary." Reggie hopped up to assist. She pulled together a few of the couch pillows and propped his feet up on them to get the blood flowing back to his head.

Reggie walked into the kitchen and returned with a wet towel for his forehead while Janey resumed her task of writing down numbers.

It seemed this interview session wasn't going to go too far. Gary was not in any kind of shape to be questioned.

"I know this is very difficult for you," Reggie forged ahead. Logan smiled inwardly. It had been a long time since he'd had what he considered a competent partner. "Is there anyone you can think of who might have wanted to cause Ann harm?" Reggie asked. "A coworker? Someone she had angered recently? Anyone at all?"

Without lifting it from the couch, Gary was shaking his head before she could finish. He held the cloth against his head and sat up slowly, cautiously. "Everyone loved Ann. She was just one of those people—how can I explain it?" He looked to Janey for help, but Logan already knew exactly what he was talking about.

"She lit up a room," Janey said. "I know that sounds cliché but that was Ann. Except these last few months. She was sullen. We usually go to lunch on Wednesdays. She found excuses every time."

Gary nodded. "She was depressed. She was dragging herself out of bed every morning. It wasn't like her."

"Do you have an exact day when this change occurred?" Logan asked. "Was it like a switch that got turned on or was it gradual?"

Once again they looked at each other to confer. "Right after her birthday?" Janey muttered.

"May 4th?" Logan asked.

Gary looked at him, his eyes rounded behind his lenses. Logan could feel Reggie's scolding gaze on the side of his face. He'd blown it but not too badly. "I saw it on the death certificate," Logan explained clumsily. "It stuck in my head because it's the same day as my mother's birthday." That part was not a lie. Logan's mother always went out of her way to buy two cupcakes, one for Becca and one for herself on May 4th. They'd sit at the kitchen table and talk and eat cupcakes. No one else was allowed to join them. Becca had told Logan more than once that she looked forward to the cupcake with his mom more than anything else on that day.

"Yes, it was right around then," Gary continued, satisfied with Logan's explanation. "I took her to her favorite Italian restaurant. I'd planned for a nice drive to the beach for a wine picnic afterward, but she barely said one word through the whole meal. She didn't want to go to the beach." Seemingly revived, he folded up the wet cloth and sat forward. "Two things I think might be important."

Logan's new partner had her purple pen ready to go.

"Ann told me that someone from her past had contacted her recently. It had shaken her up. She wouldn't tell me who it was or what they'd approached her about. She said she had to confirm a few facts first, but that never happened. I never found out who it was."

"Was it someone from her recent past or her childhood?" Logan asked, maybe too anxiously. Had someone else from their hometown discovered that Becca was still alive?

"I think her childhood, but I don't know for sure. That brings me to something along those lines. You might have noticed that Ann had a tattoo on her wrist. The name Logan."

Reggie sat up straighter with her pen and notepad. She shot a sideways glance at Logan.

"Yes, we saw that," Logan said.

"Then I'm surprised you haven't asked me who it is," Gary said, sounding a little perturbed. He pulled out of his earlier grief-filled trance. The subject of the tattoo seemed to have kicked him into gear.

"Who is it?" Logan asked, awkwardly.

"I don't know but I think you should find that out. Ann was always vague whenever I asked her about the name. She said it was someone from her past. I think that might be who had contacted her recently."

Reggie wrote down his suggestion.

Logan was disappointed that was all Gary had for them. It seemed Becca was keeping a lot of secrets from her husband. That made him absurdly glad. She had never kept secrets from Logan. At least not until the day she pretended to commit suicide. He supposed that was a big one, big enough to make up for all the secrets she never kept from him. His gaze swept toward the coat rack in the far corner of the den. A light green coat, a quilted one with a hood, hung from the top hook. He tried to picture her wearing the coat, smiling, laughing under the deep hood.

"Is that Ann's coat?" he blurted, effectively interrupting the conversation that had continued while he daydreamed about Becca in a hooded green coat.

Gary seemed perturbed again. He pushed his glasses up higher on his nose. "Yes, that's her coat."

Logan stood up and walked over to the coat rack. He knew the people on the couches were watching him but then his partner pulled their attention away with a question.

"Mr. Robbins, does Ann have a computer? It might help to look at her browsing history."

"Ann did everything on her phone. She didn't like to sit down at a computer."

Logan tuned them out for a moment. His fingers ran along the pillowy fabric of the coat. He leaned closer. The faint scent of perfume wafted off of it. It smelled different than the perfume she wore as a teenager. That was cheap, powdery but she always smelled amazing. The scent coming off the coat was sophisticated, pleasant. He closed his eyes and imagined her lifting her hair off her neck and spraying it behind her ears.

It was summer. It had probably been several months since Ann Robbins had worn a coat. Logan had found more than one good piece of evidence in a victim's or killer's coat pocket. He reached into the pocket. His fingers found a soft piece of paper. He pulled it free and unfolded it. It was a yellow cocktail napkin from the Three Boars, a bar on the outskirts of town near the turnoff to the beach cities. He'd had beers there on more than one occasion, especially right after Vicky left him.

"Did you and Ann go to the Three Boars a lot?" Logan asked. He knew he was more interested in knowing if he had somehow or another passed Becca in the dark, crowded bar. If Becca had lived so close to town, close to his apartment, how often had they driven down the same road or walked out of the same store?

"The three what?" Gary asked.

Logan carried the napkin over to where the others were sitting. He handed it to Gary.

"It was in her coat pocket," Logan added. Suddenly he wanted to yank it back from Gary. It had been in her hand. It might have touched her lips. He wanted the napkin back to hold on to, to keep in his own pocket.

Gary handed the napkin back briskly. "Never even heard of it. Becca didn't like to drink."

Logan wanted to ask how it got in her pocket, but Gary seemed to be growing irritated with the whole interview. Besides, he had the napkin back now. He pushed it into his pocket.

"Like I said—" Gary began in an agitated tone. "I think this guy Logan was the person from her past, the one who called and upset her. Find him and I think you might find out who killed Ann." His voice had taken on an angry edge.

Janey reached over and covered his hand with hers. "It's all right, Gary. They're going to take care of this."

Gary pulled off his glasses and closed his eyes. He rubbed them hard for a second. "I'm sorry. I'm just—"

"It's understandable," Reggie said as she stood. "We'll be in touch."

Janey walked them to the door. "You'll have to forgive him. He's not himself."

Logan nodded. "Thanks for your time."

They headed down the pathway to the car.

"I guess I wouldn't be doing my job if I didn't ask this." Reggie stopped before climbing into the car. "Did you kill Ann Robbins? Because the husband seems to think it's all linked to this Logan character from her past."

Logan shook his head. "Get in the car, Hawkins. And be ready. Tomorrow—you and I are taking a long drive."

They sat in the car. The summer sun had left the seats and steering wheel hot. Reggie squeezed her backpack next to her feet. "I'll make a call to get the warrant started for phone records." She pulled her phone out of her backpack. "Where are we going tomorrow?"

"To the dullest, most pathetic town on the west coast. My hometown, Layton. Before we can figure out who murdered Becca, I need to find out why the hell she was still alive."

CHAPTER
TEN

Logan tossed and turned all night. He stared up at the shiny building. He was sure some young, big shot architect was proud as hell about the cold, stark monstrosity they'd created, but Logan considered it an eyesore. Give him an old brick building with a weathered exterior and wood windows anytime. In the late afternoon, waning sunlight, the building reflected long, wavy shadows. It was the last place Logan wanted to be after the turmoil filled day. He'd woken to a regular Monday morning, smacking his alarm hard enough to lengthen the crack on the top, reheating yesterday's coffee, shoving down a piece of cold pizza, smothering his face with shaving cream, talking himself out of a much needed shave, washing the cream off, checking for his badge and pushing his Glock into his belt. Nothing about the ordinary morning told him it was going to be an extraordinary day. And not extraordinary in the good sense, like a view of the Northern Lights or a double rainbow after a spring shower. Extraordinary in the sense that nothing was the same now. The day had been an endless series of cartwheels, each event turning him upside down over and over again. It was a wonder he didn't feel dizzy. Now he had to end the wild fucking day with a staid, forced chat with his assigned shrink, Dr. Webb. If the higher-ups really cared about his mental health, after a day like today, they would have bought him a bottle of whiskey and told him to go home.

Logan had successfully avoided a second session with Webb for a few days by claiming that he was still taking painkillers for his hand and needed to get past them. After their first session, where Webb had to sit across from a smartass cop who was buzzing just enough to be completely worthless and arrogant, the doctor was in full agreement. But he'd put it off long enough. Webb would be writing a report soon to let Castillo know how he was progressing. Logan was sure the captain would frown upon a report that said there'd been no progress and no sessions attended.

Logan smacked the red button.

"Yes?" Webb asked.

It was all so formal. Logan wanted to answer with something stupid like 'pizza delivery' or 'I'm here to pick up your dirty laundry'. "It's Logan Cooper."

The door buzzed and he walked inside. Webb hadn't bothered to add anything of note to the cold, austere lobby. Medical buildings were usually over glamorized with matching leather chairs, glossy coffee tables, plastic plants and stacks of odd magazines that no one had ever read like *Golfer's Digest* and *Modern Mountain Home.* Webb's lobby was just one step above the lobby at the morgue.

Logan took the elevator up to the second floor. Webb was ready for him, the office door opened simultaneously with the elevator doors. Even though it was summer outside his cold steel building, Webb was wearing a dark blue woolen sweater and gray slacks. His face was so clean-shaven Logan wondered if the man actually had facial hair. His slick pink skin made Logan reach up to touch his own jaw. The stubble was long and rough, but he was sure he could avoid the tedious task of shaving at least one more day.

"Glad to see you, Logan. Please, come inside."

The desk was still empty.

"As you can see I haven't had any luck hiring a receptionist yet," Webb said with a light chuckle. "It's my fault really. I'm far too picky." We stepped into the therapy room. "I've got a touch of OCD." He turned to me. "Do you know what that is?"

"Obsessive compulsive disorder," Logan said, slightly annoyed. The superior doctor was certain the crude detective wouldn't know of such things. "You forget, Dr. Webb, you sit inside this comfy office having chats with people who are suffering from mental illnesses. I'm out there dealing with them in real time." Logan had promised himself he wouldn't be a prick this time, but this whole damn situation just brought out the prick in him. "Sorry, it was a long day. I'm also surprised." Logan sat on the hard, unforgiving couch and rested back. The cushions didn't sigh and relax and swallow him up like his good old couch at home. It was more like resting against a wall.

Webb sat down elegantly as if he'd attended some posh finishing school where they taught you how to sit like a gentleman and how to tilt your hat at a lady. He crossed his legs and balanced his notepad on top of his knee. "What surprises you?" he began.

Logan's head was so not into the session he had to recall why he'd even said it. "It's just I didn't realize that you guys had your own set of troubles. You know, like OCD."

Webb's chuckle was rehearsed too. Maybe the rich boy finishing school had a class solely on the art of chuckling politely. "I assure you we have more than our share of afflictions. While you're out there dealing with mental health issues in *real time*, we've got to absorb everyone's troubles, analyze their minds and come up with solutions. Just as I'm sure you've seen it all, Logan, I can assure you, I've seen it all as well."

Logan didn't respond. He felt as if he'd just been put in his place.

An easy smile appeared on Webb's face. There weren't any of the usual creases and lines that came up on people who generally smiled or laughed a lot. Logan decided either Webb didn't find much in life amusing or he was having some kind of Botox treatments. Maybe even a little of both. Webb's pen was poised as if at any moment he'd be taking copious notes and writing anecdotes and some of those *solutions* down.

"Why don't you start by talking about your long day," Webb said. "Did anything interesting happen?"

A laugh spurted from Logan's mouth before he could stop it. "Sorry but understatement of the year."

Webb sat up straighter, ears perked. Logan considered that he probably heard a lot of mundane shit, but there had to be some juicy nuggets every once in awhile or the job would be boring as shit.

"There was a murder."

Webb nodded. It seemed he wasn't going to interject any wisdom or inquiries so Logan continued.

"Some monster handcuffed a woman inside a car, then sent the car into a lake to drown the victim."

Webb's mouth pulled tight as he wrote down a few notes. He nodded. "Continue." He had posture as straight as a flagpole, but it slacked just a little bit as he wrote.

"I guess you probably don't want to hear about my job stuff. It can be a little grisly, depressing. Should I talk about my dad again?"

Webb lifted his face. "On the contrary, your job is crucial to your mental health, especially a job like yours where you constantly deal with death and monstrous killers. How is the case going? Is there any indication who might have done this? Was it possibly a suicide?"

"She was handcuffed to the wheel. From the looks of it, she put up a pretty fierce struggle." Logan had to keep the conversation cold and hard in his head as if he was talking about some strange woman and not the woman he once loved.

Webb wrote a few more notes. "What if she changed her mind about the suicide? Maybe she handcuffed herself to the wheel and threw away the key, then changed her mind as the water seeped in around her."

"I suppose that is an angle we should consider. If you don't mind me saying, you are always rather focused on suicide."

Webb's gray eyes looked up. "I'm a psychiatrist. It's discussed a lot in this room."

Logan shifted on the rock hard cushions hoping to find a soft spot, a place worn in by other clients, but there was no give. The couch was saying 'oh no you don't, no getting comfy on these cushions'.

"It seems to me that you encounter murder victims weekly," Webb said. "But this one has you on edge. Is there something different about it?"

The man was intuitive that was for damn sure. Logan was regretting bringing it up. Maybe talking about Becca would help. Maybe it would relieve that heavy, swollen ache in his chest that hadn't lifted since he realized he was looking down at Becca Kinsey's dead body.

"I knew the victim."

Webb was expert at not showing any kind of reaction or emotion. It was a required skill in his line of work. Logan's job required it too, but Logan was no expert. Maybe Webb wasn't either. His eyes rounded just enough for Logan to notice before he returned to the placid expression he usually wore.

It took Webb a second to drop out the next question, an obvious one in this circumstance. "Did you know her well?"

Logan was doing something he'd been doing all day, tamping down the memories. "We grew up together. I was in love with her."

Webb was taking it in, but Logan didn't see anything being absorbed. He was so busy writing notes, Logan almost felt as if he was sitting alone in the session. He was all right with that. As long as the guy signed off on the proper paperwork at the end of all this, Logan could go right on talking to himself.

"You know what, Dr. Webb, let's switch topics. This one just isn't sitting right with me."

Even though Webb had seemed unenthusiastic about the subject, at the same time, he seemed reluctant to leave it. "It is better to talk about things that stir up emotions. It's obvious the murder scene today did just that."

"First time I've known the victim."

"Will they let you continue on the case?"

"I'll probably have to put up a fuss, but I'm staying on

it. This is one I need to finish."

Webb nodded. "Since you aren't in the mood to discuss it any further, why don't we talk about your hand." He looked pointedly at it. "I see it's mostly healed. Let's talk about that day, the day that ended you up here, on my couch."

Logan stupidly hadn't prepared for the topic even though he knew damn well it was going to come up. The day had wiped out most of his usual thoughts. He'd been in a sort of delirium since the lake.

Logan shrugged. "I would tell you it was a routine arrest but it wasn't. I'd been on child abuse cases before. This was like nothing else I've experienced. His kids were in cages, literal cages. They were filthy and malnourished and sleeping in their own excrement. And that asshole yelled at us as we waited for social services to arrive. He told us we were trampling on his rights. He cussed and spewed shit at us, and when the innocent young woman from social services arrived to collect the girls, he shot his foot out and kicked her patella around nearly to the back side of her leg." The graphic description gave Webb pause.

"I've hurt my knee before. I can't imagine the pain she went through," Webb noted.

"She screamed in agony. That was the catalyst. I couldn't stop myself. I grabbed him and hauled him to his feet. I plowed my fist into him over and over again."

"From the report I received, you nearly beat the man to death."

Logan grinned faintly thinking about the damage he'd caused.

"You seem pleased about that," Webb said.

"Not sorry for one single blow. He had it coming. Someone else thought so too. They finished him off in the hospital. They're still looking for the suspect. Personally, I think they should get a medal instead of jail time."

Webb put the pen down for a moment. "But your job is to catch people who do bad things. Don't you consider someone taking justice into their own hands a bad thing?"

"Guess it depends on the circumstance. That guy didn't deserve justice. He deserved what he got."

Webb switched his legs so the right was now on top. "Tell me—how did you feel as you were hitting him?"

"How did I feel?"

"What were you thinking about?"

Logan thought back to those moments on the front stoop when blood was spraying everywhere and his knuckles were swelling up like balloons. "Nothing. I was just thinking about hitting the guy."

"You've had incidents like this before," he started. "Scenarios where you lost your temper with a suspect. After all, that's why you're here."

Logan wasn't sure where all of it was going. He hated psychiatry. "I get mad. It's not always easy to keep your cool in this job."

"Not trying to be contrary or agitate you. I'm just trying to peel back the layers of your character. Would you consider yourself a good detective, Logan? Do you usually, as they say 'get your man'?"

"My record's pretty good."

"So you're competent and effective, but you have this one professional flaw. You lose your temper."

Logan laughed dryly. "Show me a detective who doesn't?"

"We're not talking about other detectives. We're talking about Detective Logan Cooper. Tell me, is it fair to say that when you lose your temper, when you're angry enough, for lack of a better phrase, to pound the shit out of someone—" Webb was so pompous, arrogant it seemed the word shit left distaste in his mouth.

Logan chuckled. "Don't think there's a better phrase for it than that."

"Right. Would you say that you're almost in a trance? Are you in a blackout state while you're doing it?"

Logan sat back and was again reminded that the couch had been stuffed with bricks rather than the usual foam or fluff. "You mean like someone who gets blackout drunk?"

"Think about it before you answer. Take yourself back to that day when you were beating the suspect. Were you fully aware of everything, of your surroundings, of the man in your grasp?"

Logan wasn't loving the way this session was going. He would have rather talked about his dad, the accountant. He gazed out the window. The days were still long but a frail fog had started to float in from the coast. It was still no match for the late afternoon sun, but by this evening, when the sun had finally settled behind the horizon, a thick, damp haze would cover the town. Sometimes it crept right into Logan's joints, his bad knee from football, his knuckles...

"I guess when I was hitting the guy all I was focused on was my knuckles hitting the guy's face, breaking bones and skin."

"Several of the officers at the scene said they were calling your name, trying to get you to stop. Did you hear them?"

Logan shook his head. "All I heard was bone on bone."

Webb took a moment to write out a longer than usual note. Was he writing 'this guy is fucking crazy and should be wrapped up in a straightjacket'?

Webb rested the pen down. "I know I mentioned this last time but I'd like you to think about trying some hypnosis."

"What for?"

"So we can dig deeper into your subconscious, find out what's driving you into the kind of rage that leaves you senseless, unaware of your surroundings."

Logan stared at Webb, unblinkingly. He stared back, poker-faced, unflinching.

"There wasn't anything senseless about it," Logan said. "He took out the woman's knee. He treated his children like garbage. But he was the garbage."

"I'm not saying he wasn't or that he didn't deserve it. But we're not here to focus on him. There could probably be volumes written on the psyche of a man like that, but we're here to solve your anger issues. Give it some thought. You'd be surprised what can surface after a few sessions of hypnosis."

Logan shook his head. "Like I told you in our first session, Doctor, there are no ta-da moments from my childhood. My parents were good people. Better than I might have realized even." Logan's thoughts floated back to what Gary had said about Ann marrying an accountant. The more he thought about it, he realized that his parents were not only good people but probably the most decent couple in Layton. They were always kind to Becca. It wasn't just the birthday cupcake. Dad would always make sure to chat with Becca when she came by to see me. He always asked her about her classes and how she was doing on the track team. They made her feel something that her parents had never done, they made her feel important.

"I think you should still consider it. In fact, in my professional opinion, I think it will help us get to the end of these sessions faster."

"Well, if you're dangling that carrot in front of me, let's try it next time. Just don't be too disappointed if it doesn't work."

"I'll see you Wednesday at eight, first appointment of the day." Webb said.

"I've got a job," Logan reminded him.

"You do as long as you attend these meetings. I'm booked the rest of the day and we're already behind. They'll be wanting my first report soon."

Logan sighed. "Fine."

Webb closed up his notebook, his gentle cue that the session was coming to an end. "I'm curious, Logan," he said before Logan could push up from the couch. "You said you were in love with this woman, the victim in the car. I assume it never came to anything. What happened between you?"

A dry laugh rumbled in Logan's throat. "That story is a whole session in itself, Dr. Webb."

Webb walked him to the door but no more words were exchanged. They were off the clock, and Webb's words cost money. Logan stepped into the elevator. The steel and glass building creaked as dusk brought cooler temperatures. The elevator doors slid open into the deserted lobby, and he was pelted with the flowery air freshener. A modern, slick ghost town—that was the phrase that came to mind as Logan walked to the exit doors. There was no need to be buzzed out. The handles opened from the inside.

Logan stepped out into the fresh fog rolling onshore. It always brought the tang of the ocean with it. Tonight it was particularly sharp. He was still holding the door. A stout man with thick black hair, a double chin and an ill-fitting t-shirt with a Cabinets R Us logo printed across it had just shoved the last bite of a candy bar, a Baby Ruth, according to the white wrapper clenched in his fist and the smell of peanuts in the air, into his mouth. His cheeks were filled as he struggled to quickly chew and swallow the bite.

Logan pointed inside. "Are you waiting to go in?"

He swallowed dramatically and grinned. It was one of those kind but gooberish smiles. "Yes." He glanced at the silver watch cutting into the flesh on his thick wrist. "I've still got fifteen minutes though. Dr. Jordan is very particular about my arrival. I'm sort of hung up on never being late—one of the things that I'm being treated for, that along with an overeating problem. As part of my therapy, I'm not allowed to buzz in early. This is only my third time here. I was early on the second visit. Boy, did I get a lecture." He wiped his chocolaty hand off on his shirt and stuck it out. "I'm Quinn. Nice to meet you."

Logan released the door and reluctantly took his hand. It was sticky. "Logan, nice to meet you." He motioned with his head toward the door. "They probably don't like it if you don't buzz in anyhow."

"No, I'm sure of that. Are you seeing Jordan too?"

Logan shook his head. "Nope, I'm with Dr. Webb. Good luck with everything."

"Yes, you too."

Logan picked up the pace as he headed to his car. It had been a long day, and the cold beer in his fridge was calling his name.

CHAPTER
ELEVEN

It turned out that Reggie lived in an apartment building just a few blocks from Logan's. It was nearly as shabby but could be considered a step up because someone had slathered it with a fresh coat of paint recently and because the swimming pool was blue rather than the moss green puddle in his complex. Logan was still reeling financially from the divorce, his reason for living in a crappy apartment. What was Reggie's excuse? Had she gone through a messy divorce too? Something had her financially strapped. Logan reminded himself it was none of his business.

Logan had been determined to get an early start for the trip to Layton. When he texted, letting her know he would pick her up at seven, she was ready to go.

Reggie pulled a plastic container out of her backpack and opened it. The scent of strawberries filled the air. "Want some yogurt?" she asked.

"Since when is yogurt vegan?" They'd left the rocky, mountain fringed coast and headed inland. The landscape had flattened to farmland, each parcel defined in square patches of neatly plowed rows and brown fields left fallow for the season. The occasional group of cows lounging under a tree or crowded around a muddy hole of water was the only true sign of life. The highway stretched out in front of them, a long, monotonous ribbon of asphalt that was soaking up the late morning sun like a sponge.

"It's made out of almond milk," Reggie said spritely before digging in.

"Almonds don't make milk, and yogurt comes from cows," Logan said stubbornly.

Reggie turned slightly his direction. She'd pulled her shiny, thick hair up into a ponytail again. She had one of those incredible faces that was pretty from every angle. "Really? Directly from the cows? Are there also blueberry and raspberry cows for the different flavors?"

"You know what I mean."

"Yes, I do. You're one of those narrow-minded people who think that it's not a meal unless there is dead flesh on the plate."

"I just think if you tried a little dead flesh now and then you wouldn't have to snack all the time."

"I ran four miles this morning," she said curtly and pushed the spoonful of yogurt confidently into her mouth. Logan found his gaze lingering a little too long on her lips as she licked a drip of yogurt off of them.

"Impressive." Logan tilted his head side to side. "I used to run in the mornings until I decided my bed was far more inviting than a cold, dark sidewalk."

"You should get back into it. Might do you some good." She licked the back of the spoon. How the hell was she making a cup of yogurt look so fucking sensual?

"Yeah, maybe then I'll look my age, instead of a craggy faced couch potato," he replied.

"Running is good for your heart. It's not a medical miracle cure-all." Her lips, the same ones he'd been watching just a little too intently seconds before, turned up at the edges.

"Gee thanks. We had such a busy day yesterday, we never really got to talk. What brings you up north? Not treating you right in L.A.?" It had occurred to Logan that like Becca, Reggie was very much the type of woman a man could become obsessed with, a woman who probably had more admirers than she cared to have.

Reggie dropped her gaze to the empty yogurt cup in her hands. It was the first time he'd seen some of what he had termed her perky confidence fade. "My mom is up here."

It wasn't the answer he was expecting but then would she have told him if she was trying to get away from a stalking ex or an over-enthusiastic admirer?

"Guess you two are really close?" The tone of the conversation had turned from mocking to polite.

Reggie nodded. "We were always each other's best friend." She wrapped her yogurt up in a reusable tote and pushed it into her backpack.

"Were?"

"I mean are." She zipped up her backpack briskly. "So, you told me about the day Becca disappeared into the ocean. Tell me more about this guy Jeremy. Why are you so certain he's still living in Layton and that he's at home in the middle of a Tuesday?"

Logan felt his mouth turn up. "Jeremy West. Where do I start? You know that kid in school who was always talking about aliens and comic books and all the things that earned him a lot of ridicule?"

"Some of them were my friends," Reggie said.

Logan glanced over at her. She was staring out the passenger window with a wistful look as if the statement had taken her back to high school.

Logan turned to face the road. It was one of the ramrod straight sections of highway that could lull a sleepy driver into complacency and a soft snore. "Thought you were a varsity cheerleader?"

"I was but I didn't hang out with them much. I preferred the quirkier set, the people who talked about things other than the newest nail polish or who the quarterback was taking to homecoming."

Each minute spent with his new partner uncovered another layer. There was always a new surprise waiting beneath it. "Jeremy hung out with those comic book people, but he really had a hard time connecting with anyone. He was always freaked out about germs. Even made himself a foil and canvas suit in middle school. He didn't just talk about aliens, he created comic books featuring the extraterrestrial beings he claimed to know in person. And yet, Jeremy was the nicest, smartest, most genuine person I'd ever met. He works from home, the home he inherited from his grandmother. I'm not exactly sure what he does. I think it has to do with developing software programs. His grandmother brought him up after his parents died, both from cancer, just two years apart."

"I think I would have made myself a canvas and foil suit too if both my parents had gotten cancer."

"I'm sure that had something to do with his germ obsession. He knew everything there was to know about any disease, a walking medical handbook. I haven't talked to him in about three years, but last time we spoke, he was dealing with a pretty unmanageable case of anxiety that led to agoraphobia. That's why I'm sure he'll be at home. I texted him that I was heading out to Layton, but I didn't tell him why. I need to see his reaction to the news about Becca firsthand."

"Were they close? Becca and Jeremy?"

"I think Jeremy considered Becca his best friend." Logan thought about how often Becca would leave their lunch table to go sit with Jeremy. "Becca would occasionally sit with him at lunch or during an assembly. A smile would spread across his face, and Jeremy would jump right into some long explanation about something he'd been studying, and she would listen as if he was telling her the world's greatest story."

Logan could feel Reggie staring at the side of his face. "I think I would have liked her," Reggie said. "I think we would have been friends."

Logan nodded. "I think so too."

Logan turned up the radio when a set of Creedence Clearwater Revival popped on KPPR. It was the only station that came in clearly on that stretch of highway. Thankfully, it was a good one. Becca and Logan had cruised down that mostly desolate stretch of highway, blasting tunes and talking about the future, their future, so many times, Logan knew every house along the way, the flat gray one that was a gas station someone turned into a home, the little red one with the pastures on each side and the trail of tall sweetgum trees leading up to the house, the faded green wooden shack that had burned the summer before senior year leaving only a blackened shell. All the same houses were there, only the gray flat house had been boarded up and the sweetgum trees had shriveled from lack of water.

"Cherry slushes," Reggie said excitedly.

Logan's face snapped her direction. "What did you say?"

She looked slightly taken aback. "Cherry slushes? The sign back there said cherry slushes at Picolo Pete's Gas and Mini Mart. Do you have something against cherry slushes? Is it because they don't come from cows?"

Logan smiled thinking about how often Becca would chant 'cherry slush' on that same stretch of road until he gave in and pulled into Pete's station. "We can stop at Pete's for his cherry slush. I haven't had one in years. We need to fill the tank anyhow."

"Are we almost in Layton?" Reggie asked.

"Five more miles."

Picolo Pete's Gas Station, the only station for miles, hadn't changed much. The rounded edges of the store were still painted a bright cherry red. It seemed a new coat had been added recently. The smell of oil based paint mixed with the pungent odor of gasoline drifted through the open windows. Every year, Pete's wife Rhonda planted flats of red and white petunias in the brick flower box running along the front of the shop. But there were no petunias this year, only the weedy stems of past plantings. The giant poster boasting that the world's best cherry slushes were inside the store had faded and ripped. Yellowed pieces of tape still held it securely to the window.

Pete had never updated his station. A customer had to go inside to pay for gas. Reggie fished around in her backpack for her wallet.

"The cherry slush is on me," Logan said.

They got out of the car and headed to the door. Inland, without the onshore breeze to provide some sweet relief from summer temperatures, the heat was dry, crackly, suffocating. Logan had no idea if Pete would still be working. He had to be close to sixty. Last time Logan had driven through that way, Pete was complaining about arthritis.

Sure enough though, Picolo Pete was sitting on a stool behind his counter hunched over a newspaper crossword puzzle. "Five letter word for awry?" Pete asked without looking up.

"Askew," Reggie answered with hardly a thought.

Pete looked up through a pair of wire rimmed glasses that sat at the tip of his bulbous nose. "Very good." He wrote in the answer.

"Impressive," Logan muttered as he walked past her. He motioned over to the self-serve slush machine. Pete used to fill the slushes himself, but he realized it was much easier to let customers fill their own drinks. It was probably his only nod to new technology.

Pete pushed his glasses up but didn't take his eyes off his crossword. "Which pump?" he asked.

"Number ten," Logan answered wryly.

"We don't have a ten." Pete finally looked up. "Logan Cooper, is that you?" His cheeks pulled up with a grin as he slipped off the stool. He was shorter than Logan remembered. Lines creased his face in every direction.

"How are you doing? How are your parents? Still a big shot detective?"

"I'm good. The parents are loving Palm Springs. They're both learning how to play golf. Apparently, it's a requirement down in the desert. And yep, still carrying a badge."

Pete hopped up on his toes to look over the display of cookies and chips to the slush machine. "You might have to tap it on the top a few times. This is the first cherry slush of the day, and it gets stopped up at the spout." Pete turned back to Logan. "Is she with you?" His brows danced up and down. "You always had the prettiest ones on your arm. Wait, that's not your wife is it? That's not Vicky?"

Logan shook his head. "That's my partner, Detective Hawkins. Vick and I split up."

"That's a shame. It's hard being alone." Pete lowered his face a second and rubbed a knuckle swollen from arthritis. It was obvious something had happened to Rhonda.

"Pete?" Logan asked quietly. "Rhonda?"

Pete swallowed. "Died of cancer two years ago. It was sudden. She'd been ignoring a lump. When she finally went in to have it checked the cancer was everywhere."

Logan covered Pete's hand with his own. "I'm sorry to hear that. We all loved Rhonda."

"She was the best woman in the world."

Reggie approached the counter. Her lips were already red from the slush.

Pete's face lit up. "So you're the new partner? I've known Logan since he was a kid. Has he told you what a troublemaker he was?"

Logan laughed. "Don't think we need to rehash those days."

Reggie scooted closer. "I want to hear all about it."

"Well," Pete said enthusiastically, finishing it with an ear to ear grin. "There was this time when Logan drove his rattling old truck in here for some gas and an ice cream for his friend, Becca." Pete motioned to the cup in Reggie's hand. "Becca loved those cherry slushes too." He shook his head. "Such a shame about that girl." Pete said the same thing anytime Logan had walked into the station since Becca's purported suicide. "She was pretty as a picture," Pete said. "Like you. And as lively as a fire-cracker at the end of a burning fuse." Pete lightly scratched his temple. "Now what were we talking about?"

"This troublemaker." Reggie motioned her head toward me.

"That's right. On that afternoon, it was summer, I think. Hot as Hades out there. Even the crows had come to roost under the overhang of the shop. Logan and Becca pulled into the station, music blaring and laughing like always. Those two were always laughing and flirting and having a good time. Like no one else in the world existed but them. But on that blazing hot afternoon a truck filled with good ole boys pulled in. You know the type, shirt sleeves cut off to show off muscles and twangs in their speech even though they were just from up north."

Logan had lived the story. He didn't need to hear it. It wasn't one of his prouder moments, but it was one that had stuck with him for a long time. "Pete, we've got someplace to be."

"Oh no you don't. Pete is an awesome storyteller, and I'm fully in now. I've got to hear the ending."

Logan shot Reggie an annoyed glower and walked to the freezer section on the back wall. Pete was still stocking all the usual ice cream treats, creamsicles, choco tacos and drumsticks. He stared into the glass on the case and could almost see their reflections staring back at him, he and Becca, gazing longingly into the case trying to decide which treat to buy.

Becca bites her lip. "I can't decide. You decide for me."

"I'm getting a choco taco." I reach in for the ice cream. "I'll grab two."

I pull out two ice creams.

"Never mind, I want the creamsicle." Becca puts the taco back and grabs an orange popsicle.

A truck with dual wheels and head-banging heavy metal blasting out of its speakers pulls into the gas station. The bass is so intense it rattles the windows on the store. Rhonda puts her knitting down and walks to the small window to peer out.

A cowboy hat emerges from the driver's side. It's crisp and clean, not the kind of hat that has actually seen farm work but the kind worn to give the illusion of having done the work.

Pete hears the music and comes out from the storage room. "What on earth? Sounds like someone is playing drums right outside the door."

"Sweetie Pete." Becca made up the nickname right after Pete put in the cherry slush machine. She told him he deserved a special title for making such a brilliant purchase. Pete never seemed to mind the nickname. Rhonda always laughed about it.

"I've got a creamsicle." Becca looks my direction to let him know I'm paying. An even louder blast of music shoots inside when Becca pushes out the door.

Payday at the hardware store is once a month, and I'm down to my last few dollars. I count out seven singles to pay for the ice creams and the gas. Rhonda winks at me. "How are your parents?"

"Good. Mom's working at the bank now. She really likes it."

Rhonda tosses in a bag of Skittles for free. "You tell them hello from Sweetie Pete and me." She winks again. Pete is rolling his eyes as he's counting out change in the register. The music is still blaring. He flinches as the drumbeat gets louder.

"Wish they'd make their purchase and go," Pete mutters angrily.

I pick up my ice cream and shove the Skittles in my pocket for the drive home. The summer heat blasts me as I leave the air conditioned shop. The smell of gasoline is made even stronger by the hot air. The ice cream instantly softens in my hand. My truck is parked on the opposite side of the fuel pumps. I can only see the nose of it behind the big lifted dually.

The music reverberates like a massively loud heartbeat. I circle around to my truck. The clean and crisp cowboy hat is visible above the top of my cab. Becca is leaning against the door of the truck, nibbling her ice cream. Cowboy hat and his two sidekicks, trucker hat and shaved head, are circled around her, leering and watching her eat the ice cream as if they are watching porn.

"That's my boyfriend. Nice meeting you boys." I can barely hear Becca over the pounding music.

Cowboy hat shifts his stare from leering to ice cold as he pushes the brim of his hat up and looks my direction. His friends suddenly feel the need to hold their arms slightly away from their bodies, like the way body builders do because their muscles are too big to relax their arms. These guys aren't body builders, but it seems they spend some time lifting weights. More time than they spend doing actual cowboy work. Even their boots are slick like they just came out of the box.

Shaved head struts casually over to stand between me and Becca. I toss the ice cream onto the hood of my truck. He smells like chewing tobacco, which explains the freakish lump on the side of his face. His eyes squint at me, then he turns his head to spit. He turns back to face me. Toe to toe, he's the same height but probably fifty pounds heavier. My fists are curling, but the last thing I want is a fight.

"Just need to get to my truck," I say.

"Yeah? Well we're still having a conversation with this lovely lady. We'll let you know when you can get to your truck."

"Look, no trouble. Just get out of the way and we'll take off." I glance past shaved head. Cowboy hat has moved in closer. Becca straightens and tries to move to the side. He mirrors her movement. My dad always said diplomacy first. I gave it my best shot.

"Why don't you take your shiny boots the fuck out of my way you tobacco spitting piece of shit." Shaved head shoves me hard. I was waiting for his fist, so I'm caught off guard. I fall back a few steps, then my right hook flies out before I can stop it. Blood splatters, along with his nose and the smirk on his face.

Becca cries out as cowboy hat grabs her wrist. She shoves the ice cream into his face. His hat flies off as he yanks her toward him. I jump over shaved head. He's nursing his bloodied face. Trucker hat intercepts my lunge toward cowboy hat. I'd trained myself to use my left arm in a fight, to give my opponent a fair advantage but not today. I didn't care if I fucked each and every one of them up. If I killed them, so much the better. My right cross is no match for the knife trucker hat had hidden in his shiny new boots. He slices my arm before I can land the punch. I pull back, reset and fire right into his ugly face. Blood is dripping from my arm like a river, soaking the sleeve of my shirt and splattering red on the parched gray cement of the gas station. Trucker hat stumbles back shaking his head like he doesn't know what hit him.

Cowboy hat looks worried but not enough to release Becca's

arm. She stomps hard on his fancy boot. He yells out and releases his grip. Before I can reach him to stop his arm, he smacks her to the ground.

Cowboy hat is the biggest of the three, but I'm determined to make him fall the hardest. I block it all out, the dry tumbleweed filled field across the road, the blazing sun shooting down at us, the pounding bass from the speakers. It's just me, my right fist and the fucker who just pushed Becca to the ground. It's bone on bone, knuckles on facial bones, teeth, a nose that looks like clay with the first two punches. The slice in my arm hasn't zapped the strength of my right hook. My left hand is gripping his shirt as if the fabric grew from my fingers.

Bone to bone. Knuckles numb from pounding. Her voice pulls me free. "Logan," it comes through my red haze pleading, frantic. I look up at her face as she leans over me, her eyes glassy with tears. "Logan, let him go."

I can still feel fabric clutched in my left hand. Everything is wet, my hands, my arms, my fist. Even the cement beneath my feet is slippery. My head is swimming with the sharp, metallic smell of blood.

"Jesus." Pete's voice comes from somewhere between the groans and the heavy metal. The lump in front of me is not moving. I release his shirt. He crumples to the ground with a howl of pain.

"Just go, both of you. I'll take care of this. Get out of here," Pete is saying from behind.

Becca grabs my left hand and I'm on my feet, not entirely sure how I got there. She slides in past the steering wheel to the *passenger seat. I haul myself in behind the wheel. Out of the side of my eye, I see trucker hat wiping blood off his mouth with the back of his hand. He's holding his friend's cowboy hat. It's smeared with grease and blood. Not crisp and clean anymore, I think as I start the engine.*

Pete is helping cowboy hat to his feet. "I saw the whole thing. You three started this. Now get out of here and don't come back through this station again."

My hand aches as it tries to grip the steering wheel. Blood drips onto the ripped vinyl seat. Becca turns around and hangs over the back of the seat a second before emerging with a white t-shirt I had jammed back there. The truck rolls down the highway. I can barely keep an eye on the road. Becca scoots next to me and wraps the shirt tightly around the slice on my arm. We ride in silence for a few minutes. Bob Seger's "Like a Rock" blasts from the radio. The wind blowing into the cab cools our faces and cools the burning sting in my hand.

Becca rests her head against my shoulder. "Logan Cooper, I am always and forever your Cricket."

"Ready to go?" Reggie's voice pulled Logan from his thoughts. He looked at her in the glass on the freezer. She was staring back at him, slightly stunned.

"I told you not to listen to Pete's bullshit story." Logan spun around. "Later, Pete." He pushed harder than needed on the door.

"So it's bullshit?" Reggie asked. Her long legs moved fast to keep up with him as he lumbered back toward the car.

"Didn't say that." He climbed in behind the wheel. Reggie took the last sip of her slush and dropped the cup in the trash. She got in the car and buckled her seatbelt. Logan felt her staring at the side of his face as he pulled out of the station.

"Pete said if Becca hadn't stopped you, you might have killed that guy."

"Possibly. What's your point?" he asked harshly.

"Just want to know what kind of person I have watching my back when I'm out in the field." Her tone was tight and curt. "I've heard the rumor," she said quietly and softer. "They even knew about it down south."

Logan swallowed hard. His throat was suddenly dry. "Rumor? Then that should tell you it's bullshit. Rumors aren't exactly reliable."

"This rumor was about a detective who had a lethal right arm, and it was coupled with a bad temper."

The radio was playing quietly in the background. Logan let the music fill the silence for a few minutes. Reggie pulled her gaze away from him and was staring out the passenger window.

"Then I guess you know what kind of person you have watching your back." Logan turned up the music.

CHAPTER
TWELVE

For Logan, it was always strange coming back to Layton. Everything looked so familiar and almost nothing had changed. The sign welcoming people to Layton was faded and rust crept along the metal edges. The town had been boasting a population of five thousand, three hundred and fifty-nine people since Logan could read numbers. He was sure it was less than four thousand now. A lot of the people he grew up with had moved out the second their feet could get them out the door. Graduation hats flew and half the people were gone before they even hit the ground. It had taken Logan longer than he expected to get out of Layton. He was still reeling from Becca's death and leaving the town felt as if he'd be leaving her behind. His parents were still working and had no plans to uproot their lives. Logan was all they had left. His older brother, James, had moved out right after high school graduation. He settled across the country in New York. He rarely looked back. Logan didn't want to leave his parents entirely alone so he stuck it out, eventually managing the hardware store when Mr. Walters got too old to run it. A few years later he found a flyer to try out for the police academy. He broke the news to his parents. They were always supportive. Always. He realized that now far more than he did as a teen.

The Tucker Farm, the first set of fields and pastures that marked the official entrance into Layton, was planted with garlic. The earthy aroma filled the warm summer air. It was always more pungent when it was still in the ground.

Reggie sat up straighter and wriggled her nose. "Suddenly, I have a craving for spaghetti."

"The Tuckers are the biggest garlic growers in this region. They used to have a big harvesting party. We'd all go out there and dig up the garlic by hand. Jason Tucker, the owner, always insisted harvesting by machine was a waste of money and too many plants were ruined. He paid us each a hundred bucks for the day, then his wife and some of the moms would cook up trays of lasagna and garlic bread."

Reggie rested back. "That sounds fun. I think I was meant to grow up in a town like this. I would have loved it. I definitely would have had my own horse instead of living vicariously through my Barbie."

"We haven't reached the actual town yet. You might be less impressed."

Reggie pulled out her phone and swiped through some photos. "As I was leaving Los Angeles, I rode through my old neighborhood, thinking I might not see it again. I snapped a photo of the house I spent my first twelve years in. It's still being rented out by the same horrible man. He must be a hundred years old by now." She held the photo my direction. The house was the size of a single garage with one small window in the front. The whole roof line was flat and droopy, and the weeds surrounding the front gate looked like a menacing jungle. "Not exactly the two-story contemporary you were picturing, is it?" She sat back with her phone. "Unless the whole town is made up of lean-tos and shanties, I'll be impressed."

The Rodale Farm had been abandoned years earlier. Harold Rodale died of a stroke and his wife and daughters weren't interested in running the place on their own. It turned out that Rodale was up to his ears in debt. He'd borrowed money against the farm so often, the wife and daughters had no choice but to up and leave it. The bank tried to sell it for a few years but gave up when no offers came in. The quaint white farmhouse had yellowed and withered with age. The brick chimney was leaning dangerously to the right, and someone had nailed plywood where the front door once stood. The fields were more dust than grass, and the barn where they used to keep their cows and goats had fallen in on itself.

Logan turned left onto Main Street. The two and three

story shops were mostly brick, tan and a mismatched red. Some of the window trims had been painted in new sharp colors. The hardware store where Logan had spent more time than he wanted had been turned into a grocery store that specialized in local produce and meat. The bus stop bench had been painted a shiny forest green to go with the new paint on the street lamps. It seemed the people who still lived in Layton were determined to show pride in their town even though a chunk of the population had left.

Reggie was sitting forward, her face plastered to the side window. "I love it. There's a candy shop, an entire store dedicated to sweets. A town cannot be sad or pathetic if it has a candy shop," she said emphatically.

"Oh yes it can. Some of those candies have been sitting on the shelves since I was a kid. But I'll admit, I did drop a few bucks at that store now and then, after an allowance. The taffy was usually so old and dry, you could almost feel your teeth being pulled from your mouth as you ate it, and Becca once found a spider web in a candy bar. The Frederick family has been running that place forever."

Logan turned down Hillside Road, the road that would take them to Jeremy's house.

"Will we be driving past the Cooper house?" Reggie asked with a smile.

Logan pointed through the front windshield. "The yellow house on the left." He slowed to look at it. The people who bought the house from his parents had painted it yellow and removed the massive jacaranda that had been growing in the front yard. It upset his mom when the neighbor called to tell them that the jacaranda was being chopped down. Supposedly it had some kind of rot or fungus, but his mom figured the people just didn't want to deal with what they'd called the lavender snowstorm after the spring bloom. Logan's mom loved that the front lawn, sidewalk and road in front of the house always turned a shade of purple for several weeks a year, but some people didn't like it. His mom always said those were the same people who didn't enjoy a crisp autumn wind or a bird building a nest under their eaves.

Reggie craned her neck to get a good look at the Cooper house.

"It used to have a big jacaranda tree, but the new owners took it down."

"It's such a cute house with the shutters and white roses."

"My mom planted those roses. At least they didn't rip those out."

"Who cuts down a jacaranda tree? Someone with no heart and soul," she said confidently.

Logan smiled. "I think you would get along well with my mom. She was ready to turn those people in for being ignorant and anti-purple after she heard her beloved tree was being cut down."

Reggie laughed. It was a lyrical sound that mixed well with his thoughts. Some laughs were jarring and made funny things not funny. Reggie was sparing with her laughs, but they were always well-timed and they were never jarring.

Reggie twisted back to get another good look at the house before it disappeared from the rear view. She spun around. "I can picture you sitting at the table eating cookies and drinking milk while doing your homework."

Logan chuckled. "Homework was not always high on my priority list, but I never turned down milk and cookies."

"I already had you pegged as a guy who dragged his feet when it came to homework. I loved to do homework."

Logan nodded. "Yep, I would have guessed that."

"Not that I loved the actual work, especially not math, but as crummy as our house was, especially on the outside, my mom always had it done up really cute inside. She found everything at yard sales and thrifts stores, of course. One day she came home with this old desk. It had been some little girl's vanity set or something because it had its own satin upholstered bench. My mom sanded off the ugly white and gold paint and painted it peacock blue. I chose the color. She thought it might be too distracting for doing work, but I wasn't going to get those division problems peacock blue or not. I couldn't wait to do my homework so I could sit at my beautiful desk."

"Huh, maybe I needed one of those peacock blue desks. My dad brought me a boring old desk, one that was being discarded from his accounting office. I hated that thing because it always reminded me that I would have to do homework. They always say the only things certain are death and taxes. As a kid the only thing certain was homework."

Logan slowed the car as they reached the end of the road where Jeremy's grandmother's house sat under tall pine trees. Shingles were falling off as if the old roof was shedding its skin like a snake. The driveway was nothing but bits of crumbled gray pavers. The front lawn was hidden under a mass of pine needles and debris that had blown in either from the street or the house.

Logan parked the car. Had he misjudged Jeremy's anxiety? Was it better now? Had he left the house for good to take a nice modern apartment in the city? He couldn't imagine that was the case. What if he'd underestimated the anxiety? Was Jeremy stuck inside the house, living in complete squalor with the house practically falling down around him?

Two front windows, big picture windows where Jeremy's grandmother used to place her ceramic Christmas village during the holidays, were so crusted with dirt it was impossible to see inside. A half dozen do it yourself solar panels lined one side of the house. The wooden picket fence that used to hold in his grandmother's flower garden had been switched out to a short chain-link fence that circled the entire property.

"What did he say after you texted him?" Reggie asked.

Logan pulled out his phone. "He never responded."

Reggie's smooth dark brow arched up high. "We just wasted an entire morning. This place doesn't look occupied."

"It wasn't wasted. If we hadn't driven out here, you wouldn't have a bright red tongue and lips," Logan said as he opened the door. He needed a little sweet revenge after she insisted on hearing the whole story about his fight at Picolo Pete's.

Reggie climbed out of the car, wiping her lips with a napkin that she'd pulled from her backpack. She paused to take out a mirror and check out her mouth.

Logan shook his head. "What else do you have in that bag, Mary Poppins?"

Reggie dropped the mirror inside and pulled the back-pack onto her shoulders. They reached the small metal gate that led into the yard. The odor of stale food, sour milk and something that could only be described as rank sat in a noxious cloud over the entire lot. Logan reached over and lifted the latch. Loud, vicious barking roared across the front lawn. Logan snapped the gate shut again. The two of them searched left and right for the source of the barking. It sounded big and mean.

"Pit bull?" Logan asked.

"Something that could tear us to pieces and it sounds like multiple." They stood there for a moment staring into the weed and trash covered yard. It wasn't a big yard as far as front yards went, but the pines had grown so large they shaded half of the lot in darkness.

The barking subsided after a few minutes.

Reggie looked at him. "There's no poop."

"Huh?"

"There's a thick layer of pine needles and weeds and even some trash but no dog poop. I'm going to assume your friend doesn't come out here to walk around all the debris just to make sure the yard is free of dog poop."

Logan thought about her logic for a second. "To be honest, I can't even picture Jeremy with a big, mean dog. I once saw him startle when a ladybug landed on his hand."

Logan opened the latch. The chorus of dogs started up again. "It's a trick. That sounds far more like Jeremy than him having an actual dog."

There was no real path to follow, but someone had stomped down a narrow strip of pine needles and cones to get to the mailbox. They were halfway to the house when a voice shouted at them to get off the property.

Logan and Reggie instinctively reached for their guns when the sound of a gun cocking reverberated through the warm air.

"Now step back and keep your hands up. Keep going until you're out of that gate. I've got perfect aim. I never miss my target," a disembodied voice drawled.

Reggie had scooted closer to Logan. There was no place to hide. She muttered from the side of her mouth. "Does that sound like your friend, Jeremy?"

"Not unless he gained a John Wayne accent."

"You heard me. I said git. Now git," the voice said.

"Never heard him say git either. I think someone has seen Home Alone once too often." Logan stepped closer to the front door. "Jeremy! Hey, West, it's me, Logan Cooper."

A long pause followed where birds that had been scared off by the barking found their way back to the trees and shrubs surrounding the house. The click of several locks being turned followed. The front door, once glossy oak with four panels, had shriveled down to a splintery plank that was having trouble hanging on to its hinges. It creaked open and one of the nails in the top hinge dropped free of the door and clinked down the front steps before stopping against a crumpled piece of newspaper.

"Logan? Is that you?" a voice that sounded much more like Jeremy's slipped past the cracked door.

"It's me, Jeremy. I'm here with my partner, Detective Hawkins."

The door opened more. The voice was familiar, but the person standing in front of him was anything but. Jeremy's hair was twisted in a long braid down his back, and he wore a knitted beanie on top of his head. His loose drop shoulder linen shirt with long flowing sleeves looked like something you'd see George Harrison wearing while he was sitting with the Dalai Lama. The only way Logan could recognize the man on the stoop as the eccentric kid he grew up with were the wire rimmed glasses on his nose.

"Sorry about the sound effects," Jeremy said. "Some of the neighborhood kids have been harassing me." They walked toward the steps. "Old traditions never die," Jeremy said with a chuckle.

Logan stopped just short of the top step. "Did you get my text?"

"Your text? No, sorry, I haven't been able to find my phone." The reason for the lost phone was more than apparent once he opened the door wider. The interior was exactly what one might have expected after seeing the exterior. What Logan couldn't square was how someone with an extreme aversion to germs could suddenly live like a hoarding hermit. The putrid odor was seeping through the open doorway. It promised to make the front yard smell like a spring rose garden. Logan could sense Reggie's hesitation about stepping inside.

"Come on in, Coop. I've got some orange soda in the fridge."

Jeremy stepped back and nodded politely to Reggie as she made the first big step for mankind and entered the house. Newspapers, books, junk mail, flattened pizza boxes, empty soda cans and old computer parts filled most of the room. Just like the path to the mailbox, a walking path had been carved into the debris. It seemed that under all of the trash, Jeremy's grandmother's furniture was still sitting exactly as Logan remembered it, the floral sofas and the antique walnut sideboard with her collection of porcelain tea cups, the coffee table with the wobbly legs and the lamp with the stained glass shade that looked old and valuable. All those pieces of the past stood in their original places layered in the junk Jeremy had collected since his grandmother's death.

Reggie and Logan followed Jeremy to the kitchen. The kitchen was a level or two above the front room in being inhabitable. The kitchen table, the same table Logan had sat at to devour Jeremy's grandmother's fudge brownies, was littered with papers and mail. One place on the table had been cleared for a laptop, but there was no space to eat a sandwich or put down a cup of coffee.

Jeremy was even thinner than he was as a teenager and that was saying a lot. His dark braid swung side to side on his back. Logan had never seen Jeremy with hair past the tops of his ears. Jeremy opened a fridge that released a new kind of odor, one that made Logan consider never eating cheese again. Reggie discreetly covered her nose and turned her head from the smell.

"What do you know?" Jeremy said cheerily. "Here's my phone." He reached into the refrigerator and pulled out a cell phone. "Who wants a soda?"

"We're fine," Logan answered.

Jeremy turned around with his phone in one hand and an orange soda in the other. He smiled at Reggie. "Guess you had one of Pete's cherry slushies."

Reggie covered her mouth. "Do I still look like a clown? I may never have another cherry drink again."

"You don't look anything like a clown, Detective—was it Hawkins?" Jeremy asked.

"Reggie is fine," she added in a brilliant smile that

seemed to knock Jeremy senseless for a second. He stared at her with the same glassy eyed stare he always wore for Becca.

Jeremy dragged his gaze away and focused on clearing the stacks of paperwork and junk mail from three chairs. One chair had been used for his collection of empty soda cans. He picked them up and moved them over to the counter. Logan was sure those same cans would sit on that counter until they got pushed aside by more junk or more cans.

Jeremy sat to the right of them. Logan turned his chair toward him.

"What brings you out to Layton, Logan? Never thought I'd see you back here. Old lady Stevens, remember her? She used to bake oatmeal cookies for us on the first day of fall. She passed away last month. I couldn't tell you from what, but I imagine it was old age. She had to be a hundred."

"Hundred is a ripe old age," Logan said. He realized breaking the news wasn't going to be as easy as he thought. "Jeremy, I need to know what really happened that day down at the beach."

Jeremy's freckles had only intensified with age. They made him look younger, as if he was still just a teenager. "What day is that?"

"You know the day I'm talking about," Logan said quietly.

Jeremy fidgeted with the top on the soda can, but he

never pulled it open. He pushed aside a stack of catalogues, mostly tech stuff, and set the can on the table. "I don't know why you want to rehash all that, Logan. You and Nate were there. You know what happened. Becca swam out into the ocean and never came back." The waver in his tone could have been interpreted two ways—as old sorrow dredged up or from nerves in knowing he wasn't telling the truth. Logan was going with the latter. Two decades had passed since that day, and while Logan himself grieved when he thought of that day, it rarely brought up that level of emotion. Logan also knew that Jeremy hated lying. It made him nervous and fidgety. If he had been lying that day on the beach, then it must have taken every ounce of his stamina to make it all look so believable. Logan briefly considered that Jeremy had been just as fooled as him, that Becca had slipped away and tricked all of them into believing that she had committed suicide. But something told him that wasn't the case. Jeremy's shifty eyes looking every direction except toward them told him he was right.

"I don't know what to say, Logan. You saw the note. Becca walked out into the ocean—"

Logan slapped the table. A pile of papers fluttered to the floor. Jeremy startled. He looked entirely different and had gone the opposite on the germ thing, but he was still jumpy, nervous Jeremy. Logan hadn't meant to startle him, but he needed to get the truth.

"Becca did not kill herself that day," Logan started.

"They searched that bay until the moon came up," Jeremy countered.

Logan stared down at the floor. It was the same silver and pink linoleum that had always been there, only it was smudged with shoe prints and littered with dirt. He took a breath realizing it was still hard for him to talk about it out loud. "Jeremy, Becca Kinsey is lying dead in a Santa Cruz morgue. She was murdered last Friday." As he spoke, the color drained away from Jeremy's face. Even the toast brown freckles faded to gray.

"Becca's dead?" Jeremy asked weakly. He took a deep breath and then another, then two more in fast succession.

Logan sat forward and put his hand on Jeremy's arm. "Where's your inhaler?"

"Fat squirrel," Jeremy said as he sucked in his breath, pulling hard to get oxygen.

Reggie looked at Logan. "Did he say fat squirrel?"

Jeremy nodded hard.

"Fat squirrel," Logan muttered. "His grandma's cookie jar. We called it fat squirrel."

Jeremy was sucking in each breath as if it might be his last. He motioned with his thumb over his shoulder.

"On the counter, next to the fridge," Logan said.

Reggie raced over, pushed aside a pile of empty cereal boxes and pulled the ceramic head off the fat squirrel cookie jar. "I've got it." She hurried it back to Jeremy. He shoved the inhaler in his mouth, squeezed and drew in a deep breath. He repeated with a second dose. Eventually, his shoulders and body relaxed. The color returned to his face, but the shock of the news Logan had thrown at him still showed in his expression.

"Do you want some water?" Reggie asked. As she said it she looked around with a certain degree of cringe apparently thinking about finding a clean glass.

"The soda will do." Jeremy popped the top. Artificial orange fizz scented the air for a moment before the mix of rotten smells overtook it.

Logan let him take some sips and waited a few seconds to see that his breathing had returned to normal. Jeremy set the can down and leaned back with a woeful sigh. "I can't believe Becca's dead."

"Imagine *my* surprise," Logan said wryly. "So you knew she was alive. I thought as much."

"We haven't spoken in a few years. To be honest, I think the lie I'd been keeping all these years, it weighed heavily on me, caused some major anxiety."

"You don't say." Logan glanced around at the room he once remembered as a sweet little old lady's kitchen with pictures of cows and roosters on walls that were covered in daisy print wallpaper. The small kitchen smelled of something good, a pot roast or a pan of brownies. Now, it was a place that hazmat would suit up for. Logan was wishing for one of those head to toe suits right now.

Reggie sat forward. "Jeremy, can you tell us what

happened that day?" Her tone was far more sympathetic and less biting than Logan's, but Logan was trying to get past the fact that the guy with the long braid sitting in front of him had allowed him to go on thinking that the girl he loved, the girl he lived for was dead. Suicide had crossed Logan's mind for months after Becca's disappearance. Jeremy knew it was eating him up from the inside, but he kept up the farce. Logan knew why. Jeremy was just as much in love with Becca as Logan. He would have done anything for her.

Jeremy took one more bracing gulp of soda. It left a light orange ring around his mouth. The guy could never grow even a solitary hair on his face. His skin was still baby smooth.

"It all started when I picked Becca up to drive her down to the beach house," Jeremy began. He picked up the inhaler and folded it in his hand to keep it close. "I pulled up to the house. She ran out from her neighbor's trees with a sweatshirt pulled so low over her head most of her face was hidden. Her clothes were sticking out of her backpack as if she'd shoved in anything she could before fleeing the house. And that was what had happened. She sat down in the car and told me to go and fast." Jeremy rubbed his forehead as if he was getting a headache. Considering the heartache Logan had suffered for years afterward, he was finding it hard to work up any sympathy for the guy. Then his gaze drifted around the room again. Jeremy had suffered too. Maybe even more.

Jeremy drained the last of his soda. "Her hood came off once we hit the freeway. She had a black eye and her lip was cut. Her dad was a monster," Jeremy explained to Reggie. "She was nearly inconsolable all the way to the coast. She kept saying she didn't want to live." Jeremy looked directly at Logan. "It was the worst I'd ever seen her."

Logan knew, too well, the scenario he was describing. He remembered a dark night when rain was pouring out of the sky as if every thunder cloud in the world had settled over town. It was well past midnight when Becca tapped on his bedroom window. She was dripping wet, shivering and her cheek had a deep cut in it. Logan tried to leave, to climb right back out that window. He was determined to walk inside her house and pound her father to death. But Becca cried and begged him to stay. He held her all that night. Rather than thinking about the girl in his arms, sobbing and shivering, all he could think about was killing the man who hurt her.

"She never went into the water?" Reggie asked. Just like with the husband, Gary, Reggie took charge as Logan lost himself in every emotion on the spectrum.

"Yes, she did," Jeremy said quietly as he stared down at the empty soda can in his hand. He squeezed it flat. Apparently, lost in his thoughts, he forgot he had company. He tossed the flattened can behind him. It clanged against the edge of the counter and landed on a pile of dirty clothes. "Becca said she needed to take a walk, to clear her head. She didn't want to ruin the weekend, she'd said. She promised to be her old self once she returned. I didn't have any reason not to believe her. She had never lied to me. After about fifteen minutes, I stepped out onto the balcony to make sure she was all right. I saw her shoulders and head just before they disappeared under the water."

"Jesus," Logan muttered to himself.

"I raced out the door and across the sand. By the time I reached the water, there was no sign of her. I dove in and felt around blindly in the murky water." Jeremy looked at him. "I didn't give up, Logan. I promise, I didn't give up."

Logan nodded. "I know. You loved her as much as I did."

Jeremy covered his face and sobbed into his palms. He lowered them and swiped at his eyes. "By the time my hand smacked into her, she was unconscious. I dragged her back to shore and cried out for help, but there was no one around. I'd taken so many first aid courses, I knew CPR. It took about a minute before I heard that first sputtering cough. I collapsed in relief and the two of us lay in the wet sand crying and holding each other. I'll never forget it. Then we hatched the plan. Becca knew she could never go back to Layton. We created the story around her disappearance. She decided to write a note to add weight to the story. I can tell you, Logan, she was crying as she wrote it. Leaving you was the hardest thing she'd ever done."

"But she did. She left me." Logan heard a heavy sandpaper sound in his voice. It came from his throat being bound up in a painful knot.

"Don't you see, Logan?" Jeremy asked. "Her dad was not going to stop before he killed her. He was growing more insane each day, and her mom was one step from a padded room. She needed to fake her own death so he wouldn't chase after her. She needed a clean break to pull it off."

Logan was taking in everything he said. There was part of him that still wanted to grab Jeremy and give him a good shake for causing him so much pain, but the same caliber of hurt had hit Jeremy too. And it had festered and manifested itself into the man sitting in front of him, the man who had once been terrified of germs but who now lived in utter squalor.

"Thank you for helping her," Logan said, albeit with slight reluctance. He hoped since they'd stayed in touch for some of the years that Jeremy could help them. "When was the last time you spoke to Becca?" Logan asked.

Jeremy was always one of those people with a photographic memory who remembered every date and important event. "It was three years ago on October 29th. She had just gotten a bag of those little Hershey bars at the store, and it reminded her of me." Jeremy smiled shyly at Reggie. "They've always been my favorite."

"I love those too," Reggie added.

"What did you two talk about?" Logan asked it with the

bitter taste of envy in his mouth. Even if they hadn't ended up together, he would have given anything to have had at least one more conversation with Becca. He never got to say goodbye or tell her how much she meant to him. That regret had always felt like a solid stone in his gut.

"She mostly talked about her life with Gary." Jeremy paused with a worried frown. "Sorry to drop that bomb on you, but she was happily married... to an accountant just like your old man."

"Yes, we met Gary," Logan said.

"That makes sense. He must be devastated. He treated her like a princess. Honestly—" Jeremy lowered his voice as if he was about to reveal some big secret and others might hear. Logan had no doubt that there were at least a few pairs of rodent ears twitching nearby, but they were hardly interested in the human conversation. "Gary was head over heels in love with her, but for Becca, Gary was just security, a sense of calm after her dreadful upbring-ing. She asked about you, Logan. She always asked about you."

Logan perked up straight on the seat. It hadn't even occurred to him that while he considered her life long over that she might ask about him.

"I told her you were a detective in Santa Cruz and she laughed. She said I can't imagine Logan taking orders from anyone."

Logan smiled weakly. "Yeah, well she was right there. It's the hardest part of the job."

Reggie sat forward. "Did she ever talk about any problems in her life? People or workmates who she had beef with?" The odor in the house was getting to Logan's partner. She was moving things along. Logan would call Jeremy sometime to hear more about Becca's life, but they were there for a reason. They needed to find the fucker who killed her.

"She went through some really rough years after she left," Jeremy said. "Living on the streets and doing whatever it took to stay alive. I sent her money a few times. After a couple years, she landed a job in a department store, and she found a place to live. Things got better. Then, eventually she met Gary. She told me she wouldn't ever have to live on the streets or in fear of abuse again." Jeremy rested back. "It seems she was wrong." Tears made his eyes glassy. "All she wanted was to be safe and live a normal life. Who did this to her, Logan? You've got to find them."

Logan nodded. "I'm going to find them, Jeremy. Her husband and best friend mentioned someone from her past had tried to contact her recently. It upset her. Was there anyone else who might have known she was alive?"

Jeremy shook his head slowly. "Gosh, there's just no way, Logan. I never even told my grandmother. I can't think of who that might have been. Maybe they were talking about her more recent past, the rough years between Layton and marrying Gary?"

"That might be the case. If there's anything else you think of give me a call."

Jeremy walked them to the door. "Let me know about the funeral, would ya?"

Logan knew full well there was no way Jeremy could leave the house for a funeral, but he nodded, pretending it could happen.

"Nice meeting you, Jeremy." Reggie flashed him a smile that Logan figured was probably the best thing that had happened to him in a year.

He blushed lightly. "Nice meeting you too, Detective Hawkins. Take care of Coop, would ya?"

"I will." Reggie walked out of the house at a slow, steady pace even though Logan was sure she was ready to burst free of the house and yard to get a clean breath of air.

Logan turned back. "Jeremy, if you're ever interested in talking to someone, you know, someone who might help with the anxiety and stuff..."

"Thanks, Logan, but I'm fine. Keep me posted, please."

"I will." Logan turned and followed his partner, who had now picked up her pace to a definite scurry. She pushed through the gate, out of the trash filled yard and into fresh air.

They climbed into the car.

Reggie fished into her backpack and pulled out a tube of hand cream. She opened the cap and the fragrance of roses filled the cab of the car. She took a few deep whiffs, then held the tube under his nose. "Here, it helps clean out the nostrils, though I'm not sure my olfactory cells will ever let me forget the smell in that house." She decided to actually smooth some of the cream into her hands and up her forearms. Her tanned skin looked silky as if his fingers could just glide along her arm. Reggie put away the cream and stared up at the house. "That poor guy."

Logan looked toward the house too. "Yeah."

"How are you feeling?" she asked.

"You know, you don't have to keep asking that," Logan said sharply.

"I'll take that as an I'm feeling pissed off. I don't blame you. It seems like Jeremy would have done anything for Becca, even internalize a huge secret like her faked suicide."

Logan nodded. "Becca was the only person who was truly kind to Jeremy. I never bullied him, but I was never on his side either. I just wish he'd told me."

"Why should he have told you?" Reggie asked. Logan looked at her, briskly, defensively. "You just said it yourself. You were never on his side."

Logan sat back against the seat. It had already gotten hot enough to feel through his shirt. "No one likes a know-it-all," he said with half a smile.

"Duly noted." Her phone rang. "Detective Hawkins. Right. Perfect. Thank you so much." She hung up. "Warrant just got handed to the cell phone carrier. They said they'd send records over this afternoon. What's our next move, partner?" Reggie asked.

Logan stuck the key in the ignition. "First, a long, hot drive back, then I guess we better go through those phone lists to see if anything pops out."

CHAPTER THIRTEEN

She'd parked in his spot again. "Dammit," Logan muttered as he parked in one of the patrol car spaces. After the trip to Layton, Logan had dropped Reggie off at her apartment to pick up her motorcycle. He had to go to the clinic and get a doctor to sign off on his hand. Other than the cuts that were now thin scabs, it was feeling pretty much back to normal.

The late afternoon sun was making its slow descent on the horizon. It helped cool the air, but the asphalt on the way to the station still felt hot under the soles of his shoes. Air conditioning and, oddly enough, the smell of bananas blasted him as he stepped inside. Gregor's desk was first in the maze of detective desks behind the counter. He had just finished eating something.

"Coop, sorry buddy, just ate the last one. Reg brought some banana muffins." His tie was coated with crumbs along with the papers on his desk. "She made them herself. They're vegan," he added as if that was necessary.

"Do you even know what vegan means?" Logan asked.

Gregor shrugged. "I assume it has something to do with them having bananas. By the way, Cap'n wants to see you. He said we're switching cases."

"Like hell we are," Logan mumbled as he strode past.

"He said you'd say that too," Gregor called.

Garcia was leaning against Logan's desk, with his hands braced on the edge, trying to make his chest look bigger as he spoke to Reggie. She was sitting at her desk across the way with a highlighter in her hand and Ann Robbins' phone records spread out in front of her. She was forcing a smile and trying to look interested in what Garcia was saying. Logan only need to catch a snippet of it. Garcia was, in excruciating detail, retelling the harrowing day he had to take down two armed killers at once. It happened at his precinct in Chicago, so no one here was able to corroborate the tale. He embellished it and added even more heroic, almost superhero, details with each retelling. Logan was sure that Reggie was getting the full color version.

Reggie spotted Logan and gave him a pleading look. Logan stopped right next to Garcia and stared at him. Garcia lifted his chin at him. "Coop, I was just telling Reggie about that time in Chicago—"

"When you had to take down two armed killers at once," Logan finished for him.

Garcia's mouth pulled tight. "Hear Castillo is pulling you off a case. What happened? You lose your temper again?"

"Don't you have your own desk to lean on?" Logan asked as he circled around to his chair, plopped down and tossed his keys into a drawer. He stared up at Garcia long enough that Garcia pushed off the desk.

"It was nice talking to you, Reg. Thanks for the muffin." Garcia shot Logan a sneer before walking away.

"Have you talked to the captain?" Reggie asked.

Logan flicked on his computer. "Going in there now. I'm not going to hand off this case. No fucking way." Logan pushed to his feet.

"I'll be with you in spirit," Reggie said with a wink.

Logan walked down the scuffed tile hallway to Castillo's office. He knocked.

"Come in," Castillo called. He was hunched over his desk putting his signature on paperwork. It seemed most of his day was spent either chewing out employees, placating higher-ups or signing his name on reports. Sweat was making its way down the middle of Castillo's shirt as if he had breasts. Actually, that assessment wasn't far off.

Castillo threw the pen down as if it had suddenly grown hot in his grasp. "You're switching cases with Gregor." He put up his hand before Logan could refuse. "You can't work on a case where you know the victim.

That's always been policy, and, frankly, I think it's a good one."

Logan stood a few feet from the desk, not moving, not speaking. He needed to say just the right thing. He was determined not to lose his temper. That would only work against him. The harder Logan pushed, the harder Castillo would push back. There was no way he was handing the case to Gregor.

"I haven't seen this woman in twenty years." It wasn't exactly the gangbuster, winning start to his speech he'd imagined, but it was what rolled out first.

Castillo seemed almost relieved that Logan was going to put up some resistance. "From what I heard, you looked as if you'd gotten hit by a truck when you realized who you were looking at next to that lake."

Keep it cool, Logan reminded himself. "That's because the woman they pulled out of the lake was supposed to have drowned in the Pacific Ocean when she was eighteen. It was just a shock."

Castillo was almost flustered by Logan's calm, steady defense. "Still, I think it's better that Gregor take it over."

"When is it ever better that Gregor takes over?" Logan asked.

Castillo couldn't suppress the short laugh. "Right, well, in the words of Donald Rumsfeld 'you go to war with the army you have, not the army you want'. Stupid words but they work in this context. Now go talk to him so he can fill you in on his case. It's a business partnership turned deadly." Castillo never liked to lose. He was stubborn, but Logan wasn't going to lose this time.

Logan pulled out his badge, walked to the desk and calmly placed it on the stack of papers Castillo had been signing. "I quit." He turned around and headed to the door. He saw Castillo's shocked expression in the reflection on the window. He let Logan get all the way to the door and halfway through it.

"All right. Fuck. Pick up your damn badge."

Logan walked back to the desk and reached for the badge. Castillo placed his hot, sticky hand over Logan's before he could pick it up. He peered up at Logan. "I hate this, you know. I hate that you're pulling this shit. If you try it again, I'll pick that badge up and throw it in the fucking trash. If you give me even one tiny reason to regret this decision, you're off the case and back on patrol."

Castillo removed his hand. Logan picked up the badge and walked out of the office. Gregor was at his desk with a folder. "I guess I'll work with Reggie since she knows about the case." There were still banana muffins crumbs on his tie. "Here's the one I'm working on."

Logan pushed the folder away. "We're not switching." Logan was sure he heard Reggie release a sigh of relief. She'd already discovered that Gregor was an idiot.

Gregor looked as if the wind had just been taken out of his sails. "What the hell? Castillo told me I was taking over."

"Well, you're not." Logan ignored the long face he

was getting. He rolled his chair over to Reggie's desk. "Have you found anything on the phone records?" Gregor stood over them flummoxed and pissed for another minute before stomping off toward the captain's office. Logan knew it wasn't the case as much as it was the possibility that Gregor would get to work alongside Reggie.

Reggie had pulled out a variety pack of highlighters. "I've highlighted all of the husband's and friends' numbers in pink. I included the work numbers in that group. I used blue on these numbers that seemed to always come in at two on Thursdays. They're different each time, so I'm going to guess someone was using a burner phone. They're quick calls too. Just two minutes."

"That's definitely a red flag. Why would someone use a burner phone to call her at the same time each week and have a two minute conversation? Anything else?"

Reggie pointed out the yellow. "This number in yellow was not on the list Janey gave us. The person called three times since May 4th." Reggie looked at him. "That was when Gary and Janey noticed Ann's abrupt change of behavior. The Thursday calls started on the third Thursday in March, so it seems they weren't a catalyst for her change in behavior."

"Good work." Logan pulled out his phone. "I'm going to call Gary and find out if there's anything we should know about two o'clock on Thursdays." The phone rang a few times. Logan was expecting to leave a message, but

Gary eventually answered. He sounded low, like someone deep in the throes of grief.

"Mr. Robbins, this is Detective Cooper. I'm here with Detective Hawkins." He put the phone on speaker. "We just need a moment of your time."

Gary cleared his throat, but his voice was still gravelly when he spoke. "Is there a break in the case?" he asked hopefully.

"You'll be the first to know when there is. We noticed calls with different phone numbers coming to your wife's phone at exactly two o'clock every Thursday since the third week of March. Each call lasted approximately two minutes. Do you have any idea what those calls were about?"

"Two o'clock every Thursday?" He sounded confused and a little out of it. "No, she would have been at work at that time. I have no idea." He grunted in aggravation. "I'm sorry I'm not more help. Ann and I had a good marriage, but I worked a lot and she was very independent. She liked to do her own thing."

Logan wasn't surprised by that. Becca had always been a free spirit. It seemed she'd found a husband who gave her that peace and security she was looking for without killing her love for independence. Logan knew deep down he needed to be happy that she'd found all that. He was just pissed that she hadn't found it with him.

"We don't want to keep you, Mr. Robbins—"

"I was just writing down a list of people to call. Janey is

dropping by to help with that. Like I mentioned, Ann had cut off contact with her parents, with her entire past, in fact, so there aren't too many people to notify. It's mostly my side of the family. I've told my parents. They're devastated. They adored Ann. But before I go, I wanted to mention something, something that might be important."

Reggie picked up a pen. "Go ahead."

"I picked up Ann's personal belongings from the morgue. It wasn't much of course, her wallet and a lucky coin she always kept with her."

Logan smiled. "The lucky penny," he muttered absently to himself.

"Yes, a lucky penny. How did you know?" Gary asked.

Reggie rested her elbow on the desk and her chin on her knuckles waiting with a tilted smile to see how he would squirm out of this one. Logan hadn't considered how hard it would be to pretend to know nothing about a woman that he probably knew more about than any other person on the planet, including her husband.

"Just a lucky guess. My Uncle Harvey has a penny he carries with him everywhere because he thinks it's lucky."

"She never left home without it," Gary said.

Reggie tipped an invisible hat at Logan to congratulate him for making it out of the mud cleanly. He had to be more careful.

"There was something I'd expected to receive with the personal belongings," Gary continued.

"Go ahead," Reggie prodded. Sometimes the noise in

the precinct outweighed any phone call. They both leaned closer to the phone, hoping a new revelation would give them the spark they needed to get the case going.

"For our wedding anniversary, I gave Ann a platinum and diamond watch. She always put it on first thing in the morning and took it off before bed. I looked in her jewelry box to see if she'd forgotten it that day, but it's not there. I don't see it anywhere in the house."

"Did she wear it on the right or left wrist?" Reggie asked. Logan felt stupid for not thinking it. Becca had rubbed multiple layers of skin off her left wrist trying to free herself from the handcuff. A watch would never have survived the struggle.

"She wore it on her right wrist. Do you think she was robbed?" Gary sobbed once. "My god, did they kill her for that damn watch? She insisted that it was far too extravagant of a gift, but I was being a big shot. I wanted to make sure she knew how much I loved her. I think she was just wearing it to make me happy." Another sob.

"If they wanted the watch they could have held her at knife or gunpoint and taken it," Logan said. "You can't blame yourself," Logan said it thoughtfully, but several times in the past two days he'd wanted to shake the guy hard enough to make his glasses pop off. He wanted to ask him what the hell he was doing out of town instead of being at home making sure Becca was safe.

"What about her wedding ring?" Reggie asked. "She

didn't seem to be wearing one when she was found. Did they take that too?"

There was a long pause and some sniffling that Logan would have preferred not come so heavily and wet through the phone. "That was me being a big shot again. I should have known Ann wasn't the type to want a big, glittering diamond." Could have told you that, Logan thought smugly. "She told me it was just too impractical. She only wore it when we went out for dinner or to a party. It's still sitting in the jewelry box where she always kept it."

"We'll have a team do another search of the recreation area and the car for the watch," Reggie suggested. "One more thing, Mr. Robbins, before we let you go. I'm going to read you a phone number that came up three times on the calls report. I want to know if you recognize it." Reggie read out the number slowly and repeated it. "Does that sound familiar?"

"Not at all. I wrote it down. I'll ask Janey and let you know if we figure it out. Anything else?" he asked.

"That's it for now," Logan said. "We'll keep you posted. Take care." He hung up the call. His phone rang right after. It was Fran.

"Hey, Fran, what's up?" Logan asked.

"Good news. The owner of that Toyota didn't have any camera on his property, but a neighbor two doors down got a pretty good video of some guy checking his car to see if the doors were unlocked. They weren't so he left to try the next house. It seems he was just looking for an unlocked door then hit the lotto with the Camry, not only an unlocked door but keys still in the ignition. Thought you might want to check out the video. The neighbor just sent it to me and he's right. It's a pretty clear shot of the guy."

"We'll be right there, Fran. Thanks."

Fran's curly red hair was visible over the top of the computer monitor. She was wearing her signature purple t-shirt and matching purple high-tops. She glanced up once, then her face popped up again. "You must be the new detective." She stood to greet Reggie.

"Reggie, but you can call me Reg."

"And you may call me Fran or Frannie. Whatever suits you. Have a seat." She motioned to her own chair. Logan grabbed a spare chair from the neighboring desk and sat down next to Reggie.

"The neighbor"—Fran leaned over to look at her notepad—"Mr. Brian Trumble, said this was from last Thursday around midnight. Just click play. Now, of course it's not Hollywood caliber, but for one of those porch cameras it's pretty good. Unfortunately, the car thief had anticipated porch cameras and had his head covered with a hood," Fran explained.

The first few seconds showed a blue Honda sitting in a dark driveway. The sidewalk and road in front of the house were quiet as one would expect at midnight in a suburban neighborhood. After thirty seconds, a figure crept into the frame wearing a black hooded sweatshirt with the hood pulled so far over his head it hung over his eyes. His hands were jammed in the pockets of oversized jeans. The lower half of his face was somewhat visible when he turned slightly to look around.

Reggie paused the video and pointed at the screen. "A goatee."

Logan leaned in closer, squinting his eyes to see through the graininess.

Reggie grinned at him.

"I think you need some of those readers that are obligatory once you reach forty." Fran snickered behind him.

"I'm thirty-nine and I don't need glasses. I see the goatee. Push play."

The figure appeared to be a young male, thin and of average height. He walked around to the passenger door and tried the handle. It was hard to see anything except the goatee. It was something, but it wasn't a lot to go on. Hands back in pockets and hood still pulled low, he looked around and seemed to pause at a sound. He stood for a moment, like a prey animal waiting to see if the predator was nearby, then he moved around to the driver's side. He pulled his hand out of his pocket and reached for the driver's side door.

"Pause it right there," Fran said.

Reggie paused the video. Fran leaned over, hit a few keys and zoomed in on the hand. This time even Reggie squinted. "Is that a spider web tattoo?" she asked.

"That's what I see," Fran said.

"Yep," Logan said. "That's a spider web."

Reggie looked at him. "Do you know who it is?"

"No but it'll be much easier to find him now. Let's go see Jimbo at the liquor store. He'll know the guy." Logan stood up. "Good work, Fran. You're the best."

"Then don't forget that 'the best' likes her maple bars."

"I'll bring you one tomorrow," Logan said as they walked out.

CHAPTER
FOURTEEN

Logan turned onto Tuscany. Reggie held out a celery stick stuffed with peanut butter but he declined. It crunched between her white teeth.

"You're like a hummingbird, constantly needing sustenance," Logan noted. "If you ate a steak for lunch, you wouldn't be hungry again for hours."

"That's because a steak takes twelve to twenty-four hours to digest. It just sits there in your gut, gluing up your entire digestive tract. My digestive tract is like a fucking race car."

Logan put up his hand. "No need to elaborate and new rule, we never ever talk about our digestive tracts again."

"You're just jealous because mine is a Ferrari and yours is a Model A with four flat tires. The watch puts an interesting new angle on this," Reggie noted. "We should get a picture of it and check out some of the local pawn shops to see if it's shown up."

"Good idea. Can't imagine someone would go through all the trouble getting rid of their robbery victim by hand-cuffing them inside a car and sending them into the lake. There are easier ways to get rid of a material witness. Just shoot them at the point of robbery. It was risky too. The lake area is closed after dark, but there are no gates. I know teens like to park there at night to mess around. The police cite you if they catch you there after hours. It takes awhile for a car to sink. It wasn't a quick crime. It was slow and insidious." Logan swallowed back the bile that filled his throat as he thought about the horror Becca experienced as she sank into the lake. "This person was sadistic. This was a planned, theatrical event. The killer was getting off on watching his victim's terror as she realized her death was imminent."

"Maybe we should get the park rangers to put up some signs to see if anyone saw something that night," Reggie suggested.

Logan nodded. "Yep, I know someone to talk to."

"See, that's what I need to build up in my career. Knowing people to talk to. Guess once I'm forty, I'll have a nice collection of those names too."

"I'm thirty-nine."

Reggie smiled at him. "It's just too damn easy."

Logan parked the car around the corner from Jimbo's liquor store. "Mitch sent his report on that Jane Doe in the alley," Logan said as they climbed out. It seemed like so much had already happened since the start to that morning it was hard to believe it was just yesterday. "Her real name was Carrie Burke, a missing teen from Ohio. It was a clear heroin overdose. They had to release our runner."

They reached Jimbo's liquor store. Two teen boys were trying to talk Jimbo into selling them a six pack of beer. Jimbo spotted them walking in the door and flashed his crooked grin. At least two of his teeth were missing. "Like I said, boys, come back when you're twenty-one. And you might want to skedaddle because law enforcement just walked in."

One boy laughed, thinking Jimbo was pulling his leg, but the second boy, with lanky hair dyed green and a vintage Grateful Dead t-shirt, turned to see if it was true. His face blanched. He grabbed his friend's arm. "Let's get out of here." They both scurried out like mice the farmer was chasing with a carving knife.

"Detectives, welcome." Jimbo hopped up on his stool. "What can I do for you? Nice to see you again, Detective Hawkins."

"You as well," Reggie said.

"What's up?" Jimbo did a short little drumbeat on the counter with his hands.

Logan leaned one arm on the counter. "We're looking for a young man who has a goatee on his chin and a spider web tattoo on the back of his hand."

Jimbo's bushy eyebrows did a little dance, assuring Logan he knew the guy.

Jimbo stood up on tiptoes and glanced around the store to make sure there was no one else inside. "That's Mickey James. On the street, they call him Razor. What's that kid up to now?" He shook his head again. "He's always getting himself into trouble."

"Is he the murdering type?" Logan asked bluntly.

Jimbo laughed. "No way. He's just into small stuff like car theft, shoplifting. His dad disappeared about five years ago, presumed dead. His mom is in a wheelchair, a car accident. He's got two younger sisters. Mickey makes money any way he can to take care of them. His mom's disability check only goes so far." Jimbo rubbed his chin. "Murder, no way. But that doesn't mean he hasn't gotten himself tangled up with people who *would* murder for money."

"Do you have an address?" Reggie asked.

"You won't find him home at this hour. He hangs out with the Dixon brothers over at Charlie's Pool Hall. Watch out too. Those Dixon brothers, now, they are the murdering type."

"Yeah, I know them," Logan said. He tapped the counter. "Thanks for your help."

"Maybe you'll return the favor sometime," Jimbo said.

"I'm already ignoring that little gambling house you're running in the back room of the laundry mat so consider us even," Logan called as they walked out the door.

"The Dixon brothers?" Reggie asked as they headed to the car.

"Mel and Rocco. Their older brother, Cal, is doing a life sentence at the state penitentiary for murder. It was a botched bank robbery. Cal got antsy and pulled the trigger. Killed a security guard. Mel and Rocco both just got out, so I assume they'll behave."

The sun had dropped and a cool ocean breeze flowed between the buildings, fluttering through the few trees in the neighborhood. Reggie stood outside the car for a second, seemingly enjoying the breeze. "We occasionally got an ocean breeze down south, but there are so many tall buildings and so many cars there was no way to enjoy it or, for that matter, to even feel it on your skin." She opened the door and climbed inside.

Logan started the car and drove toward the pool hall. After the rocky start in Castillo's office, things were going pretty smoothly. So far she was easy to work with and she knew her job. That was all he asked for in a partner. It was hard to know what she thought of him, but he hoped she was finding him to be a good partner too. It figured the first case they landed together was one with a bizarre twist and a strong connection to his past.

Charlie's Pool Hall was the very definition of a dive. Its yellowed exterior walls had cracks and mold running in every direction. Several sizable chunks of plaster had fallen off and long since been washed away in the gutter. The once vibrant green lettering on the front window had been scratched away leaving only the letters Char Po.

The clack of billiard balls echoed through the place as

they stepped inside. The smell of stale beer, sweat and whatever the hell Charlie was cooking on his little stove in back flowed around the room like a giant rancid cloud. Elvis was playing on the jukebox in the corner. The music box shone like a silver and red jewel in the otherwise dank and gray toned room. The green felt on the tables was so scarred and hastily repaired with massive pieces of silver duct tape, it was hard to see how anyone could play a legitimate game of pool. The brass light fixtures that swung over each table were flickering. The light emanating from them was no better than wavering candlelight.

Rocco Dixon, the biggest and by far stupidest of the brothers, made a point of resting the butt of his pool cue on the gritty floor. He leaned on it like a shepherd with a staff. His dark eyes skewered Logan and Reggie as they moved farther into the hall. He muttered something to his brother. Mel looked up from the shot he was about to take. Mel straightened, said something to his brother and they both made a point of surveying Reggie from head to toe.

"I take it the two guys who look like Mr. and Mr. Potato Head are the infamous Dixon brothers," Reggie said from the side of her mouth.

"That's right." Logan stifled a chuckle. "I was just thinking those two guys remind me of someone. I just couldn't think of who but you're right. They look like Mr.

Potato Head. Especially Rocco, who is the big pile of muscle and blubber leaning on the cue."

"Either of you seen Razor?" Reggie asked. She strode confidently toward them, not the least bit intimidated by size or ugliness.

Rocco's lip lifted with a leering sneer. "Who's asking?"

Reggie pulled out her badge. "Detective Hawkins. Have you seen him?"

Mel rested his cue down too. "We prefer not to talk to cops."

Reggie laughed lightly. "What a coincidence because we prefer not to talk to you either." She glanced at Logan. "Isn't that right, Detective Cooper?"

"Personally, rather be speaking to lumps of shit but there aren't any around. Oh wait, maybe I'm wrong." Logan kept his eyes on them, figuring they were probably armed, and if not, the pool cues could do plenty of damage even from a distance.

A layer of red hot anger swept up from under the stained collar of Rocco's shirt. He badly wanted to swing that cue or, at the very least, throw it like a javelin. That third strike hanging above his head was probably a good deterrent.

"Anyone in here seen Mickey? Better known as Razor," Logan added. There was no response, but several customers glanced fleetingly toward the men's room. Reggie and Logan exchanged slight nods. They were already communicating like partners who'd been together for years.

Reggie took off first toward the men's room. Rocco stuck his cue out and poked her lightly in the stomach to stop her progress. Logan could have intervened anytime, but he decided to hold back and watch how she handled it.

She stared down at the cue tip that was just barely touching her. Rocco grinned in a lurid way, exposing some nasty brown teeth to go along with his potato shaped face. "Never seen a pretty detective before."

Reggie looked partially over her shoulder. "Hear that, Cooper, Rocco here says you're pretty." Before the words had finished rolling off her lips, she grabbed the tip of the pool cue and shoved it hard. It hit Rocco square in the jaw. His teeth snapped shut, presumably on his tongue, because a feral grunt roared up from his throat. The groan of pain was followed by blood trickling from the sides of his mouth. Reggie tossed the pool cue on the table, disturbing their game and sending balls in every direction, before continuing her trek to the bathroom.

Logan stopped to grin at Rocco. He was holding his hand against his mouth. "And the moral of that story is never underestimate a woman," Logan said glibly. He followed Reggie, all the while keeping an ear turned back toward the Dixon brothers. It seemed they'd decided not to follow.

Reggie pushed open the door and immediately

covered her nose and mouth. "Holy shit," she mumbled behind her hand.

"You got part of that phrase right." Logan pushed past. "Mickey, police here. We need to talk to you." Reggie was right, Logan thought. Holy shit. He covered his nose and mouth as he kicked open the two stalls. The third one didn't have a door, and the source of the atrocious smell became quite evident. A honk outside pulled his attention to the small window. It had been pushed open.

"Shit." Logan raced to the window and yanked himself up. Mickey was stumbling across the alley, heading toward the sidewalk. "Here we go again," he muttered. "Out the window." He pushed past Reggie mostly because he wanted to get a head start on her this time. It was a useless attempt. They weren't five yards outside before Reggie's long legs carried her ahead. She sprinted after Mickey. The kid glanced back once. The look of horror when he saw Reggie catching up to him was priceless. If Logan hadn't felt like a fat, lazy sloth for being so slow, he might have enjoyed it more.

People were ducking out of the way as the two raced along the sidewalk. They reached a corner. The light turned red. Mickey jumped right into the street. Reggie grabbed the back of his shirt and yanked him out of the path of an oncoming car. He fell down on his back and stared up at her, somewhat thankful and equally terrified.

Logan caught up to them.

Reggie couldn't keep the smile to herself. "Glad you could make it."

Logan shook his head. "If I'd known they were pairing me up with the roadrunner, I would have started working out."

"Never too late to start," she quipped. She offered Mickey a hand. Even with the goatee, he looked younger than expected. He stared at her hand unsure about whether it was a trick.

"We just need to ask you some questions," Logan said.

Reggie pulled him to his feet. He was gaunt, greasy and looked about as scared as a rabbit who just met up with a pack of wolves. Dusk was on its way, but the disappearing sun was blasting that section of sidewalk with its last energy of the day. Logan motioned with his head, and the three walked around the corner to the shade and out of view of the main stream of traffic and pedestrians.

Mickey stood with his back against the wall of the building, a brick two-story that had been everything from a drug store to an office space to a low rent apartment. Now it was boarded up and waiting for its next endeavor. Mickey was fidgety. His feet couldn't stay in one place, and his eyes darted back and forth.

"The silver Camry," Logan started. "The one you stole last Thursday night."

He looked close to puking. "I don't know nothing about a stolen Camry. I drive my mom to her bible study on Thursday evenings. You can ask her."

"Does the bible study go until midnight because that's when the car was stolen?" Reggie noted.

He crossed his skinny arms defensively. "Yeah, sometimes they go until midnight. It's a long book."

Reggie lifted her hand to discreetly cover her smile.

"Look, Mickey, we have video of you stealing the car," Logan said. It was not exactly the truth but close enough. "We're not going to arrest you for it, but we might have to haul you in for murder."

His chin dropped. "I didn't murder anyone, I swear. I was just paid to get a car, any car."

Logan stepped closer. "Paid by who?"

He shrugged his thin shoulders. His t-shirt was so threadbare it was almost see-through. "Don't know. Sometimes we get requests, you know."

"We?" Reggie asked.

Mickey looked nervously side to side. "You can't rat me out. They'll kill me. I just work for them a few nights a week."

"Auto theft ring," Logan said to Reggie.

"Please, they'll kill me. There'll be no one to take care of my little sisters."

"We just want the information, Mickey," Logan said. "We're not going to rat you out. A woman was killed in that Camry."

Mickey's feet were doing a frantic tap dance. Logan noticed his shoes had so many holes all of his toes were exposed.

Logan pulled out his wallet and took out two twenty dollar bills. He held them up just out of Mickey's reach. "It's yours after you talk."

"The person left an envelope at the garage. It had four hundred dollar bills and a note."

"What did the note say?" Reggie asked.

Mickey closed his eyes to think. "Uh, let's see. It was typed. My mom says I have a photographic memory." He smiled proudly about that and squeezed his eyes shut again. "It said here is four hundred. You'll get four hundred more if you drop a car off at Crystal Lake on Friday after the park closes. Nothing special just a small car. No car, no more cash and I let the police know what you're up to." Mickey opened his eyes. The forty dollars had made him far less fidgety. "That was it. My boss—" he paused. "I won't tell you his name cuz he'll kill me and then no one—"

Logan nodded. "Yes, yes you already pleaded your case. We're looking for a murderer not a car thief. What did your *boss* say?"

"He said 'Razor, go out there and find a car. Bring it back here and we'll deliver it Friday night to Crystal Lake.' He promised me half but he only gave me fifty bucks."

"Nice boss," Reggie said. "Who delivered the car to the lake?"

Mickey pointed to himself. "I did the whole thing myself. That's why I should have gotten at least half."

"Did this boss of yours have any idea who you were

working for?" Logan asked. "What if it had been a set up by the cops?"

Mickey straightened his posture. "See, that's what I told him, but he said money was money. He's kind of stupid, to be honest. When he sees dollars that's all he sees. You know what I mean?"

"Yeah, I know what you mean," Logan said as he held tight to the bills. "When did you deliver the car? Did you see anyone or anything? Do you have any idea who you were working for?"

Mickey stared longingly at the cash. "I drove the car there at ten o'clock. Didn't see anyone. I just left the car in the parking lot and walked back to the bus station. Two days later there was another envelope with the rest of the money. The person kept his word," he said.

"Very honorable of a cold-blooded murderer," Logan muttered.

"I didn't know it was going to be used for that. Honest," Mickey said. His gaze fell to the money in Logan's hand.

Logan handed it to him, but before he released his grip on the bills, he looked Mickey straight in the eye. "No booze or drugs. Take this to the store and buy some decent food for the family."

"I will." He grinned. "Looks like it's gonna be hot dogs and frozen French fries for dinner," he said gleefully. He grabbed the money and shot off like he'd been freed from a trap.

"Why does this feel like a dead end?" Reggie asked.

"Because it's a fucking dead end. Let's talk to his boss just in case he knows anything."

Reggie strode next to him as they headed to the car. "Do you know who this boss is?"

"Yeah, I'm pretty sure."

"What if he takes it out on Mickey?" Reggie asked. Logan had already noticed that Reggie had a soft spot. He did too when it came to people like Mickey. As long as her soft spot was saved for the right people, he was good with that. In fact, better than good. He'd worked with plenty of assholes who lacked even an ounce of compassion. He'd had to grit his teeth with a lot of partners.

"We'll make it in the boss's best interest that Mickey stays safe," Logan said as they climbed into the car.

CHAPTER
FIFTEEN

Big Sam, that was the only name ever given for the rotund, slob who ran a legitimate garage as a front for a chop shop. Logan was sure he had some deal with the local cops for ignoring the illegal half of his business. Logan didn't care what Big Sam did up front or in the back. He just wanted to know who paid for the stolen Camry. Logan hadn't dealt with Big Sam in years. He'd forgotten about the thuggish crew of thick necked goons he employed for security until one of them, a hulk of a man, stepped out from behind the front desk. His big arms stuck out in ape-like fashion. Apparently, the man's intuition told him the two people who just stepped inside were not there for a car repair or hard to find part.

The guy had been downing a massive burrito when they opened the door. There was still hot sauce on his square chin. Logan figured the burrito was just a light snack. The man, Logan was mentally calling him Hulk, circled around the counter. "Can I help you?" he said in a brusque tone that indicated anything but helpfulness.

They simultaneously pulled out their badges. Logan shot Reggie a sly little smile about how in sync they were.

Hulk's arms went out wider. His face pillowed with anger, which, considering he already had a head the size of a beach ball, was saying a lot. "You got a warrant?"

"For what?" Reggie asked. "You doing something illegal?"

He de-puffed his chest some, becoming more defensive than offensive. "Nope, it's all good here, so why don't you be on your way."

Logan looked at Reggie. "Why, I'd almost think something criminal was going on in this establishment with the way this guy is reacting." Logan turned to Hulk. "We need to see Big Sam, so if you'd just take your twinkle toes to the back room to find him that'd be grand."

Hulk was shaking his head before he finished. "Boss isn't here." Then Hulk made a big mistake. He reached for Logan's arm. Logan snatched his wrist. It was as thick as Popeye's. Logan had to grind his fingers into the flesh to keep a grip on it as he swung the arm around Hulk's back and wrenched it painfully toward his shoulders. Hulk leaned over grunting in pain.

"As far as I see it, there are two different endings to this story," Logan growled into Hulk's ear. "Either I cuff you and drag you off to jail for obstruction of justice with a possible broken arm or, at the very least, a dislocated shoulder, or I release you and you take a leisurely stroll to the back to let Big Sam know we need to talk to him. Which will it be?" Logan jerked the arm for good measure.

"I'll get Sam," he groaned.

Logan released Hulk but was ready to throw a fist if needed. While Logan had the guy in his grasp, Reggie had decided to go to the back room herself. She leaned out of the hallway. "I think I've found Big Sam. Is he big?" she asked with a smile.

"You can't be back there," Hulk growled.

Reggie glanced around. "Looks like I already am."

"It's all right, Tank," a deep voice said from behind her. "Let them through."

"Tank?" Logan said to the guy as he passed him. "I had you pegged as Hulk. Thank you so much for your help. If you put some ice on that shoulder you should be feeling right as rain in no time." Tank's mouth was drawn in a straight line. Logan could almost see his thoughts vividly portrayed in thought bubbles floating over his giant head.

A shoe scuffed tile hallway led to an office where Big Sam sat behind a desk. He took up nearly all of the office space with his girth. The small space was stifling hot, and all the oxygen had been taken up by Sam and the over-whelming smell of cumin and onions. A Styrofoam container holding the last remnants of what looked like a family sized portion of enchiladas sat on top of a messy pile of papers. The shelf behind Sam's chair had been hung crookedly. It was filled with sports memorabilia, a signed baseball, a signed glove and a signed photo of Mickey Mantle. Sam didn't look like the sporty type.

Big Sam's chair creaked loudly as he sat forward wiping his mouth and multiple chins with a paper napkin. He dropped the napkin next to the container and sat back, again causing severe anguish to his chair.

"Detectives, what can I do for you?" He reached forward. There was no muscle or joint definition left in his massive arm. "Here's a flyer we just printed up with our new prices. Inflation is hitting all of us, but I've got to keep my bottom line."

"You're keeping a bottom line all right," Logan quipped. Hulk had put him in an ornery mood.

"We're not here about car repairs." Reggie said. Sam took a moment to brazenly look her up and down. She was good at ignoring lascivious stares, but Logan had no doubt that it irritated her. "We're here about a stolen car that was used in a murder last Friday."

Big Sam's laugh matched his size, big and round. "Now, what would I know about a stolen car and, for that matter, a murder?" He picked up his fork to let us know he was so unbothered by the topic he was going to go right on with the last bites of his party-sized enchiladas. He sawed off a forkful and plowed it into his mouth.

"Look, we don't give a shit about your rinky-dink back-room operation," Logan said.

Sam swallowed faster than he anticipated. Logan worried he'd have to give him the Heimlich. He briefly tried to reason out exactly how he could manage that with a man of his size. Sam grabbed his massive soda, a cup that probably held a liter, and took a few draws on the straw.

"Why don't you get to the point then, Detective? You're interrupting my lunch."

"Wouldn't want to get in the way of that," Logan said. "You received an anonymous envelope with money and a note asking you to deliver a freshly plucked car to Crystal Lake last Friday night. A woman was sent to a watery grave in that car. Who sent the envelope?"

Big Sam's eyes were set deep in his pillowy face. He stared up at both of them, shifting his gaze from Logan to Reggie and back. "Don't know who sent it. We delivered on our end and they paid up. That's all I know."

"Do you still have the note or envelope?" Reggie asked.

"Why would I keep something like that? You never know when a nosy cop might come barging into my shop to harass me."

"I hardly find this harassment," Logan noted.

"You just about popped Tank's shoulder just now," Sam pointed out.

"That's because he wasn't very cooperative," Logan countered. "You're saying you have no idea at all who sent the note. Not some usual customer?"

Sam shook his head slowly. "No idea at all. Like I said, we just delivered on our end of the deal. Most of my customers prefer to remain anonymous. I like it that way. Keeps my hands cleaner."

Reggie didn't even try to hold back her laugh.

Sam's brows bunched up. "Who told you about the envelope? I'll bet it was that little weasel—"

Logan picked up a paperclip and unfolded it. "About that." He jammed the newly straightened paperclip right through a pile of papers. "If we hear that anything happens to Mickey, I'm talking even the smallest thing, like you ruffled his hair or shucked him on the shoulder, then I'll make sure this whole place is closed up, legitimate half included. And why don't you think about paying the kid a little more? He's so thin, a strong wind would take him out all while you're sitting there shoveling in enough food for his whole family. This is your community, Big Sam. People look up to you around here. Why don't you give them a reason to."

Logan and Reggie walked back down the small hallway. Tank pretended to be engrossed in the magazine he was reading. He'd covered his shoulder with a bag of ice.

"Later, Hulk," Logan said as they walked out.

"That would be two dead ends in one afternoon," Reggie said.

"Yep, I've about had it with this dead end shit too."

CHAPTER
SIXTEEN

Logan was starting to feel like a lazy, butter drenched dumpling next to his partner. He got up an hour early, charted out a two mile run, made it halfway, then dragged his ass back to his apartment. Just a few years ago the two miles would have been a warm up on the way to the gym for an hour of weights. He needed to find that old Logan again. He was sure he was somewhere beneath the layers of pizza and binge-watching.

The fog would burn off soon enough, but this morning it was drifting past his windshield in gray cotton puffs. Webb's building, with its presumptuous exterior, was easy to spot even through the pea soup. It was a shitty way to start his day, a day that he hadn't really planned out yet. They knew that someone paid Big Sam to steal a car and deliver it to Crystal Lake. That anonymous person was the killer. That much was clear. Without anything else to go on, that narrowed it down to anyone in a fifty mile radius who owned a computer, some envelopes and knew about Big Sam. It was easy enough to find an auto theft ring in the middle of the city. Most snitches would sing for a twenty dollar bill.

Logan pushed the button.

"Yes?"

"It's Logan Cooper." He released the button. Logan hoped that Webb had forgotten about the whole hypnosis thing. He wasn't in the mood to pretend, even though he'd seriously considered pretending to drop into a trance only to reveal something stunning, something that would make the doctor think he'd gotten to the root of the problem. He was now rethinking that idea. If Webb thought it worked, Logan would have to sit through more bullshit hypnosis sessions.

The door to the office was ajar. Logan stepped inside. He could hear the murmur of Webb's voice in the office across the hallway. He was talking to Dr. Jordan. Logan sat on the uncomfortable reception area chairs. There were no windows. Logan leaned back and, by habit, stuck his hands in his pockets. His fingers brushed the soft paper napkin he'd found in Becca's coat pocket. He took it out and breathed in the scent of it, hoping he could find a trace of her perfume or hand cream or lipstick. It was a fairly clean napkin, neatly folded in half. He opened it up and stared at the silhouette of the boar on the logo. He hadn't been to the bar in months, but maybe it was time for a visit. He pulled out his phone and texted Reggie.

"Ask Gary if he can send over a recent photo of Ann."

"Sure thing," she texted back.

A door shut and Webb came across the hall to his office. He looked at the napkin in Logan's hand. Logan folded it up and slid it in his pocket.

"I recognize that napkin," Webb said. "The Three Boars, right?"

"Yep. Can't picture you hanging out there. You seem more like the top of the Four Seasons type."

"I haven't been there for several years. A few colleagues and I used to meet there on Friday nights to unwind, exchange ideas."

Logan followed Webb into the therapy room and sat on the hard couch. "Ah ha, I knew it. You shrinks get together to compare levels of lunacy, don't you?"

Webb smiled. "Not exactly but it helps to talk to your peers when you have a stressful job. Surely, you understand that with your line of work."

"I don't have too many peers I respect enough to bounce ideas off of. However, I do have a new co-worker. So far she ticks all the boxes of an excellent partner."

"A she? I've always found women are easier to work with than men. Do you go there often?"

Logan was confused. "Where?"

"The Three Boars."

Logan chuckled lightly. "If you're trying to assess whether or not I have a drinking problem, I like a beer or two in the evening. I haven't been to Three Boars since St.

Patrick's Day when some of the guys talked me into a pint of green beer."

"I've tried green beer too. Of course it's just food coloring, but the color just didn't match up with my perceived notion of beer so it tasted funny." Webb sat down and crossed his legs at the knees. He picked up his notepad and paper. "How is the case going? Were you allowed to continue after they learned you knew the victim?"

"I put up a good protest, and I didn't lose my temper," Logan added, then decided he sounded like a petulant little kid.

"Good to hear. So you'll be continuing on it. How is it going?"

Logan shrugged. "Not great yet but we'll find the killer. I won't stop until I do."

Webb flipped back a few pages. Considering Logan was only on his third visit, the man sure did have a lot of notes on him. What he wouldn't give to be looking over the man's shoulder to see what he'd written.

"At the end of the last session you mentioned that your relationship with the victim was a story in itself. Why don't we start there?"

Logan was surprised that the session would start with that topic but then he did leave somewhat of a cliffhanger at the end of Monday's session. "Becca and I—"

Webb looked up. "That's her name? Becca?"

"When I knew her. She was going by a different name now." Logan didn't fill in that detail. He never liked to discuss a case with outsiders, not even a shrink who had to keep it all confidential. He also wasn't in the mood to narrate the whole damn story, so he gave a quick, abbreviated edition. "We grew up together in a town called Layton. We weren't just high school sweethearts. There was never doubt in either of our minds that we would be together forever, long after high school. Becca had a terrible family life. Her father was an abusive monster, and her mom suffered from some major mental health problems. Her husband never allowed her to get proper help. He was master in that house, and the two women were essentially his prisoners. His brother was with law enforcement, a corrupt cop who managed to make case files and calls to social services disappear. One day it became too much for Becca. Some of us were heading down to the beach for a weekend, and when we got there the beach was covered with emergency vehicles. Our friend, Jeremy, had been there with her. He said she'd gone for a walk on the beach, and she just walked into the Pacific to commit suicide."

Webb's neatly shaped brows inched together in confusion. "I don't understand."

Logan nodded. "Trust me, I was right there with you when I saw her lying on the grass, newly dead. It turns out she tried to commit suicide but Jeremy saved her. He was one of those kids who'd been traumatized by his parents dying successively from cancer. He was brainy and book smart, and he studied everything having to do with medicine and first aid. Becca knew she could never go back to Layton, to the house of horrors she grew up in."

"So they made up a story that she was dead, gone forever, and Becca moved on to start a whole new life?" Webb provided.

"That's it in a nutshell."

He finished writing down a few notes, then looked up and rested the pen on the side of his clean-shaven chin. It reminded Logan that his own beard stubble was getting past the point of no return. No return meaning he'd either have to grow a beard, or he was going to have to involve scissors.

"How did that make you feel? You must have been pretty hurt when the girl you loved just took off without looking back?"

"I thought she was dead. I was in anguish afterward, even suicidal myself for a time."

Webb shook his head lightly. "I mean now. How did it make you feel when you realized she was still alive, living a new life and that she never tried to contact you?"

"How would you feel?" Logan asked.

"Not talking about my feelings here but I'll play along. Guess there'd be shock first, at discovering she was still alive, then hurt that she hadn't felt the need to contact me followed by anger. Are you feeling angry?"

"It's hard to be angry at someone you loved your entire life, someone who died a horrific death. But yeah, there was some anger. Guess I'm disappointed she never felt she could come to me for protection. But then I was never able to fully protect her in Layton. There were plenty of times that I came close to taking on her asshole of a dad."

"But you didn't?"

Logan chewed on that sentence for a long moment. But he didn't. He stared out the window. Daylight was breaking through the coastal gray. It promised to be another blistering summer day. He looked at Webb. He sat there in all his elegance and indifference waiting patiently for Logan's response. "It's a regret I will live with my whole life."

Webb set the pen and paper on the side table. His movements were always so slow and thought out, Logan wondered if the man ever got agitated or frantic? Did he ever get angry?

"Last session we talked about hypnosis."

Logan nodded unenthusiastically. "Don't think it will work but I'll humor you."

Webb grinned but it was only slight. Logan supposed a big show of emotion would be unprofessional.

Webb walked to a closet and pulled out a small pillow that was covered in a disposable pillowcase like the kind they used in a doctor's office. He placed it at the end of the couch. "You're tall so feel free to rest your feet up on the arm of the couch. I apologize that the couch is not more comfortable, but I've found that when a couch is too cushiony, too cradling, my patients doze right off into a snore."

"Why stop here? Why not get a bed of nails like Uncle

Fester had in Addam's Family?" Logan chuckled at his joke as he stretched back on the couch, resting his head on the pillow and propping his feet up on the opposite arm.

"I'll keep that suggestion in mind." Webb pulled a stool from the corner of the room and sat down.

Logan peered up at him. "No shiny gold watch to swing back and forth?"

"No, this isn't a Hollywood movie. I want you to close your eyes and start thinking about every part of your body relaxing. We'll start at the top of your head. Relax your scalp, your forehead, your ears." Webb's voice took on a smooth almost surreal tone, as if no one was in the room with Logan and his voice was coming from all around. Logan gave in to the directions deciding it wouldn't help to resist. If the doctor thought he could do something with hypnosis, something that would move him faster through therapy, then Logan was good with that. Surprisingly, as his body relaxed, he felt his mind empty, as if he was drifting toward a blank daydream. His body felt heavy on the couch, almost as if it could sink into the rock hard cushions. For those few minutes, life was lacking the usual garbage that kept him up at night. Webb's voice drifted over him like warm water as his body melted into a boneless mass.

"Logan, I want you to think of a time in your past when you were really angry."

The suggestion made his muscles harden slightly, but

Webb quickly worked the kinks out reminding him to
relax every part of his body. Visions of his old neighborhood crept from the edges of his mind, becoming slowly
clearer with each new frame, like a film coming into focus.

"Where are you at?" Webb's disembodied voice flowed
over him

His mouth relaxed and the words didn't form easily.
"I'm in Layton. I'm in front of Becca's house."

"Tell me what's happening. What's going through your
mind?"

"I'm mad as hell. I want to kill him..."

The sky above looks apocalyptic, like I'm standing in a
movie where the world is about to come to an end. The
massive wildfire burning a hundred miles north has
blown its billows of toxic smoke our direction. It erases
the blue and replaces it with a murky gray. Not the cold
bone chilling mist of a deep fog gray, a suffocating, steamy
gray that turns the sun an unnatural orange and makes
the trees sag and weep from lack of oxygen. It's the perfect
day for killing someone with my bare hands. Ray Kinsey
has been in my sights since I was eight years old when
Becca showed up to school with a fat lip.

I stand on the sidewalk staring at the house, opening
and closing my fists, like I'm priming a weapon. Becca is in
my room, buried under my covers crying her eyes out.

This time Ray took his wrath out on Becca's mom. Linda locked herself in the bathroom, rocking and crying and sobbing about the two angels. Becca ran out the front door and down the street to my house.

Smoke from the sky is burning my eyes. My throat stings with the taste of it, like I've been standing in front of the barbecue too long. There's no movement in the house, but Ray's truck is there. He's home. He's in the house menacing his wife, waiting to take another swing at her.

My feet move forward without me thinking about it. I stomp along the broken cement path leading to the front door. I don't know how it will all end, but one of us will be dead. I don't intend to leave until one of us is ready for a body bag.

As I approach the house, ashes start to fall from the sky. It really is like an end of times day, perfect. The front door opens slowly. My heart slams wildly against my chest. My fists have stopped flexing. I'm holding them tight, in iron knots. I'm expecting Ray's big, hard edged face, but Becca's mom, Linda, slips past the small opening. She's holding a washcloth to her mouth. It's covered with blood. She smiles weakly. "Hello, Logan. Becca's not here. You go home now okay?" Her thin, reedy voice trembles. "Go back home. Everything is fine. I'll tell Becca you stopped by." She backs up toward the door.

"Are you fucking kidding me, Ray?" I yell so loud the ashes dash off as if a blast of air has hit them. "You're sending *her* out, you fucking coward!"

"Now go on, Logan. We don't want any trouble." Linda sobs into her bloody washcloth. It leaves streaks of red across her face. She's holding tentatively on to the door until it's smacked from her hand. It flies open. My nemesis is standing in the doorway. Linda curls her shoulders over into the walking fetal position I've seen her in so often. She ducks back inside. Ray is wearing a stretched out gray t-shirt that's stained with sweat and blood. He's still got his steel-toed work boots on. I hadn't considered the fucking boots. They'll hurt. That's for damn sure.

"This is over now, Ray." My voice isn't nearly as steady as I hoped, but my body is rigid with anger. I'm in that tunnel I create when I'm mad as hell and I need to pound someone. The smoke, the ashes, the sounds of Linda sobbing from the house, they disappear and it's just me and my prey. "I'm going to fucking kill you, Ray. Someone's got to stop you."

Ray turns his head slightly to the right. "Linda, get out here," he bellows into the house.

"This has nothing to do with her," I say. "You've hurt her enough."

Ray's smile is never kind or happy. It's one of pure evil, like the Joker. "You telling me how to run my family, boy?"

"I'm just telling you this has to stop. Since the authorities don't have the balls, it's down to me. And mine are feeling like fucking titanium right now."

His laugh is worse than his smile. Linda peers around the edge of the door, looking about as afraid as I've ever seen her. She shrieks as Ray reaches back and yanks her out to stand next to him on the porch. I take a few steps forward until the glint of a gun sparks through the smoke and ash. He presses it to Linda's temple. She cries uncontrollably. Her knees give way, but Ray yanks her back to standing.

"Let her go." I am losing it now. My voice shows it and I hate that.

"I will let her go just as soon as you back yourself off my property. Otherwise, this thing might go off accidentally."

My eyes flit toward the neighbors' house. One side is vacant. The Millers moved out the second they had a chance to leave. No one wants to live next door to Ray Kinsey. It is like living next to a madman. The other side belongs to an older couple, the Rossmores. They can barely hear or see and never step outside. Stay inside. That was the warning from the health department at school and on our phones and people listened. It is just me and the man I want to kill... and his wife. Linda is hysterical. I worry he'll shoot her just to shut her up.

"Get out of here and don't come back, and when you see that tramp daughter of mine tell her to get her ass home and quick."

It takes all my willpower to step back. I can't be the cause of Linda's death. It figures Ray would use his own wife like a hostage, a human shield. He only swung his fist at women. Too fucking coward to come out and have a real fight with someone who can swing back hard. I get to the sidewalk and just start walking. No outdoor activity, the health department warned. Air quality was dangerous. I take off at a full run. I run hard and fast until all I can breathe and taste is smoke. I run until I drop to my knees in anguish and puke my guts out.

Webb's tone reminds Logan of vanilla ice cream, smooth and cold and monotonous. His words flow through Logan's ears, but they seem to slide right past his muddled thoughts. Layton was gone. Ray was gone. The rage still clung to the edges of his mind.

"What do you see now?" Webb's voice came from nowhere in particular as if he was floating around the office like a ghost.

"It's dark. There are a lot of people, drunk people. I can smell the beer and wine and stale peanuts. Walt is behind the counter. It's the Three Boars. People are elbowing me and trying to order their drinks. It's crowded. A band is playing "Sweet Home Alabama" in the corner. There's a line for the dart board. My gaze is drawn to something, someone at the bar counter." Logan felt his heartbeat in his chest. Not a normal pace, accelerated, urgent. "She's leaned over the counter talking to Walt. He's grinning back at her." Logan could feel his mind sweeping down. There is a pair of cutoffs, flip-flops. "Those legs. I'd know them anywhere." Logan felt he was being pulled down, out of his own body, into the hard couch cushions. "She turns. It's her. It's that smile I have etched in my brain." Logan fell silent, lost in a scene he so badly wanted to stay in... forever. She was there, alive, smiling. Then she laughed but the sound wasn't the one he knew, the one he could still hear in his dreams. It was a clap, a sharp clap.

Logan opened his eyes. He stared up at the shiny chrome light fixtures.

"How do you feel?" Webb asked. It was no longer the monotonous, vanilla tone. His doctor tone wasn't much different, vanilla but with the occasional swirl of flavor.

"Fine." Logan sat up still feeling as if he weighed three hundred pounds and the couch, hard as it was, might swallow him up. "Did it work?" he asked, sensing that it had but wanting to know for sure.

A cool, confident smile crossed Webb's face. "It was a successful session." He walked over to his notepad and jotted down a few words. "Friday? Same time?"

"Three in one week?"

"Well, if you want to draw this out longer—"

"I'll be here on Friday." Webb walked him to the door. Logan glanced back at him. "Should I be feeling better?" He asked because he was feeling different but not neces- sarily as if he'd made any steps toward managing his anger. He wasn't sure how a doctor, even an adept one like Webb, could show him how to turn off the valve. It had always been there, ready to flip on at a moment's notice. It just didn't seem like something that was ever going to switch off for good.

"It's a little too soon for that, but I think today was a big step forward." Webb walked him to the outer door. The hallway was empty.

Logan motioned to the door across the way. "Your co-worker doesn't have many clients. It's so quiet over there."

"Dr. Jordan has a steady stream of patients. Good luck on the case. We'll see you Friday." With that, he shut the door.

Logan raked his hair back with his fingers. He felt energized, ready to work. He pulled out his phone. There had been a missed call from Reggie. He hit dial.

"Hey, Coop." Should her voice already have sounded so damn familiar, like he was talking to an old friend?

"Anything new while I was stuck on the shrink's couch?"

"A couple of things. I tried the number, the one that came up three times on the phone records but that Gary didn't recognize. It went to a Google voicemail box. I left a message for them to call the precinct in regards to an ongoing investigation. I left some numbers and an address. I'll try again later."

Logan stepped into the elevator.

"Now for the bigger nugget. I let Gary know we needed a current photo, which he sent to me via text. I'll send it to you too. He called me right after to let me know that he'd called Ann's workplace, Morgan's Fine Jewelry, to let them know what happened and to tell them about the funeral. He was a little confused about why they hadn't called to find out why she wasn't showing up to work. That confusion was cleared up when they informed him that Ann had been fired from her job in April. They didn't want to tell him over the phone what had happened."

Logan pushed out the exit. He was always glad to be free of the austere, sterile building. The fog was gone and a blue summer day loomed ahead. The sidewalks were crowded with shoppers and people rushing in to work. Logan had to walk a wide berth around a woman with a double baby stroller as she forged ahead making it clear he was going to have to move and not her.

"Guess we'll be stopping at the jewelry store first this morning. I'm on my way to the station, all cleansed and exorcised and free of guilt and anger."

"Sounds like I'll be working with a saint instead of grubby five-o'clock shadow Coop."

He climbed into his car and glanced up at the rearview. "Think I passed five-o'clock a few hours ago. You women are lucky you don't have to shave."

Reggie laughed into the phone.

"Right, that sounded stupid to me the second it came out of my mouth. See you soon, and I better have a parking spot."

"You'll have a spot. Just not the one you want. I'll send the photo once I hang up on this ridiculous conversation."

Logan hung up. The photo came through as he turned

on the car. Without thinking, he grabbed his phone. A breath got caught in his throat. It was Becca. She was standing at a park with green grass and trees surrounding her. She had on a light green sundress that tied behind the neck. Her thin, tanned shoulders glowed in the sun. Her thick brown hair flowed in the wind as she tilted her head to the side. She'd perfected the flirtatious head tilt in high school. She used it as a secret weapon against any unsuspecting male, even gruff old Principal Halbert, when she wanted to avoid detention.

As if she knew he'd been staring at the photo taking it all in with no small amount of heartache, Reggie sent a text. "She's incredible. I'm still going with my first hunch. She was someone's obsession."

"You might be right," he texted back. He was feeling slightly obsessed himself. Logan snapped the phone into its holder.

"All right, Cricket, let's nail this monster."

CHAPTER
SEVENTEEN

Reggie met Logan in the parking lot. Logan preferred not to walk into the precinct if it wasn't necessary. She was carrying a box filled with three blueberry muffins, the good kind with chunks of brown sugar on top. Logan's fridge had been a total disappointment this morning. He always looked in it with a degree of hope, as if in the middle of the night a refrigerator fairy had come to restock it with sliced meats and cheeses, fresh eggs and a gallon of milk. It was an old habit from being married. Vicky never let the fridge run low. He could always count on a cold beer and a load of groceries staring back at him from the shelves. This morning, the only thing staring back was a moldy block of cheese that could almost have been literally staring at him because it was that close to coming alive. The egg carton jammed in the back corner had long since passed its expiration date, and the package of lunch meat was no longer recognizable as edible. The muffins were making his mouth water.

"You going to share those muffins with a hungry friend?" he asked.

"You can have one, but we need to stop somewhere before the jewelry store. It's on the way."

"Deal."

Reggie handed him a muffin. "Eat it before you get inside. They're super crumbly." She leaned her slim hip against the side of the car, crossed her arms and watched him devour the muffin from behind her sunglasses. "Guess one of those steak dinners didn't hold you over like you thought," she quipped.

Logan was enjoying the muffin too much to care about the barb. He finished the muffin in three bites. "Now I need a cold glass of milk, dammit." He squinted one eye at the backpack on her shoulder. "Miss Poppins?" he asked hopefully.

"If I did have milk in this backpack, it wouldn't have been squeezed from a cow. It would have been squeezed from a soybean."

They climbed into the car. "I told you, if it doesn't come from a cow it's not milk."

"Said the man who complained that women don't have to shave."

"That was a major step back for mankind. In my defense, I'd just come out of a pretty intense therapy session with hypnosis and all the crap that goes on with a shrink." Logan drove the car toward the exit. Reggie pointed for him to go right.

"So hard-headed Logan Cooper was under the spell of the swinging watch," Reggie said.

"No watch. That's from movies, apparently."

"Did it work? Did you go under?"

Logan thought about it. "You know what? I think I did." An inkling of what he'd experienced under hypnosis stayed in the creases of his mind. There was a confrontation with Becca's dad, a bad one from what his subconscious was telling him, and somewhere in there was a trip to Three Boars. He figured that had to do with the fact that he'd been looking at the napkin before the session started.

"Turn right here," Reggie said.

"Exactly where are we going?" Logan asked.

"I need to drop these muffins off for someone. The jewelry store is this direction too, so it's not even a detour, just a pit stop."

The closer they got to the beach, the more people there were on bicycles and dressed in swimsuits. One guy had his boogie board strapped to the back of his bike. Logan had to switch lanes to avoid smacking the board and, subsequently, the rider right out of the bike lane.

"Turn in here," Reggie pointed.

"Here? This is an assisted living home."

"Wow, you read that on your own?" she teased, but her

voice had taken on a more somber tone. "Be right back." She climbed out with the box of muffins. The Sunshine Home was a series of olive green buildings sitting under a line of tall pine trees. A large expanse of grass started at a chain-link fence and worked its way to fill a courtyard between the buildings. The courtyard had a big three-tiered fountain and some tables and benches. Several of the patients were sitting in wheelchairs, closely attended by medical assistants.

Logan leaned back to rest, wishing he had a second muffin and hoping that there wouldn't be too many more sessions with Webb. Out of the corner of his eye, he spotted the distinctive long, graceful movements of his new partner. Reggie walked out to the courtyard with her muffins and stooped down in front of a woman in a wheelchair. The woman had thin gray hair brushed back into a bun. From the distance, with the wheelchair, the blanket over her knees on a warm summer day and the gray hair, Logan was sure he was looking at a much older woman, eighties maybe ninety, but as he focused on her face, he realized she was much younger. She stared down at the muffins Reggie set on her lap. Reggie peered up at her and placed her hand on the woman's arm. There were a few words exchanged between Reggie and the caregiver, then Reggie stood, leaned over the woman, kissed her forehead and headed back across the courtyard. It was all becoming clear, the reason why a young detective would put in for a transfer just a year after her promotion. The shabby apartment, the motorcycle, it was all so she could afford a place for her mom.

Reggie returned and settled quietly into the passenger seat. Logan didn't ask questions, he just looked her direction and waited to see if she wanted to talk. Reggie pushed her hair behind her ear, giving him a clear view of her amazing profile, the long lashes, the small round nose, the lips and slightly cleft chin.

"She was only fifty-six when she started to forget where we lived, where she put her keys and purse, where she worked. We'd survived at least three break-ins, one where my mom fought off the guy with a frying pan, and two shootings right outside our house. I joined the force thinking, if nothing else, I'd finally have the skills to keep her safe. But I couldn't protect her from this. Early onset is what they told us. Rare but it happens. It seems we beat the odds, but not in a good way. It seemed a lot of people were beating the same terrible odds down south. I couldn't find a decent place for her. They either had a waiting list or they cost more than my year's salary for a month's rent. I found this place. At first, I considered just moving her up here and staying down south for work. I was just getting in the swing of things." She turned to him. There was no self-pity in her expression, only an edge of anger for the crap life had handed her. "I couldn't leave her up here alone. The rest is history. I transferred and somehow ended up with a partner who I wasn't too sure about at first but—" She reached across and flicked something off Logan's chin. "Muffin crumb," she explained.

"But—" Logan prodded.

"But I think he's all right," she finished.

"Probably the nicest thing anyone has ever said to me. Which probably tells you a lot." Logan put the car in drive and rolled out of the parking lot. "I'm sorry, by the way. I know you're very close to your mom. It has to be hard seeing her..." He couldn't find words to finish. He was realizing how lucky he was to have two parents who were still happy and independent.

"Hard seeing her disappear right before my eyes," she said quietly. "It sucks worse than anything I've ever experienced." Reggie leaned down to her backpack and pulled out her thermos of water. She took a long swig. "Sorry, turn right. Forgot to tell you."

Logan made a quick right. A block of shops rolled out in front of them. They were for the wealthier tourists and people from up in the hills. Antique stores, an art gallery with some of the creepiest looking paintings in the window, and, at the end, on a corner, in a shop that was trimmed with gleaming marble and green stone sat Morgan's Fine Jewelry. The front windows glittered with diamond filled displays.

They got out of the car. Two women were walking out, admiring a gold watch in a black box. They were both dressed as if they'd just stepped out of a glitzy fashion show. There was an outer door, which led to a small space where Logan and Reggie stood sandwiched between the outer and inner doors. They were close enough that Logan could see the individual freckles on Reggie's nose. A voice came through the intercom that could only be described as snobbish.

"May I help you?" a woman dressed in a blue jacket and matching skirt asked from behind a chin height counter.

They simultaneously pressed their badges against the glass of the inner door. The woman, who appeared to be someone who refused to get ruffled, became obviously ruffled.

"We just need to ask some questions about an ex-employee, Ann Robbins," Reggie said.

"One moment." The woman stomped off on blue heels that matched her pristine suit. She hurried into the back.

Logan looked at Reggie. "I think we scared her."

"She did scurry away rather quickly."

Seconds later, an old man with thick gray hair, bushy eyebrows and an expensive pinstriped suit emerged from the back room. He looked decidedly less frightened than the woman. They pressed their badges against the glass again. He pulled a small pair of spectacles out of his top coat pocket and took a moment to check out the authenticity of the badges.

"In the meantime, two detectives are going to suffocate in his little security barricade." Logan quipped. There was no lack of oxygen, but somehow, being so confined with his partner, who smelled like freshly squeezed citrus, was making him antsy.

The inner door clicked open. Logan and Reggie stepped inside the shop. The entire room was surrounded by gleaming glass cases, each one overflowing with gold and silver. Their feet practically glided across the extra plush hunter green carpeting that filled the room. The walls were decked in heavily patterned wallpaper and the speakers in the corners dribbled out some sort of classical tune. Logan couldn't picture Becca working there. Nothing about it reminded him of the wild child he grew up with.

"I'm Gerald Morgan," the man said. He circled back behind one of his glass counters to put some distance between them. "I understand you have some questions about Ann Robbins." He put on a properly sad face, though it looked staged. "I was very sorry to hear about her death. For two years, she was a model employee, and the customers loved her. She had a spirit, an energy that was infectious." His words sounded genuine.

"Her husband mentioned you fired her in April," Logan said.

"That is correct." He had the kind of big expressive brows one might see on a Muppet, and it was hard not to keep watching those brows. "One day in March, Ann went out to lunch. It had been a normal morning, a few engagement ring purchases and some window-shoppers. She was late coming back from lunch, about twenty minutes or so. I didn't mind because, like I said, up to that point she'd been an exemplary employee. She came back so flustered, so upset that she couldn't even answer customers' questions properly. Naturally, I asked her if everything was all right. She said she wasn't feeling well, that she'd developed a headache. I sent her home early. She returned the next day looking as if she hadn't slept. Dark rings under her eyes, and she was agitated, anxious." As he spoke, the woman in the blue suit nodded along in agreement. "I assumed something was going on with her husband. A week passed and she gradually seemed better, more herself. Then she received a phone call—"

"Was it on a Thursday?" Reggie asked.

His brows did the surprised dance. "Yes, and I know that only because after that she received a call every Thursday at two. I don't normally mind a call as long as it's not lengthy and it doesn't happen while a customer is at the counter. The calls were quite short. She claimed it was her husband and that was his break time and the only time they could chat, but Margaret and I—" he glanced toward the woman with the nodding head. "We thought there was something suspicious about them."

"Why is that?" Logan asked.

"For one thing, if it was her husband she was never happy to talk to him. She was curt and irritated and rarely spoke. She mostly listened, and when she hung up she would jot a few things down on her phone. The first call that came at that time on a Thursday—" he looked at Margaret, whose face turned a darker shade of pink.

"I wasn't eavesdropping," Margaret stated emphatically, but her face turned even darker assuring everyone in the room that she had indeed been eavesdropping.

"It's all right. Please, if you *overheard* anything important," Reggie said putting special emphasis on the diplomatic term overheard.

Margaret's face lost some of the pink. "That first call I just happened to be checking my hair in the mirror on the door in the back room. Ann was here at the counter in front of the door when she answered her phone. I heard her whisper angrily, asking the caller how they got her number. It seemed like an odd question for her husband."

"Agreed," Logan said. "Did you ever happen to *overhear* anything else during one of those calls? Anything at all, a name, a place?"

Margaret nodded and moved closer to them. "One time I think she slipped and said the person's name." She paused for dramatic effect, but Logan wasn't in the mood.

"And," he asked impatiently.

"I might have misheard, but I could have sworn she called the person on the other end Drax."

Logan straightened. "Drax? Are you sure?"

"That's what I heard," Margaret said.

Logan nodded. He returned his focus to the owner, Mr. Morgan. "Did you fire her because of the phone calls?"

That made the two of them fall silent, exchanging looks that showed it was more than the phone calls.

"Please, a woman has been murdered, and we need to find the killer," Reggie said bluntly.

Morgan cleared his throat. It was a forceful, take charge kind of throat clearing. "I caught her trying to steal a diamond."

Logan felt as if he'd been slapped. Becca was not one to stay out of trouble, but with as little as she had growing up, she never stole. It wasn't in her nature.

"Are you certain?" Logan asked.

Morgan's brows bunched in an insulted expression. "Yes, I'm sure." He waved his arm around the store. "There are cameras everywhere. She knew that so she had to be quick and clever about it. Her change in behavior and the strange phone calls had me suspicious. Frankly, I didn't trust her after awhile, so I kept an eye on her when she didn't realize I was watching. I was showing a customer some watches, and Ann was showing a young man diamond engagement rings. She had seven of our most popular rings out on black velvet." He reached into a box at the end of the counter and produced a piece of black fabric. It was lush and silky. "We find that jewelry always looks best when displayed on contrasting black."

"So you were keeping an eye on her while you showed a customer watches?" Reggie asked.

"That's right. Like I said, I was starting to feel uncomfortable having her behind the counter."

"Yeah, you said that." Logan hadn't meant to sound so snippy, but he was having a hard time listening to someone talk about Becca as if she was a common thief. It just didn't make sense.

"In the end, she didn't make the sale. The young man decided an antique ring might be more to her liking." Morgan looked a little miffed. "I think Ann suggested it after she saw a photo of the girlfriend. She was wearing some kind of vintage dress."

"Then she was probably right," Reggie pointed out.

"Her job was to sell a ring not give unwanted advice. And I was about to tell her exactly that when I noticed that as she placed the rings back on their stands, there were only six. I confronted her. She tossed the ring she'd been hiding in her hand on the counter. I fired her on the spot. She grabbed her things and walked out without another word. I considered pressing charges, but she never actually left the store with the ring... thanks to my vigilance."

Logan liked the pompous jewelry store owner less and less. A couple walked into the security area behind the inner door. Morgan motioned for Margaret to get to the intercom.

"If there's nothing else," Morgan said. "They're here to pick up their wedding rings."

"That's it for today, but we may need to ask you more questions later," Reggie said. Logan was already making his way to the door. The classical music droning through the store was getting on his nerves.

Morgan groaned in irritation at the notion that they might be back. The inner door opened allowing in the happy couple and letting the two detectives back out onto the city sidewalk.

"I got the feeling you knew the name she gave. Drax," Reggie said as they walked back to the car.

"I know of a Drax." They climbed into the car. It had been sitting in direct sunlight. Both of them had to lightly finger the seatbelts and door handles so as not to scald themselves. Logan turned on the engine and blasted the air. It was warm still but it helped cool down the steering wheel. "He used to run a kink dungeon, Dracula's Palace, a place where people could go and live out their sexual fantasies, capitalize on their fetishes."

"Doms, whips and chains, the whole shebang?" Reggie asked.

"Yep, the whole shebang. Drax, short for Dracula, was a real piece of work, greedy, ruthless, but he ran a pretty tight ship. That was when I was a young, enthusiastic, clean-shaven whelp in a patrol car. Other than a few incidents, where someone got a little too much of what they were begging for and then there was one bad reaction to latex—" Reggie looked at him with wide eyes. "Yeah, that one wasn't pretty. Guy nearly died in his latex suit. Otherwise, it was mostly young women, even college students, in the Dom roles and professional men, men who were probably respected but who were hiding their dark sexual fantasies from the public eye as clients." Logan sat back as something occurred to him.

Reggie read his mind. "Do you think Becca might have been moonlighting as a Dom? Maybe she had a dark side that her all too respectable and prim husband wouldn't have approved of?"

"Not sure. Let's pay a little visit to Dracula's Palace and find out what good ole Drax is up to these days."

CHAPTER
EIGHTEEN

Everyone in the area knew that Dracula's Palace existed, but it was well hidden from view in the sprawling basement of an old business complex. Drax had provided an entrance and exit that came up from the cement steps and emptied into an alleyway behind the building. There were a few parking spots in the alley that were marked reserved on plain white signs for their clients.

"A basement in earthquake riddled California," Reggie noted. "Wouldn't want to be chained up and gagged when the big one hit. I once knew a girl who made good money as a Dom. She was perfectly content with her career and even bragged about it. She also drove a Porsche 911 and owned a sweet little house in Newport Beach, so no one frowned on her career choice."

The industrial metal door was locked. Logan knocked and had his badge ready. The door creaked open. "Password?"

"Detective Cooper, just here to ask a few questions." He anticipated the door slamming shut and shoved his foot inside. It slammed right on cue and right on his foot. "Ouch, fuck," he muttered. "Don't give a damn about the business. I'm just looking for Drax."

The door shut and before they could knock again, it reopened. A tall, middle-aged woman with jet black hair that was streaked with white motioned them inside with a smile shrouded in bright red lipstick. "I'm Julia, the owner of this establishment. I didn't catch your names," she said before they took more than a few steps into the dark, narrow hallway.

They flashed their badges again. "I'm Detective Cooper and this is Detective Hawkins."

Julia, if that was her real name, surveyed Reggie from head to toe. "All that stunning beauty wasted on a job with law enforcement. You could make four times your salary here."

Reggie grinned. "I'll keep that in mind if I ever get tired of this job."

"Follow me to my office. We can talk there."

They headed down a narrow hallway that was lit with antique brass wall sconces. Doors lined both sides of the hallway, some with signs that said 'do not disturb' and others with signs that said 'welcome'. Some small sounds could be heard through the doors, but it seemed the rooms had been soundproofed for extra privacy. Before they reached Julia's office, a door with a welcome sign opened and a young woman wearing a shiny black leather corset and not much else came out drinking a can of cola. "Julia, I'm going to take a break. I need to call my professor to find out if I passed the final. The med school is waiting for those transcripts, and this one class is holding me up."

"Fingers crossed that you passed," Julia said as she motioned for them to step into a small room. The walls were covered with oil paintings of grand landscapes like mountains and a rocky coast line. It wasn't exactly what one would expect to see. However, her desk chair was upholstered in red leather and metal studs ran across the top and arms of the chair. A half empty glass of red wine was sitting next to a bowl of trail mix. She pushed her computer monitor aside as she sat down and motioned to two chairs that were covered in cheetah print fabric.

Julia's nails were as red as her lips as she crossed her long fingers. "Now what can I do for you?"

"As we told the person who opened the door"—Logan sat forward—"We need to talk to Drax."

Julia's painted on brows lifted. "Drax? The former owner?"

"So Drax doesn't own Dracula's Palace anymore?" Logan asked.

The red lips turned up like a bow. "We don't call it Dracula's Palace anymore. It's just Palace. I was one of Drax's best Doms back in the day. I saved up my money. When he decided it was time to retire, he sold it to me."

"Do you know where we might find him?" Reggie asked.

Julia's instant reluctance showed on her face. "Is he in some kind of trouble?"

"No, his name just came up in the middle of an investigation," Logan said smoothly. That seemed to allay her concern.

"Drax bought himself a big, fancy house up in the hills. We haven't spoken in several years, but I assume he's still there."

"You wouldn't happen to have his address?" Reggie asked. Logan knew her answer before it left her mouth.

"If I did, I don't think Drax would take too kindly to me handing out his address. You're police officers. Surely, you can find that out on your own."

A door across the hallway opened. Heavy metal music poured out of it. A short squat man with a ring of hair around his otherwise bald head hurried down the corridor in his sensible trousers and shoes. He kept his face down to avoid being seen. Not that there was anyone around to see.

"Yep." Logan rubbed his temple. "Let me see. His real name is—Dan, hmm, Dan—it was something famous, Dickens right? Dan Dickens. I remember it because I always thought it was a name that would have been tough to grow up with."

Julia nodded but didn't confirm or deny. "Now, if there's nothing else."

Logan was just as anxious to leave as Julia was to have them vacate her establishment, but he knew there was one more question that needed to be asked. It was one he didn't want to hear the answer to. Reggie looked at him, silently, thoughtfully telling him it was his to ask when he was ready. He doubted he'd ever be ready. He pulled out his phone and brought up the photo of Ann Robbins. He didn't have to scroll for it because he'd looked at it more than once since Reggie sent it.

"Do you know this woman?" he asked as he held the screen toward Julia.

She pushed on a pair of bright purple framed reading glasses and looked at the picture. "Yes, I know her or knew her, I should say. We used to be Doms together about twenty years back. She was Drax's favorite. She went by the name Angel. I don't think I ever learned her real name. I haven't spoken to her since she left the Palace. Is she in some kind of trouble?"

Logan put the phone away. "She's dead."

Julia shook her head. "I'm sorry to hear that." Her expression smoothed with comprehension. "Is that why you're looking for Drax?"

"We just need to talk to him," Reggie said. She stood up first. Logan sprang to his feet, glad to be heading to the exit.

Julia walked them back down the hallway. The place was still cold and creepy like Logan remembered. He knew the rooms were more welcoming with thick rugs, painted walls, mood lighting and every device imaginable to give the clients what they desired, but the hallway reminded him of a hallway prisoners might walk down on their way to execution. He was just as happy to be out in the sunshine and fresh sea breeze. He felt the same relief from his partner.

"She was trying to survive," Reggie said as they walked to the car.

"Yeah, I know," he said, but it didn't make the bitter pill any easier to swallow. The shocks kept coming. He found himself ready for just about anything.

"I don't know about you, but I can't imagine living out my sexual fantasy in that dungeon." Reggie shivered once.

Logan peered over at her. "Now you've got me trying to figure out just what that sexual fantasy would entail. Not that I don't agree. It's always been a cold, dark place. I suppose it probably fits the mood of the people who go there. It's sort of a punishing atmosphere, you know, like doing penance. They're obviously there because they fear that polite society would shun them for their desires, so it should be a place that reminds them of that. Of course, that's just me with my community college level bullshit psychology. It could be that Julia is too cheap to hire a decorator. The rooms are much more inviting."

Reggie smiled at him over the top of the car. "And you know this because...?"

"The latex incident, remember? The guy had passed

out still chained up to the whipping apparatus, or whatever it's called."

They got inside the car. He looked at her. "Care to elaborate?"

Reggie reached for her water. "Elaborate? Oh that. Let's just say it involves Chris Hemsworth dressed as Thor and some chocolate covered strawberries. That is all I will say, so let your imagination run wild."

"I don't have to. There's just nowhere to run to with that." Logan picked up the phone. "Let's see if Fran can get us an address for dear old Dan Dickens."

CHAPTER NINETEEN

Dan Dickens, better known as Drax, lived in a nice modern home at the top of a long curvy road in the lush hills above the city. Jacarandas and flowering plum trees lined the road up to the property. The house was mostly windows on the front, a midcentury modern with flat roof and white cinder block entrance. Massive date palms lined the driveway up to the house. There were two lifted blue trucks in the driveway parked on either side of a black Mercedes sedan. A small green midsized Honda was parked off to the side and looked out of place next to the other expensive vehicles. A black wrought iron gate blocked entry into the driveway.

Logan stopped the car just short of the gate, opened his window and reached for the button on the intercom.

"What can I do for you?" a voice asked.

Logan lifted his badge for the security camera. "Detectives Cooper and Hawkins here to see Mr. Dickens. It's important," he added.

"One moment."

"What do you want to bet Mr. Dickens will be unable to see us," Logan said.

Seconds later, the voice on the other end returned. "I'm sorry but Mr. Dickens is not able to—"

"Tell him it is in regards to a murder investigation and that it would be in his best interest to speak to us," Logan countered.

"One moment." The woman returned seconds later. "He can only spare a few minutes."

The gate lock clanged and the ornate iron gates swung slowly open. Logan parked next to the Honda. There were cameras in every corner of the eaves as they walked along a strip of cement pavers to the double front doors. A large man with a neck as thick as his head met them on the front stoop. Nothing about his square jaw and brooding forehead said welcome. He had a leather shoulder holster strapped around his fuselage sized torso. A shiny Glock was nestled in the holster.

"Badges?" the man grunted.

They showed the badges, which he studied as if getting ready for an exam. "This way. Don't touch anything," he growled.

As they walked behind, Reggie pretended to touch everything they passed. Abstract art, the kind that really took some figuring out, lined the long, wide hallway. A

Persian rug runner ran the length of the slate floor. They passed a sitting room that was filled with white leather furniture and had a waterfall cascading from the top of a fireplace mantel. It seemed Drax had done well for himself. He made plenty at the Palace but enough for this type of lifestyle? Logan doubted Julia would have paid an exorbitant price for the business.

What had Drax gotten into after the Palace? Logan made a mental note to find that out. The armed guard stopped at a door and knocked with his massive knuckles. An older woman answered. She was wearing light blue scrubs and latex gloves. The distinct smell of a hospital, rubbing alcohol, antiseptic, sanitizer and, if his nose wasn't deceiving him, the acrid smell of blood, seeped through the opening. It wasn't exactly expected after a stroll through the expensively decorated house.

"I'm Tilda, Mr. Dickens' nurse. Please, not too long. It will tire him out." She opened the door, and the hospital smell was instantly explained. The entire room had been transformed into an exact replica of a hospital room complete with the rolling bed, beeping monitors and wheelchair. The last time Logan had seen Drax, he was still the purveyor of Dracula's Palace. He was a robust forty something man with thick black hair he wore slicked back like a vampire. He wore t-shirts from rock concerts and lots of gold chains around his neck. The few times Logan met him he had a highball glass half filled with whiskey clutched in his hand. The man in the bed hooked up to the kidney dialysis machine was bald and withered and sallow skinned. It seemed it wasn't just his kidneys that had given out but his liver as well. Maybe the whiskey had caught up to him.

Drax motioned for his nurse to lift the bed up. She hurried over to the side panel of buttons. The top half of the bed gradually lifted Drax to semi-sitting. The interim was slightly comical as everyone in the room waited for his slow ascent. The bed stopped with a jolt.

"I told you this bed needs replacing," Drax snapped. "It's a piece of shit. The hospital needs to send over a new one." After his short tirade, Drax rested back against his pillows as if that small rant had zapped him of all energy. His breathing was shallow and sweat beaded his forehead.

"If it isn't Officer Cooper. I hear you're a big shot detective now."

"I'm a detective. Not sure if the phrase big shot necessarily goes with it. It's a little more rank, but there are still plenty above me to tell me when I can piss and for how long."

Drax's laugh was frail and hoarse. It led to a small coughing fit. Tilda was highly attentive and immediately handed him a glass of water. He pushed it away. "Stop coddling me. I'm fine." He refocused on the two detectives standing in the room. "Who is the pretty woman standing next to you?"

Reggie nodded. "Detective Hawkins."

"You don't look old enough to be out of college let

alone a detective. What's this about a murder investigation? Who died?" He coughed again, but this time Tilda refrained from offering water. She busied herself with the numbers on the monitors, writing them down on a chart she plucked off the side of the bed.

"A woman named Ann Robbins was murdered," Reggie said.

"She worked at Dracula's Palace and went by the name Angel," Logan added.

Drax sat up a little but didn't have the strength to stay up long. "Yes, I know who she is. I didn't kill her. If I had, I would tell you right now."

Reggie and Logan exchanged puzzled looks.

"I assumed it was obvious. Don't let these machines fool you. They're not really keeping me alive just making it a little easier descent into the hell that awaits me."

Tilda gasped slightly.

"Oh, come on, Tilda, you know I'm not going that way." He lifted his eyes to the ceiling, then looked at Logan. "I've only got a few weeks according to my last exam. A combo of rich food, alcohol, smoking and all the shit that goes with living a fun life. Caught up with me a few years back but took a big turn for the worse about three weeks ago when the final kidney stopped working. Liver's shot too, which you can probably tell by the fact that I look as if someone rubbed a yellow highlighter all over me. I'm sorry to hear about Ann though," he said. "She was always a favorite."

"About five months ago, Ann started getting calls at work," Reggie started.

"Every Thursday at two," Drax supplied.

Logan and Reggie were both temporarily stunned into silence.

Drax chuckled but shut it down fast before it morphed into a cough. "That was when I told her where to meet me and how much to bring. You see, I was blackmailing her. That call would be to tell her where to drop off the money. Tried to get one of those fancy diamonds from that jewelry store too but she got caught."

Reggie looked over at Tilda.

"Don't worry about Tilda," Drax said. "I've been slowly confessing all my sins to her deciding I should get them off my chest. Isn't that right, Til?"

Tilda's grimace assured them Drax was telling the truth. Logan could only imagine the tawdry narrative a retelling of his life would be. "I've asked him if I could call him a priest," Tilda said weakly.

"Pfft," Drax muttered. "Those priests have even more to confess than me. I much prefer talking to you."

Poor Tilda looked as if she'd been bearing the burden of his confessions for sometime.

The large tubes of blood flowing up and down each side of the bed had been enough to keep Logan a few steps back. He'd even felt a wave of nausea between the sight of all of Drax's blood surging through clear tubes and on full display and the chemical odors circulating the room. But he'd passed that point of nausea and stepped closer to the side of the bed.

"Why the fuck were you blackmailing her?"

Drax shrugged nonchalantly. "I was blackmailing a lot of the women who used to work for me in Dracula's Palace. I'd track them down. If they were doing well, living what society would consider a respectable life, a life they wouldn't want disrupted by a scandalous secret from the past, then I'd ask them for money to keep quiet. How do you think I kept up this lifestyle? It certainly wasn't from the sale of the business." His dry laugh was irritating. In fact, even as withered and as close to death as he looked, he was entirely irritating. He spoke about ruining these women's lives as if he was talking about the weather. There was no sense of guilt or remorse. He was just stating it as plain fact. "I happened to run into Angel, I guess her real name was Ann, on her lunch break. She wasn't too happy to see me. I followed her to find that she worked at a fine jewelry store and decided it was time to see just what Ann was willing to shell out to keep her nice, prim life intact. She was upset, of course. They all were, but I only picked on the girls who could afford it. Those with good jobs and wealthy husbands."

"I see," Reggie said sharply. "You've been a heinous asshole for all these years. You think that as long as you tell everyone about it, you might not go straight to hell. Good luck with that," she added.

Drax shrugged again. "I'm giving it all back to them

once I'm gone. I don't have family. My entire estate will be divided between the women I blackmailed. I'm considering the money they gave me a loan that will be paid back with interest. They don't know that yet, of course, but it'll be my little surprise from the grave, so to speak. I'm just sorry that Angel won't be around to enjoy it. Why would someone kill her?" he asked.

"That's what we're trying to find out," Logan said. He was a little less irritated when he learned the money would eventually be repaid.

"I'd confess to that too only the real killer would still be out there. I hope you nail the bastard. Angel was always a good kid."

"Any idea at all who might have wanted her dead?" Reggie asked. She was still talking with a tight jaw to show Drax she disliked everything about him.

"If it wasn't the husband, then I imagine someone else who became obsessed with her. Happened more times than I could count when she was working at the Palace. Angel just had that thing, that magic that drew everyone to her." Drax looked up at Reggie through bloodshot, fading eyes. "You'd probably have it too if you didn't have that stick up your cute ass."

Reggie took an angry step toward the bed.

Logan placed his hand out to stop her from getting closer. "Don't fall for it. He's just a frail, dying old man who's trying to get his last kicks." Logan turned back to Drax. "This"—he waved his hand around to encircle the tubes and the machines—"All of this—I'm glad you're not getting off easy, you know, with a slipping away in your sleep kind of thing. And if by some miracle you survive past the end of this month, then I'm coming back to arrest your ass. We'll just drag all these machines down to the county jail with ya." Logan turned and prodded Reggie to walk out ahead of him. The guard led them to the door.

"That coward is still paying for protection right up to the end," Reggie said. "What a jerk." She tromped to the car. It was the first time Logan had seen her angry. He was glad to know she had it in her because trying to always stay positive in this job could eat at your very soul.

Logan sat behind the wheel and gripped it at two and ten o'clock. He sighed dejectedly.

"Ditto," Reggie said. "If nothing else, we're uncovering Becca's life, her second life, that is. I'm not sure what I would have done if I'd had no home, no family, no prospects. I might have worked for a creep like Drax too." Her phone beeped with a text. "It's Ann's friend, Janey. Funeral is set for tomorrow afternoon at two." Reggie looked at Logan. "I think we should be there. Maybe the killer will show up. Aside from that, you should be there. You were one of the few people in her young life that mattered."

Her words hurt his chest. Logan started the car. "She had prospects. She had me," he said angrily. "I would have moved heaven and hell for Becca." Somehow, knowing that she was willing to do anything just to stay free of

Layton made his heart sink. Was it the same for him as it was for Gary? Was he head over heels about a girl who only stuck with him for security? That was her big mistake because he wasn't able to provide that security. If he had, then she wouldn't have left.

Reggie's phone rang. "Detective Hawkins," she answered. "We're about twenty minutes away. Can you have her wait please? Get her some coffee or refreshments and tell her we're on our way. Thanks." Reggie hung up. "A woman showed up at the station to see us. It was her phone number on Ann's phone records. She got my message and came into the precinct to find out what was going on. I imagine most people aren't used to getting a voicemail from a detective. Hope I didn't freak her out too much. I'll bet she's a hairstylist or something as innocuous as that."

Logan smiled. "Innocuous," he repeated. The gates rolled open. He drove out to the street and turned left.

"What are you smiling at?" she asked. "Never heard of that word?"

"I've heard of it. It's just nice having a partner who can already read my mind and who uses four syllable fancy words. I've had some real Neanderthals sitting in that passenger seat."

Reggie reached into her backpack and pulled out a baggie with apple slices. "Don't forget that I share my healthy snacks."

He reluctantly took a slice of apple. "Yeah, that part I'm

still getting used to." He took a bite. "Hmm, forgot how good these are."

Reggie settled back with a slice between her fingers. "I just hope your body doesn't reject it as a foreign substance."

"Me too because that would not be pretty. I'll take the freeway back. It'll be quicker. Maybe this next step in our investigation won't just be a circular piece of shit cuz I'm starting to feel like we're chasing our tails."

CHAPTER
TWENTY

"Why do all the good looking women migrate to you?" Garcia asked as Logan and Reggie walked into the station.

"What are you blathering on about, Garcia?" Logan asked with no mild dose of annoyance.

"A woman came into the station, a hot woman," Garcia added sounding like a middle school kid. "I swept in to see if I could offer my assistance, but she wanted to see Detective Hawkins or Detective Cooper. She's in the first visitor room. Dottie set her up with a cold drink."

"Thanks," Reggie said.

They headed down the hallway to the visitor room. It was a sparsely furnished room with a table and four chairs. There were no two-way mirrors, recording cameras or harsh lights like the interrogation room, but the visitor's room was just a step above it in hospitality.

A woman was sitting at the table with a can of cola

next to her. She was staring down at her phone. When she heard the door open, she looked up. The air pushed out of Logan's lungs as if someone had struck him in the chest. It was one of those moments when he considered that he might have still been sleeping, having a weird dream, but even after surviving his first hypnosis, visiting a BDSM den and listening to the deathbed confessions of a complete and utter asshole, this part of the dream was really the fucking kicker.

Logan sensed that Reggie was equally stunned, and she'd never seen Becca alive. Just from the photo Gary had sent, it was obvious they were looking at a nearly exact replica. The woman at the table didn't exude that same energy and magic that Becca had, but everything else right down to the perfectly shaped lips was Becca.

Reggie regained her composure way ahead of Logan. "I'm Detective Hawkins and this is Detective Cooper." They pulled out chairs on the opposite side of the table and sat down. Reggie had to discreetly elbow Logan to get him to stop gawking at the woman.

"I'm Allison Morton. People call me Ally. What's this about? I have to say, hearing a message from a detective has me a little anxious. Did I do something wrong? I've been out of the country for the last three weeks. Just arrived last night."

"Do you know Ann Robbins?" Reggie asked first. "Your phone number came up on her phone records."

"Yes." A serene smile crossed her lips. She looked so much like Becca it was hard for Logan to focus. "At least I hope to get to know her. We were waiting for the DNA test results to confirm our suspicion."

"Your suspicion?" Reggie asked.

Another serene smile. It was not as breathtaking as Becca's, but it was enough to make Logan hold his breath and tamp down that ache that reminded him how much he'd lost.

"Ann Robbins and I are sisters. Not just sisters but twin sisters."

Logan sat back and released the breath he'd been holding. "Becca had a twin," he muttered, realizing too late he'd spoken out loud. Ally's face snapped his direction.

"Yes, Becca," she said softly. "That's the name I found in my research."

The woman was talking in bits and pieces. It made sense considering she'd just been pulled in to sit down with two detectives right after coming off an international flight. Anyone would have been struggling to get their thoughts in order.

Reggie sat forward, her hands clasped on the table in front of her. "If you wouldn't mind starting from the beginning. Let's say, from the start of your research."

Ally's eyes, sparkling blue just like Becca's, shifted back and forth between them. The serene smile faded. It seemed to finally dawn on her that she was there because something serious had occurred. "Has something happened to Ann? We were supposed to meet once we got the DNA results. I planned on calling her the second I got back home."

Logan and Reggie exchanged glances. It was a silent back and forth over who was stuck with the terrible responsibility of telling Ally that she'd already lost her newly discovered sister. Reggie knew Logan was still too stunned to be sitting across from a woman who looked and sounded just like Becca.

Reggie wriggled her bottom on the chair, squirming a little to work up the courage. Telling people they'd lost a loved one was always the toughest part of the job. Ally had only just found out she had a twin sister. It seemed they hadn't even met in person yet. It made the task a bit easier.

"Ms. Morton, Ally," Reggie said quietly. "I'm afraid Ann Robbins is dead."

Ally's hands flew to her face. She shook her head behind her hands. "That can't be. We only just found each other," she muttered into her palms. Logan wasn't getting any sense that the woman across from him had anything at all to do with Becca's death. She had just coincidentally stepped into Becca's life at a time when things for Becca went horribly wrong.

Logan got up and walked over to the box of tissue sitting on a small desk in the corner. He carried the box back to the table and placed it next to Ally's elbow. She lowered her hands. Her face was red. She sniffled and plucked a tissue from the box. "I can't believe it. It seems that we were just never destined to meet. For a brief moment, I allowed myself the joy of thinking I had a sister." She sniffled and wiped her eyes with the tissue. "I was already picturing us going shopping, having a girls' weekend down at the beach, sitting in a coffee shop sipping mocha lattes and filling each other in on our childhoods."

That statement caused Reggie to look Logan's direction. Ally had no idea the bullet she'd dodged by not being raised by Ray and Linda Kinsey. As he thought the name, another comment fell from his mouth before he could stop it. "Two angels," he said quietly.

Both women looked at him. He wasn't ready to explain it, but he had just solved a major Layton mystery. Linda Kinsey had two babies and she knew it. Someone took the second baby away. That would make any woman sink into a mental health crisis. The entire time that Linda had shuffled around town mumbling nonstop about two angels, she was crying out for her second baby. God, there were so many fucking things he needed to talk to Becca about. How was he going to get through the rest of his life never having that chance?

"How did you find out you had a sister?" Logan asked. If he wasn't going to get to talk to Becca, he would at least get answers from the next best thing, her twin sister. Becca had a twin sister. Shit. Heads would have spun in Layton if there had been two Kinsey girls.

Ally took a bracing sip of cola, wiped her eyes again and sucked in a deep breath. "I knew I was adopted... two wonderful people. I'll never think of anyone else as my parents. They're loving and perfect in every way." Logan felt a thump in his chest as she spoke about her loving parents. Becca had a one in two chance of being brought up by the parents she always dreamed of rather than the nightmare childhood she'd had to endure. "As I got older, naturally, I grew curious about my real parents. I think every adopted child goes through it. Nowadays, with all the ancestry sites and DNA tests, it wasn't too hard to track down my original birth certificate. Rebecca's came up at the same time. We were born just five minutes apart. She's older. I understand Ray and Linda Kinsey are both dead. Becca didn't have much to say about them in the few short conversations we had. She said she'd explain more once we confirmed we were sisters. Now I guess I'll never know."

Logan looked at Reggie. She nodded slightly.

He turned back to Ally. Her face stole his breath for a second. "It's better you don't know too much."

Ally's brows lifted. "Oh? Did you know them? Did you know Ann Robbins?"

"I grew up with Becca in the town of Layton."

Her face brightened some. "Really? What was she like? I sensed so much energy from her over the phone."

"She was the most beautiful girl in the world," Logan said. He'd never been asked to describe Becca to someone. So many things came to mind, he was afraid he wouldn't be able to stop. "Everyone in town adored her. She always had a smile for anyone who needed it. Energy and light swirled around her. I can't explain how but she was just this star that had dropped from the sky to light up an otherwise dreary town." His throat thickened. He decided he'd said enough.

"She sounds wonderful..." Ally's voice trailed off. "If only I'd found her earlier. Maybe I could have somehow kept her from dying." She stared down at the can in her hand. "If you're detectives—" she was putting two and two together. "Was she murdered?"

"I'm afraid so," Reggie said. "We're trying to piece together her life over the last few months to figure out who killed her. Her husband didn't recognize your number, and it came up multiple times."

"Yes, that makes sense. When I first contacted her, she thought it was some kind of joke. I'm afraid I might have upset her. It was more than a bit shocking to hear I'm sure. She seemed excited then, once I sent her a copy of my birth certificate. We decided to both take DNA tests to confirm, you know, in case there was some mix up in the records office or some bizarre clerical error at the hospital. I already had a trip planned to Europe. We agreed we'd meet afterward, after we knew the results." She smiled faintly. "We decided we'd meet regardless. After talking on the phone, there was this instant connection." She leaned back and took the tissue with her. She ruffled it between her fingers as her hands rested in her lap. "My whole life, I felt as if there was someone else out there, someone connected to me spiritually, subconsciously. I can't explain it but I felt her." Her blue eyes lifted. There was sorrow in her expression. "I know this sounds crazy, but I think I felt her suffering. Sometimes, I'd be waking up or sitting in a class and I felt this profound ache." Her eyes glazed with tears. "Was it really very bad?"

Logan nodded. "You were very lucky."

She wiped her eyes. "Poor Becca and now this. I hope you find them soon."

"We will," Reggie said.

They stood up. This had been the last thing Logan expected. It might have answered a few questions they had about Becca's last few months, but it didn't bring them any closer to the killer.

They reached the door. Logan opened it for Ally. She stopped halfway through and looked at him. "Did you know my mother?"

Logan nodded. "She was kind and beautiful like you and Becca."

She took in a shuddering breath as if she was keeping back more tears. "Why do you think she gave me away?"

Logan's stomach knotted. "I don't think she did. I think she spent the rest of her days wishing and dreaming about her lost little girl."

A small sob escaped. She reached over and hugged Logan. For a second he was holding her again, for that brief moment he imagined himself holding Becca in his arms. Ally took another shuddering breath and stepped back. "Please let me know when the case is over."

"I can let her husband know what's going on. It seemed Becca hadn't mentioned anything," Reggie said.

"We both agreed we wouldn't tell anyone until it was confirmed. Please, if you don't mind. Give him my number. I would love to talk to him."

Reggie nodded. "I'll do that." She led Ally down the hallway and pointed her toward the exit. Logan was still standing in the doorway of the visitor's room trying to take in the shock of it all. Reggie reached him.

"Do you think Ally was the person from her past who contacted her?"

"Could be."

"But this wouldn't have made her depressed," Reggie noted correctly. "This would have been something exciting, something to look forward to. I know this because growing up I had a make-believe sister named Noreen. Don't ask me where I came up with the name, but Noreen was an expert horse rider and she could bake chocolate chip cookies just by snapping her fingers. My reason for divulging that embarrassing detail is to add weight to what I just said. Finding out you had a sister would be amazing."

"Something else happened to Becca around May 4th,

something that might have had to do with someone from her past or not. Whatever happened, it upset her enough to darken her mood drastically. And you're right. I don't think it had anything to do with Ally."

"Unless she was angry that Ally had escaped the hell, and she was left with a monstrous father," Reggie suggested.

Logan shook his head. "No, Becca wasn't like that. She was never the type to be green with envy. She would have been happy for her sister, knowing that she was raised by loving parents. Something else happened to Becca. It wasn't even Drax. He started his blackmail plan before May 4th. She was fired before that too so it wasn't the job."

"So we find out what happened to her the first week of May and we find the killer," Reggie suggested.

"I sure hope so because we're coming to the end of a lot of threads that lead nowhere."

Reggie paused in the hallway, before they reached the desk area where nosy people with big ears would overhear. Her eyes were cocoa brown in the brightly lit hallway. "This is a lot to take in. I thought you'd fall over from shock back there. How are you doing?"

"It is a lot to take in, and yep, I was pretty much ready to fall face-first in that room. I'm fine. Just aggravated that we can't seem to turn a corner on this."

"Right there with you on that, partner." She continued on but Logan stopped her.

"Hey, Hawkins—"

She looked back at him expectantly.

"Thanks for asking. Can't remember the last time someone asked me how I was doing and actually meant it."

A smile faintly crinkled her lips before she spun back around.

CHAPTER
TWENTY-ONE

The chill of the morning was set deep in his bones. It was hard to believe the foggy dawn would eventually dissolve into a summer day, so hot, barefoot kids would have to hop quickly across the sandy beach to avoid burning the soles of their feet. It was also hard to believe he'd allowed his partner to talk him into a pre-dawn run. After his attempt the day before, an attempt that ended in embarrassing defeat, he was determined to prove to himself he could run three miles without keeling over dead. He'd finished the run a good mile behind his partner, and if he hadn't felt like throwing up at the end of it, he might have felt triumphant.

They reached the corner in front of her apartment building. He'd parked in one of the visitor spots. Reggie was stretching her arms and legs looking almost as refreshed as when they'd started off. Logan came to a full stop and bent over resting his hands on his thighs and swallowing in some of the dank, briny air. He'd decided before he reached the finish line that he would rather choke on his own puke than throw up in front of Reggie. Fortunately, it didn't have to come to that. The two cups of coffee he drank to wake himself up for the run stayed where they were supposed to stay, but it was a sharp reminder for him not to down cups of coffee before a run. If there was a run again. At this point, that possibility looked slim.

"That wasn't too bad, was it?" Reggie asked. The run had energized her, and he was finding it annoying.

"I'll tell you at about two this afternoon when my brain and limbs are no longer numb."

"Do you want to come up for some breakfast?" she asked. "I make a mean tofu scramble."

Logan pressed his arm against his stomach. "Nope, nope, nope. I don't think my stomach is saying tofu scramble right now. Thanks for the offer. I'm going to go home and shower... for about three hours," he added. "See you at the precinct and don't take my parking spot," he called as he lowered himself *gently* behind the wheel. He glanced up in the rearview mirror. His dark eyes stared back at him. When did those lines in his forehead get so deep? "Fuck, Coop, thirty- nine? You might as well be sixty-nine," he muttered in disgust as he started the truck.

Max, the supervisor of his apartment building, was

zipping around on his jalopy of a golf cart. He'd found it sitting on a sidewalk one day, dumped by its owner along with what Max insisted was a perfectly good couch, give or take a few rips in the cushions and a missing foot. Max brought the abandoned golf cart back to life and painted it a bright yellow so he was easy to spot as he coasted through the parking lot. He drove back and forth between the two wings as if he had to navigate a massive multi block apartment complex. Logan figured even the two wings were a distance for someone like Max who was carrying around at least a small person in extra weight. His knees were even starting to cave in toward each other as if surrendering to the burden of the weight above. Max's jowls shook as he waved enthusiastically to Logan from across the lot. The buzz of his electric cart whirred as he raced toward him. Max was clad in his usual work coveralls. This pair was stretched over his belly. The coveralls were always stained with grease despite the fact there were numerous things around the complex that needed fixing. The light above Logan's door had blown out months ago. He'd filled out the proper paperwork and reminded Max about the broken light every time he saw him but still no new bulb.

One thing Max always had time for was chatting with tenants. The man could talk a zombie right back into the grave. When he wasn't cruising back and forth on his golf cart like a comical security guard, he was talking and gossiping with the neighbors. It seemed, this morning, Logan was the only person out and about early enough to get caught in his chatty snare.

Before Logan could tell him he was late and needed to get ready for work, Max shouted, "I found them!" just a few feet before he reached Logan. He was holding the metal ring with all his supervisor keys in his chubby fist. That was another thing Max spent his time on—misplacing things. Everyone had to keep an eye out for his special wrench for months. He even put up photos of the wrench with a reward of an extra trash dumping for the week if it was found. Max didn't care for the way the tenants were tossing the garbage, sometimes not even enclosed in a bag, into his trash bin, so he came up with a schedule. Tenants left the trash outside, at the foot of the stairs for those on the second story. Then he picked them up with his trusty golf cart and carried them to the bin for what he considered proper dumping.

"You lost your keys?" Logan asked. Great, he thought but didn't add.

"Yeah, remember when I was telling you the day before yesterday that they'd gotten away from me?" He smacked his head with his hand. Luckily, it wasn't the hand holding the mass of keys. "Nope, never mind that wasn't you. I was telling Carl down in 12B. Yep, lost the darn things. Looked all over for two days, then whammo, there they were, right where I left them on the hook inside my office door. Can you believe it?"

Unfortunately, Logan could.

"My sister tells me I'm not getting enough of those B vitamins in my diet."

Logan couldn't imagine that Max's diet was lacking in anything.

Logan raked his hair back with his fingers. It was still wet from the run, a mix of the fog and his sweat. His body was starting to cool down. He badly needed a hot shower.

"I'm glad you found them, and I'm glad the most valuable thing I have in my apartment is an electric can opener," he quipped.

Max had a barrel laugh. It was a low rumbling sound that seemed to be coming from deep inside his belly. "Now, now, your valuables were never in danger. You know I'm patrolling this building night and day. No thieves are going to get past me, no way, no how," he said with a confident smile that made his mouth nearly disappear into his round cheeks. "By the way, you can thank me. I found your hat. It must have fallen into your trash can. Brand new one too."

"What hat?" Logan asked.

Max pointed a thick finger at him. "See, you've already forgotten it. I was tossing your trash, and I saw the bill of it pressing against the plastic bag. Good thing I noticed it or you would have lost a nice new hat. I stuck it in your apartment."

Logan had absolutely no idea what Max was talking about, but he wasn't in the mood to debate it. He needed a shower and food and another cup of coffee. "Thanks, Max, and don't forget about that light bulb over my front door."

"I've got it on my list." It was the same answer he'd been giving for six weeks. It must have been a helluva list.

Logan climbed up the stairs to his apartment. He unlocked the door. It was always the same smell that hit him, the scent of cheap carpeting and stale air. The windows were nearly impossible to open, yet another repair request he had filled out the week he moved in and yet another repair that had not been done.

A black baseball cap, one that was most assuredly not his, sat on his coffee table. He picked it up and looked to see if there was a name or something to point it toward its owner. Like Max said, it was brand new, hardly worn. Even the inside rim was still clean. There was no logo, no distinguishing mark, just a solid black baseball cap. He was certainly not going to wear someone else's hat. He placed it outside on the railing. Someone would recognize it.

Logan walked to the refrigerator. He'd added in a loaf of bread, cheese and a package of sliced turkey. It wasn't ideal for breakfast, but it was better than nothing. After a three mile run, he was going to be hungry. While warming up, he'd decided their first stop would be a visit to the Three Boars. If Ann Robbins had a napkin in her coat pocket, it meant she'd visited the bar at least once. Logan knew Walt, the owner. Maybe he knew Ann Robbins.

Maybe another incredible layer of Becca's life would be peeled back. He wasn't sure how many more of those layers he could endure. They were giving him quite the narrative. Hopefully, the next layer and possible surprise would get them closer to the killer.

CHAPTER
TWENTY-TWO

The silhouette of a wild boar stared down at them over the door of the bar. Walt's father, Jake, had started the bar as a traditional style pub based on the pub Jake grew up near in Scotland. Walt took over after Jake was diagnosed with Parkinson's and his hands were no longer steady enough to pour a drink. It wasn't modern and shiny and without character like some of the other bars in town. Its charm came from the beat-up pine tables and the mismatched chairs and stools. The countertop bore the scars of shot glasses being slammed down, beers mugs sliding across it and the occasional drunken fight. The bar didn't officially open for another two hours, lunch hour to be exact, when Walt offered some ham and roast beef sandwiches to go along with the lager. Considering the only fare offered at night were stale peanuts and chips covered with a runny cheese sauce that was more water than cheese, the sandwiches were pretty tasty. Walt piled fresh rye and pumpernickel high with wafer thin slices of meat and slathered that with mustard, mayonnaise and a dollop of homemade sauerkraut, his late grandmother's secret recipe.

The early morning rise and run was catching up to Logan. His stomach was in the mindset of lunch even though it was barely ten.

As one would expect from the owner of a pub-style bar that served lager and ale, Walt was a big, burly man with thick red hair and freckles that ran over every inch of his skin. His blue eyes were set deep in his face. It was rare to see him without his signature smile. Although, this morning he was wearing more of a grimace as he wheeled a dolly weighed down with crates of wine through the side door.

Logan hurried to catch up to him and hold the door.

"Logan, good timing. You know we're not open for two more hours." He wheeled the dolly into the side room where stacks of boxes lined a cinder block wall.

Logan put the rubber stopper down to hold the door. "Need some help with the rest of those boxes?" he asked.

Reggie was already lifting a big bag of shelled peanuts from the back of Walt's truck.

"Thanks," Walt said as he unloaded the dolly. His face was red from the task as he rolled the dolly back out the door. He spotted Reggie for the first time. "Well, hello." He put on a bit of the Scottish brogue he saved for the women in the bar. As far as Logan knew Walt left Scotland at the age of two, but he knew how to put on an accent when he thought it might impress the ladies.

"Walt, this is my new partner, Detective Hawkins."

Walt wiped his hand off on the apron he had tied around his waist. He shook her hand. The way he looked at Reggie, Logan was half expecting Walt to kiss it. A loud, rumbling motor pulled our attention to the road. A vintage cherry red Camaro pulled into the parking lot, complete with tinted windows and two white racing stripes from front to back. Music was blasting through the windows.

Walt put his hands on his hips. "Who's this?"

The car engine shut down. The instant quiet that followed made them realize just how loud the car was. A tall, lanky kid wearing a green fedora and black shirt with a red skull on the front climbed out.

"What on earth?" Walt said to no one in particular.

"Do you know him?" Logan asked.

"That's Tyler. He's my stock boy and tech expert. He looks like a goofball, but he knows computer stuff." Tyler glanced back at the car, then tossed the keys on his palm a few times as he lumbered toward them on long legs.

"Tyler, how come one minute you're complaining to me that you don't have enough money to fix the brakes on your old truck and the next you're driving a fancy red Camaro? Did you win the lotto or something?"

"Uh, yep, the lotto," he said.

Walt crossed his arms. "No, really. Are you stealing from me? Got your hands in the till?"

Tyler looked insulted. "I wouldn't steal from you, Walt. My aunt lent me the money, that's all. I'm going to finish installing that new accounting software, then I'll come help you in the stockroom." He disappeared inside.

Walt shook his head. "He sure as hell never mentioned his aunt before."

They finished carrying the last few boxes into the storeroom. "Can I get either of you a cold drink? Some soda or tea?" Walt asked as he finished unloading the last box of wine.

"We're fine," Logan said. "If you have a minute, we need to ask you about a possible customer."

"I figured. Man, if I had a dollar for every time a member of law enforcement showed up here to find out whether or not someone had been hanging out at the Three Boars. That's why I keep all my security footage for at least six months."

Walt led them through the small hallway to the barroom. Tyler had his earbuds in as he sat in front of a computer in a small office and plunked away on the keyboard. The bar looked different with the lights fully on and daylight seeping through the small windows. The place looked a little less charming and a little more raggedy than it did under dim lights. Security cameras poked out of two corners, something Logan had never noticed when he was there chugging a few beers. The cameras might come in handy.

Logan pulled out his phone. "We're wondering if you know this woman."

Walt placed a pair of reading glasses at the end of his nose and squinted at the picture. "Yes, yes I know her. She comes in here every Friday night. Her name is Ann. Is she in some kind of trouble?"

Reggie spoke up first. He hated even speaking the words. She'd figured that out. "I'm afraid she's dead. Murdered," she added.

Walt's head shook, his shoulders hunched and his usual smile flipped upside down. "Can't believe it. She seemed like such a nice woman. She was always smiling and friendly, although I know she suffered a setback."

Logan and Reggie both straightened to attention. "How's that?" Logan asked. Were they about to get to the dramatic event that sent Ann Robbins into a depression?

Tyler popped his head into the barroom. "That software is downloading. You know that message on the screen that warns you not to turn off the machine, don't ignore it like you always do when there are updates. Otherwise, I'll have to start all over again."

Walt waved his arm. "Yeah, yeah, now go unpack that wine. I need two of each up front." Tyler left. Walt scoffed. "Twenty-somethings. They know a little bit more about computers than us boomers, and they lord it over us like we all just fell off the turnip truck. If I'd grown up with a computer at my disposal, I would know that shit too." His face reddened. "Sorry. Cussing is a bad habit. And I apologize if you're twenty-something. I'm sure you're a perfectly polite one," he said directly to Reggie.

"No problem. About that setback," Reggie said, also anxious to hear.

"Right. Hope you don't mind if I dry these glasses while I talk. The morning always gets away from me when I have a delivery."

Logan was starting to grind his jaw together in anticipation. "No, that's fine," he said curtly.

"Like I said, Ann came in here every Friday night for about the last year and a half. She would order one glass of white wine, sip it, chat with people and then leave well before midnight. It was just her way to unwind after a work week was what she told me. About two months after she started coming to the Three Boars, she started showing up with a friend, a young man named Derrick."

Logan's ears perked. Was Ann Robbins having an affair? Was she cheating on poor, dull Gary? And why had he determined that Gary was dull? He had to have been if she was cheating on him. Had Becca been cheating on Logan in high school? She was the one who'd decided they should keep their relationship secret. Had she done that so none of her other boyfriends found out? Was there a whole group of guys who had been duped? But she had his name on her wrist. He was mentally kicking himself for heading down that rabbit hole.

"Do you know what the manner of their relationship was?" Reggie asked with a hesitant eye flick Logan's direction. She was so intuitive, he was sure she knew exactly what he was thinking.

"I would catch their conversations sometimes. I believe they were both seeing therapists. They'd talk about their sessions and whether or not they were doing any good."

"Becca—" Logan cleared his throat. "Ann was seeing a therapist?"

"That's the impression I got. I know Derrick was on some kind of medication that would react with booze. He always ordered a virgin daiquiri. And that brings me to the setback." Walt set the glass he'd just dried on the tray and sighed sadly. "Derrick hung himself a month ago."

"Tragic," Reggie said sadly. "So he was suffering from depression?"

"I think he was being treated for something like that," Walt said. "Ann took it real bad when she heard the news. She was waiting for him and texted to see where he was. His husband called her right back to let her know the bad news."

"His husband?" Logan asked, stupidly relieved. "So Ann and Derrick weren't romantically involved?"

Walt chuckled. "If they were that would certainly be a surprise to me. I think they were just good friends. Ann was devastated. She sat right there at that table in the corner. Had a few shots of tequila, a good long cry and walked out. I didn't see her for a week, then she showed up again. She sat mostly alone after that. Had her glass of wine and a bit of conversation before heading home. She told me her husband worked late a lot, and she didn't like to be home alone."

"Derrick died a month ago?" Reggie asked. She took out her notebook and pen and pulled a calendar up on her phone. "Sometime in June?"

"Don't know the exact day, but it was between the second and third weeks of June. He was here on the second week. We were celebrating one of the server's birthdays. Derrick was here that night, sitting right there with Ann." He pointed to a counter high table near the small stage area. "He had a beautiful voice, loved to sing along with the band, so he started off the birthday song. Ann was sitting right next to him. She looked a little glum. In fact, of the two, I thought Ann was the one suffering from depression. For a few months, she came in here not wearing her usual smile. She just wasn't her radiant self at all. Whereas, Derrick seemed just fine. I never would have suspected he felt suicidal."

Walt was forking out a lot of information. It was hard to tell if any of it was pertinent to the case, but they'd added at least one more previously unknown person into her social circle. Unfortunately, Derrick was gone now, so he wouldn't be able to add anything. Maybe the husband could provide some insight. One thing stood out more than anything. Walt had noticed Ann's change in mood too, and it had started before Derrick's suicide. While that loss might have piled on top of her already darkened mood, it was not the catalyst. Logan was sure that starting spark would lead them to the killer.

"Do you happen to know Derrick's last name?" Reggie still had her notepad and pen at the ready. Logan envied that she could carry out this investigation like a true pro without the terrible emotional pull Logan was feeling. It was making him shitty at his job, but he couldn't shake all the feelings. There had been too much history between him and the victim. Maybe Castillo was right. Maybe it wasn't ideal having him work the case, but there was no way he was giving it up now.

Walt walked to the back office to pull up some old credit card receipts with Derrick's name.

Reggie took a moment to admire the rustic décor in the bar, the tin pendant lights hanging over the carved oak bar, the old-fashioned mirrors lining the wall behind the liquor, each one etched with a wild boar, the antique spears crisscrossed over the mirrors and pewter pint mugs lined up on a shelf by the tap.

"I could almost imagine myself in merry old Scotland listening to fiddles and red nosed men signing loud songs in their kilts," she mused.

"It's got character and the beer always has a good thick head," Logan said.

"What do you think? Should we talk to Derrick's husband?" she asked. "I wonder how much Derrick talked about Ann because something tells me if we bring him up to Gary, he won't have heard of Derrick. Or about the therapy sessions," she added wisely.

Logan nodded. "You're right. Gary mentioned something about her being very independent. I'll bet she never mentioned her friend Derrick or the therapy. Seems like Gary, or, at the very least, Janey would have brought either of those things up at the first interview."

"Aronson," Walt said as he came out from the office area with a folded receipt in his hand. "His husband's name was James." He handed the receipt over so Reggie could copy the name correctly.

"Was Ann here last Friday night?" Logan asked.

Walt rubbed his temple for a second. "Hmm, was she here last Friday? I was in and out of the bar. My water heater at home had broken. I was cleaning up the big mess and waiting for an emergency plumber, but yes, I think she was sitting a few stools from the end at the bar."

"I guess you have video from that night," Reggie said.

Walt beamed. "Like I said, you'd be surprised how often I have to hand over security footage."

"Can we see the footage from last Friday?" Logan asked.

"Tyler," Walt shouted without warning. Reggie startled and then chuckled about it.

Tyler stepped into the barroom. "Yeah, Walt?"

"I need all the security footage from last Friday night."

Tyler's eyes rounded. "All of it? Last Friday night?"

"See, you're listening to that music in those tiny ear

pieces so loud you're losing your hearing. Yes, all of it and yes, last Friday night." Tyler looked at Logan and Reggie almost as if they were asking him to do something extraordinary or even illegal.

His head was a little big for his long thin neck, so his nod was slightly cartoonish. "I've got to wait for that software to download before I can access the security footage. It's still got at least an hour."

Reggie was already writing down her work email. "That's all right. Send it to this email when you get access."

Tyler nodded his big head again before lumbering off like an ungainly young giraffe.

Logan placed his hand on the bar counter leaving behind his card. "Thanks for your time, Walt. Call if you think of anything else that might be important."

"Sorry I wasn't here much Friday night, but I'll ask the girls if anyone saw her or if she was talking to anyone in particular. Could you go back out the way we came in? The doors are still locked. Some of my patrons have their hearing honed to listen for the distinct click of my locks. If I open the doors, they'll be swarming the lot begging to get in early."

Logan was sure it wasn't all that much of an exaggeration.

"Thanks again," Reggie said.

"Hey, catch the bastard who did this, eh?" Walt called as they walked toward the side door.

Tyler was placing wine bottles in a rack. He lifted his head. "I'll send those the second I have time."

"We'll be looking for them," Logan said.

The sun was bright and warming the air fast. "Lunch before the funeral?" Reggie asked as they climbed into the car.

"That run really made me hungry." Logan started the car.

"I'll send information over to Fran so she can find James Aronson's phone number." Reggie pulled out her phone. "Let's eat someplace where the food isn't lethal. I didn't have time to make my hummus sandwich."

Logan laughed and picked up his phone. "Non-lethal restaurant," he said into the phone.

"Not legal restaurant," the phone repeated back. They both laughed as they rolled out of the parking lot. With the week he'd been having, Logan was more than a little grateful that Reggie was sitting in the passenger seat and not Gregor or Garcia.

CHAPTER
TWENTY-THREE

Logan had changed into a black suit, gray shirt and dark gray tie for the funeral. Never in a million years would he have thought he'd be pulling out his funeral suit to watch Becca's casket be lowered into a grave. The first time he'd gone through the nightmare of losing her, there had been no body. Now the reason for that was more than clear. Her parents were too messed up to pull together any kind of a memorial, so the school held a cheesy prayer thing in the cafeteria. The cafeteria workers were cooking something that smelled like a cross between ground beef and dog shit, and the whole place smelled and felt like grease. Ray sat stiff as a board behind a pair of dark sunglasses, not even acknowledging the principal when he told him how much we'd all miss Becca. Linda was a crumpled ball, barely human as she rolled in on herself, hunched down under the thick collar of a coat. It was ninety degrees outside the putrid smelling cafeteria, which meant it was at least ninety-five inside, and Becca's mom had worn enough layers for an Arctic expedition. It seemed it was her way of letting the world know that without her daughter she was being erased, she was melting into a puddle of despair and that soon she'd be gone too.

Most of Becca's friends had their own memorial, no adults, no creepy preacher waxing on about how she was with God now, no Ray and his aura of menace, just the people who loved her. Jeremy, the weasel who knew she was alive, had set up a slideshow with all of Becca's favorite music to go along with pictures of her having fun. Becca had two modes, misery and fun. When she wasn't in despair about her family, she was having a good time with her friends, with him, with Logan. They'd all sat in Jeremy's backyard, watching the slides, listening to the music, chugging fruit punch laced with rum and eating salt and vinegar chips. Becca's favorite. Logan had gotten home in the middle of the night so drunk he climbed in through his bedroom window not to wake his parents. He puked his guts out and fell asleep on the bathroom floor with a stuffed bear someone had brought to the memorial clutched in his arms.

Logan pulled up to Reggie's apartment building and texted to let her know he was there. He was busy scrolling through bullshit on his phone when he heard the gate to the apartment complex snap shut. He glanced up and was more than a little annoyed that a breath stuck in his chest. Reggie had changed out of her jeans and t-shirt. The dark blue dress she was wearing hugged her curves and stopped a few inches above her knees. She was wearing heels and a pair of dangling pearl earrings. Her thick, dark hair covered her shoulders.

"Fuck," Logan muttered to himself.

Reggie got into the car. "I've got James Aronson's address and phone number."

Logan looked at her confused. He was still getting over the dress. "Who?"

She arched a brow. "Oh my god, is this what I can expect when I reach the ripe old age of forty?"

"I'm thirty—" He shoved the key into the ignition. "Nope, I'm not going to fall for it again."

She laughed. "Think you already did. So do you remember who James Aronson is?"

"Yes, he's the husband of Becca's friend, Derrick."

"Technically, he's Ann's friend." She smoothed the dress over her lap. "Feels weird to be wearing a dress."

He could feel her gaze on him.

"What?" he asked.

"You shaved. And you got the grunge off. Nice. You're quite presentable when you put out a little effort."

"For someone who is standing in the dark, grim shadow of forty," he quipped.

Logan pulled onto the road and headed toward the cemetery.

"I'll call him after the funeral," Reggie said. "James, that is, in case you've already forgotten."

"Maybe he'll be at the funeral," Logan said.

"Only if Gary knew about Ann's friendship with Derrick." He could feel her gaze on him again. "This is going to be hard for you," she said.

He nodded. "I won't know anyone there. No one from her past will be there. It's so weird. She lived an entirely different life once she left Layton. Nothing of the Becca I grew up with was left, and yet, something tells me everything about her was the same. She was still adored. Everyone knew she was special. It was the same in Layton. Even the teachers loved her. The only people who didn't realize how amazing she was were her parents."

Reggie's phone beeped. "Fran's got the video from Three Boars cued up for us to watch when we get back to the precinct. Maybe the killer was somewhere in the crowd that night. The people in that bar were probably the last people to see her alive."

"Where the hell are people going at this time of day?" The streets were packed with mid-afternoon traffic. Logan stuck the light on top of the car and turned on the siren to get people out of the way. He wasn't in the mood for a California traffic jam this afternoon. Clouds had moved in over the shore, ending the beautiful summer day a few hours early. A gray gloom was settling over the city. It seemed appropriate for the occasion.

The verdant green hills of the cemetery rolled into view. There were several gravesite services taking place. Ann's was the smallest. Logan parked behind a short line of cars, mostly expensive, luxury sedans. A shiny ivory coffin, piled high with an arrangement of pink roses and white lilies, hovered over the six foot deep rectangle where Becca would rest for eternity. This time she was truly gone. He'd seen her dead on the grass, but somehow, seeing the coffin struck him as if someone had thrown a bowling ball at his chest.

Gary was standing between an older woman and a younger woman, who resembled Gary enough to assure Logan it was his sister. An elderly man was sitting nearby in one of the chairs set up for the family. A silver tipped cane leaned next to the chair. Janey was standing with a man who was undoubtedly her husband. She held on to him tightly as if letting go might result in her knees giving way. There were a few other business-y type people, Gary's coworkers, no doubt. No one looked suspicious or out of place. Logan scanned the area in case someone was standing in the distance, hoping not to be seen. A group of crows, with their shiny black feathers and menacing beaks, lined up on a small wrought iron fence that circled a family plot. It was almost as if they were there to add ambience to the event taking place in front of them. A row of sparrows would have had an entirely different effect.

Logan glanced back toward the road. Aside from two cemetery workers pulling dead flowers from nearby graves, there was no one else. No possible killer coming back to witness the grief he'd caused, no murderer waiting for the gravediggers to finish the job he'd started by erasing Ann Robbins from existence for good.

None of the people standing around her coffin looked like people Becca would have befriended. Even Janey seemed like the kind of person she would have avoided, polite, traditional, dull.

Reggie and Logan stood nearby but opposite of everyone else. They didn't interact with the others. They were there to pay respects to a victim they were now trying to avenge, but the family and friends were there to provide each other comfort. Gary finished talking with a woman who had held his hands tightly the entire time she spoke to him. His gaze flicked their direction, but it didn't look appreciative or kind. He almost looked irritated.

Reggie leaned her head closer to talk quietly. "If I didn't know any better—"

"You'd think Mr. Robbins is pissed that we haven't made an arrest?"

"Took the words right out of my mouth," she muttered.

A preacher started the ceremony. The only time Logan remembered Becca being in church was when they were handing out free cookies at Christmas. She always joked that if Ray Kinsey walked into the church, lightning would bolt down from the ceiling and strike him dead. How badly Logan wished that scenario had played out.

Banal, bland, almost offensively boring words were spoken about a woman who was anything but banal, bland or boring. The preacher read with almost no emotion, like a robot dressed in black, off of a paper that had apparently been written by Gary. There was mention that while no one knew much about Ann's youth, it could only be imagined that she was a bright, energetic young girl. Logan wanted to storm over, push aside the preacher and let everyone know just how Ann Robbins was in youth. He'd let everyone know how she lived with a monster yet managed to always be kind, especially to underdogs. Becca was always on the right side of a fight, no matter who the opponents. She knew the stark difference between good and bad, and she never strayed to the dark side though she had every reason to.

The entire ceremony was for someone else, not for the girl he loved. She wouldn't have stood for such a sham funeral. Becca would have asked to blast Pearl Jam through a set of speakers while everyone told their funniest story about her.

Logan and Reggie stayed long enough to watch them lower the casket into the grave. Even the ivory white coffin and flower arrangement seemed entirely wrong. "I suppose it would be rude to leave without at least talking to the husband," Reggie said.

"I suppose." They circled the grave. Logan stood over it for a moment staring down into the perfectly carved rectangle as Reggie continued on to give her condolences. It was Gary's sharp tone, a tone that didn't match the setting one bit, that pulled Logan from his thoughts.

"I thought there would have been an arrest by now," he

said. Janey stood nearby still clutching her husband's arm. Her frown seemed to be aimed at Gary.

"I assure you, Mr. Robbins, we are turning over every leaf, looking in every corner," Reggie said.

Gary laughed harshly. He was certainly less weak and helpless than the first time they met. "Turning over leaves? Why don't you find out who the hell killed my wife and bring him to justice? I don't need leaves turned. I need results. Have you tracked down that Logan character? It can't be too hard to find someone with that name. She grew up in a small town for fuck's sake."

The woman who seemed to be Gary's sister took hold of his arm and said something quietly to him. He glanced over at his parents but ignored his mother's look of distress. Logan was sure Gary wasn't the type of guy who tossed the f word around easily.

"Find that guy, Logan. He's your man. I'm sure that's the person from her past who contacted her."

Reggie's brown gaze flicked Logan's direction. Logan stepped closer. "We'll find him," Logan said. "We'll find who did this."

"Empty words I've heard before," Gary said sharply. He took his sister's arm, and they headed back to the line of parked cars.

Reggie looked a little more slammed than Logan felt but then she was newer at this. He'd been berated by plenty of unhappy family members during his time on the force. Although, this time was remarkably different because the unhappy husband wanted him to chase down the man named Logan and he was Logan.

Janey walked over. "You'll have to excuse him. He's just so distraught." The woman seemed to make a habit of apologizing for a man who wasn't even her husband. "I think we were both hoping there'd be word this week of an arrest. It's hard knowing the person is still out there somewhere, lurking in shadows or whatever it is killers do when they think they've gotten away with murder. He's particularly obsessed with this guy Logan," she started.

Reggie flicked a sideways glance his direction. "Tattoos happen," Reggie said. "I'm sure there are thousands of regret tattoos, names or symbols people chose when they were young. It doesn't mean much."

Janey glanced around to make sure Gary and his family had walked back to the cars. With his father shuffling along on the grassy knoll with a bad limp and a cane it was taking them a long time, but they were well out of earshot.

Janey turned back to them. "Honestly, whoever Logan is he's been somewhat of a ghost hovering over their marriage. Part of it was Ann's fault. She refused to tell Gary about the name she had tattooed on her wrist. She told him he was from her past, and she didn't want to look back, only forward. I think if she would have just laid it out there for him, that Logan was the boy she loved in her hometown, it wouldn't have bothered him so much."

Logan was so dumbstruck by the conversation, he

couldn't speak. It was almost as if he was a ghost, listening in on a conversation where he was the topic.

"It sounds like she must have talked to you about Logan," Reggie said.

"Not much. She was always pretty secretive about her past. She never even spoke about where she grew up. When I asked her about the tattoo she just smiled and said 'he was the boy I loved when I was young'. It would have been easy enough for her to put Gary's jealousy to rest by telling him as much, but she refused to speak about Logan with Gary." Janey looked down and fiddled with the purse on her shoulder.

"There's something more," Reggie started for her.

Janey nodded. "Yes, a few months ago, after Ann's mood changed, Gary told me she woke up in the middle of the night from a bad dream." Janey paused. "She was calling out to him."

"To Gary?" Reggie asked.

Janey shook her head. "No, she was calling out to Logan."

A hammer was smacking Logan in the chest. He was finding it hard to take a decent breath, all while still trying to look as if nothing she was saying fazed him.

"When Gary asked her about it she just laughed it off. She said she must have been having a dream about her hometown and the name just came out. But Gary wouldn't let it go. He was really upset about it. Poor Gary always felt he was—how do they say—punching above his weight when he met and married Ann. He was crazy about her, and she loved him too... in her own way. I think he knew the passionate love was coming more from his side than hers. Somehow, he'd gotten it into his head that this mythical Logan person was standing between them."

Reggie nodded along. "I can see that. While we have you here, Ms. Moore, did Ann ever talk about a friend named Derrick?"

Janey turned to her husband. "Go ahead and bring the car closer, Nick. I'll be right there." She turned back. "She mentioned something about a young man who was suffering with mental health issues. She said the poor man killed himself."

"Yes, that's true. I assume she was very upset by that," Reggie said.

"Of course. Who wouldn't be," Janey said. "She didn't talk about him much. I think he was more of a casual acquaintance than anything."

"One more thing," Reggie said. "I don't want to keep you. Did Ann ever mention that she was going to therapy?"

That question caused her to look around. There was no one in earshot except the two cemetery workers who were filling in the grave.

"I know about a year ago she told me she'd started talking to a therapist on one of those online mental health sites. She said it was mostly to throw off the burdens of her past. She had a terrible childhood apparently. She never elaborated, but I assumed there was abuse. I know she didn't want Gary to know about it. She didn't talk about it much. When I asked she said it was helping, but she wasn't sure if talking to someone over the computer was as effective as sitting across from a therapist."

"Did she find a local doctor?" Reggie asked.

"I don't know. Like I said, she didn't want to talk about it. She said it was all about her early life, and she liked to keep the two halves separate. Ann was a very private person. I was her best friend, and even I didn't know everything going on in her life." A low honk startled the birds from nearby trees. Janey huffed in irritation. She shook her head at her husband who had just pulled their Land Rover up to the site. "Doesn't he realize it's bad manners to honk in a cemetery?"

Reggie shrugged. "Not like he's going to wake anyone up."

Janey gave her a motherly disapproving scowl.

"Sorry, bad timing," Reggie said. "Thanks for this information. Every little bit helps. And we'll let you know the second we have a suspect."

Janey held her purse against her side and walked cautiously down the grassy slope on high heels.

"Well, partner, I assume this little chat has left you stunned," Reggie said.

"Stunned has been my go-to emotion all week. Let's head to the precinct and watch that surveillance video. Maybe our suspect is sitting at the bar having a beer."

CHAPTER TWENTY-FOUR

"I want an update on the Robbins case," Castillo barked as he walked out of the lunchroom wearing some of his lunch on the front of his shirt.

"When we get a chance," Logan answered back.

"Find that chance soon. The husband's been calling. I've been holding off on talking to him," he said before snapping shut his office door.

"Shit." Logan dropped his keys on his desk and pulled out his chair. "That husband is starting to get on my nerves."

Reggie clicked open the email with the video. "Fran says we should watch the video on her computer. She's got all the fancy software for zooming in and all that. She said we should hurry. There's something we need to see."

"Yeah? Sounds promising." Logan rolled his chair back and stood up.

They headed down to Fran's office. She was just

finishing a phone call and waved for them to come into her little media room, which was really just an old office set up with more electrical outlets than usual and dark blinds that could be drawn to drown out light.

Fran hung up the phone. "Pull up some chairs, guys," she was speaking in her serious, professional tone. Most of the time she was just good ole funky Fran, but when she had something important to share, she took on a more somber tone. This was definitely her somber tone.

Logan pushed a chair over for Reggie then grabbed one of the fold-out chairs used for meetings from the corner. It had been sitting under the air conditioner vent, and the metal was icy cold. Aside from a multitude of electrical outlets, the room had been set up with extra vents to counteract the heat blowing off various devices.

"I'm going to press play then let you two scoot in to watch. I've got my remote. I'll stop it at the important parts."

Logan rubbed his hands on his thighs. The room was ten degrees colder than the outer offices and he was feeling it. "If you've got video of the killer looking right into the camera, Fran, then I might just kiss you." Normally, that would have elicited a flirty response. Fran loved to flirt and joke around, but she didn't say a word.

A somewhat fuzzy video started up. The bar was crowded. People were draped along the bar counter and leaning with their elbows and drinks on the counter height tables near the stage. A band was playing country music. Walt liked to mix things up with the music. Sometimes it was rock, sometimes country, sometimes jazz and occasionally folksy music one might hear in a true pub.

A few minutes in, a woman walked into view of the camera. Logan sat up straight. "There she is. That's her," he said the second part to himself, quietly, as his gaze glued to the thin, graceful figure approaching the bar.

Becca was wearing the jean cutoffs and flip flops they found her in. The Three Boars was probably the last place she visited before she died. Ann leaned up against the bar with her long tanned legs and slim hips. The diamond and platinum watch Gary had mentioned was draped around her tiny wrist. Seconds later, two beefy guys who had their hair slicked back and who seemed to be there only to scope out the women approached her. There was a short chat. She smiled. It was her smile, the one Logan remembered, the one that always gave him a jolt of adrenaline. He was watching her, still alive. She was twenty years older, but everything about her was familiar. The two men left cheerily enough.

Gary had mentioned that Ann didn't care for her big diamond wedding ring and rarely wore it. The lack of ring would have made her quite the target in a place like Three Boars.

Ann Robbins walked out of the camera's view. People were moving in and out of the shot. The band shut down for a break and people headed toward them to meet them or comment on the set. The camera had lost sight of

Becca. There was the slightest blink in the video, then the chaos resumed at a new camera angle. It had been a particularly crowded night. Walt barked an order to Sherry, one of the servers.

"There's Walt," Reggie said. "He said he was in and out that night because of a water heater failure."

There were swirls of people, but Ann Robbins was out of the shot. The video paused. Logan could hear Fran's breathing, as if she was anxious. "I'm going to zoom in," she said in the same serious tone. With a push of her remote button, it seemed as if the bar scene was being dragged forward, closer to the camera. There it was, the piece of the video that had Fran so uptight.

Logan leaned in even though the video was zoomed in so close he could see the nostril hairs of the face on the video. It was a face he knew better than anyone's. It was the face that stared back at him in the mirror.

Reggie looked at him. "That's you," she said unnecessarily.

"I see that." Logan shook his head. "I was not at the Three Boars last Friday night."

"The kid sent me video from that night. I double checked the date," Fran said.

Logan sat back and shook his head again. "Last Friday night I was sitting on my couch, drowsy and feeling good from painkillers, with my left hand under a bag of ice and my right wrapped around a cold beer. Zoom back out. My left hand will be big as a grapefruit if this was last Friday."

Logan leaned in again, sure another closer look would show that they were watching the wrong video. His right hand was clutching a pint of lager. He was turned with his left side to the bar and his left hand wasn't visible. "Can't you do something to turn the picture so we can see my left hand?"

Fran raised a brow. "When you've discovered software that will actually make individuals in a video turn around please let me know. It would really come in handy."

A group of people walked in front of Logan at the bar. By the time the shot cleared, Logan was no longer in it. Logan sat back feeling as if the wind had been knocked out of him.

"I wasn't there that night. There is no way in hell I wouldn't have seen Ann Robbins."

"You haven't seen the woman in twenty years. And you thought she was dead," Fran reminded him. Privileged information sure became unprivileged fast in the precinct. Logan was convinced his new partner hadn't been talking.

Logan looked at Fran with a questioning brow lift.

Fran shrugged. "Sometimes Sara Vaughn and I have lunch together."

That explained it. For a well-respected coroner, Sara tended to be loose with information.

Reggie was keeping silent about the video, taking in the discussion without wanting to step into it.

"I would have known it was her," Logan said, confidently. "I would have been shocked, after thinking she was dead all these years, but if I had seen her I would have recognized her instantly, even twenty years older. She was that kind of person, one of a kind. Even with an identical twin, she's impossible to replicate."

"You were drinking and taking pain meds," Fran noted. She was stepping over the line. She figured that out just seconds after letting the comment slip. Her cheeks were red. "Sorry, let's get to the rest of the video. You two are the detectives. You can sort this out."

"Could the video be doctored?" Reggie asked. It was the first smart thing to come up in the conversation.

"Yeah, I guess so, but that kid who sent the clip would have to be pretty skilled," Fran said.

"He wasn't exactly the quintessential computer nerd," Reggie said, "but Walt mentioned the kid was really good with technology."

"Let's set aside the last few seconds of the video for now," Fran said as she lifted her remote. "There's a part you'll definitely want to see." Logan almost dreaded what might come next. He was still trying to absorb what he just saw.

The video started again. "There's Ann Robbins," Fran pointed out unnecessarily. "She is no longer holding a drink. It looks as if she's heading out." Ann moved closer to the camera. The shot passed over her head and then she was gone. Just seconds behind, a figure dressed in a dark shirt and pants followed closely at her heels. It was impossible to see the face because the figure, most likely a man, was wearing a black baseball cap. The bill was pulled low over the face, so low it obscured all his features.

"Stop the video and back it up, could ya?" Reggie asked.

A rewind and repeat of the video didn't give them a clearer view of the suspect, and with the way the person followed right behind Ann Robbins, he was definitely a suspect. Logan was sure they were looking at the killer.

Reggie pointed at the monitor. "That's him." She glanced at Logan. "That looks like a man, don't you think? The walk, the set of the shoulders."

"That would be my guess too," Logan said. "See if you can find out whether the video has been doctored." Logan was still a little miffed at Fran, but he needed her. He'd learned early on in his career to never burn bridges, and Fran's skills made her the Golden Gate.

"I'll see what I can find out."

Reggie and Logan stood up. The still shot of the suspect remained on the screen.

"A black baseball cap," Logan muttered. Just like the black baseball cap Max found in his trash. What the fuck was going on? Was someone trying to frame him? Logan kept that chilling prospect to himself.

"Do you recognize it?" Reggie asked hopefully.

"Just trying to commit it to memory. Let's find out who was working that night. Maybe they know the man in the black hat."

CHAPTER
TWENTY-FIVE

Logan combed back his wet hair and stared at his reflection in the milky, damp mirror. He felt as if he'd aged a decade in one week. Nothing was straight in his world right now. He was Alice and he'd fallen through the damn rabbit hole. After a quick debriefing with Castillo, one that left the captain grunting his disappointment about the lack of progress, Logan and his partner had stopped by the Three Boars. Reggie showed several of the servers from that evening the video of the man with the hat, but no one recognized him. It wasn't too surprising considering how many people had been crammed into the bar that night. The detectives left their cards with instructions to call if they thought of anything or came up with a name.

While in Castillo's office, Logan brought up the fact that he had to take valuable time out of the investigation to sit on the shrink's couch hoping it might persuade the captain to reconsider his punishment, and he was definitely considering it a punishment. Logan hadn't minded Webb at first, but his arrogance was starting to wear on him. He was never going to be comfortable laying out his feelings to a guy who sat as primly as the Queen at tea. The hypnosis shit was weird too. The sooner he got done with therapy, the better. It was the last thing he needed.

The smell of burnt toast reminded him that he'd put two pieces of bread in the toaster. It also reminded him that he needed a new toaster. The slices always came out raw on one side and black on the other. He was late enough that he wasn't going to have time to choke down burned toast anyhow. Webb was a stickler for punctuality. Logan figured if he buzzed into the building too late, Webb would consider it an affront and ignore him. That actually sounded like the best possible scenario, if only Webb wasn't reporting back to Logan's direct superior. Gary, the aggravated spouse, also had a phone call arranged with his direct superior yesterday evening. Castillo was not impressed with what they had so far, and he grumbled that he'd have to embellish and let Mr. Robbins know that two stellar detectives were working on the case and that an arrest would be made soon.

Castillo had texted early, before Logan had even lowered a foot out of bed, letting Logan know he needed to see him the second he got to the precinct. He let Castillo know he'd be late because he was stuck going to his therapy punishment. Castillo just responded with a see me ASAP. That could never be good news, but Logan had decided to ignore it for now. He had more important things on his mind. Like the video and the black hat. Someone had picked up the black hat he left on the railing. It might have been the actual owner or someone who just decided they found a nice new hat. Now he wished he'd kept the damn thing. Something wasn't right. The word that kept popping into his mind was gaslight.

Logan poured himself a cup of coffee. He made it extra strong, lamely hoping it would ward against any impending state of hypnosis. He was blaming the crazy week he was having for how easily he got lost in the doctor's suggestions. He didn't like losing control like that. If anyone was going to control his already fucked up head, it was going to be him.

Logan hurried into his bedroom. He stepped over a pile of dirty clothes and then turned around and toed them to see if a matching pair of socks was hidden somewhere in the pile. He needed to do laundry, but there was nothing he hated more than going down to the communal laundry room. Only two of the washers worked, and there was almost always a line of baskets waiting to be next.

No matching socks. Logan was certain Webb would notice if he was wearing two different socks. He'd probably write up an entire page of notes about the slovenly detective who was too lazy to find matching socks. Webb, he was certain, would never consider leaving the house with mismatched socks.

Logan grabbed his phone to text Reggie. He shot off, "did you get the wake up text from Castillo about seeing him ASAP?" He yanked open his sock drawer. A gray sock with a black stripe was perched on top of the pile. He just needed the twin. He plunged his hand into the pile of cotton socks and fished one out. It was black with a gray stripe. He actually considered that this could be a creative match, then tossed it back in and kept searching. His phone beeped with Reggie's text. Before he could read it, his fingers hit something hard, something that was absolutely not a cotton sock. He pulled the hard thing free. For the millionth time that week, the breath was knocked from his chest. A platinum and diamond watch hung from his fingers.

He could hear his heartbeat in his ears. It reminded him of the Edgar Allen Poe story "The Tell-Tale Heart". Was he nuts like the narrator of the story? Had he committed murder, and was he now trying to convince himself it never happened?

He lifted the watch to give it a better look. It had been on her wrist. It had touched Becca's skin. He shook the insane thoughts from his head. Reggie's words 'like someone a man could become obsessed with' sliced through his mind. There was something rough on the inside, where the watch had been pressed against Becca's wrist. He turned the delicate watch over. It was an inscription. "To my Ann, Love Gary."

Logan dropped the watch as if it was molten hot. It landed with a clatter on top of his dresser. The room spun sharply around him. He backed away from the dresser, from the watch, until the backs of his knees hit the bed, and he fell backward onto the mattress. He stared up at the ceiling. The mold stains that he had memorized from nights when he couldn't sleep swirled around as if they'd come unmoored from their spots. They drifted across the cracked and crumbling plaster like dark clouds in a grim white sky.

His phone vibrated again to remind him there was a text. He peeled himself off the bed, but what he really wanted to do was climb back under the covers and curl into a ball. The room had stopped spinning, and the lightness in his head had been replaced by a heavy, solid anger. Someone was fucking with him. He had no idea who or how or why, but he was going to find out.

The watch, an expensive trinket for sure, glittered in the sunlight streaming through the blinds. He swept it back into the sock drawer for now. He hadn't decided how to handle it. After a vigorous face washing with ice cold water, he marched through the room, picked up his phone and keys and headed to the door.

He glanced at his phone as he settled behind the wheel. "I didn't get one of those texts," Reggie wrote. "Maybe I'm not important enough."

"Shit." He tossed the phone onto the passenger seat and drove toward Webb's office. It was the last thing he wanted to do this morning. Then again, maybe he needed a shrink more than he realized. He was definitely losing his fucking mind.

CHAPTER
TWENTY-SIX

A shroud of gray clouds had moved into the coast and clung there like wet wool. A thin, cold drizzle lingered in the air and made everything smell like mildew. The stark, modern building looked even less inviting in front of a dark gray sky. He wondered if he would like the building better if it wasn't the place he had to sit and bullshit with an imperious doctor about his anger issues. Were they really anger issues, or was the world just screwed up enough to warrant the occasional fit of rage? Logan was going with the latter.

Logan rubbed his forehead. It was wet from the mist. He smacked the intercom button just a little harder than necessary.

"Yes?" Webb asked.

"It's me," he said curtly. Webb knew he had an appointment. He'd heard Logan's voice enough. It was time to dismiss the formalities. The door buzzed. The sound of it agitated Logan enough that his shoulders jerked up and down. Pavlovian conditioning, Logan thought.

Due to a job where one day could bring a horrific grisly murder and the next could be a long drawn out afternoon of paperwork, Logan was expert at compartmentalizing things. He'd tucked the confusing, disturbing realities of the past twenty-four hours away. Reggie and Fran had seen the video, but for now, he was going to keep the rest to himself. If someone was fucking with him, it could be anyone. Even his new partner. That notion left a bitter taste in his mouth. Had his initial impressions of the woman been clouded by the fact that she was easy on the eyes and incredibly smart? Was she a plant to try and get him to fly off the handle again? Were the higher-ups looking for a way to get rid of him after all? But then why wouldn't they just ask for his badge? He would have handed it over if they'd asked. Growing up he'd imagined himself a contractor building houses, beautiful buildings, not the metal, glass eyesore he was walking through but cool buildings that mimicked the amazing architecture of old Europe. He'd pushed aside those dreams to join the police force. After seeing how corruption in the force allowed an asshole like Ray Kinsey get away with everything short of murder, Logan wanted to prove to himself that there were good, honest people in law enforcement, people with integrity and the grit to do what was right even if it was hard. He'd always stuck to those principals.

Look how far it had gotten him. He stepped out of the elevator.

Webb opened the door but didn't wait to greet him. Logan took a deep breath and headed across the hallway to the office door. He glanced back at the other doctor's office.

Webb was wearing an olive green sweater. Something told him the doctor was thrilled to see the cold and clouds because it meant he could pull on one of his expensive wool sweaters.

"You're late so let's get started," Webb said coldly.

Logan glanced at the clock behind the desk. He was about two minutes late. The man really did have a problem with OCD.

"Are you going to write that on the report?" Logan asked adding in a grin.

Webb ignored the sarcasm. He apparently still had his briefs in a bunch about Logan being two minutes late.

"How is the case going?" Webb asked before Logan could settle his ass gently on the rock hard couch. Logan looked up, surprised.

"I'd prefer not to talk about an ongoing investigation."

Webb's stony expression winced just a bit. "Everything you say in here is confidential. I'm not about to step outside and flag down the nearest reporter to relay all the details. But suit yourself. Let's leave the case off the list. I do think we made a breakthrough last session that I wanted to talk to you about." He methodically flipped backward through his notebook. The man had reams of notes on Logan already, and this was only his fourth time on the Flintstone couch.

Webb took a few minutes to refresh himself on notes he wrote just two days ago. Logan glanced at the clock. That was two minutes. He could have used the two minutes of Logan being late to refresh his memory on the notes, then it would've been a break even situation. Logan was close to telling him that but decided to keep his sarcasm to a minimum. Webb didn't seem to be in the mood, and Logan needed a good report to cross Castillo's desk. The captain had already made it clear he was disappointed with the work they'd done this week. Logan wasn't sure what they could have possibly done differently. They followed leads and kept hitting brick walls. It happened.

"This is just a hypothesis based on a few sessions, but I think you're holding onto some deep rage from your past."

"You mean Ray Kinsey? The guy who I would like to kill, even now, ten years after his death? Yep, I think that's right. Is that it? Have we found the key?" Logan regretted his derisive words the second they left his mouth. "Sorry, I'm just feeling some anxiety this morning."

Webb crossed his legs at the knees and sat forward with interest. "Tell me why."

Logan had opened his mouth too far, but it was easy enough to snap it shut. "It's just the pressure I'm feeling from the top to get this case solved."

"Are you closing in on the killer?" Webb asked as he picked up his pen and jotted down a few notes.

"We'll get him," Logan said with the confidence he wished he was feeling.

"Him?" Webb asked. "So you've narrowed it down to gender. Guess that eliminates at least half the population." He added in an arched brow and a slight grin.

"Ah ha, it seems the doctor is hitting back with a little sarcasm of his own. Well played."

His nondescript expression returned instantly. "Is there anything else that has you feeling anxious?"

Logan shook his head. "Nope, just that."

Webb stared at him for longer than usual, waiting apparently for Logan to elaborate, but Logan had said enough. He was going to kick himself later for bringing up his anxiety.

Webb set aside his notebook, signaling the hypnosis part of the session was about to take place. "Let's get you comfortable, and we'll see where your subconscious takes you this morning."

"We can follow my subconscious, Dr. Webb, but getting comfortable is not going to happen on your granite couch."

Webb chuckled lightly as he brought out the paper covered pillow. Logan rested his ankles on the opposite arm of the couch and wriggled until he felt reasonably supported by the cushions.

Webb started with his relaxation techniques, a

soothing tone telling Logan, gently but firmly, to relax every muscle from his head to his toes. It took Logan a lot longer to relax this morning but then he'd started it wound up like a spring.

"Let's go back to your youth, your time in your hometown of Layton," Webb said, his voice was starting to sound disembodied, as if it was coming from some other dimension.

"Let's start with a pleasant memory, perhaps one that involves the girl you loved. The girl you wanted to protect..."

Logan let go of the tension of the morning, the bizarre incidents that had caused so much anxiety. Becca was pulling him back to days when he was fit as a fucking gladiator, and he had the most amazing girl at his side. The diamond watch flickered through his mind pulling him back to the present.

"You're fighting it." Webb's deep voice flowed over him. "Go back to Layton, go to her." Logan easily slipped back over the line, the line between now and then. Layers of haze peeled back and he was staring at the Fight Club movie poster hanging on the wall opposite his bed.

The television is blasting The Sopranos in the downstairs den. It's one of Dad's self-indulgences, a show mom has deemed too brutal for her tastes. I'm surprised Dad likes it, but something deep down makes me glad he does.

I toss my world history textbook down to the floor. The assignment was three chapters with notes. I managed to get through one and a half before I felt like chewing the cover off the book. I reach into my dresser and pull out the last half of the cakey donuts I bought from the vending machine at school. They had one vending machine filled with fruit and little paper cups of oatmeal and one filled with cakey powdered sugared donuts and cellophane wrapped pastries that looked like they'd been run over with a car tire. Kids didn't just avoid the machine with the fruit, they walked a wide berth around it as if they worried that a banana or apple might jump out at them if they got too close.

I lean against the headboard on my bed and take a bite. Powdered sugar falls on my t-shirt like snow. I hop out of bed to brush it off. A light clicking sound pulls my attention away from the sugar mess and to the window. "Cricket." My bare foot accidentally kicks the history textbook across the room. I reach the window and pull it open. It's not a cold night but it's not warm either. A sliver of moon is just starting to peek through a tangle of light clouds. Becca's incredible face is turned up toward the window. The lights from my bedroom illuminate her smile and sparkling eyes.

"You've been eating powdered sugar donuts," she says as she steps on the cinder block and heaves herself up onto my window ledge. She sits there for a second, stuck between inside and out, the glow of night backlights her. For a second it feels like I'm looking at a picture. She swings her long legs over the ledge and into my room. She's wearing shorts and a pink tank even though it's still early spring. She shivers once as she stands up from the ledge. "Colder than I thought out there. I was going to grab a sweatshirt, but he who must not be named was sitting in the den watching television, and the sweatshirt was hanging over the back of the couch."

I watch her as she walks over to my nightstand and takes the last donut. The way she moves is mesmerizing, long liquid movements that stir every inch of me. She pushes the donut past her lips and stares down at the blizzard of white on her chest. She laughs and some of the sugar spurts out around the donut. She swallows the bite and goes to flick the sugar off her shirt. It's clinging to the skin on her chest. "A gentleman would help a lady clean this mess up," she says with a coy blink of her lashes. She's added in a Southern accent for effect.

"Are you studying?" she teases as she toes the book.

"Not all of us can just skim a book and get an A. Some of us actually have to study. Not that I did much of it." I flop on the bed and pull her down next to me. Sometimes she's there to hide from her dad, to hide from the world. I like it best when she's just there to be with me. She rests back against a pillow and stares up at the ceiling. As a kid I was obsessed with constellations. One day while I was at school, my parents decorated the whole ceiling with glow in the dark star constellations. I was so excited about having the night sky in my room, I almost couldn't sleep. And they were so excited about the surprise, I knew I'd leave those darn stars up forever, even when I was close to being an adult and had a girl in my room. Becca loved the stars on the ceiling. It was another thing I loved about her.

"North Star right? Is that the one I can use to make a wish? Or is that only a falling star?"

I laugh. "Considering I've reattached that big North Star to the ceiling more than once, we can consider it a falling star too."

Becca's laugh is not one that just splashes against you and fades away. It's a sound that washes over you, fills your senses and then settles itself inside your soul forever.

She turns to her side and rests her head against my shoulder. Her hair smells of minty shampoo and her skin of some sweet smelling perfume that I want to drown in. "I've made a wish to be someone altogether new," she says matter-of-factly. "I know that's impossible, but if my wish does come true do not be surprised if I don't answer to my usual name tomorrow. If the falling star does its magic, I will wake up as Stella Higgins, a twenty-five-year-old with thick black hair that is so long it has to be rolled up so I don't sit on it. I'll own a doggie boutique where snooty dog owners can come in and buy expensive designer doggie pajamas and engraved silver food bowls. I'll have a chef who fixes me orange flavored cinnamon rolls for breakfast and big fat cream cheese sandwiches for lunch."

I groan about the cream cheese sandwich. She elbows me. "Don't put a damper on my dream with your unwarranted hate of cream cheese."

"I have nothing against the stuff in cheese cake or in cookies. It just doesn't belong between two slices of bread, like the way you eat it."

She lifted an imaginary sandwich to her lips. "Hmm, but the bread gets so squishy from the cream cheese it almost morphs into a liquid."

I groan again.

"All right, enough about cream cheese. What about you? Who would Logan Cooper like to wake up as tomorrow morning?"

I roll my eyes. Becca loves games that take her out of reality, but I've always been a practical, reality based guy. The difference worked well for us. My eyes flit past the movie poster. "I'd like to wake tomorrow as Brad Pitt."

She elbows me again. "You don't get to be a person who already exists."

I roll over and pull her into my arms and kiss her. Her blue eyes open as the kiss ends.

"Now tell me," I say, "wouldn't you like it if I woke up tomorrow morning as Brad Pitt?"

She laughs and curls her body against mine. "Cricket," I say softly as I kiss her forehead. Her warm body slips away. The bed is filling with cold slimy water. Becca rolls to the edge of the bed. She grabs for me but slips off into the murky water that has filled my room. The stars peel off the ceiling one by one, dropping into the dark water that surrounds me, that weighs down on my chest. I can't move my limbs. I struggle to gulp air above the water. It's filling my mouth. I gag from the bitter taste of it. In the distance, the clicking sound, the tapping of Becca's house key on the rain spout next to my window, the sound she uses to let me know she's outside my room reverberates in my ears. Her hand flails through the air. I grab it to pull her back on the bed, but she shies away in fear. She screams.

Logan's eyes popped open and a worried looking Webb was hovering over him.

"You're back," he said. There was some strain in his otherwise chill tone that seemed to indicate that he was slightly worried about my journey. He took a deep breath and relaxed back. "You went deep this time," he sounded almost surprised about it.

Logan's limbs started to feel lighter, normal again. He moved his arms first, then swung his outer leg to the floor. It felt good to have ground beneath his shoe. His head wasn't ready to pop up though. He collapsed back against the pillow, rubbed his temples and squinted against the lights in the office. He swallowed and found the bitterness he tasted in his subconscious was still there.

"Would you like a glass of water?" Webb still sounded like a doctor who just had the shit scared out of him by a patient.

"Yes, please." Logan's throat was crackly, harsh. He pushed to sitting and rested against the back. Nothing in the room had changed, yet he felt as if he'd taken a long trip around the world and returned back to the same couch.

Webb regained his composure. Not that it was really a loss of composure, more a fleeting second of worry. He handed Logan a paper cup filled with cold water.

Logan chugged it back, enjoying the relief it provided to his parched, bitter throat. Webb grabbed his notepad as if he was a writer who'd just had an incredible revelation, one that had to be written down before he forgot it. He sat down and made some fast scribbles, then placed the pen calmly down as if he wasn't just writing furiously with it. His seemingly unflappable countenance had returned. Logan knew better now. He knew Webb had a cracking point. It actually made Logan like him better knowing he was a mere mortal too.

Just like after the last session, most of what he'd experienced came in short fuzzy clips. It was a confusing mix of visions, memories and emotions. One where happiness seemed to cross paths with abject horror.

"What are you feeling now?" Webb asked.

"Not sure." Logan rubbed his forehead. A slight headache seemed to be creeping up from somewhere in his skull looking for a place to settle. "I remember laughing with Becca. We were in my bedroom. She used to sneak out of her house and come to my bedroom window."

Webb's brows moved, so slightly, it could have just been a muscle twitch. Still, it seemed he was trying to regain his usual stone-faced expression.

"And then what?" he asked.

Logan allowed some of it to surface, but each bit felt like a spike of iron in his head. That was the source of the impending headache. Becca was drowning. His subconscious had recreated her death, so he could experience it in real time. Another sharp pain in his head. He winced.

Webb sat forward slightly. "Are you feeling all right? You look a little pale."

Logan rested his head back for a second. "Just a headache. I'm not too sure about these sessions. I'm here about my anger. Hypnosis is just shaking up my brain."

"It takes time to peel back the layers before getting to the heart of the problem. I'm focusing on your past because of Ray Kinsey. I think that's where your anger issues began. Is there anything you want to relay about your time under hypnosis?" He glanced down at the notepad balancing on his top knee. "You were calling to Becca at one point. You sounded angry. That was when I brought you out of it."

More of it was coming back. Slimy pond water covered his bed as he watched Becca slide away into its murky depths. "It was a bad dream," Logan said, not feeling the slightest need to elaborate. "I'm sure it was just a metaphor for me not being able to find Becca's killer."

"Care to add any details about it?" Webb asked.

"Details?" Logan's gaze drifted to the window. Rain was spitting against the clear glass, obliterating the usual view. That was what you got with impractical modern design, Logan thought. In their attempt to go ultra-minimal, they forgot the overhang that protected windows from rain. Webb waited, pen in hand, for Logan to narrate what he visualized. The headache had settled around his forehead. It was a dull ache with the occasional jarring twinge.

Logan looked at Webb. "Can't remember any details. Guess you put me under too deeply."

"I assure you that was not the case." He sounded somewhat insulted. "You're working unconsciously or possibly consciously to repress the images because something about them has upset you." There it was again, the look that showed something had knocked the usually balanced doctor off kilter.

"Why am I getting the feeling that there's something *you're* not telling me," Logan said. "Did something happen while I was off in my other dimension?" He asked the question facetiously.

Webb's response was anything but humored. His

nostrils had a touch of flare in them as he glanced down at his notes.

Logan sat forward. "There is something. Did I say something embarrassing while I was under? Whatever it was, I don't remember it. Why don't you tell me? Maybe it'll help me remember some of those lost details." Logan wasn't sure it was wise to push this. Maybe it was better if he didn't know. Still, he couldn't imagine what might have come out of his mouth that would have put Webb in such an agitated state.

Webb was avoiding eye contact. He skimmed his notes. Logan was sure it was a ploy to avoid looking at him. Logan's stomach was twisting up with hunger and the uneasy feeling this therapy session was leaving him with. His thrumming headache was starting to morph from manageable into something only aspirin and a dark room was going to kick. It was the last thing he needed before his work day. Then there was the dreaded meeting with Castillo waiting in the wings to add to his misery.

"Die, bitch, die," Webb said quietly, and a little too elegantly, given the words.

"Excuse me," Logan asked. That feeling of dread that always hit him just before shit hit the fan had gripped hold of him. He tightened his hands into fists and loosened them.

Webb finally found the courage to look at him. "That's what you said. That's why I brought you out of the hypnosis." He looked at the notepad again as if they were words one had to read again to remember. He repeated them. "Die, bitch, die."

Logan stared at him, hearing what was being said but finding it impossible to absorb. Finally, he rested back with a weak smile. "You must have heard wrong. I woke feeling upset and frantic. Becca was slipping away from me. I was in despair."

Once again, Webb looked at the stupid notes. Logan wanted to whisk them off his knee and hurl the notebook out the rain smeared window. "You were speaking clearly," Webb insisted. "Now, it doesn't mean anything. Obviously, you had nothing to do with her death. Perhaps, you were still feeling resentful about Becca faking her death to get away from you."

Logan sat forward so fast, the solid couch cushion came with him. "She wasn't trying to get away from me. She was running away from her father." Logan could hear that his tone was laced with rage, but he couldn't stop himself. Webb was supposed to be helping him not pushing him into a fit of anger. Or was he? Was this his method? Was he saying all this just to stir Logan up to get him to exhibit some of the uncontrollable anger he was being admonished for.

Logan squinted at him to see if he would break character during an impromptu game of chicken, but Webb's stare held his back. "Are you shitting me here? Are you trying to get a glimpse of that infamous anger, so you know exactly what you're dealing with?"

Webb wrote down a few notes. Logan decided it was a damn rude way to treat a client who was in the middle of something upsetting.

Webb set down the pen. "I'd like to finish the session with a few easy questions. A lot has happened this morning. I want you to leave here feeling better than when you came in."

A laugh shot out before he could stop it. "I don't see how that's possible. And it makes me wonder—are these sessions helping or hurting me?"

Webb looked taken aback by the question. "The results aren't always immediate. I assure you, this will help you solve some inner conflicts. You seem to have a few of those at the moment."

"Really? Thought I was here because I beat the crap out of a lowlife who caged his daughters and murdered their mom right in front of them. Didn't realize there was an inner conflict problem."

Webb's expression grew cold. "I realize you're upset about what transpired today. If you'd prefer a different doctor—"

Logan shook his head. This morning was going from fucked up to ultra fucked up. "I just want to get through this, and I'm sure you're feeling the same way. I think we can end it there today. I need to get to work. I've got to hunt down a killer."

Webb hurriedly closed his notepad as if Logan might catch a glimpse of something he'd prefer to keep to himself on his precious notepad. He half walked Logan to the door.

"I'll see you Monday, same time," Webb said hesitantly. Webb hated these sessions as much as Logan.

"Sure," Logan said curtly and walked out the door. He stepped into the elevator and saw his reflection on the shiny steel doors. What the hell just happened? Whatever it was, he was feeling even more uneasy than he was when he got there. To top it off, his head hurt, and there was no way he was going to avoid seeing Castillo this morning.

Logan leaned back against the cold, metal wall of the elevator. "Fuuck."

CHAPTER
TWENTY-SEVEN

Logan was absurdly glad to see Reggie's motorcycle, even if it was parked in his spot. He'd contemplated, for all of a second, that Reggie had been some kind of plant sent to get him to mess up big time. She was just too real, too genuine. His intuition was better than that. If she was there to trip him up or gaslight him into losing his cool, he would have sensed it. The whole thing was too farfetched anyhow. The higher-ups could just fire him. Why bother going through all the hoops to do it. But how the hell did the hat and bracelet get into his apartment? Then there was the session at Webb's office. Had he really yelled out die, bitch, die? Webb wouldn't make something like that up, but who was he talking to? He never would have said anything like that to Becca, no matter how hurt he was that she left him. Nothing was making sense, but he knew one thing for sure. He needed to get to the bottle of aspirin in his desk. His head was on fire.

More eyes turned his direction than he was comfortable with as he stepped into the precinct. Garcia glanced up from his paperwork and immediately returned his focus to his report. Reggie wasn't sitting at her desk. Maybe she'd been called into Castillo's office too. Logan sat at his desk, yanked out the drawer, tapped three aspirin onto his palm and tossed them into his throat. He swallowed them dry, but it wasn't easy. He was still feeling the effects of his session in Webb's office.

Pairs of eyes flicked his direction, like wolves watching from shadows in the night. Sometimes the precinct was just like his sappy hometown, gossipy and judgmental.

Logan got up and marched to Castillo's office. The door was ajar. He knocked.

"Come in," Castillo bellowed. It was a small office and an even smaller hallway, but he always felt the need to bellow. Logan pushed open the door and was disappointed not to see his partner inside.

Castillo's face pinched into something that almost looked like pain when he saw that it was Logan. He waved a thick, hairy forearm toward a chair. "Close the door and have a seat, Cooper."

Logan shut the door. He wondered how long it would be before the aspirin relieved the pounding in his head. He grabbed the chair with even legs. The expression on the captain's face told him it was a stable chair kind of meeting.

Castillo had been sucking on one of his throat

lozenges. It gave off a medicine-y cherry scent as he grabbed a tissue and spit it out. He wrapped it up and tossed it into the trash. It was another indication that shit was about to fly. Castillo never wasted a perfectly good cherry lozenge.

The captain pushed some papers aside and crossed his arms on the desk as he leaned forward. "Had a talk with the husband of your victim, Gary Robbins."

Logan nodded. "Yeah, that's the husband."

"Why didn't you tell me Ann Robbins had the name Logan tattooed on her wrist?" Castillo drummed the desktop with his fingers as he waited for Logan's response.

"I told you I knew her."

"You didn't mention the tattoo."

"Didn't think it was important," Logan said. He had no clue where this was leading, but from the look on Castillo's face, it wasn't leading anywhere good.

"You didn't think it was important?" Castillo sat back hard enough to make his chair groan. "Well, I wish you'd said something to me because I unwittingly told Gary Robbins, after he berated me for having incompetent detectives on the job, that Detective Logan Cooper was my best detective."

Stupidly, Logan didn't put together what Castillo was trying to tell him. He was going to blame it on the drumbeat pounding in his head. He responded tentatively with a thank you, wondering, only briefly, if the captain had called him in to let him know that he told the husband not to worry because his best detective was on the case.

"I'm not telling you this to boost your ego, Coop." A spray of cherry colored spittle shot from his mouth. "Robbins practically leapt through the phone at me when he discovered your first name was Logan. I can only assume your full name never came up during the interview, which leads me to the conclusion that you never told the husband you knew his wife." The flush of red was creeping up from his collar to slowly swallow his whole face. "Considering she had your name tattooed on her wrist that was probably a good call. It would have been nice if I'd been given a heads up about the tattoo and the whole keeping the husband in the dark part of the story because then I wouldn't have stepped my foot into a big pile of shit."

Logan rubbed his temple. He could feel his pulse pounding there. He wondered if that was it, if an aneurysm was going to take him out right there. He could only imagine the story making its way around the precinct —Castillo yelled Logan right into an aneurysm.

"You're right, Cap'n, I should have told you about the tattoo and the secret we were keeping from Robbins. But we've been so busy with the case—"

His hand went up like a big white stop sign. "Nope, none of that matters now. Certainly, you knew that Mr. Robbins considers this mysterious man from his wife's past a suspect. He thinks someone from her past contacted her recently and upset her. He thinks it's the man whose name was tattooed on her wrist. Now, he knows that man is you, and I can tell you he is raving mad. He went straight to the chief because guess what—he happens to be Police Chief Riley's accountant."

Logan felt himself sinking deeper into the chair as he finally clued in to where this was going. "Don't take me off the case, Captain. Please." He felt the word *please* all the way down to his bones.

Castillo's eyes dropped. He absently picked at some invisible speck on his desk. "I'm putting you on administrative leave."

Logan froze in the chair, convincing himself that he'd heard Castillo wrong.

Castillo finally grew a pair and looked across the desk at Logan. "It's been decided. It starts this morning."

"All because I didn't tell you about the damn tattoo?" Logan hopped to his feet and paced across the office before spinning back and stopping in front of Castillo's desk. "She was eighteen when she got that tattoo. I haven't seen her in twenty years. Hell, I spent the last two decades convinced she was dead."

Castillo was giving him a sort of puppy dog look for empathy. "I know this isn't what you were expecting. I wasn't expecting it either, but—" He rolled his lips in to stop the next words from leaving his mouth.

"But what? What the hell is going on?"

Castillo no longer seemed comfortable having Logan

stare down at him in his chair. He stood up and walked to the window that looked out on the hallway. It gave a partial view of the desk area. He turned back to Logan.

"I was just going to reassign you, but this morning, we received the first report from Dr. Webb."

"That asshole, what did he say?"

"First of all, you can't take this out on him. He didn't make the decision to put you on leave. He sent a report that stated he was worried that progress wasn't good and that you were having a hard time because of the case you were working on. He thought the personal connection to the victim was too much for you."

"What the hell does he know? He's just some polished, scholarly prick who looks down on all of us as beneath him and gets his panties in a bunch if you're two minutes late. I can handle this case. I would tell you otherwise. Reggie and I are getting along great. We work well together. We're going to get this done."

"I'm sorry but you're absolutely off the case. Gary Robbins is insisting on that."

"Maybe we need to look at that guy again cuz he sure has been giving us a hard time. He sure as hell is trying to pin the murder on Logan. And we both know Logan didn't do it."

"Thought the husband had an ironclad alibi," Castillo said.

"You know as well as me that ironclad alibis can be bought."

"Doesn't happen often," Castillo said. The few paces around his office were more than enough exercise for one morning. He circled back to his chair and sat down with a grim expression. "I'm sorry, Logan. The decision's been made. I sent Reggie off with Gregor this morning to continue the case. Robbins was even fighting to take her off the case, but I told him then we'd be back at square one with two newly assigned detectives."

The headache had lightened but now the pain was in his gut. He was getting chopped down at every turn, and Reggie was stuck working with Gregor.

"Enjoy the time off." Castillo tried to sound light and airy about it. "Take a few bike rides or a trip down to the beach."

"Right, a trip to the beach." Logan slapped his badge and gun on the desk then turned to leave.

"Just stay away from the case, Logan. Is that clear? I know she was someone you cared about, but let Gregor and Hawkins cover it."

Logan didn't say a word or look back as he walked out of the office.

CHAPTER
TWENTY-EIGHT

The aspirin had kicked away the headache, but they were now burning a hole in Logan's empty stomach. He pulled the leftover fried chicken from last night's fast food dinner out of the fridge. He picked at the crumbly coating but left the meat on the bone. It was too cold and greasy, and his stomach was already warning him that things weren't great.

The stained walls of his crappy apartment looked especially drab this afternoon, but he wasn't in the mood to push back curtains and let in light. He didn't deserve daylight. The smell of the chicken was getting to him. He carried it to the trash and dumped it, then grabbed the milk out of the refrigerator. There was just enough for a glass, so he decided not to bother with one. He tipped the carton back and chugged it hoping it would ease the burning sensation in his stomach.

Logan's phone rang from the coffee table. He walked over and picked it up. It was Reggie. "Hey," he said quietly.

"Hey, partner," she said just as quietly. Traffic noise shuffled through the phone around her voice. "How are you doing?"

"Just great. I'm going to Disneyland. Isn't that what they say after they've won the Super Bowl? Think I'll go hang out with Mickey and Donald, that's how fucking awesome I'm feeling. Where's your new partner?"

"Ew don't call him that. We stopped for lunch early because, according to Gregor, he gets low blood sugar and then he can't think straight. And I'm thinking—but they gave you a gun with that volatile blood sugar thing? Anyhow, he's eating a ham sandwich the size of Manhattan with all the gusto and manners of a medieval king. I just couldn't watch anymore. I told him I was going to take a little walk. I wanted to see how you were doing. What case are you on now?"

Logan plopped onto his couch. It was getting old enough that springs were starting to poke his ass when he sat too hard. "Guess you haven't heard the latest. They've decided to put me on administrative leave."

"What? You're kidding. Why is that?"

"Apparently because I'm nuts, and you know what, they might just be right." There was so much he wanted to tell her, but he held it back, just in case. As badly as he wanted to trust her, he was feeling alone enough now with his misery and confusion that he decided not to trust anyone. It was paranoia, but that was how he was feeling —paranoid.

"Look, before you spend too much time at your pity party, I promise I'm going to find the killer, even if I have to keep a continual supply of candy bars in my pocket to keep Gregor's blood sugar spiked. When Castillo called Gregor and me in this morning to tell us about the assignment change, he had me stay after Gregor left. He said Robbins put together that you were the Logan from Ann's past. He wanted me off the case too. I guess I can't blame the guy."

"I'm wondering—did we brush off the notion of him being the killer too easily? I know he had an alibi but—"

"It's rock solid," Reggie said. "I was able to get a list of the names of some of the people running the financial conference he attended. There's video of his speech. He was there."

"What if he paid someone?"

"That's always a possibility, but it's harder to prove. One thing is certain—he's been trying to throw this mystery man from the past, Logan, under the bus from the start. I guess that theory is no longer going to hold water."

"Yeah," Logan said hesitantly as he rested back.

Reggie laughed. It was short and brisk. It was followed up by someone honking a horn. "You don't sound convinced. Did you forget that you were Logan, or is there something else you're not telling me?" She said it with a joking air, but there was just enough seriousness on the edge to assure Logan that Reggie sensed something was up.

Logan hated bringing up the subject. It was that damn video that had started his downward spiral. Reggie seemed to read his mind.

"Fran said she hasn't had time to check the video. She got inundated with other work this morning. But she promised to get back to me as soon as she has it sorted out."

"Where are you heading to now?" Logan asked. He dropped his feet one at a time on his coffee table. "Or has Castillo warned you not to let me in on any details about the case?" Her pause answered his question. "That's all right. I don't want to get you in trouble. I'll just sit here and go stir crazy. I was thinking I might redecorate this hellhole of an apartment. Maybe throw up some paisley wallpaper or a bright color or two."

"You are far less likable when you're being pathetic," she said. "We're going to talk to Derrick's husband, find out exactly what happened and what his relationship with Ann was."

"Almost forgot about that guy." Logan sighed. "I'm thinking it'll be another dead end."

"You and me both, but we've got to cover all the angles and, honestly, there aren't too many that we haven't already covered. Do you think we should go back over some of them?"

"You might need to." Logan was devising his own plan. There wasn't any way he could sit around and not do anything. His suspicions kept going back to the husband. If someone hired Razor to steal a car, they could certainly hire someone to cuff Becca to that steering wheel and drown her.

"Gotcha, I'll go back over the list. It won't be as easy because you're the guy with the contacts. Something tells me Gregor doesn't have many."

Logan smiled for the first time all day. "I don't know about that. He probably knows the name of every donut and coffee shop owner in a twenty mile radius." Talking to Reggie was the first time he felt all right since he woke up, burned toast and found an incriminating piece of evidence in his sock drawer.

"Speaking of Gregor, here he comes," Reggie said quickly. "He's got a big spot of mustard on his shirt." She giggled into the phone. "The whole car is going to stink like a deli. Talk to you later, and try to leave the pity party sooner rather than later."

Reggie hung up. Logan hauled himself off the couch. He very nearly decided to drop back onto the couch, grab the remote and spend the rest of the day flipping through the billion channels at his fingertips. He smiled thinking about how often his parents would tell him they grew up with four channels to choose from and three of them were news shows for two hours an evening. There was some general whining about rabbit ears or something that had to do with the reception as well, but they'd always lost him at the four channels thing. It seemed so absurd, he'd pushed it off into the pile of tall tales parents generally told about the twenty mile trek through snow just to get to the school bus stop.

The couch and television begged him to stay. Against his good judgment, Logan pulled on his hooded sweatshirt and grabbed his keys. The morning drizzle never left, and the gloom above had turned more menacing. Raindrops that were far past a drizzle had started to fall. Max buzzed toward him in the golf cart as Logan crossed the cracked asphalt to his car.

"Detective Cooper, we don't usually see you home in the afternoon. What happened? Did they already round up all the bad guys?" Max had a good belly laugh to himself as he punched it and zipped across the lot.

Logan got in his car and headed toward Gary Robbins' house. He wouldn't be able to do much. If he was just going to sit on the couch staring at shows he'd seen before, he figured he could do just as much sitting in the truck staring at the Robbins house.

His stomach had improved so he drove through his favorite burrito joint and picked up a burrito and some of that hot salsa to confirm Reggie's guess about his salsa habit. The aspirin had finally stopped burning his stomach, and now it growled like an empty cave. Robbins had only seen him in his detective car, so he wouldn't recognize the truck. The house was in a quiet, typically ideal suburban neighborhood, which meant eventually neighbors and even Gary himself would get suspicious about a strange truck sitting on the street. Logan parked under the shade of a massive mulberry that hung out over the street in front of his neighbor's house. He hoped the thickly leaved tree, the dark skies and the unusual summer rain would make his truck less noticeable. It was California and rain, especially heavy rain, tended to make people drive slowly, cautiously, focused like they were driving with blinders on.

Gary's car was in the driveway along with a few others. It was possible his family was staying with him after the funeral. Logan felt that sense of disappointment he got whenever a lead didn't pan out. Why was he there? Like Reggie said, Gary was out of town last Friday, the day of the murder. Would a nerdy little accountant really have contacts in the underworld, contacts with car thieves and assassins?

Logan pulled the hood up over his head and slumped down lower in the seat. Raindrops helped camouflage him inside the cab of the truck. He pulled the hood farther forward and lifted his face to the rearview when he saw headlights in the reflection. The car rolled slowly past. Logan peered past the edge of his hood to get a glimpse of the driver. It was an older woman, so tiny she could barely see over the dash. She looked horrified to be driving in the rain.

Logan unwrapped his burrito and poured on the salsa.

He was hungry enough to finish it in four bites. It landed in his stomach just as he expected, like a rock. He glanced at his phone in the holder. No calls. Everyone on the force knew by now that he was on leave. Badly, he wanted Castillo to call and tell him they'd made a mistake and that he could get back on the case. But he knew that was a fantasy thanks to Gary Robbins and Dr. Webb. He really wanted to know what Webb's notes said. He fleetingly dreamed up a plan of getting one of his contacts on the streets to set him up with the guy everyone called the notorious Houdini. He could pay the guy to break into Webb's at night so he could read that stupid notepad.

There was no one entering or leaving the Robbins house. It was going to be the world's dullest stakeout. Without a badge to back him up, he had absolutely no right to be there, let alone to consider approaching anyone leaving or entering. Somehow, he'd gotten a wild notion that Gary Robbins was trying to get them to focus on Logan because he was hiding his own guilt. But, the truth of the matter was, if Logan had married a woman with another man's name tattooed on her wrist, a man she refused to talk about, a tattoo she refused to fully explain, he would have felt the same way. Especially if there was someone from her past who recently contacted her. From what they'd uncovered, it seemed there were two possible answers to that mystery. One was Drax, her old boss who was blackmailing her to keep her past life from floating to the surface. The other was her twin sister, Ally. It would have been a huge shock, after all these years, to discover that you had not only a sibling, but an identical twin. If there was someone else from her past that had contacted her, it had not come up in the investigation. One thing was sure, Logan knew it wasn't him.

Logan relaxed back and stared at his phone. He snatched it up and dialed his dad. His parents had gone golfing in Scotland, and they got back to Palm Springs the night before. If there was one thing he was learning from this week, it was that he hadn't given his parents nearly enough credit for being good people. Growing up he'd been almost embarrassed about the fact that they were so straight and polite and not involved in any of the scandalous shit some of the other parents had been. Now he felt ashamed.

His parents would be shocked to hear the news about Becca. He nearly hung up realizing he was going to have to hold back a lot of truths about his current situation, which meant he'd probably have to lie. He hated lying to his parents.

"Logan, is that you?" Dad always asked that. Logan wasn't exactly sure who else it would be calling from the private number of his phone.

"Yeah, Dad, it's me. I just wanted to make sure you got in okay."

"Oh yeah, yeah, got here with all our parts and luggage." His familiar chuckle tickled the phone. His dad would chuckle at the silliest things, the paper boy landing the paper in the tree, a neighbor pulling out their trash even though it was a holiday or his mom if she forgot where she put down her keys. He was an avid chuckler. Logan had never appreciated it enough.

"Everything all right, son? You sound a little down. Are you getting enough sleep and eating right?" His dad always assumed a detective job was a nine-to-five with a leisurely hour for lunch like an accountant's job.

"I'm getting enough sleep. Probably not eating right but don't tell mom. The last time she sent me a bunch of healthy eating plans."

Another chuckle. This one made Logan feel a little homesick. He hadn't made enough effort to drive down to the desert and see them. "All I know is she's counting my servings of fruits and vegetables." Another chuckle. The comment made him think about his new partner and her healthy diet. Was she trying to avoid what her mom was going through? He didn't know a lot about early onset Alzheimer's, but he knew enough about science to figure it was probably tied to genetics... and lifestyle. Seemed like all the bad ones were tied to lifestyle.

"Glad she's taking good care of you. Hey, Dad, I have some news. It's sort of shocking and upsetting, but I thought you'd want to know. Remember Becca?"

"Of course I do, Logan. You two were in love. We always liked Becca. What a tragedy her life turned out to be. Just mad at myself for never confronting that awful Ray Kinsey."

Logan had to pull the phone away to make sure it was still his dad on the other end. He'd never seen his dad confront anyone. He used to just say 'let the police handle things' when Ray was on one of his tirades. That might have been the one thing Logan could look back on and feel disappointed about his parents. But it wasn't just them. The whole town was afraid of Ray. People avoided him like a plague.

"Dad, it turns out Becca didn't drown in the Pacific. She tried to commit suicide, but Jeremy West saved her. She ran away after that, not wanting to go back to Layton, to her father."

To me, Logan thought then dashed the notion from his head. Webb had filled him with some serious doubt, and it had been eating at him. Was Becca fleeing him too? Had she sensed that he was going to propose and rather than say no she just took off?

"I don't believe it," his dad said. "That's wonderful. Have you talked to her? Gee, we'd love to see her too. Are you two getting back together? Wait until I tell your mom. She just stepped out for some groceries." Logan was losing control of the conversation. He should have started with her much more recent and far more confirmed death, but how did you tell someone that a person had died when that person had already been assumed dead for years?

"Dad, dad," he had to say it a little more forcefully to get his attention. "Dad, she showed up as a victim on a murder case."

Heavy silence on the other side of the call. "I don't understand. So she's dead?"

"I'm afraid so. She started a whole new life." Logan couldn't hold back a smile. "She married an accountant. She told her husband that growing up her friend had a dad who was an accountant, and he was one of the only nice men in town."

More heavy silence.

"Dad? You still there?"

A light sniffle came through the phone. "That poor girl. She just couldn't get a break, could she?"

"Seems not." Logan glanced up toward the suburban house where Becca had lived the last years of her life. Even in the cold drizzle, it looked inviting, like it was a nice, comfortable place to live.

"What a shame," his dad said. He'd been in such good spirits. Logan hated that he had to tell him bad news. His mom and dad were definitely more good news people.

"Dad, I've got to go, but I just wanted to say thanks." Logan's throat tightened.

"Thanks for what, son?"

"Just thanks for being totally cool parents. Becca was right. You were the nicest guy in town, and mom was great too. I got lucky."

Another sniffle. "Gee, I don't know what's wrong with me," he said briskly trying to hide another sniffle. "I guess I'm getting a cold. Wouldn't be too much of a surprise.

After living in Palm Springs, Scotland felt like the Arctic, even in July." He chuckled.

"I've got to go, Dad."

"All right. Stay safe. Oh and, Logan—"

"Yeah?"

"Mom and I got lucky too."

"Thanks, Dad. Give Mom a kiss for me."

Logan relaxed back against the seat and pulled the hood forward to hide half his face. It didn't take long in the warmth of the truck and with only the pitter patter of rain on the hood as music for him to drift off to sleep. The rumble of a loud motor woke him.

The sticky grogginess in his head assured him he'd slept for a good hour. Logan rubbed his face then sat up and stared through the front windshield. An old Subaru with a loud motor tuned to make the most noise possible vibrated his truck as the driver swung a fast U-turn at the end of the road and stopped in front of Gary's house. A young guy with tattoos running in every direction up his arms and a black t-shirt climbed out of the car. He left the obnoxious motor running. It sounded almost worse idling. He climbed out of the car holding something in his right hand. Logan sat up but couldn't see what it was through the rain on his windshield. The kid swiped rain off his face with his free hand as he ran up to the front door. Gary came out to meet him halfway.

Logan sat forward practically leaning his chin on his

steering wheel. Gary handed off something that Logan was sure looked like money.

"Here we go," Logan muttered. His heartbeat sped up like it always did when he was sure he was closing in on something important, and a sketchy looking kid who Gary met halfway out the door, out of view of the family members inside, seemed important. Gary hid something under his raincoat and hurried back to the house. The kid ran back to the car.

Logan stepped out of the truck and stood in the middle of the street to stop the car. He held up his hand. "Stop, police!" The kid looked scared as shit. For a second, Logan thought he might whip around the madman in the street, but he put it in neutral and hung his head out the window.

"I'm getting a new muffler this week," he said shakily.

Logan approached the car. The smell of cannabis and onions hit him as he leaned down toward the window. "I noticed you just exchanged something with the man in that house." Logan motioned with his head toward Gary's house. He hoped the noisy car wouldn't bring Gary to the window. Logan would probably lose his badge for good if Gary spotted him, but finding Becca's killer had become more important than his badge. The killer was screwing with him too, and he needed to find out why.

The kid looked totally confused. "Is it illegal to deliver food to this neighborhood?"

"Food?" Logan asked.

"Burgers from Benny's Malt Shop." He pointed to the corner of his front windshield. "I'm an Uber Eats driver."

Logan nodded. "Right. Then carry on."

The kid stared up at him still unsure of whether or not he should drive off.

"Go on, before I arrest you for disturbing the peace. And get a fucking muffler."

The kid pushed the car into first and rolled off slowly.

Logan walked back to his truck, climbed inside and looked up at himself in the rearview mirror. "Not your finest hour, Coop."

Logan had just started the truck when another car pulled up to the house, a small white sedan with a sunroof and nice rims. The driver climbed out of the car. Logan couldn't catch his breath. The long legs, the perfect, dollish profile, the smooth way she moved. "Becca," he said on a sigh. But it wasn't Becca. It was Ally, her twin sister. She fidgeted with her raincoat and smoothed her hair back before heading up to the door. It opened. Gary stood in the doorway looking stunned as if someone had just tased him. A few words were exchanged, but Logan couldn't make them out. Gary wiped his eyes and reached out to hug Ally. She walked into his arms. They stood in the doorway in a long embrace before Gary motioned her inside. The door shut on the house... and on Logan's worthless stakeout.

He put the truck in drive and swung it around to head home.

CHAPTER
TWENTY-NINE

The rain was coming down hard. It seemed California was going to get a much needed drink for a change. Logan sat on the couch, nursing a cold beer and staring up at the wet stain on the ceiling that spread out like blood on a cotton sheet. After one of the most humiliating moments of his career, though it technically happened when he was off duty, Logan decided drinking himself into oblivion might be his best bet. With any luck, he could fall into a drunken coma and wake up on the other side of this nightmare.

One thing he knew for certain, sitting alone in his apartment staring at spreading stains on the ceiling was only leading him to the darkest corners of his mind. How the hell did the diamond watch get in his sock drawer? Why was the hat in his trash? Was someone trying to frame him or, worse, did he have something to do with Becca's death? Webb had insinuated that his fits of rage caused him to black out, to ignore his surroundings. It was true. If he thought back about moments when his fist was flying, the only thing motivating him was anger. He blotted out what was happening around him. What had Webb noticed in the last session that led him to write such a damning report, a report that led to his administrative leave?

The dark thoughts were taking far too much hold. Logan walked to his bedroom. The rain had cooled down the air. A dreary fog had coasted in and mixed with the rain. Logan considered a sweatshirt for all of a second. After an unseasonably hot June and July, he was looking forward to feeling the cool, wet air on his skin. It was just what he needed to clear the heaviness in his head.

The corner bar was close enough to walk to, even in rain. The brisk walk was as necessary as the cool rain. He planned to get plenty wasted, so getting behind the wheel was out of the question. The roads were unusually empty especially for a Friday night. That was what rain did to Californians. A little adverse weather and people stayed home. A summer rain could hardly be considered adverse compared to storms the East Coast and Midwest endured. It worked well for his plans, getting as drunk as possible all while seeing as few people as possible.

His phone vibrated in his pocket. He pulled it out and shielded it with his hand. It was a text from Reggie.

"Call me when you can."

Logan was standing by his limited interactions with

humans decision. Even texting with his partner was stepping out of that boundary. He pushed the phone back into his pocket. There hadn't been many cars on the road, but there were plenty of people, wet people, huddled into Mick's Bar. It was the quintessential dive with gritty floors and questionable lighting. The dank smelling wood paneling on the interior walls smelled even worse than usual in the wet weather. Darkly tinted windows gave the place a cave-like feel. There was no space for a band, not that any self-respecting cover band would take a gig there. Raspy speakers had been hung overhead by thin wire. The music for the night was whatever the owner, Mick, had chosen. Mick was an oversized, ex-marine who still wore a buzz cut and military style boots. The buzz cut, he told Logan, was because he hated fussing in a mirror, and the boots were for Mick to literally kick people who got on his nerves out of the bar. Logan had seen him give the boot more than once, and he had resolved never to be on the receiving end of Mick's temper.

The wobbly bar stools were all taken. Logan managed to find himself a corner of the bar counter to stand at. Dripping wet from the unexpected summer rain, everyone looked tired after a long work week. People cradled their drinks and their beers in their hands like babies holding bottles. It seemed he wasn't the only person nursing away his blues with booze.

Mick was playing some good tunes for a change, old rock and some borderline country stuff like Lynyrd

Skynyrd. After three shots of tequila and three beers, Logan was feeling almost loose enough to dance. He was fairly drunk but not so out of it that he missed the flirty smiles of a woman with big dark eyes and glossy pink lips leaning against the wall with her drink. Her skin tight jeans were dotted with raindrops, and her blonde hair was drying into a mass of wavy curls. He decided one more shot might help pry him off the bar and onto the dance floor. He spun around and flagged down Mick.

"Another shot of tequila, Mick."

Mick walked over with a disapproving scowl. "Are you sure you're not pounding those back too fast?"

"I'm fine. I walked here. I'll be sober before I reach my door. That is, if I can find my door."

His scowl returned.

"Just kidding." Logan slapped the counter. "One more."

Mick returned with the tequila. It burned a trail down his throat as Logan tossed it back. He smacked the shot glass down and wiped his mouth with the back of his hand. His next plan was to walk over to the woman with the glossy pink lips and ask her to dance. Van Morrison's "Brown Eyed Girl" trickled down from the speakers. That was his cue. He spun around and smacked right into her, and hell, if her eyes weren't brown as chocolate.

"You remind me of the guy who keeps popping up in my sex fantasy daydreams." She stroked his arm lightly with her fingertips.

"Maybe that's because I *am* that guy."

She laughed gently. "Want to dance?"

Logan nodded, took her hand and navigated his way through the drunken crowd to the small space in the corner where a few other people were dancing. It wasn't meant to be a dance floor, but somehow, on Friday and Saturday nights, the patrons managed to carve out the space for some inebriated dancing. Logan pulled the woman into his arms. She circled her arms around his neck. He swayed more to the sloshing in his brain than the beat of the music. Her body moved right along with him. She pressed against him. Logan decided then and there that he was overdue for a good fuck.

"What's your name?" he asked, his mouth against her ear.

"Brenda. How about you?"

A sharp smack on his shoulder startled him. He'd had just enough tequila to take an unsteady step back. He was still holding Brenda. The source of the shoulder smack stepped into view. He was a big guy with a scar cutting through his right eyebrow and a tattoo that seemed to be a rattlesnake wrapping clear around his thick neck. He was equal in height to Logan, but outweighed him by a good seventy pounds, some of it bulk, some of it too many plates of nachos.

"Hey, buddy, you can have the next dance," Logan said. He wrapped his arms tightly around Brenda. Since she didn't put up any resistance, he assumed everything was good. The next shoulder tap was more of a grab. The guy's fingers pinched Logan's shoulder, and dragged him back a few steps. Logan was just unsteady enough on his feet to allow it to happen.

Logan put out his arms. "What's your problem? We're just dancing."

"Sam, you're ridiculous," Brenda said angrily and stomped away.

Sam stared at Logan. Either he was grinding his teeth together or he was chewing on his tongue. It could have been both. "I've got to agree with Bren," Logan quipped. "You're ridiculous, *Sam.*"

"You're lucky I don't kill you," Sam said. Spittle dripped from the side of his mouth. "That's my woman."

"That's your woman?" Logan laughed. "What are you, a fucking caveman?" Logan knew damn well he was antagonizing the guy. He wondered if he was just looking for a good reason to pound someone. The more he thought about it, yeah, that was what he was itchin' for. Only he couldn't show up to Webb's office with cuts and bruises, or he'd be finished for sure.

"She's all yours," Logan said, his gut heavy with disappointment that he didn't get to throw his fist. He could feel Sam staring at him as he headed back through the crowd. Another shot and then he would head home to pass out on the couch. It wasn't going to be enough tequila for a coma. At least he'd be out for the night.

Mick cast him another dirty look as he poured the

shot. "Seems that someone had a rough week. You don't usually get this hammered."

Logan lifted the shot. "Rough week is an understatement." He dropped the tequila back. His throat stung as the bitter liquid seared it yet again.

Mick wiped the counter in front of him. "Want to talk about it?"

Logan shook his head slowly. Even slowly, he nearly lost his balance. In his twenties, he could down an entire bottle of tequila and still stand on one foot. It seemed he really was catching the middle aged train.

"It's a long story, started all the way back when I was a kid, so I think I'll skip it and just meander out of here while I can still walk." He tossed his money on the counter and turned around... cautiously. It seemed the entire exit and walk home was going to be in slow motion.

He held the door for two young women. One smiled and tucked her caramel colored hair behind her ear. "Aw, you're leaving?" she asked. "We're just getting here, and you look like you need some company."

"Sorry, ladies, guess the timing wasn't right tonight." He nodded at them, slowly... again.

The rain was coming down heavier than when he walked in. Instead of the cool air feeling refreshing, it had a bite to it. Logan wished he'd opted for the damn sweatshirt. He turned the corner from the bar and was passing the drug store, now dark from being closed, when someone slammed him from behind. He stumbled forward and fell to his knees. He glanced up from his shock just in time to see three men in the reflection of the drug store window. One had his fist raised. Logan rolled out of the way before it came down on his head. Because his reflexes were dulled by alcohol, his attacker managed to slam his shoulder. Excruciating pain shot across his left shoulder.

He jumped to his feet, not entirely sure how he managed it. His right fist, the torpedo as his friends in high school called it, pulled back. Thanks to the tequila, his aim was off, but Sam was a big wall of a guy. His fist struck somewhere between Sam's shoulder and neck. He gasped and stumbled back, apparently, not expecting the impact.

One of the other men standing in the shadows lunged at Logan before he could pull his arm back again. The guy shoved him so hard, Logan fell against the window. It didn't break but his head gave it a good slam. Logan was too drunk to make a plan. He swung out wildly hoping he'd make contact, but he was outnumbered. He lost count after three and was too drunk to count to five. He tried to wind up his right hook again but found his arms were being constrained. Sam's ugly face appeared for a second before his meaty fist slammed Logan in the jaw. Blood filled his mouth. He couldn't tell if it was coming from his tongue or lost teeth, but the taste of it mixed with the alcohol made him puke. Even in his haze, he had the forethought to turn his head and make sure the bloody tequila landed on the shoes of the asshole holding his right arm.

"Fuck, look what you did!" A fist flew at the side of Logan's head. The entire night sky seemed to loop around him. He dropped to his knees with his two assailants still holding tightly to his arms. Logan groaned in pain and worked to get back to his feet. He'd just gotten the soles of his shoes beneath him when Sam slammed him in the stomach three times hard. The wind rushed out of him, and he gasped for air.

Before Logan could catch his breath, a fist hit him square in the jaw. His teeth clacked together so hard, it reverberated through his skull. By the time the wind returned to his lungs, Sam slammed his stomach again. Logan realized then that he'd stopped fighting back. If these fuckers were there to kill him then so be it. The beating had urged the darkness that hovered in the corners of his mind to swoop in and take over. He deserved a painful death. His head filled with the images of Becca sinking below the surface of the murky lake water. Another blow, this one to a rib. He felt the rib give way. As they pounded away at him, he found himself calmly cataloguing all the damage they were doing as if he was watching the beating from a spectator seat. Was this that disconnection Webb was trying so hard to put in his head? It was almost as if there were two of him, the coherent, reasoning Logan Cooper and the madman who couldn't stop himself from being destructive.

Somewhere between the ringing in his ears and the weak groans, his, he assumed, he heard Mick's voice. Logan squinted through his right eye. The left was swollen shut. Mick was holding his signature sawed off baseball bat. When his big black boots didn't do the trick, Mick pulled his secret weapon out from under the counter. Logan had never seen him use it. The flat edged bat being held in Mick's meaty fists was enough of a deterrent.

"You boys realize you're beating the shit out of a cop?" Mick tapped the bat on his hand.

"This guy's a cop?" the guy holding his left arm let it go instantly. "Fuck, Sam, what have you dragged us into?" Logan fell to the ground as they raced off, their feet splashing on the wet sidewalk. Sam took off too. The sidewalk was slippery like oil from the mix of rain and blood. Every breath assured him he had a few broken ribs.

Mick walked over to Logan and stood over him with the same scowl he'd been wearing over the shots of tequila. "You look a right mess. Should I call an ambulance?"

Logan shook his head. "Nope, I'm just going to sit here until the ringing in my ears stops. Thanks though."

"Yeah? Wasn't sure you'd appreciate what I did. For a second there, it seemed like you were just waiting for them to kill you." Mick crouched down. "Whatever it is, Coop, it'll pass. I've always learned that if you take life by the balls, you can survive anything."

Rain sprayed his face as he looked at Mick. "Yeah? First you've got to decide whether or not you even want to grab those balls."

Mick chuckled. "Sure you don't want me to call someone?"

"Nope, I'm good." Only, he was anything but good.

CHAPTER
THIRTY

The relentless rain only added to the surreal night. It poured down Logan's face, washing away the blood, but doing little to cool the fire in his head. Logan's feet felt heavy. Every step sent jarring pain through his body. He stopped twice to throw up. By the time he reached his apartment building, he was sober enough to feel every spot that hurt, and there seemed to be a lot of them. He'd mentally blocked out some of the beating, leaving his state of consciousness to twist his mind into knots.

Rain flowed down the gutters like a wild river. He imagined jumping into the torrent so the rushing water could carry him out to sea and beyond. How often he'd imagined himself walking into the Pacific to follow Becca. Fuck Jeremy for letting him go on thinking that Becca was dead. Fuck Becca for it too.

Logan walked right past his apartment building. The only things waiting inside were the shitty remnants of a life he once lived with Vicky and the stained walls of a crappy apartment. It wasn't a home. He hadn't had a home since Vicky told him to pack his stuff.

Water ran everywhere, from driveways, rain gutters and rooftops. California was getting its thirst quenched for a change. His body was going into that weird shaky shut down mode one suffered after a beating. He was shivering almost uncontrollably by the time he reached Reggie's building. He stood there looking at the place, a rectangular stretch of buildings with air conditioners jutting out from tiny windows. Lights sporadically lit up the covered hallway over the top story. Most of the windows were dark, including Reggie's. She was sleeping. He turned back around, telling himself to go home. He wasn't sure how the night would end if he sat alone in his apartment. It wasn't a place of comfort or security. It was a place that reminded him how much he'd lost and how pathetic his life had become.

Logan spun back and moved slowly toward the stairs, slow motion no longer from the booze but from the physical and mental anguish. He wasn't sure which was worse, but together, they'd brought him to the lowest place he'd ever experienced in his life. A walk into the Pacific was sounding a little too inviting.

The climb up the stairs was pure agony. Halfway, he considered turning around but he kept going. He stood at Reggie's door staring at the number 23 long enough that the vision through his one good eye grew blurry.

He knocked two times and waited. The door cracked open. Reggie peeked out over the chain. "Logan? Holy shit." The door shut and the chain dropped.

She opened the door. Logan's feet were frozen in place. Her flawless tanned skin was barely covered by a white tank shirt and a pair of shorts. She had her gun in her hand.

"Come in," she said as she surveyed him from head to toe.

Logan finally willed a foot forward. Two steps in, he dropped to his knees.

"Coop." Reggie locked the door and put down her gun. She dropped to her knees in front of him. He knew right then she was the best partner he could ever have. "What the hell happened?"

"I didn't kill her, Reg. There's no fucking way I killed Becca. I loved her. I loved her so much it hurt."

Reggie touched the one small spot on his face that wasn't swollen or bruised. Her gentle, warm touch was better than a dose of morphine, though he wouldn't have said no to that either.

"Of course you didn't. That video—it's bullshit. That's what I texted you about."

"But that black hat, the guy who followed her out, that hat wound up in my trash. And the watch—it was in my sock drawer."

His shocking admission caused her to sit back on her

heels. She still looked at him with sympathy and concern, not the revulsion he expected.

Reggie shook her head in disbelief. "Why didn't you tell me? Someone's trying to frame you."

Logan's shoulders slumped. He was quickly reminded of the broken ribs. "Webb hypnotized me. She was there. Becca was there waiting. First, it was good. She always came to my room. It was a night she came, not to hide from her parents, just to be with me. Then she was drowning—" Logan reached up to scrub his face, something he did when upset or frustrated. Reggie's warm fingers wrapped around his wrist to stop him.

"Your face needs ice. Don't touch it. I need to get you dry and to the couch, so I can fix you up. Leave all those bad thoughts alone for now." Reggie pushed to her feet. She lowered her hand.

It took him a second to allow himself to be helped. Earlier, he was sure he was spending his last night on earth. Something had pushed him to seek help, and there was only one person he could trust for that. He'd only known her a few days, but he'd come to the conclusion that everything about her was genuine.

Logan reached up and she took hold of his hand. It took some effort and a few gasps of pain, but he got his feet under him. He swayed forward. Reggie placed her hands on his chest to stop him from falling face-first onto the dingy carpet. It was just as crappy as his place, but with her standing in the middle of the room, he could have been standing in a palace.

His face leaned toward hers. She stared up at him with those big brown eyes. He could have died right then and been happy.

"Come on, Coop. Hope you can walk on your own to the bathroom because I don't think I can carry you." She headed toward the short, dark hallway on her long, smooth legs and bare feet. He watched her, enjoying the way she moved gracefully, confidently before willing his own feet forward.

"I don't happen to have an extra set of men's clothes here in my apartment, so you'll have to pull on a towel. She turned to look at him. "Actually, a few towels. Mine are kind of skimpy." She reached into a shelf in the bathroom, pulled down two lilac colored towels and handed them to him.

The towels were soft and smelled of fresh air.

"Shower off all that blood. I can't afford new furniture. I've got a first aid kit under the kitchen sink." She shrugged. "I'm sort of clumsy with a knife. Looks like you could use some hot coffee too."

Again, he watched her, transfixed. He was cold, wet, bloodied and depressed, but standing near her made him feel as if there was still light to be found.

CHAPTER
THIRTY-ONE

The hot water felt better than he expected. Blood swirled around his feet and slowly disappeared down the drain. The icy shiver in his bones disappeared. Every breath hurt from the cracked ribs, but he was feeling far more human. He patted himself dry, and, at the same time, avoided looking in the mirror. He knew he wouldn't recognize the face staring back at him and not just because of the black eye and fat lip.

The towels felt embarrassingly inadequate, but he managed to cover the important parts. A black bruise was snaking its way along his right side where the ribs had cracked.

Reggie had placed a steaming cup of black coffee and a blueberry muffin on her pine coffee table. Her couch looked too nice for his miserable ass, but standing in the towel was starting to make him feel like he'd gotten up in front of class to do a book report and realized too late he'd forgotten to wear clothes.

He adjusted the towels to make sure everything stayed where it was supposed to stay as he sat down. The tequila, the blood and the puke had made his throat rough and sore, but black coffee went down smoothly. Between the hot shower and coffee, he felt as if he'd just stepped into heaven. It was comfort after a beating in the cold rain.

Reggie walked out of the kitchen with a cup of coffee for herself and a white metal box with the words *first aid* written across the top. She set the kit down on the table next to her coffee cup, then sank to her knees in front of the couch. She winced when she noticed the big bruise on his side.

Her small nose crinkled as she looked up at him. "Broken ribs?"

Logan took a shallow breath, and shut his eyes against the pain. "I'd say so," he grunted as he breathed out.

"I could try and wrap them. Maybe we should get you to an emergency room."

"They can't do much for cracked ribs. They'll heal. Not my first time breathing through broken ribs. It hurts like hell but they heal fast."

Reggie relaxed back a moment and surveyed his face, biting her lip in thought. "I'm going to start with the cut on your forehead and work my way down."

"There's a cut on my forehead?" Logan asked. "Guess that would explain why blood kept getting in my eye."

Reggie opened the box and pulled out cotton gauze and an antiseptic solution. "This might sting a little bit."

"I'll just take a deep breath, then the pain in my ribs will drown out the sting."

She was biting her lush bottom lip again as she rose up on her knees and pressed the antiseptic covered gauze against what he reasoned must have been a pretty good gash.

She leaned over and that sweet lemony scent that he'd already come to count on washed over him. "I think you're going to have a scar."

"I hear women like scars," he said.

"Guess they didn't beat the cockiness out of you." She pulled the gauze away. A thin line of blood remained on the gauze. She fished around in the kit. Again, he found himself watching her. She was a little less sure of herself than usual but then she probably wasn't used to wet, beaten men showing up at her door in the middle of the night. She unwrapped a butterfly shaped bandage and leaned back over him to apply it. "Do you want to tell me what happened?"

"Not much to tell. I danced with a girl. She had brown eyes," he added unnecessarily, but he was sure it had to do with the brown eyes gazing down at him right then. "Apparently, she has a boyfriend who gets jealous easily and who has a lot of friends to back him up."

She sat down with a sigh. "Logan, you do manage to get yourself into a lot of trouble."

"Guilty as charged." As he said it that heavy feeling overtook him again. Was he guilty?

Reggie with her incredible intuition sensed what he was thinking. "I'm going to clean up this cut on your lip, then I want to show you something. I think it'll help put your mind at ease." She paused and touched his hand. "You didn't kill her, Logan. I saw your reaction when you found out it was Becca lying on that grass. Every woman in the world wishes she could be loved like that."

His throat tightened. He knew Reggie was right. His love for Becca had been all-consuming. Back in Layton, he woke up thinking about her, spent his school day looking for her and went to bed hoping she'd be at his window. It wasn't an obsession. It was pure unadulterated love. There was no way to know Becca and not feel it.

Reggie carefully blotted the cut on his lip. "I recommend you avoid hot salsa and salt for a week."

"Yes, doctor." He smiled and flinched. "Ouch. I guess I have to avoid smiles too."

She pressed cotton gauze against his lip again. "Yep, that just got it flowing again." She reached for his hand and lifted it to press against the gauze. "Hold this while I get my laptop."

Still holding the gauze to his lip, Logan relaxed back against the cushions. The soft, velvety fabric felt nice against his skin. His good eye surveyed the room. There were a few framed photos of Reggie and a woman who looked remarkably like her. They were standing in different locations, at the beach, in front of Disneyland, on a bridge over a river. Logan was stupidly glad there were no photos of Reggie standing with a man. Even if she'd been attached to someone down in Los Angeles, it seemed she was unattached now. Not that it mattered, he reminded himself harshly. The quickest way to ruin a great partnership was to fire up a romance. If he kept his job, and, at this point, that could go either way, he planned to fight like hell to keep Reggie as a partner. She was the first positive thing in a long list of negatives. He needed that more than ever right now.

Reggie returned. She sat on the cushion next to him. Her thigh pressed against his as she straddled the laptop between them. "I talked to Fran today. She was so busy she hadn't had time to do any forensic work on the video, but she doesn't need to because I know it was doctored."

"Really? How is that?"

She clicked play, then fast forwarded to the part where he made his starring debut. She paused it just as Logan was about to take a drink of beer. His head dipped to meet the pint.

"Look," she pointed at the screen. "Look at the shelf behind your head, the one with all the bottles of liquor."

Logan leaned forward to get a clearer look at the grainy shot. "Shamrocks," he muttered. He sat up quickly and immediately hunched until the rib pain subsided. "St. Patrick's Day," he said between gritted teeth. The shock of pain lessened, and he was able to take a small breath. "Fucking Sam."

Reggie looked at him. "Sam?"

"The guy who broke my ribs. A bunch of us went to Three Boars on St. Patrick's Day. Haven't been there since. Other than when we talked to Walt about the case." He leaned down to get a better look again and reminded himself not to sit up too quickly. There was nothing like broken ribs to make you move like a ninety-year-old. "Yep, shamrocks. Walt put food coloring in his beer and hung shiny green shamrocks all around the bar. St. Patrick's Day is a big deal at Three Boars." Leaning forward was putting too much pressure on his rib cage. He relaxed back. He stared longingly at the cup of coffee he'd left behind on the coffee table.

Reggie picked it up and handed it to him. "Good thing you're on leave. You're going to be pretty useless for a few days, at least until those ribs heal. And that face—" she looked at him half-sympathetic and half-amused. "You are not going to be sweeping anyone off their feet this week, that's for darn sure."

"Worst part is I'm going to have to explain this face to Dr. Webb. He's already writing shitty reports on me."

"Just tell him the truth. I can see by the lack of swelling on your knuckles that you didn't even fight back. Maybe it'll show him you can control your anger."

Logan looked at his hand. He'd gotten in one shot, but it mostly missed the target. It seemed he had spared himself that pain for a change. "You're a good detective. You're right. I didn't really fight back."

Reggie picked up her cup and sat down on the floor, leaning against the side chair. She peered at him with some scrutiny over the brim of her cup. "Just out of curiosity, why didn't you fight back?"

Logan thought about those long, torturous minutes, cold rain pouring down from the sky and Sam's big, meaty fist pounding him over and over again. His arms had been constrained, but he knew how to get out of that kind of situation. Logan looked at Reggie but didn't say anything.

Reggie put her cup down and brought her knees up, wrapping her arms around them. "Because you'd convinced yourself you did it," she supplied the answer for him.

"All the stars were sure as hell lining up that way," Logan said. "But the video—that proves someone is trying to make me think I did it."

Reggie snapped her fingers. "The kid, Tyler, the one who does all the tech stuff at Three Boars. Remember how shocked Walt was about Tyler's new car. It was pretty sweet and definitely expensive, especially for a kid working part-time in a bar."

Logan figured out where she was going. "Unless someone hands you a nice pile of cash to doctor up a security video."

"Exactly. But how did they get the hat and watch into your apartment? Had you left it unlocked, or did you notice anything unusual like an open window or broken lock?"

"Nope and even though I have exactly zero valuables in that apartment, I still always lock up when I leave." Just as he said it something occurred to him. "Of course, that probably doesn't matter when you have an absentminded apartment manager. Max told me he'd lost his keys for a short bit then found them again hanging exactly where they were supposed to be."

"Sounds like whoever is behind this is clever and determined to make sure you get charged for the murder."

"I'm really going to miss working on this case. How is it going with Gregor?" Logan asked.

Reggie paused. It seemed she was searching for the right words. "You know that terrible itch you get on the bottom of your foot when you're driving? That sort of sums up Gregor."

Logan pressed his arms against his ribs and hunched forward. "No fair. Don't make me laugh."

"Oops, sorry. Let's just say you better get your ass clear of all this trouble soon because I need my asshole partner back."

"See, the asshole part kind of grows on you, doesn't it?"

Reggie shook her head as she stood up. "I'll get you a pillow and a blanket for the couch. Try not to get in any more brawls while I'm gone."

CHAPTER
THIRTY-TWO

Logan turned slightly and opened his eyes. Only one was cooperating. Dim early morning light seeped between the curtains, casting the room in shadows. It took him a second to remember where he was. Reggie's apartment was crummy, but she'd hung curtains and covered her small kitchen table with a yellow checked tablecloth. There was even a brightly colored rug at the entrance to the kitchenette. She was obviously spending most of her salary keeping her mom in a nice full-time care facility. From what he'd learned about her childhood, she'd grown up dirt poor. She was finally making decent money, not grand money but enough for a decent life, and she had to pour all of it into keeping her mom cared for. It wasn't fair but then such was life, a whole shitload of unfairness.

The front door opened. Instinctually, he sat up fast and reached toward his side for his gun. He was quickly reminded of the broken ribs.

Reggie strolled inside dressed in running shorts and a sweatshirt. She dropped his clothes on the coffee table. "All washed and fluffed. Couldn't get one spot of blood out of the jeans, but I figure old bloodstains coupled with that future scar should help you score with the ladies. You just have to come up with a better war story than Sam beat the crap out of me because I danced with his brown-eyed girl." She put her fists on her slim hips. "How are you feeling this morning?"

"On a scale of one to ten?" he asked. "Like something the cat threw up."

"Did not realize cat barf was on the one to ten scale. Maybe they can add a cat hawking up a hair ball on that stupid little chart they have in triage in the emergency room. You know, the one with all the smiley faces in different degrees of distress."

"I know that chart and I've been on both ends of it. Today, I'm somewhere near the guy who has his eyes squeezed shut and his mouth pulled into a straight line." Logan reached for the clothes. They were still warm from the dryer and smelled as if he'd just run through a field of flowers. "Thanks for this. I wasn't loving the idea of walking home clad only in your tiny lavender towels."

"I've got yogurt and granola, or I can make you a bowl of oatmeal," she said as she filled her coffee pot.

"Coffee only please." He rubbed the side of his jaw. "Now that I'm totally sober everything hurts a lot more. I think I just about bit a hole through my tongue." Logan pulled on his underwear and jeans.

"I do have some leftover blueberry muffins if you're interested. You could break off tiny bites and tuck them carefully into your mouth."

He padded across the floor shirtless and barefoot. Four muffins had been carefully wrapped in cellophane. "Guess those are your mom's favorites," he said.

Reggie nodded gently. "For some reason, when I bring her blueberry muffins, she has this quick moment of clarity where she still knows me." Her voice wavered but only for a second. "It's just nice to hear her say my name."

"Can't imagine how hard it would be, Reg. I'm so sorry."

She sniffled discreetly. "Enough about that. We need to get you in the clear on this case. I'm talking to Derrick's husband this morning. We're having a zoom meeting. Turns out he was so devastated by Derrick's death, he didn't want to stay in California. He packed up and moved back home to North Carolina. You can sit in but you're a silent partner at the moment."

"Speaking of partners, where is Gregor this morning? Leaving you on your own?"

"He had to go to his niece's sweet sixteen brunch. We're meeting up later at the precinct." She said it with a little twist of her mouth. "I was just as glad to do this interview alone. Gregor tends to—"

"Rub people the wrong way?"

"Yeah, poor guy. I feel bad for people who don't realize they're irritating."

"Not sure how much of your sympathy he deserves." Logan walked back to the coffee table, bent over like a ninety-year-old man and picked up his t-shirt. He stared at it dauntingly as if it contained a nest of wasps. "Next time I get beat up, I've got to wear a button up shirt. Much easier to put on with broken ribs."

"Do you need help?" she asked.

"Nope, I got myself into this, and I'm going to suffer through putting on a t-shirt all by myself."

"Great. I'm going to shower."

After a long, cautious process of putting in one arm, his head and then the second arm, Logan was finally dressed. He walked across the room to the kitchen to refill his coffee cup. The kitchenette was no more than a hot plate, an apartment sized fridge and an oven under a cracked tile counter, but there was a basket of lemons and limes in one corner and a cute little rack of various spices sitting next to a wooden cutting board. Two ceramic salt and pepper shakers in the shape of chubby cats sat on the ledge of a small window. The window had a view of the parking lot and the concrete block wall that mostly hid the trash bin. Like his apartment, it was a depressing place to live, only, somehow, Reggie had made it anything but depressing. She'd grown up without much and knew how to make any place a home. For him, home had meant the two bedroom bungalow Vicky and he had bought the year he was promoted to detective. Vicky was like Reggie, she could make any space livable, comfortable. Moving out of the bungalow, moving away from Vicky, he'd somehow convinced himself he'd never live in a comfortable place again. Even now that Vicky had remarried and he was no longer handing out alimony payments, he'd remained in his shitty apartment. How could any place be home without Vicky?

Reggie's couch was so comfortable, Logan found himself drifting off into a late morning snooze. Sleep was the only time he could forget that every inch of his body was sore. He'd only just started a weird dream where the chubby cat salt and pepper shakers had come to life when Reggie returned. Her long, thick hair was wet and brushed back from her face. She was incredible to look at. She sat down on the floor between the couch and coffee table.

She pulled her laptop toward her and placed her badge, a notepad and pen next to it. "James Aronson, Derrick's husband, should be logging on any second." She ripped off a piece of paper and handed me an extra pen. "Take notes so I don't have to interrupt the flow of conversation by awkwardly pausing to write down details." Logan's mind went straight to Dr. Webb and his annoying note taking habits. "If there's something you want to ask just write it. It's probably better if you stay off camera and silent. We don't want Castillo to find out you were involved."

Logan smiled at the side of her face as she logged onto her video conference. "I'll bet you were one of those kids who never disrupted a class, never broke a rule and, worst of all, never missed a homework assignment."

She lifted her finger in the air to draw three check marks. "Your point?" She tapped his knee. "Never mind. He's logging on."

A thirty something man wearing a blue polo shirt and a neatly trimmed mustache came into view.

"Mr. Aronson?" Reggie asked.

"Actually, my name is Preston, James Preston. Derrick was Mr. Aronson. We kept our own names. Too much hassle to change them."

"I apologize," Reggie said politely. She picked up her badge. "I'm Detective Reggie Hawkins from the Santa Cruz Police Department. How is the weather in North Carolina?"

The badge caused his expression to tighten, a common response from people who didn't get a close-up view of a cop's badge too often. Her casual question about the weather caused the tightness to disappear.

"It's hot and humid. I miss the nice, cool summer weather in Santa Cruz."

"Do you think you'll come back?" she asked.

He shook his head. "I don't have any reason to be there. Every place reminds me of Derrick." His voice broke. He reached for something and brought his hand back with a tissue. "Promised myself I wouldn't cry but you'll have to excuse me. The pain is still very raw and intense."

"Absolutely and please feel free to cry as much as you need."

Logan was getting a rare opportunity to watch his partner interview someone without his input, almost as if he was observing from another room. She was expert at putting people at ease. She had such a natural charm about her there was no way to feel uneasy, badge or not.

"Mr. Preston, did you ever meet Derrick's friend, Ann Robbins?"

"I never met her, but Derrick talked about her a lot. He said she was one of the most honest and refreshing people he'd met in a long while." His cheeks grew pink. "Aside from me. They had a lot in common."

"Oh? How's that?"

Preston discreetly wiped his nose. "Derrick grew up in an abusive household. His father was a horrid person. His mom didn't know where to turn, so she just ignored a lot of what was happening. From what Derrick said about Ann, she grew up in the same kind of household, a terrible father and a mother who had no control over the situation. They met at Three Boars on Fridays just to hang out. I know Derrick really looked forward to seeing her, and I think Ann was quite fond of Derrick. He was a gentle soul, the kind of person you wanted to be around if you were feeling like the world was closing in on you." He paused to swallow and catch his breath.

"I'm sorry to broach the painful subject, but I understand Derrick committed suicide?"

"Five weeks ago, Thursday. I got home from the office and found him." His voice grew thin and reedy. "He hung himself." Reggie paused for Preston to collect himself. Just like the day they discovered Becca's body, when Logan needed time to gather himself, she sat quietly, patiently. "Derrick had a lot of problems with depression. It was a result of his childhood. When his abusive father found out Derrick was gay, he threw him out of the house with only the clothes on his back. Derrick lived on the streets for awhile, but he pulled himself up by his bootstraps, so to speak. He was determined to remake his life, out from under the shadow of his father."

It was easy to see why Derrick and Ann formed such a tight bond. They had a lot in common, most of it hardship and tragedy, but sometimes, those commonalities were more binding than good things.

"So the depression became too hard to handle? Or was there something that triggered Derrick to commit suicide?"

Logan was feeling a little antsy. She was spending too much time on Derrick when what she needed was to find out information on Ann Robbins. He was about to scribble out move on to Ann Robbins when James said something significant.

"No triggers. Just a lifelong struggle with depression. A while back Ann had mentioned that she was attending therapy sessions that included hypnosis." Logan sat up a little too straight and was quickly reminded by his own body to knock it off. "She said it was helping her peel back some of the painful memories. He wasn't ready to try it though."

Logan scribbled out the question. "Who was her doctor?" He slipped the paper in front of her.

"Do you happen to know what doctor Ann was seeing for hypnosis? Was she recommending anyone in particular?"

James rubbed his chin. "I don't think any name ever came up. By the way, you mentioned triggers."

"Yes?" Reggie asked.

"A few months back, Derrick told me that Ann had become despondent. Something had happened but she wouldn't tell him what it was. He was quite upset because they always confided in each other. He was a little hurt I think. Whatever it was, it had changed Ann's mood entirely."

"Did Derrick ever mention anyone in Ann's life, anyone who might have been causing her anguish?"

James was polite enough to give it some thought. He'd never met Ann Robbins, and he only knew about her through discussions with Derrick. "He did mention that awhile back, Ann was feeling anxious about something that had to do with her past. I could have sworn he said she was close to finding out whether or not she had a twin sister. She was waiting to find out for sure. She mentioned to Derrick that if it was true, it explained a lot about her mom's mental health problems. I figured it was like those three guys back in the eighties, the triplets who found each other and then discovered they'd all been adopted out to different families. Only the strange thing about that was Ann insisted she wasn't adopted. The whole story was pretty wild. Ann wasn't entirely sure it was going to pan out, but I know she spoke of it a lot to Derrick."

"I can tell you that it is true. Ann did have a twin sister who was adopted by another family."

"Wow. It would be shocking enough to discover you had a sibling but even more so if the person was your twin."

"Unfortunately, Ann was murdered before she found out the truth," Reggie noted grimly.

James's face dropped. "Such a tragedy." His voice was breaking again. He looked up. "It's hard, you know? Life. Derrick and Ann survived brutal childhoods. In the end, they died too soon."

"I don't want to take up any more of your time, Mr. Preston. You have my number. If there's anything else you think of, please don't hesitate to call."

"I hope you find this monster soon," he said. "Goodbye, Detective Hawkins."

The call ended. Reggie leaned back against the couch. "I wonder if Ann ever mentioned anything about a specific therapist to her friend Janey? I'll call her today to see if she knows anything. I'm also going to go have a talk with Tyler at Three Boars. I'm hoping he'll be the golden ticket to this whole case." She pushed up to her feet. "I've got to take the muffins to my mom. She has physical therapy in the afternoon, so this is the best time to see her." Reggie looked down at him and crinkled her nose. "You still look like something a cat threw up. You're welcome to stay here on the couch and rest."

"Nah, I think I'll go home, take some aspirin and sink into my bed for the rest of the weekend. Do you think you could give me a lift home?"

"On my motorcycle?" she asked.

"That's right. I forgot about that. Yeah, why not? It's only a few blocks, and if they pull us over for me not having a helmet, I know someone who can help us get out of the ticket."

CHAPTER
THIRTY-THREE

Aspirin, the kind with the added bonus of a sleep aid, helped Logan sleep through the rest of the weekend. His ribs were still sore, but as long as he didn't make any sudden moves or take any deep breaths he was good. A long hot shower, three cups of coffee and a piece of toast helped clear his head for his therapy session. The black eye, fat lip and gash in his forehead were going to give away the obvious, that he got into yet another altercation. Only this time was different. Like Reggie pointed out, his knuckles were fine. He didn't fight back. Webb didn't need to know that he'd gotten so drunk and had sunken so low Friday night that he didn't care if someone beat the life out of him.

Reggie had helped ease some of the despair he was feeling. The video was proof that someone was trying to frame him for Becca's murder. But who the hell could it be? He was drawing nothing but blanks. The husband was still at the top of his list. If it weren't for that rock-solid alibi, Logan was sure Reggie would be pursuing that lead too.

The deluge of rain that had swept into town Friday was long gone. The weekend had warmed right up to the usual summer heat. There wasn't a puddle or wet gutter to be seen. Monday mornings were usually rough for traffic, but on this particular morning he glided right through to Webb's hideous building. He'd made his mind up that he wasn't going to be hypnotized again. It just wasn't sitting right with him, and it made him feel like shit. How cocky he'd been thinking that hypnosis wouldn't work on him. He couldn't remember a lot about the hypnotherapy but the progression of time and the odd memories left behind had assured him he'd not only slipped under but slipped under good.

This morning there hadn't even been a coastal fog to cool the air. The sun was stroking every inch of the city as he climbed out of his truck. After spending most of the weekend alone in his apartment, drifting in and out of a heavy, sweet sleep provided by the sleep aid, Logan had a lot of time to think. Aside from determining that he would no longer submit to being hypnotized, something else occurred to him. So far, everyone who was close to Ann, her husband, her best friend, Janey, and her friend and confidante, Derrick, had noticed a sudden change in her mood. It had happened around her birthday, May 4th.

Derrick's husband, James, had mentioned she was

trying hypnosis. What if the hypnotherapy had pushed some horrid memories to the surface? Repressed memories came out in therapy. Logan knew that Ray was always abusive with his fist and his mouth, but what if he'd done more than hit Becca? She'd never said anything about him molesting her, but what if that was hidden somewhere in a locked box of memories? Could it be that something even uglier came out in her therapy session, and it was bad enough to throw her into a depression? He planned to bring it up to Reggie. It would solve the mystery of why her mood had suddenly darkened.

Logan pushed the button and said 'it's me' before Webb could say a word. The door buzzed and he walked inside. The short trip in the elevator pushed an idea into his head. He was off the case. Sometimes not having the trappings of being official was better. He had the freedom to do whatever the hell he wanted. He was pretty sure Webb had not been seeing Ann Robbins as a patient. It seemed as if it would have come up when they were talking about the murder and Logan's relationship with Becca. Then again, doctors weren't allowed to discuss anything about a patient. During investigations, he'd met some doctors who would bend that code of ethics just a bit, some that would ignore it altogether and some that stuck to it by the letter, not allowing even a name to slip unless there was a warrant. Webb seemed like the latter, a real tight ass who prided himself on sticking to the rules.

Logan surmised it wouldn't hurt to glance at his appointment book.

Webb had the door ajar when he reached the office. Logan walked inside. The appointment book was splayed open, he assumed to today's date. It was a thick enough book that Logan felt confident there would be a few prior months of appointments in the pages. This was going to be a big nothing, but he could at least check one hypnotist off the list of hypnotherapists available in the city.

"Uh, Dr. Webb—" Logan began his simple plan. "There was a woman pacing the sidewalk in front of your building. She looked distressed and was talking to herself. I could have sworn I heard her mumble something about Dr. Webb. I thought maybe it was a patient having some kind of meltdown."

Webb looked utterly baffled. "Really? Are you sure she mentioned my name?

"Webb is pretty easy to recognize. Maybe I'm wrong and she's fine."

He grunted quietly. "I'd better check it out. Go on in and have a seat. I'll be right back." Webb rushed out.

Logan waited for the elevator doors to close and start its short descent. He raced over to the appointment book. Names, dates and times were written in perfect handwriting, and each page had been methodically ruled into perfect squares. Logan would have expected no less. He flipped back a few months to April and May. By his calculations, Webb was already out at the sidewalk discovering that the mystery lady was long gone. It would only take him two minutes to get back to the office.

Logan pulled out his phone and took pictures of the April and May pages. The rumble of the elevator heading back up startled him. He'd overestimated the time. He flipped the book back to the current week and slipped into the therapy room. He sat down so hard on the solid couch, it jarred his ribs. He was bent over just catching his breath when Webb stepped inside.

"Are you all right, Logan?"

Logan nodded and sipped some breaths in between gritted teeth. The pain subsided and he sat up straighter.

"Good god, you've been in a fight. I hadn't even noticed. By the way, there was no woman, but I have a few patients that it might have been. Did the woman have red, curly hair by any chance?"

Logan hadn't anticipated a detailed question. "She might have. She had a hat pulled down over her head. You know what? Maybe I misread the whole scene. Sorry."

"Well, it seems you had a rough weekend. Do you want to talk about it?"

"I danced with the wrong woman at a bar, and her jealous boyfriend took it out on me." Logan lifted his hand. "But look. My knuckles are pretty as a picture. I didn't fight back."

Webb stared at him, tapping his pen against his chin. "That might be a story in itself. Maybe we can delve deeper into that during hypnosis."

"No can do, Dr. Webb. No offense but that hypnosis is messing with my head. I'm in here to get it straightened out not more twisted."

While he worked hard not to show any reactions, Webb's disappointment was clear even on his smooth forehead. "On the contrary, I think we are making progress, Logan. Sometimes you have to go through some rough sessions to get to the heart of the matter. Does this have to do with you being taken off the case?"

"Yes, thanks to you, I'm on administrative leave."

"Of course, I didn't make that decision. I just let Captain Castillo know that we'd been making break-throughs but that we still had a long, hard path in front of us." Webb sat forward. "I think you've been having black-outs during your fits of rage. Those can be very danger-ous. We need to deal with that."

"First of all, fits of rage is an overstatement. I might be zeroed in on my opponent when I'm angry, but I don't think I've ever blacked out."

Webb sat back pulling his mouth in as a way to show he didn't agree with Logan's assessment. "Without the hypnosis it might be harder to know one way or another. Since you want to skip hypnotherapy, let's talk about the fight you had."

The session felt interminably long. It occurred to Logan that hypnosis had helped the time fly. He told Webb about the bar and the many rounds of tequila and even added in a little dig that Webb was responsible for the shots because he got him put on leave. He told him how he'd felt so low about everything, about losing Becca before he even had a chance to talk to her again and how the case had become a twisted mess. He left out the pieces about important evidence showing up in his own apartment.

Webb seemed as bored with the session as Logan. When he gave the silent signal, the traditional closing of the notebook, discarding of the pen and uncrossing of his legs, Logan was eager to leave. While he was retelling the story of the fight outside the bar, another notion popped into his head. He wasn't sure how many hypnotherapists there were in Santa Cruz, and he had a feeling Reggie was already working on that list, but he was inside a building with two therapists. So far, he'd only ever met one. The other had been as invisible as a ghost. Logan knew he existed because he'd met one of his patients, Quinn, the guy with the punctuality obsession and candy bar habit. Those seemed like issues that hypnosis might help.

Logan reached the outer door. "Is your partner across the way a hypnotherapist too?"

"Dr. Jordan is not my partner." Webb sounded uncharacteristically agitated that I would even suggest it. "We just work in the same building." Logan wasn't getting any vibes of camaraderie or exchanging of professional ideas from his response. "And yes, Jordan dabbles in hypnotherapy." Webb obviously didn't have a great deal of respect for his colleague across the hall.

Logan nodded. "Building is still pretty empty, eh?"

Webb's mouth pursed tightly as he glanced down at his appointment book. "I've found people are very cheap when it comes to leases. I've finally gotten two tenants for the first floor. I'm expecting them next week. If you don't mind, I have just enough time to transcribe some notes before my next patient."

"Right. I'll get out of your hair."

"And, Logan, try and stay out of trouble. I'm going to have to include the bar fight in my next report."

Logan nodded. "I was pretty sure that was the case. See you Wednesday." Logan made sure the outer door was shut behind him, then he headed toward the elevator and pushed the button. It arrived. He pressed the down button without stepping inside. Then he slipped around the corner to the next hallway. There was nothing easier than hiding out in a mostly empty building.

He wasn't sure where the hallway stakeout would lead, if anywhere at all, but he was on leave and didn't have a damn thing to do all day except think about the fact that he was on leave and that goober Gregor was working on his case with his new partner.

The hallway and the elevator stayed empty for what seemed an eternity. His phone showed only ten minutes had passed. He decided to check out the photos he took of Webb's appointment book. Before he could open the picture wide, a door opened and shut around the corner. He peered one eye around the corner and saw Webb march across the hallway and enter Dr. Jordan's office without so much as a knock. The deep rumble of their conversation rolled toward him, but he couldn't make out the words.

Logan crept quietly down the hallway and stopped just short of Jordan's door so he could dash around the corner again at a moment's notice.

"I've told you again and again, I won't keep covering for you." Webb sounded irritated.

An angry laugh followed. "You must be joking. With everything I do for you, you have the nerve to complain." The second voice, Dr. Jordan's presumably, was less smooth, higher pitched than Webb's. Logan couldn't get a good visual in his head of what Jordan looked like or whether he was young or old. One thing was certain, there didn't seem to be any big friendship between the two doctors, even if they were the only two doctors in the building and they were both therapists. "Don't come over here lecturing me, Ben. I don't have time for your nonsense."

"I just need you to do your job," Webb said. "We can discuss this later. I have an appointment to prepare for."

Footsteps neared. Logan took off fast around the corner, then stooped over to stop the pain shooting through his rib cage. He held his breath and waited for it to pass and for Webb to cross the hallway and shut his own door. He peeked around the corner again. The coast was clear. He hurried to the elevator, punched the button and flinched when it made its characteristic ping. He looked over his shoulder. Webb's door was still shut. The elevator opened and he stepped inside. He'd hoped to run into a client for either doctor entering the building so he could ask a few questions, but he never saw anyone.

He was just as glad to step into the fresh air. The pain in his ribs wasn't nearly as bad, but he wasn't anywhere close to a hundred percent. His phone vibrated as he sat in the truck. It was Reggie.

"Hey, Reg, what's going on? Anything new?"

"Gregor is out sick. He ate a bad piece of chicken at his niece's party."

"Guess you got lucky," Logan quipped.

She laughed. "I wouldn't wish food poisoning on anyone, not even Gregor, but I'm just as glad to be on my own. First of all, how is the guy who is supposed to be sitting next to me?"

"Good. Healing up. I just left the therapist. I took pictures of pages in his appointment book back a few months just to see if Ann Robbins was his patient. By the way, you should—"

"Find a list of hypnotherapists in the area?" she finished for him. "Working on it. There are at least fifty therapists in a twenty-five mile radius but only twenty or so who mention hypnotherapy on their web pages. I'll get to work contacting them. Not sure how many will be willing to release the name of a patient even if she's no longer alive. I also put in a call to Janey, Ann's best friend, just in case she can remember a doctor's name."

"What did the kid with the cherry red Camaro have to say about the doctored video?" Logan asked.

"I was just getting to that. First of all, I thought Tyler was going to pee his pants when I asked him about it. He got so nervous, Walt had to bring him a paper bag to stop him from hyperventilating. It was just like with the kid, Mickey, who stole the car. Tyler found an envelope stuck under the windshield wiper on his old car. It was a typed note. No cash this time but a promise to give him four grand if he spliced the St. Patrick's Day security footage with the footage from the night Ann Robbins was murdered. Tyler was to send proof of the video splicing to a cell phone. I checked out the number. It was a burner phone, cash transaction."

"This is no nitwit killer. He had all his bases covered. I fucking hate that." Logan eased back against the seat. His ribs relaxed with him. He groaned as the ache floated through his whole body.

"You sound like you're a hundred years old," Reggie commented. "You should take a long walk today. Fresh air and movement would do you good. Much better than gluing yourself to the couch."

"Sure thing, ma," Logan said with a Southern twang.

"Anyhow," she huffed, "here's what I came up with that doesn't have to do with hypnosis. Whoever paid to have that video doctored must have known you were in Three Boars on St. Patrick's Day."

Logan turned on the truck to start the air. It blew warm air against his face and it smelled like engine oil. "I guess that makes sense. Otherwise, the kid would have had to sift through a lot of video footage to find me standing at the bar. Well, shit," Logan said as the weight of that finally dawned on him. "I was there with about half the precinct that night. But who would want to frame me? And why?"

"Is there someone itching to have your position?" she asked. She sipped something through a straw.

Logan laughed. "Uh, every other guy on the force."

"Really?" she asked confused.

"Yeah, it's not my position as much as my partner."

"Oh, right," she said dryly.

It was just as he'd expected. She was so used to being ogled by men she waved it off as annoying, like a persistent fly or mosquito.

"And I used to have a prime parking spot," he continued. "But I lost that too."

"Is there anyone in the precinct who might be moonlighting as a cold-blooded killer?" she asked, ignoring the mention of his parking spot. He'd already resigned himself to never parking there again. He just hoped he'd come out of this whole case with a job. The parking spot seemed trivial now.

"I mean, I know some of them are idiots and some

have cheated on their spouses, but they know I don't give a shit about their personal lives. I don't know everyone well and stranger things have happened, but it's hard to think someone in the precinct is a killer. If so, how did they know Ann Robbins?"

"I've watched that video multiple times. There isn't anything about the guy in the black hat that looks familiar, his walk, his posture, the way he moves. It's all normal, nothing unusual or unexpected. Just need to see his damn face. Whoever he is, I think we can safely say he was also at the bar on St. Patrick's Day, and he must know you. I guess that means it could have been anyone in the bar that night and not necessarily someone we work with."

"That place was packed, and I'd had enough beers that the faces were probably mostly a blur."

"That's what I figured. Since you have so much time on your hands, try to write down the names of people who were out drinking green beer with you. It might help you to look at a list."

"I do happen to have spare time today."

"Later and send the list when you have it."

Logan hung up. No one had entered the building yet. Considering there were only two doctors inside that wasn't too surprising. He opened the photos of the appointment book and zoomed in on the first one. Each page showed a week at a glance. The one he opened was for the second week in April. The writing was precise, like the kind of print an architect or draftsman might use. It was exactly the style of writing he expected from the fussy, prim doctor. Session times were written on the left and names on the right. Interestingly, Webb had used two colors of ink, black and red. Every other entry was in red ink. It seemed Webb had five appointments each day. Logan skimmed the names on a few of the pages from April and May. Not surprisingly, there was no patient named Ann Robbins in his appointment book. It would have been strange to find it considering Webb and Logan had discussed the murder case more than once. It would have been bizarre for Webb to not show any reaction at all. The more he thought about it, it would have been just like Webb to sit stone-faced while Logan talked about her. But Ann Robbins had not been Webb's patient. They could cross one doctor off the list. He wasn't entirely sure how much finding her therapist would help. Extracting information past the brick wall of doctor's confidentiality was a slow, painstaking process. Logan hated to see the case drag on much longer. Like her husband had so aptly mentioned the day Ann's body was found, the farther away you got from the crime, the harder it was to catch the killer.

Logan started his truck. He had no place to go but home and home was shit. This time off was the last thing he needed. The report about the bar fight was only going to assure the assholes sitting in their sweaty offices that they'd made the right choice putting him on leave.

CHAPTER
THIRTY-FOUR

Logan rarely took advice from anyone, but he'd gotten to his apartment and found himself putting on his shoes for a walk. What he really needed was a long, hard run to ease the layers of frustration building up from not being able to work on the case. But his ribs weren't going to stand for a heavy run. After a few miles of a fast walk, he remembered just how fucking boring walking around a city, and not the scenic end of town, could be. At one point, he was keeping pace with a garbage truck. He tried slowing down and speeding up to avoid the noise and odor of the truck, but it was almost as if the driver was going out of his way to ruin his walk. He spun around and headed back home. He was surprised to find Reggie at his door with two brown paper bags.

"Tell me that's whiskey." He motioned toward the bags. "And you will quickly become the best partner a cop could ever have."

"I brought you a sandwich, a vegetarian sandwich," she added with a pointed look that said don't argue just eat it.

"Guess you're trying to convert me. I've got to say, don't get your hopes up." Logan unlocked his door.

"Not trying to convert you. I've already written you off as hopeless. I just don't spend my hard-earned money on meat... ever." She placed the bags on the wobbly little table sitting near the window. It was his dining room. The sight of it, lopsided and strewn with empty chip bags and beer bottles, embarrassed him. He hurried over and snatched up all the garbage and carried it over to the kitchen trash.

Reggie had her arms crossed when he looked up from the trash. "No recycling?" she asked. "Our entire planet is going to shit."

Logan leaned into the trash and pulled out the three empty beer bottles. "You're pretty bossy when you have the upper hand, you know that?"

She sat down with a smug grin. "That's funny. I always have the upper hand. You just haven't figured that out yet."

He tilted his head side to side. "I'm starting to come around to that conclusion." He sat down harder than his ribs expected. The jarring pain made the breath stick in his lungs for a second until the ache subsided. "I fucking hate broken ribs." Logan picked up his sandwich. All kinds of green stuff was sticking out the sides. "Now, barbecued ribs, that's a whole other story," he said with a teasing wink before biting into the sandwich. He nodded as he chewed and swallowed. "Not bad for a salad tucked between bread. Anything new?" He picked up a fallen piece of lettuce and considered pushing it back between the slices of bread, then decided there was more than enough of it on the sandwich.

Reggie twisted open the top on her water flask. "James left me a message to call him."

It took me a second to remember who James was. "Oh right, the husband of Ann's friend, Derrick. What did he have to say?"

"He said he might have something, but he didn't say what on the message. I tried calling him back but got his voicemail. So we're in a game of phone tag. I'm going to try again later." She chewed, swallowed a bite and sat back with a frustrated sigh. "The truth is I need my partner. I'm new here. I don't know my way around yet. It really sucks that they took you off this case, and I've learned that Gregor is about as helpful as a splinter under the fingernail. He called me an hour ago sounding as if he was at death's door. I think he was just being dramatic. To embellish his story, he started in about details of sitting on the toilet all morning. I told him I didn't need to hear any more and that I hoped he felt better soon."

"That sounds like Gregor." Logan took another bite. He wasn't hating the sandwich, crunchy greens and all.

"Speaking of Gregor, actually speaking of all our coworkers—" she started.

Logan shook his head. "I haven't written out the list

yet. And before you can give me a disapproving scowl, I didn't get to it because, as you might have noticed"—he pointed down at his athletic shoes—"I took your advice and went on a walk."

"Good for you." Reggie picked up a leaf of fallen spinach and ate it. "How was it?"

"Would have been better if I'd been walking along the beach or on a hiking trail, but it did loosen up some of the parts that hurt. I hoped it would give me some clarity about the case too, but frankly, I'm baffled about the whole damn thing. I've worked cases where someone tried to frame someone else but never when the killer was trying to frame me."

Reggie wrapped up the second half of her sandwich.

"Seriously?" Logan asked. "The thing was mostly leaves and you've had enough with one half?"

"Do you want my other half?" she asked.

"I think my body might go into shock with so many leafy greens."

Two sexy lines always creased the right side of Reggie's mouth whenever she smiled. "I was thinking, maybe the list will be a waste of time. At least that list." She lifted her gaze. It was a serious, enough of the banter kind of expression. "Logan, is there anyone from your past, anyone who wanted to get back at you? You told me all your friends in Layton had a thing for Becca. Is there someone who might have held onto an obsession with her? Someone who knew the two of you had been involved? What about Jeremy, the guy we visited? He's probably one of the few people who knew Becca was still alive. He knew she'd taken on a whole new identity. It's obvious he loved her."

Logan was shaking his head before she finished. "You met him, Reg. He's a neurotic, housebound guy with a hoarding problem."

"But you said he was the smartest person you knew," she reminded him. "If we've learned nothing"—she paused—"and that's an understatement, we've learned that the person who killed Ann Robbins is smart, calculating and pays attention to details."

"Jeremy is incredibly smart, but he's one of those gentle souls who picks up spiders to carry them outside. And his house—the way he was living—he's got some major mental health issues, always has. But a cold-blooded killer? It's just too far of a stretch. Just like me, he would never have hurt Becca."

"All right, all right. I'm convinced it's not Jeremy, but anyone else you can think of?" She picked up her water. "I'm just grasping at straws here." Reggie's phone rang, and Logan had a ping of envy. When he was off work, he hardly ever got phone calls. Vicky called but rarely. His parents were too busy with their golfing and retirement to spend much time on the phone, and most of his friends were also attached to Vicky. They'd all migrated her direction, leaving him without much of a social life. Most of the time he was fine with that, but when he wasn't at work, he realized how small his world really was.

"I think this is James," Reggie said. "Hello, Detective Hawkins." She mimicked using a pen. Logan hopped up and scrounged through his kitchen junk drawer for a pen. He carried three back, scratched a few on the crumpled paper lunch bag and found one with ink. Reggie reached for the pen, pulled the bag closer and scribbled something down. "Right, that's great. Thank you so much for calling. If there's anything else you can call me anytime." She hung up and put the phone down. "James was going through some of Derrick's personal papers trying to put things in order, and he came across a page where Derrick had scribbled down a name. James had never heard the name, but he thought it might be the doctor Ann had mentioned." Reggie picked up the brown paper bag. "Dr. Francis Jordan," she read.

Logan sat forward so fast, he wrenched his ribs. He pressed his arm against them and gritted his teeth in pain as he spoke. "That's the doctor who works across the hallway from my therapist, Dr. Webb. I haven't met him or seen him. Webb leased a huge, modern building, but he's been pricing his rent so high, he hasn't been able to get any takers, just Dr. Jordan. They practice the same kind of medicine, including hypnotherapy, but I don't get any sense that they're buddies."

Reggie was scrolling through her phone to find the

phone number for Jordan's practice. "If you haven't met the man, how do you know that?"

"Webb always gives curt, irritated answers when I ask about the doctor across the way. So I sort of hid out in the hallway this morning."

Reggie's smooth, dark brow arched.

"What can I say? I'm bored. I thought I'd catch a glimpse of Dr. Jordan. Webb told me he was a hypnotherapist too. I guess I thought I could find a way to his appointment book." Logan waved his hand. "Like I said, I'm bored. I didn't see Jordan, but after Webb thought I'd left the floor, he marched across and had a few terse words for his tenant. Something about covering for him. Jordan was just as terse back."

Reggie sat forward and tapped the screen on her phone. "There's a cheaply done website with a contact number and an email." She waited. "Damn, it's going to voicemail." She scoffed. "It's just the Google lady telling me to leave a message. Guess the doc is too busy to personalize his voice mailbox. "Hello, this is Detective Reggie Hawkins of the Santa Cruz Police Department. I'm looking for information about a former patient of yours. If you could call me back at this number as soon as possible it would be greatly appreciated." She hung up. "I guess I'll have to make a trip over to the doctor's office."

"Now I'm really pissed about this bullshit leave," Logan said.

"Maybe I could talk to Castillo, you know, let him know I really need you for this case," she offered.

Logan balled up the sandwich wrapper. "Nah, I don't want you to stick your neck out too early. It's only your second week. Just keep me posted, eh? I want to hear all about the elusive Dr. Jordan."

CHAPTER
THIRTY-FIVE

Morning light squeaked through the slim gaps on the bedroom mini blinds. Tanya's thigh brushed against his. It stirred Logan awake in every sense of the word. His arm wrapped around her and he pulled her naked body against his. She moaned lightly and stretched in his arms. "I can't stay," she said softly. "I'm going to be late for work."

His disappointment was purely physical. He removed his arm. Tanya leaned up on one elbow and smiled at him. She had jewel colored green eyes and a tiny scar just over her top lip from when she was a little girl and she tried to put a doll's dress on her grandmother's cat. Logan had dated Tanya a few months after the divorce. What they had was nice, although it was mostly physical. She'd just ended a long relationship too. They'd found exactly what they needed in each other's company, human touch without the emotional attachment. They still saw each other every month or so whenever Tanya was in town and horny.

"You look bone weary, Detective Cooper," she teased. "I noticed you were not quite your, how should I put it, your stellar self last night."

"Ah, that would be the broken ribs."

"Seriously? Why didn't you tell me?"

He reached up and traced his finger around her nipple. It puckered instantly. "You called and said you needed, and I quote, a good solid fuck. Who was I to deny you that? I did consider mentioning the broken ribs except a good solid fuck sounded just as good to me. Sorry if I was a disappointment."

She laughed and kissed his mouth lightly. "Not a disappointment. On a scale of one to ten you're usually at nine or ten. Last night was a seven."

He absently rubbed the stubble on his chin. "Huh, a seven with broken ribs. I can live with that."

"I'm going to take a quick shower." Tanya climbed out of bed. Logan allowed himself the pleasure of watching her stroll naked across his bedroom to the bathroom. His phone rang as the shower turned on.

It was getting easier to sit up. Logan rested back against the wall behind his bed. Somehow, the coolness of the plaster eased the ache in his ribs. "Hey, Reggie, what have you got?"

"First, you might have mentioned that getting into

your doctor's fancy schmancy building was like getting into Fort Knox."

Logan sat up straighter and raked his thick hair back with his fingers. "Right. Sorry about that. Modern buildings come with all the bells and whistles."

"Either that or your Dr. Webb is a paranoid prick."

"Uh oh, I take it he wasn't too friendly?"

"Cold would be a good word to describe my greeting. I know people tense up when a detective shows up at the door, but it wasn't like I was there to arrest him. Hell, I wasn't even there to see him at all." She sighed. "I guess I interrupted one of his sessions. Anyhow, with a little forcefulness and a few meaningless threats he allowed me into the building."

"That sounds like the Dr. Webb I've grown to—to not have any feelings about at all if I really think about it."

"Here's the kicker. I got inside, went up the elevator and Webb greeted me in the hallway holding his phone. He said Dr. Jordan wasn't going to be in all day. It had to do with, of all things, a wisdom tooth being removed. I asked him why he didn't mention that when I asked specifically through the intercom for Dr. Jordan. Dr. Webb said that he thought he might be able to help. I told him I needed to find out if Jordan had Ann Robbins on his patient list. His expression grew taut, and he muttered something about doctor confidentiality. He did say that it could probably be overlooked in light of the situation and since Ann Robbins was dead, but he said he wouldn't feel right looking through Jordan's appointment book. He thought Jordan might be out for a few days because the surgery was quite extensive and involved an impacted tooth."

"In other words, the whole trip was a waste of time," Logan said.

"Not entirely," Reggie said. "Webb was quite anxious to get back to his client. That made sense considering they were on the clock, but he did invite me briefly into his office while he retrieved the address Jordan used on his rental application. I'm going to check it out. Gregor is supposed to meet me here at the precinct. I'm just waiting for him and his delicate constitution to arrive."

"You'd better give it a few hours," Logan noted. "I've had oral surgery before, and it takes a couple hours until you can see straight."

"Good point."

"Here's another good point—" Logan started. He realized he was already feeling so connected to his new partner he was about to ask her to do something that was outside the boundary of 'by the book'. "If you just happened to tell me the address that Webb gave you, you know, in casual conversation, then we could consider it a brief exchange of information between friends."

There was a long pause on her end. Logan had pushed the boundaries of their new partnership too far. Maybe Reggie was more 'by the book' than he thought.

"So we're friends then?" she asked. It wasn't the

response he was expecting. The one he expected was 'hell no I won't do that'.

"Well, you did clean my cuts and bruises, and I readily ate your salad sandwich. There is the matter of my parking spot, but I think I can overlook that for now."

"Not just for now. If I happened to mention that Jordan's home address was 1813 Finch Street, then that would make the parking spot permanently mine."

A cloud of fragrant steam followed Tanya out of the bathroom. Her short hair was wet and brushed back behind her ears. She'd pulled on the shorts and tank shirt she'd arrived in the night before. She strolled over and kissed his mouth. "Until next time, Tiger," she said with a wink before walking out. Logan hadn't pulled the phone far enough from his mouth.

"Tiger is it?" Reggie teased. Her phone paused with a beep. "Got a call coming through. I'll have to hear more about your tiger antics later."

"Yeah, those antics aren't for a public forum."

"I think this is Gary Robbins on the other line. I'm not looking forward to this call. I just don't have enough to tell him."

"You might tell him that the whole case has slowed down because you're working alone."

"Since I have little to tell him and that will make him angry enough, I think I'll keep the wisecracking part out of the conversation. Later... *Tiger*."

CHAPTER
THIRTY-SIX

Logan poured himself a bowl of cereal. It was the sugary kind with lots of food color. It turned his milk pink. It was also stale, but he muddled through it, knowing it was the only thing semi-edible in his kitchen. A long night with Tanya had given him an appetite along with new energy. Release that came with a night of sex was always like a double shot of espresso for Logan. The last thing he wanted to do was waste his newfound vigor by pacing the creaky floor of his apartment.

Admittedly, and without any real reason, he was highly curious about Dr. Jordan. His interest in the elusive doctor might have stemmed from the fact that Webb so obviously disliked the man, or it might just have been because up until now he was merely a name on a brass plate. Logan had been inside the mostly empty building several times, but he'd never seen a trace of the man. He'd only heard him through a closed door.

Logan stepped outside for the first time all morning. An onshore breeze had salted the warm summer air with a briny tang. It even cut through the stench wafting from the trash bin below. His ribs were feeling much better. Maybe later he'd take that run. He needed to do something. Tanya had teased him mercilessly by grabbing a small handful of his stomach fat that hadn't been there just a year ago. He could either slump back on the couch with his cold pizza and beers and let forty snatch him from the bowels of youth, or he could fight it and go into middle age kicking and screaming. It might just have been the great sex or the nice weather, but this morning, he was opting for the latter.

The buzz of Max's zippy little golf cart made Logan look back as he reached his truck. A yellow haired dog, the kind that you might see in a kid's movie about a scruffy little scalawag looking for his way home, was sitting next to Max looking quite content in the bumpy golf cart. Max stopped the cart. Logan walked over slowly. The dog sat up instantly and wagged its tail.

"Who is this?" Logan rubbed the dog behind its half flopped ear.

Max patted the little dog's back. "I found him sleeping in the utility room. Poor little bugger. He was so hungry, he ate two cans of tuna. I was just driving around with him but no one seems to recognize the little guy."

"What are you going to do with him?" Logan asked.

"Think I'll keep him."

Logan raised a questioning brow. Not that Logan had any time for a dog, but one thing he really missed after the divorce was having a dog to greet him after a long day at work. "Thought there were no pets allowed," Logan said.

"The owner lives halfway across the country. I figure what he doesn't know won't hurt him. And Buck is quiet and well-behaved. He's a good watch dog too."

"You've already named him and figured out his character. Guess that means you were meant to be together," Logan said teasingly. "Actually, it'll be nice having a dog around."

"I noticed you were on vacation," Max said. "You should get out of this town, go someplace fun like Vegas."

Logan laughed. "You and I have very different definitions of fun. See you later, Buck."

Logan climbed into his truck and typed 1813 Finch Street into the map app on his phone. Finch Street was across town, but traffic was light at this hour. Beachgoers had already rolled through town to get a parking spot near the sand and most working people were already at the office.

During his time on the force, Logan was sure he'd driven at least once along every street on the city map but Finch wasn't familiar. After a few blocks of the small but stylish and always overpriced turn of the century bungalows, the houses and gardens slowly deteriorated to small midcentury homes with chipped plaster and missing roof tiles.

Green lawns and annual flower gardens morphed to over-grown weeds and cracked asphalt driveways. Logan double checked his phone to see if the lady barking out directions had steered him wrong. It wouldn't be the first time the Google Map lady, as he called the robotic female voice, had led him astray. According to the map and the arrows, he was heading right to Finch Street. He assumed the neighbor-hoods would improve once he reached Finch. There were plenty of neighborhoods in the city that switched from high dollar single family homes to low rent duplexes and apart-ments with a turn of the corner. But this wasn't one of them.

Logan turned onto Finch Street. It was lined with dilapidated houses, many of them boarded up. The road itself was scarred with potholes the size of truck tires and most of the sidewalk curbs had been chipped away. A half dead oak sprawled its gnarled, thirsty branches out over the street. Aside from a pit bull barking wildly behind a gate and several crows picking at a dead rabbit in the road, the tree was the only sign of life on Finch Street. It dead ended at an industrial park, which explained the monster sized potholes in the road.

Logan pulled up to the house that Google insisted was 1813 Finch Street. The address on the curb was faded but it seemed Google was right. Logan was sitting in front of 1813 Finch Street. The house was boarded up, including the front door. The front yard was a swath of dirt and debris, and the roof had been worn down to mostly tar paper.

Logan picked up his phone and dialed Reggie. He'd planned to stake out Jordan's house early, mostly to appease his curiosity and get a gander of Webb's mysterious tenant. It seemed the mystery was only growing.

"Hey, Coop," she said. The tinny, hollow sound behind her assured him he was on speakerphone. He didn't need Gregor to know what he was up to. As much as Gregor liked to kiss up to all his peers, he was even a bigger ass kisser when it came to the higher-ups. Castillo would blow a gasket and suck in a cough drop if he heard that Logan was dangling his toes in the water with the Robbins murder.

"Take me off speaker," Logan said bluntly.

"Copy that." The tunnel sound disappeared. "What's up?"

"I should be privy to this conversation if it has to do with the case," Gregor said loudly.

Reggie ignored him. "We're in the car driving to Finch Street. Figured we'd wait and catch Dr. Jordan when he got home."

"Good luck with that," Logan said. "I'm sitting in front of 1813 Finch Street right now, and I can tell you the only inhabitants are rats and spiders. This place hasn't been lived in for a long time."

"No way," Reggie said.

"What?" Gregor asked. "What's going on?"

Reggie ignored him. Logan liked her more and more

each day. "Are you sure you're at the right place?" she asked.

"According to Google Maps, I'm sitting in front of the right house. Although, house is a loose term for the four attached walls I'm looking at." The crows had picked the rabbit clean and landed one after the other in the empty, dry lot surrounding the house to hangout and digest. "I guess since you're heading this way to see for yourself, I'll take off before you get here. I don't want nosy Gregor to see me."

"Ten-four, roger and out, and eat something with fiber for lunch," she added with a gentle laugh. It was a sound he'd already logged as one that made him think not everything in the world was shit.

Logan was sure the next few minutes in the car would be Gregor whining about the phone call and a game of twenty questions about what I was up to. He wasn't worried. He knew Reggie would handle it.

It was the quickest stakeout he'd ever conducted and that was even after once arriving at a stakeout right as the subject was beating the shit out of his neighbor for trespassing. Logan turned the truck around in the industrial park. It looked mostly deserted and covered from one end to the other with graffiti.

He contemplated both the lunch of fiber and a long run, but by the time he reached his apartment complex, he was yawning from his *active* night with Tanya. Logan trudged up the stairs, let himself into his apartment, tossed the keys aside and flopped on his couch. His laptop was still sitting open from the night before. Suddenly and stupidly, it occurred to him that he could easily satisfy his curiosity about Dr. Jordan with a simple Google search. It wasn't quite clear why he was so interested in him. He supposed Jordan could be the one link to some of the mysteries they had yet to uncover. Since the discovery of the body the Friday before, a long string of mysteries, and some pretty major ones at that, had been solved, but there was still one major question. Why had Ann Robbins' mood changed so drastically at the beginning of May? What had happened to her that made everyone in her life notice an abrupt change? Logan was sure whatever it was it had been the starting spark for her eventual murder. Had she witnessed something? Had someone done something to her that shamed or terrified her? Had Jordan helped bring out some repressed memories that were so heinous she couldn't cope?

Logan got up and walked to the refrigerator. He looked inside. Fiber was as scarce as actual food. He pulled the last two pieces of bread out of the bag, inspected them briefly for mold and popped them in the toaster deciding a good char would hide the staleness. He pulled the peanut butter jar out of the cupboard and waited to pop the toaster up at the first smell of burned bread. He smeared the slices thick with peanut butter and briefly wondered how much fiber was in bread and peanut butter as he carried his plate to the coffee table.

He finished one slice by the time he typed in the keywords. Google came up with the entries for Dr. Francis Jordan. He clicked open one that mentioned hypnotherapy deciding that had to be the right Francis Jordan. His first shock came from a small photo, a grainy, older picture of a woman with short curly hair and a white smile. The title beneath the photo said Dr. Francis Jordan. Logan quickly flipped back through every conversation he'd had about Dr. Jordan. There was nothing concrete that said Jordan was a man. He had just assumed it. The voice he'd heard behind the closed door could have gone either way. It seemed a little gravelly for a woman, but it was definitely higher pitched when compared to Webb's.

He skimmed the article and came to his second and bigger shock. According to the article, Dr. Francis Jordan had disappeared while on an excursion in South America. Logan dropped the toast on the plate and sat forward with interest. He hunched over the laptop and scrolled up to see the date on the article, June 13, 2003. Logan read through the whole article for more details. Dr. Francis Jordan was a well-respected psychiatrist who attended USC for her undergraduate degree and Yale for her PhD. She was on the cutting edge of the world of hypnotherapy. According to the article, Dr. Jordan had gone on a month long vacation with a group of colleagues. The tour would take them across the South American continent, with a focus on the Amazon River. One week into the trip, the group and their guides emerged from their tents for the next leg of their tour. Jordan was gone. Her clothes and supplies were still in the tent, but there was no sign of her. It had rained heavily the night before, so it wasn't possible to look for footprints. A wide search of the area was conducted for a week, but the dense foliage, rough terrain and harsh weather made it nearly impossible to do a clean sweep. Dr. Jordan was never heard from again. Seven years later she was declared dead.

Logan's phone rang. It was Reggie.

"You weren't kidding," she said. There were voices and noises in the background, but they weren't the usual sounds from the precinct.

"Where are you at?" Logan asked.

"We had to stop at a burger stand. Gregor was hungry after his day on the toilet. He's in line ordering food, and I'm leaning against the hood of the car waiting for him to eat. Anyhow, I was doing a little research while I was waiting, and I found out something pretty wild about Dr. Francis Jordan."

"We must have been reading each other's minds. The article about Dr. Jordan going missing in the Amazon?" I asked.

"You found it too. I figured there must be more than one Francis Jordan. It turns out I was right, only none of the others are psychiatrists. One is a holistic healer who dabbles in hypnosis but that Francis Jordan lives in Connecticut. I called to confirm it. I'm baffled and my partner is no help at all. He claims he's not thinking straight, you know, because of the entire day on the toilet. If I have to hear about his toilet adventures one more time, I'm going throw a good old-fashioned hissy fit, and I have not thrown one of those since I was thirteen and my mom insisted I needed a bra."

"Exactly what does a hissy fit entail?" Logan asked. He realized he'd smiled more in the short duration of knowing Reggie than in the past three years combined.

"A great deal of hissing and crying. That last one was ineffective. I still had to get the training bra. I'm thinking we should head back to Webb's office and look over that rental agreement. I also need to get a description of the Francis Jordan in the office across the way. Did you know the doctor was a woman?"

"I didn't. I heard her voice behind the door. It was sort of an odd voice, one that could have gone either way. Like I said, Webb never talked much about her. She was strictly a tenant. What I do find odd is that he's one of those fastidious, meticulous, attention-to-detail people. He's having a hard time finding tenants for his building, yet, it seems, he didn't go through any kind of vetting process with Dr. Jordan, or whoever the woman across the way is. Seems sort of reckless for someone like him."

"Wait, he would have had to at least have done a credit check on Jordan. He must have some more solid information about her. I'm going back there after Gregor stuffs his face." A soft groan rolled through the phone. "He just sat down with a burger that looks as if it has half a cow stuffed between the buns."

"Ah yes, you must be at Yonker's Burgers. That would be the triple patty, triple cheese super burger. I can say with confidence that once you've eaten that thing, you're rendered useless as a slug for the rest of the day."

"Don't think that will make much difference," Reggie quipped. It was stupid but Logan was heartily enjoying the fact that even with him being on leave and with a substitute partner at her side, she was calling him. "Do you have Dr. Webb's phone number? I can't find it. I thought I'd give him a heads-up so we can get there at a time when there's no patient on the clock."

"Now that you mention it, I only have his email. That's how we communicated from the start. I know he doesn't have a receptionist yet. I figured with no one to answer the phone it would be too much of an interruption."

Logan sat back against the couch slightly stunned that he hadn't questioned it before. "He told me he'd only just leased the building but that's a lie. His appointment book went all the way back to March of this year."

"That could possibly fit in the category of a new lease. Send me his email. I'll write him."

"All right. Case aside, this whole thing with Dr. Jordan sure is weird. It seems that someone has stolen her identity and her profession to practice medicine. I suppose, of all the medical specialties, the one that could be pulled off by a good actor would be psychiatry. It's good money too," Logan noted.

"This whole thing might be a new case on its own. The big question is—do the inconsistencies with Dr. Jordan have anything to do with Ann Robbins' murder? Francis Jordan was just a name on a note that James came across in Derrick's personal belongings. We don't even know if Ann Robbins had any connection to Dr. Jordan at all. And that's annoying because it means I'm sitting in the hot sun, watching Gregor down a burger as if it's his last meal on earth and, at the same time, I'm chasing shadows instead of anything that will lead me to a killer."

Reggie sounded rightfully frustrated. Logan hated to bring up another sore subject, but his curiosity won out. "What did you tell Gary Robbins?"

She blew out a puff of air. "What could I tell him? I said we were chasing down every lead. I asked him if he'd ever heard of Dr. Francis Jordan, but he had no idea what I was talking about. It seems Ann kept a lot of secrets from him, and Gary is just figuring that out. I brought up the part about the case being set back some because you were taken off the investigation." She grew quiet.

"That dramatic pause tells me that didn't go too well," Logan said.

"Understatement. He blew a fuse. I had to hold the phone away from my ear and let him go on a long tirade about how deceptive we were. He said he wanted me off the case too, but Castillo told him then they'd be back to square one with the whole thing. Guess it took some convincing. I don't blame the guy. We weren't exactly holding back a little white lie. You were sitting there listening to him talk and grieve about his wife when the whole time you'd known her intimately. Your grief was palpable too, but they never picked up on it because there was no way they could have known what was going on in your head and heart."

Logan's throat tightened as he thought back to that dreadful day. Reggie had held it together for him. It was her first day on a new force, with a new partner, a partner who was going through a silent fucking breakdown, and she stayed cool through it all

"You know I never got a chance to thank you, Reg. It was a tough first day for you, but you sure didn't show it. Thanks for letting me fall quietly apart. You were exactly the kind of partner I needed that day." She was exactly the kind of partner he needed every day.

She didn't say anything, but he could sense her reaction through the phone. It was silent but there. "Jeez, that has to be a record. Gregor is wadding up the empty wrapper. Don't forget to send the email. I'm sure Webb will be thrilled to hear from me again."

"I see him in the morning, so if you don't get through to him, I'll let him know something isn't right about the doctor across the way."

"Here comes my partner," Reggie said. "He looks quite satisfied after that meal."

"Hey, I'm your partner," Logan reminded her. "Keep me posted."

Logan stared at the last piece of peanut butter toast. That three layer burger sounded better than ever. Instead, he pushed off the couch and went to change into his running shorts and shoes.

CHAPTER
THIRTY-SEVEN

Logan had envisioned himself in a Rocky style run through town and up the steps of city hall with an uplifting music score blasting through his earbuds. In reality, he made it a mile and it was a sluggish mile. The sun was beating down on his head and every jarring step reminded him that he still had a couple of cracked ribs. The lack of decent food hadn't helped either. On the slow jog back one of Becca's favorite songs, Springsteen's "Human Touch", came on. It pulled him down into a sadness that was edged with frustration. Thinking about that terrible day at the lake when he realized he was staring down at Becca's body reminded him of the few minutes alone with her in the autopsy room. He'd promised her. He promised to find the monster who killed her, and he was stuck running a shitty mile and looking things up on Google.

Every lead so far had been a dead end. The mystery

surrounding Dr. Jordan might very well be another dead end, but what if it wasn't? What if they'd finally stumbled on something important? Reggie was going to have to unpeel the layers with burger stuffed Gregor at her side.

That was bullshit. There was no reason he couldn't stop by and talk to Webb, let him know that he was curious about Dr. Jordan and that he looked her up on the internet. He could make it seem he was there to warn Webb that something wasn't right with the doctor he'd let into his building. If nothing else, he might be able to glean a few more details about Jordan.

Logan hurried back to the apartment building. He showered and changed then headed out to his truck. Days off sure left him with plenty of time to do whatever the hell he wanted.

Reggie had texted that she'd sent an email to Webb but hadn't heard back yet. In the meantime, they had another dead body to check out, another overdose, apparently. They happened with more and more frequency each year, and there didn't seem to be a way to shore up the dam.

Webb's building sat gleaming in the midday sun like a metal and glass thorn in the middle of a busy street sidewalk. Logan figured he'd grown to hate the building even more since his sessions had done little to alleviate his supposed affliction of anger and had led to his involuntary leave of absence. He pushed the intercom button several times, long and hard, but there was no response. Without the elusive Jordan in the office for the day, Webb was alone. It was entirely possible he'd stepped out for lunch or left early. Logan pulled his phone from his pocket and opened up the photos of Webb's appointment book. He didn't have a photo of this week's appointments, but in prior weeks, it seemed he had a break between sessions at one o'clock. It was fifteen past one. Logan could wait for Webb to return, or he could move on with his little shadow investigation. He knew one person for certain who had sat across from Dr. Francis Jordan, Quinn, the candy bar, time obsessed guy with the Cabinets R Us t-shirt. Most people didn't display a company logo unless they owned or worked at the company. It was worth a shot. Cabinets R Us was a warehouse of mismatched kitchen cabinets, cast-offs from kitchens that had been designed wrong or changed at the last minute. If a person was diligent, they could get a nice set of cabinets for a good price. The warehouse was in an industrial center at the edge of town. Since Logan's calendar was clear for the rest of the day, he climbed back into his truck and drove in the direction of the cabinet warehouse.

Traffic was heavy from a fender bender where, rather than clear off of the road, the two drivers decided to leave their dented vehicles in the middle of the street as they argued about who was at fault. Logan's old days on patrol reminded him that he should probably get out and intervene before things got too heated, but he quickly remembered he wasn't a cop at the moment. Just a guy without a job or a purpose. Only he had a purpose. He was more determined than ever to track down Becca's killer. Then he could tell Castillo, Webb, Robbins, the whole lot of them, to fuck off. If he got fired, it would be worth it. But he wasn't doing this for self-satisfaction. He was doing this for Becca.

There were only a few cars parked in the large Cabinets R Us lot. A big box truck was in front of the warehouse. Three workers were loading cabinets into the back. Logan spotted Quinn standing away from the action with a clipboard in his hand. He was checking off a list as Logan walked up.

"Quinn, right?"

Quinn's face popped up. He gave Logan one of those looks that said 'where do I know you from?' "Yes, hello, can I help you?" he squinted. "Were you here last week for the white shaker cabinets?"

"No, actually, I'm sure you don't remember me, but we met in front of Dr. Jordan's building."

His face blanched and his wide eyes shot toward the workers loading the truck. They were busy pushing a heavy box into the back and hadn't heard the conversation.

"Uh, I'll be right back, Tony. Just need to show this customer something inside." He motioned quickly with his head for Logan to follow him inside. "I'll be in my office for a minute, Pauline," Quinn called to a woman standing at a counter writing up an order. She didn't look up from her task as Logan and Quinn slipped down a short, tiled hallway to a small office that was crammed full of cabinets and a desk. The shelves behind the desk were filled with three ring binders and framed family photos. Quinn, it seemed, had a cute young wife and two little boys.

"Nice family," Logan said.

"Thanks." Quinn was still fidgety. He closed the office door. "Look, I never told anyone that I was seeing a shrink, not even the wife." His candy addiction was probably not helped by the large glass bowl of mini candy bars on the corner of his desk.

"I understand. I'm not here to out you."

Quinn shrugged shyly. "I'm not going anymore anyhow. Too expensive and, truthfully, the hypnosis sessions just left me feeling—I don't know—violated. Like Jordan was looking into my deepest thoughts without actually freeing me of my need to eat candy." He waved his hand toward the candy dish. "Please, help yourself. I decided there are far worse addictions than sugar. I'm starting a gym membership this week. And I'll be right on time for every exercise class," he said proudly. "I've decided I made too big a deal about what I perceived as problems. They are pretty minor compared to some people's mental health issues. Dr. Jordan, herself, well, she didn't seem altogether normal either. At first, I was sort of good with it. I thought, at least she's not one of those judgmental shrinks who looks down their nose at their patients. At least she was kooky like the rest of us in the general population."

Logan's ears were perked. "What do you mean?"

Quinn hesitated at first, then reached for a mini Kit Kat bar. "Guess I can tell you since I'm no longer seeing her. First of all, I'm not entirely sure Dr. Jordan was a woman." His cheek was filled with a Kit Kat as he put his hand up. He chewed quickly, swallowed and wiped a tiny bit of chocolate off the side of his mouth. "Not that I have any problem with that. I have a good friend and his teenage daughter is going to therapy to work out the kinks for transitioning to become a boy. I get it. There's something that happens genetically and there's confusion and all that. I'm pretty sure Dr. Jordan wore a wig. Occasionally, she would reach for a notepad or pen, and the hair piece would shift just slightly. And there were times when I felt as if she would slip into a different voice, a much more manly voice. Just something about her seemed manly, her whole demeanor, posture. Nice legs though from what I could see through the nylons, and she always crossed them at the knee, you know, like women do."

The Jordan mystery grew. "When was the last time you saw Dr. Jordan?"

"Last Thursday. I left there feeling so down I went straight to the store and bought one of those six packs of Hershey bars." He laughed. "You probably thought I was going to say a six pack of beer but that's not me. I go for the Hershey multipack. Had the whole box finished before I even pulled in my driveway. But that was my last big sugar binge. I even gave up sodas. Haven't had one in three days," he said with a boastful chin lift as if he'd just climbed Everest. Logan liked Quinn. He was sure the guy hadn't been an asshole even one day in his life. Logan certainly couldn't say the same about himself.

"I'm curious, why are you asking about Dr. Jordan?" It had finally dawned on him how bizarre this unexpected visit and conversation was. Logan didn't want to bring up the murder case or the fact that he was a cop. He shuffled a few thoughts around and came up with a plausible answer.

"The truth is I'm not getting much out of my sessions with Dr. Webb. Same thing as you. I leave those hypnosis sessions feeling almost violated. They haven't moved me forward at all. I thought I'd give Dr. Jordan a try, but I haven't seen her once."

"Well, they've got that place sealed up like a maximum security prison." They both laughed. "I'd keep looking if I were you," Quinn suggested. "If you don't mind me asking, and feel free not to tell me. Why were you seeing Webb? You seem like a normal, straight up kind of guy."

Logan smiled weakly. "Anger issues." That caused Quinn to take a small, not so subtle, step back. Logan had to tamp down a chuckle. "I won't take up any more of your busy day."

"Anytime and I hope you find a good doctor. There must be a few respectable ones out there." He laughed. "I guess if we only knew who psychiatrists went to with their problems. Those are probably the doctors to see."

"Good point." Logan nodded and walked out of the office. He stepped out into the sun and let its warming rays wash over him for a second while he sorted things out in his head. A few wild notions were starting to take hold, but they were so outlandish he didn't even want to share them with Reggie. He needed to get back to Webb's office, but first, he needed some sustenance. The entire unraveling of Dr. Francis Jordan was making him feel very uneasy about Dr. Webb.

CHAPTER
THIRTY-EIGHT

Logan sat at an outside table eating his chicken salad sandwich. Two things stuck out in his mind after the conversation with Quinn. The major one, was that the person posing as the late Dr. Francis Jordan may or may not have been a woman. A wig meant little, but Quinn had mentioned Jordan occasionally slipped into a manly voice. Whether the imposter was a cross dresser or transgender or someone in transition didn't matter. What mattered was that there was no real Dr. Jordan. Someone was playing the part. A bigger question stuck in his mind —was Ann Robbins seeing Dr. Jordan for her hypnotherapy sessions? Did the imposter have anything to do with Ann Robbins or was he just on a weird tangent that was unrelated to the investigation?

He pulled out his phone and texted Reggie. "We need to talk." There was no immediate response. He chided himself for feeling instantly insulted. His finger inadvertently popped open the photo of Webb's appointment book. He stared at it for a second. Logan didn't understand the need for posting times and names in two colors, but he'd passed it off as some organizing trick Webb was using. Logan's gaze floated over the names framed in the screen of his phone. One suddenly stood out.

"Stella Higgins," he muttered to himself. Adrenaline stiffened his muscles and his heartbeat sped up just enough for him to feel it in his sore ribs. He didn't know anyone named Stella Higgins, but he knew the name well. Becca loved to fantasize about being someone entirely different, someone with a life away from Layton, away from the nightmare she was living at home. She'd come up with the name one day and decided it suited her perfectly. When the two of them were alone, lying in the back of Logan's old truck bed staring up at the stars or alone in his bed staring up at fake stars on his ceiling, her half naked body curled into his, Becca would make up a new persona for Stella. She might be a prominent surgeon in a posh hospital or a backup singer in a major rock band. Sometimes she was just simple, sweet Stella married with a wonderful husband who brought her a box of candy every Friday night and a dozen roses on her birthday. It was amazing how clear her fantasies remained in Logan's mind. It might have been because he was always imagining himself in Stella's life. At the same time, she'd never mentioned him as part of her fantasies and that had hurt him. It seemed, more than ever, that she had always been dreaming of a life away from Layton, away from him. She'd probably avoided using the name Stella Higgins for her new life because she worried he might be able to find her. It was starkly and painfully obvious she never wanted to be found. Not even by him. She also didn't want her husband knowing she was seeing a shrink. So she used the name Stella Higgins. The name on the appointment book was in red ink.

"We're going to meet with Webb now," Reggie's text pulled him from his thoughts.

Logan quickly swiped to call her. He wasn't sure where any of this was going yet, but unless the name was a big coincidence it seemed Webb had been seeing Ann Robbins as a patient. If so, he had never mentioned it to Logan. It seemed it should have come up, or, at the very least, Logan should have gotten some kind of indication that Webb knew her.

Reggie answered. "Hey."

"I think Webb was Ann Robbins' doctor." Logan was talking fast. He felt as if he needed to get out a lot of information in a short bit of time. "I noticed the name Stella Higgins on his appointment book. I want to kick myself for not noticing it earlier, but I was concentrating on the name Ann Robbins."

"Who is Stella Higgins?" Reggie asked, rightfully confused.

"Becca used to love to make up entirely new lives for herself. She imagined herself in all kinds of cool scenarios, and she was always Stella Higgins. She just thought it was a fun name and that a woman named Stella Higgins wouldn't take shit from anyone. Webb was seeing a Stella Higgins in April."

"Great, then I can ask him about that after I ask him about the mysterious Dr. Francis Jordan. I'm beginning to think she never even existed. Only you heard her talking angrily with Webb."

"And I just talked to one of her patients. He doesn't see her anymore and she might be a he. There's a whole thing about a wig and a voice change. How close are you to the office building?"

"We're just around the corner. Webb said he had fifteen minutes to talk before his next patient, so we've got to hurry."

"Shit, I'm twenty minutes away, fifteen if I put my foot down hard and don't hit all the lights."

"Just as well. You're not supposed to be working on the case, and I'd say Webb is well aware of that fact. I'll call you as soon as we're done talking to him. Stella Higgins, right?"

"Yep. It's got to be her." Logan was climbing in his truck to head that direction. "This whole thing is getting pretty fucking twisted so watch your back."

She laughed lightly. "We're just pulling up. Talk to you soon."

The first leg of the drive, Logan made good progress. The lights were working in his favor. It was that time of day when people were already back in the office after lunch and tourists and beachgoers were still at the coast. But one of those big electronic signs with the pointing arrows telling everyone to merge left assured him his smooth journey was about to hit a road construction snag. It was all right. Reggie and Gregor needed their fifteen minutes with Webb. She was right. He was not supposed to be on the case. Webb held all the magic to his release from administrative leave in his expensive gold pen. With any luck, Reggie would be leaving the building as he arrived. Then he could slip inside and not bother with the intercom. Something told him Webb would not be keen on buzzing him in when it wasn't his appointed time slot.

As predicted, street traffic slowed to a crawl as everyone was forced into one lane. Logan came to a complete stop about a mile from the construction zone. The sidewalks were mostly empty. This was the time of day when panhandlers took to corners to scrape up enough cash for a meal or a drink. An older homeless man, a guy Logan had seen many times in his black beanie and long grease stained trench coat, an ensemble he wore even through hot summer, was checking out some of the city trash cans for edibles. As usual, he was having an animated conversation with himself. Today, he seemed to be angry at himself, with his weathered brow scrunched in scorn and short, clipped words shooting from his mouth.

The worker stuck holding the stop and slow sign

moved the few cars in front of Logan ahead. It took a honk from the guy behind to stir him into action. He put his foot lightly on the gas and rolled forward. His gaze kept sweeping up to the rearview mirror where the homeless man was still in the reflection. He had discovered something in a crumpled brown bag that made his scowl disappear, but he continued his conversation.

A new, more impossible idea pushed into Logan's head. He thought back to the few minutes in the hallway between the doctors' offices where he listened to the terse conversation between Webb and Jordan. What if there was no Jordan? What if Webb had been talking to himself? Logan laughed. Webb was somewhat of a character, but was he psychotic? He replayed the conversation with Quinn in his head. Jordan crossed her legs at the knees like a woman. So did Webb. That heartbeat that had gently tapped his sore ribs earlier returned with more vigor.

Everything since the discovery of the body was slapping back at him. The thing that slapped the hardest was St. Patrick's Day at the Three Boars. Webb had seen him absently fingering the napkin from Ann's coat pocket. Webb recognized it and admitted to going there with colleagues. More importantly, Logan had told him he'd last been there on St. Patrick's Day. Webb knew he was there that day.

Adrenaline and the frustration of traffic made him pound the steering wheel. "Come on, let's fucking move!"

He was gritting his teeth by the time he rolled past the last cone. The hypnosis, the strange visions of Becca drowning right in front of him, Webb was outside his conscience craftily placing ideas in his head.

Logan grabbed his phone and dialed Reggie. It went to voicemail. "It's Webb. Get the fuck out of there. I'm on my way." He dialed Gregor but got voicemail too.

If he'd been in his official car he would have stuck the light on top and switched on the siren, but he was stuck in his truck. The last few minutes of the drive were the longest in his life. No one called back.

Logan's car, his detective car, was parked about a block away from the building. He pulled his truck behind it and jumped out. If all his suspicions were right, then Webb was nowhere near in his right mind, and the mind he was working with was diabolical. Only someone truly disturbed could handcuff a woman in a car to drown her. Only someone truly disturbed would pretend to be two different people. Unless it wasn't pretend. The argument behind Jordan's door, if it had just been Webb, meant they weren't dealing with your typical murderer. Logan had heard tale of suspects with multiple personalities, changing back and forth, wildly, frighteningly, while sitting in an interrogation room, but he'd never dealt with it firsthand.

Logan hit the intercom button hard. It buzzed loudly, urgently, at least to his ears, but there was no response. He tried again and, at the same time, called Reggie. It was pure frustration from all angles. Logan hurried around the corner of the shiny building. A patch of weeds and two trash cans sat in the alleyway between Webb's building and the office building next door. There was one door, metal, with no window and it was bolted shut. Logan expected nothing less from the paranoid shrink. Now the reason for all the security and sticking to a strict time schedule was coming clear. Quinn couldn't buzz in early. It just so happened that he was working on his obsession with being on time, but Logan was sure Webb wanted schedule adherence for another reason. He didn't want clients to cross paths, to exchange experiences. He was working two offices and playing two different characters. That was what Logan was calling him now—a character, a sick character from a horror novel.

Logan raced to the front of the building and pushed the buzzer again. This time he heard the familiar click of someone holding the intercom on the other side. "Coop," a shaky voice came through like light dust. "Is that you, Coop?" Logan looked up at the security camera just above the door to show his face.

"Gregor?"

"Yeah." He sounded unsteady, in pain.

The door opened and Logan pushed inside. He raced to the stairwell and took the steps two at a time. He slammed through the door and ran down the hallway to Webb's office.

Gregor held on to the open doorway of Webb's office.

He was holding a blood-soaked tissue against the side of his head and looking plenty out of it.

"Where's Reggie?" Logan asked as he hurried toward Gregor. Gregor was unsteady on his feet, the kind of unsteady you get when you've taken a blow to the head. Logan took hold of Gregor's arm and led him to the front office couch. There was no sign of Webb or Reggie. Gregor was just getting his bearings enough to remember what'd happened.

Logan dialed dispatch. "This is Detective Cooper. We need an ambulance and backup to 202 Harbor Boulevard." Logan finished the call and walked into the therapy room. It looked different empty. It felt almost sinister. Logan's eyes swept past the rock hard couch. He wondered, briefly, what things had transpired on that couch or on the one across the hall. The two colors of ink must have been to keep Webb's patients separate from Jordan's patients.

Logan grabbed the entire box of tissue and carried it out to Gregor. He crouched down in front of him to get a good look in his eyes and make sure he wasn't suffering from something more severe than a cut on his head.

Gregor was focused. "I think he took her. Reggie, he's got her." His voice was thin and he was breathless from the shock of it all. "We thought we were just here to get some information on Dr. Jordan, but it was an ambush. We stepped off the elevator and something hit my head, hard. Pain went right through me. The room was spinning and I dropped to my knees. All I saw was Reggie's blue sneakers. She was kicking him, giving it her all. He must have had her mouth covered because I heard her trying to yell but it was muffled. Then it stopped and her feet weren't kicking." Gregor sat back. "Think I might puke."

Logan glanced around for the trash, then motioned to the cushion next to him. "Just puke on this ugly couch. Might improve it." Gregor leaned over to get sick. Logan took the opportunity to search around the room for a clue of any kind, something that might tell him where Webb took Reggie. His eyes swept past the framed diplomas on the wall. "USC and Yale," he muttered.

"There's a sticky note," Gregor said, breathlessly. "By the door." He waved weakly at it.

A light green square sticky note was stuck right at the edge of the doorway. Logan pulled it off the wall. "1813 Finch St."

"Why does that sound familiar?" Gregor's face was a sickly green.

"That's where Jordan was supposed to live," Logan said.

"Odd, it's almost as if he wants us to know where he took her," Gregor said. He was not the sharpest guy on the force. The blow to his head hadn't helped him.

"Not us," Logan said. "Just me. He wants me." Logan walked over to him. "I'm going after her. I'll prop the door open downstairs. I left instructions with dispatch on how to find you."

"Coop, don't go alone. Not if he's waiting for you. Besides, you're not on duty."

Logan handed him another tissue to stop the big drip of blood rolling down the side of his face. "I'll be fine. I've got to go. And, Gregor, thanks for worrying."

Logan raced down the stairwell. He grabbed one of the big potted plants and dragged it across the slick floor, leaving a nice long scratch. He jammed the plant in the doorway and raced to his truck. The man was clearly insane and capable of anything. It seemed Ann Robbins wasn't his first victim. Who knew how many women Webb had killed in his lifetime? Logan shuddered deep inside, worried that he was already too late.

CHAPTER
THIRTY-NINE

Logan didn't need Google to lead him to Finch Street this time. His truck jumped off a deep pothole as he hit the crumbling asphalt at top speed. A gray sedan was parked far enough back on the worn down driveway that it was half hidden by the house. Logan kept his personal handgun in the locked glove box. He pulled it out and kept the gun gripped tightly in his hands. The front door and windows were still secured by boards of plywood. Logan kept close to the side of the house, avoiding the debris and trash that had piled up against it. Every window was boarded up until he circled to the back. The yard was no bigger than his front room and it was surrounded by a block wall. It was the perfect hideout for a killer, Logan thought with another shudder. No nosy neighbors, no neighborhood watch and everything boarded shut. The only exception was a white door at the back. One small spot on the door had been cleaned of the many layers of dirt so a light green note would stick to it. "I can see you but you can't see me. Put your weapon down in the middle of the yard, then we'll see about meeting face-to-face."

Logan held the gun up, walked cautiously toward the center of the tiny yard, lowered his gun to the dried weeds. He lifted up both empty hands. The sun made him squint as he waited. The small door creaked open an inch. He heard footsteps and voices echo through the empty house.

Logan's instinct was to push inside and call for Reggie, but he was dealing with a calculating monster. One wrong move could mean danger for his partner. He squeezed his eyes shut for a second and took a deep breath. "Please let her be alive," he whispered.

Logan moved toward the door. He pushed it open. A musty, rotten smell hit him. It was the odor of a house that had been closed up for months, maybe years. The door led into a small area with pipes sticking out of the walls, an old laundry area or possibly where a water heater once stood. As he reached the corner, he heard two voices. His moment of relief was fleeting when he realized the second voice was not Reggie. It was the high-pitched, unusual voice of Dr. Francis Jordan, Webb's other half.

"What will you do now, Benjamin? This is too much. You ask too much of me," the strained voice said.

"Shut up, Francis. Just go away," Webb replied sharply.

Logan stepped around the corner. A terrified breath caught in his lungs. Reggie was collapsed on the floor with a thin piece of rope hanging loosely around her neck. Her hands were tied together. It took Logan a second to steady himself. He surveyed her from head to toe. She was as still as a... He couldn't bring himself to even think the word.

Webb was far better off. Logan expected to find him looking half-crazed, sloppy, not himself, but he was just as composed as ever. Not a hair out of place and no wig in sight. Even his grip on the gun he was holding was steady, like a man in complete control. He stood behind Reggie's limp body wearing a smile that conveyed the pure evil in his soul.

"Sorry about your new partner, Logan. It seemed as if you rather liked her."

Logan felt a wave of nausea go through him as he pressed his eyes shut and waited just long enough, he hoped, that when he opened them he'd find himself in his crummy, shadowy bedroom. He opened his eyes. Another wave of nausea swept through him. This was all too real. He stared down at Reggie's body, then lifted his eyes. Some of that trouble causing anger was swelling up inside of him. He curled his right hand into a fist. He didn't need a gun. He carried his best, deadliest weapon with him wherever he went. If he could just find a way to use it before the bullet shot through him. One punch—that was all he needed to splatter the asshole's face.

"I will kill you," Logan said. "I'm not on duty, thanks to

you. Far as I'm concerned that leaves me every option available. Nothing by the book when I kill you."

Webb shrugged. "Seems like I have the advantage at the moment." His gaze swept down to the body in front of him. Reggie's long lashes shaded her soft cheeks, and her lips were slightly parted. Webb had murdered another incredible woman.

"Would you like to hear how Ann Robbins begged for her life? Or is it Becca, in your mind? Or Stella Higgins, that was the name she used to keep her therapy sessions from her husband. Would you like to hear how she cried, screamed and begged for her life?"

Logan shook his head. "Bullshit. She didn't scream and beg. Becca lived her entire life in fear that she would die by her father's hand. She was hardened to the idea of dying a violent death. She didn't beg. She denied you that insidious satisfaction, didn't she?"

An odd grin appeared on his face. His nose crinkled and he smirked. "Get rid of him, Benjamin," the shrill tone was creepier than anything he'd ever heard. "I want to go home. I'm tired of this horrible house." The smooth, composed expression returned.

"You killed Dr. Francis Jordan too," Logan said. "You were on that tour of the Amazon. I'm thinking you were not only in love with her, but you were obsessed. But she didn't return the affection because who the fuck would? Look at you." Logan's only hope was to throw him entirely off guard with the hideous truth. But Webb had a hard shell.

"She was a whore," Webb said calmly. The only sign Logan's words were getting to him was the tightness in his jaw. "She was sleeping with one of the guides. I caught her sneaking out of his tent." He sighed almost as if bored talking about it. "It's amazing how many places there are to hide a body in the Amazon. I strangled her. Just like your partner here." He looked down at Reggie. "Shame, she was a beauty too."

Logan was working hard not to focus on the heart-wrenching scene on the floor. He was either going to die right next to her in this squalid house, or he was going to beat Webb to a bloody pulp.

"You were obsessed with Becca," Logan started. "You think you were the first, you sick fuck?"

"Becca came to me to get rid of the nightmares she carried with her from her youth. Why didn't you protect her, Logan? You loved her but you didn't protect her."

The tables were being turned. Webb was trying to throw him off too, but Logan wasn't having it. "I was a kid. I wanted to just like I want to tear you to fucking shreds right now, you piece of human garbage."

"You never saved her. That was why she had to fake her own death. She wanted away from Layton, from her father, from you. She thought you'd save her from his wrath, but you were too weak. That's when the real anger started, isn't it? You couldn't take care of the one person who counted on you. That's why you became a cop. You couldn't help Becca, but you were going to take care of all the other bad guys, and when they turned out to be particularly onerous, you beat them with your fist. After all, what could be more satisfying than crushing someone's bones? They were all Ray Kinsey. Everyone you beat the shit out of was Ray."

Logan was out of his element. Webb was a master manipulator of the human psyche. Everything Webb said was inching into Logan's soul, picking at his conscience. He was right. The fucking psycho was right.

Logan's gaze swept down to the floor. It erased all the tightness he was feeling in his chest. All the dark thoughts brought on by Webb's words became lighter, easier to toss aside. He had to finish this right, not just for Becca but for Reggie. Right then, more pieces of the puzzle snapped together.

"You raped Ann Robbins right there on your couch. You had her under hypnosis, and you couldn't keep your creepy hands off of her. You're pathetic."

Webb didn't shrink back or look shocked by his words. Instead, a disgusting grin crossed his face. "Ah, but she was with Logan on that couch. She'd spoken about you so much, it was easy to become you while she was under. It made her quite willing. For those few minutes she was back in Layton with her Logan. A car honked on the road below, and she popped out of her hypnosis. She wouldn't drop it. She told me she would ruin me." Webb shrugged. "Fortunately she had told me so many of the secrets she'd been keeping from her husband, I had a little blackmail game of my own going."

"Why'd you kill her?"

"I decided I couldn't trust her."

Then something clicked, something straightened out in his thoughts that was almost too much to believe.

"You planned this from the beginning," Logan said. "You knew about Logan Cooper because Becca had told you all about me."

He laughed dryly. "Imagine my surprise when your name came up on the list of law enforcement employees in need of therapy. I couldn't believe my luck. Naturally, I cleared my calendar just for you. When they found the body, I knew I had to frame you, make you believe you'd killed Becca. Now I'll just kill you too and disappear. I find it's quite easy to become someone else when necessary." Another evil grin. He was playing at the insanity thing. If he was arrested, the whole thing would go down much smoother with an insanity plea. He knew Logan wasn't on the elevator that day when he listened at Dr. Jordan's door.

"Why two doctors? Why two practices? Guess the IRS can't go after someone who doesn't exist."

Webb pretended to look shocked. "I don't know what you're talking about." He was going to keep up the multiple personality act, just in case. If anyone could pull off the insanity plea it would be a doctor who knew all about insanity.

Sirens whined in the distance. "Guess this is the end of the line for you, Cooper." Webb lifted his gun. A flash of movement distracted both of them. Before Logan could figure out what had happened, the gun went off, hitting the ceiling and sending an avalanche of old plaster down on their heads. Webb flew back yelling in pain as he reached for his leg. Reggie hopped to her feet and pulled the rope off of her neck. For good measure, she lifted her foot and brought it down on the knee she'd just kicked. Webb yelled out again. He was writhing on the floor, holding his leg and spewing out spit laced curses. Logan was frozen to the spot staring at the scene in front of him, wondering again if he was just dreaming.

Reggie strolled over and held her arms out . "Untie my hands. I've got an itch."

Logan untied her hands and grabbed one before she could snatch it away or scratch her itch. Her brown eyes blinked at him as he held tightly to her hand. He had no words. He was sure his expression said it all. He let go of her hand. She picked up the gun, careful not to smear prints.

"Well, partner, that was the longest damn confession I've ever sat through. I thought I was going to have to play dead on that moldy floor for the next hour while you two cleared the air of everything that's happened in the last ten years."

Logan looked at Webb. There was no way he was going to be walking out of there. Logan shook his head. "How the hell—?"

Reggie shrugged. "I used to attend this crappy camp in the summer. It was free for us low income rugrats. There was very little supervision. We used to have contests to see who could stay underwater longest. I always won. Turned out I could hold my breath for ninety seconds. And then there was the end of summer play. We did Bonnie and Clyde one year."

Logan was so relieved to be talking to her, to see her up and alive and smiling he wanted to pull her into his arms. "Bonnie and Clyde at summer camp?"

"Guess you missed the part when I said it was free and there was little supervision. Anyhow, I made a pretty darn good Bonnie. We rehearsed the final scene, when they get shot to death, a hundred times because that was the part we all liked best. I learned how to die on cue. I admit, I was a little freaked out. Webb seems like a pretentious, fastidious asshole. I worried he'd hold the rope long after I appeared dead."

Webb was moaning in pain. "You got him good," Logan said.

The sirens shook the house now. Fists pounded on the plywood across the front door. "Come out, we've got you surrounded." Tools were prying at the boarded up door.

Reggie waved toward the back of the house. "There's a

door right there." She shook her head. "Almost forgot," she started.

"Gregor's fine. I called an ambulance." He took her hand again lightly. "You did good, partner."

"You had this thing all figured out. I took him out physically, but it's going to be you who brings him down for good." She winked. "Becca would be pleased."

Logan nodded, his throat tightened just thinking about the past few weeks of hell starting with the heartbreak of Becca's second and final death. A groan rolled out from the corner where Webb was still whining like a baby.

"She would be pleased, but..." Logan walked to Webb and stood over him. He glared up at Logan, no longer the picture of perfect composure. His face was contorted and red. His eyes looked wild with fear.

Logan lifted his fist. All he needed was one good punch down into the killer's face. It wasn't as effective as when someone was standing right in front of him, but Logan was sure he could do major damage and inflict some good old fashioned agony.

Webb's face paled and his eyes rounded. "I'll sue the whole fucking department. Don't do it." If Webb had learned anything from their sessions, he'd learned that Logan's right fist was something to fear.

"Logan," Reggie said softly. The officers outside were still shouting to surrender. The plywood on the door was being removed.

Logan lifted his arm a little higher wanting to make sure he had plenty of room for thrust.

Webb tried to block his face with his arm. "No don't. Please. Don't do it," he pleaded.

Logan stood over him, like a dark, cruel shadow, his fist clenched like iron.

"Don't hit me," Webb sobbed. "Please," he sobbed again.

"If I ever meet up with Becca," Logan said calmly, "somewhere in the universe, somewhere in a place that you'll never end up even after they toss your wretched remains into a grave, I'm going to tell her how Dr. Webb begged and pleaded and cried for his life."

Logan lowered his arm just as sunlight and fresh air flowed into the house.

CHAPTER
FORTY

The early morning salty mist had dried into a sparkling summer day. It was Becca's favorite kind of day. She used to say nothing shitty could happen on a day like this. But plenty of shit had happened to her on bright, sunny days. She'd figured out a way to escape her abusive father, only to unwittingly land in the grasp of an equally monstrous man, someone she'd trusted to help her.

Logan placed the bouquet of flowers in front of the gray headstone. It was short and simple. *Ann Robbins, beloved wife. Cherished forever.* The dates of birth and death were too close together. It wasn't natural.

"You loved her too," a voice said from behind.

Logan looked over his shoulder. Gary Robbins looked older, thinner than the first time they met. It seemed he'd aged years in a few weeks.

Logan nodded. "Never loved anyone like it since." Just saying it out loud brought it clearly into view. He was madly in love with Vicky, but he'd never felt the same connection he'd felt with Becca.

Gary stepped closer. He was wearing a black sweater even though the temperature was rising fast. "Thank you. I know you were the brains behind finding the killer. I'm sorry I had you removed from the case."

"I would have done the same. I should have come clean with you from the start."

Gary pulled in a deep breath and placed his flowers in front of the stone. "For what it's worth, whenever I brought up the tattoo, she teared up. Not sad tears. Tears evoked by memories that could never be erased. It made me jealous." He chuckled sadly. "It was just a tattoo, but I knew it meant more than the ink on her wrist."

Logan's chest and limbs felt heavy. "I was envious of you too. You had her to yourself, happy and free of the horrible childhood she had in Layton."

"I should have protected her." Gary dropped his face and his body shook. Logan walked over and put a hand on his shoulder.

"We all failed at protecting her." Logan's voice was tight and dry.

They stood in front of the headstone for a few silent minutes. The flowers were already wilting under the summer sun.

"What was she like?" Gary asked with a sniffle. "Growing up. What was she like?"

Logan smiled. "Becca was starlight on a foggy night.

She—she could reach in and take hold of your heart with just a smile. It was like the whole world was kicked off balance when she stepped into a room, but it was a good off balance. The kind you never wanted to set right."

"Would you like to get a cup of coffee?" Gary asked hesitantly. "I'd love to hear about Becca. I knew Ann but something tells me Becca came with a whole other story. I could tell you about Ann." He shook his head. "No, I'm sorry. I'm sure you have better things to do than—"

"I'd like that. Let's get some coffee."

"Coop, Coop, Coop," the precinct chanted as Logan stepped inside.

Reggie greeted him with a plate of blueberry muffins. "They're vegan," she said with that great smile.

Logan bowed to the cheering crowd and carried his plate of muffins to his desk.

"Cooper," Castillo bellowed before he even sat down.

"Go get em, Tiger," Reggie said as Logan headed toward the captain's office.

Castillo was scribbling something with a pen as Logan knocked on the half open door. "Get in here, Cooper." It was early but his office already smelled of sweat and menthol. He put the pen down as Logan sat. This time he picked the wobbly chair with the uneven legs. He leaned back and the chair dropped onto its shorter leg. Logan rested his arms on the arms of the chair and stretched out his legs. He was feeling just cocky enough to wish he'd had a toothpick to stick in the corner of his mouth.

"In light of what happened with the therapist—" Castillo cleared his throat.

"You mean the psycho murderer you guys sent me to so that I could clear my head of all that anger shit?"

"Don't be cocky. I can't stand you when you're cocky. Anyhow, you're officially back at work. And there's a dead body at Foothill and North Road. Dispatch can get you the exact details."

Logan got up from the chair and headed to the door.

"Welcome back, Coop," Castillo said.

Logan nodded and walked out. Reggie was picking the crumbs of a blueberry muffin off her plate. "Reg, we've got a body."

She tossed the plate in the trash and grabbed her backpack. Her long legs caught up to him at the door. "Can I drive?" she asked.

"Nope."

Reggie skipped a few steps to keep up with Logan's fast pace. "Please. I'm gonna hold my breath until you toss me those keys," she teased. His mind flashed back to those terrible moments when he thought she was dead. He wanted those moments to be erased forever, but he knew it was going to take time.

Logan pushed out the door and tossed her the keys.

If karma doesn't get you, *someone else* will.

CRUEL IRONY

A LOGAN COOPER NOVEL

ELLIOT **YORK**

Detective Logan Cooper Book #2